Steve Cockayne was awarded a certificate of commendation by the National Book League for a story he wrote at the age of four. Following this, he took a forty-year sabbatical from literature to concentrate on a career in television as cameraman, manager, teacher and freelance consultant. He also managed to find time for some involvement in fringe theatre, music, puppetry and hypnotherapy. He lives in Leicestershire.

Find out more about Steve Cockayne and other Orbit authors by registering for the free monthly newsletter at www.orbitbooks.co.uk

By Steve Cockayne

Legends of the Land
Wanderers and Islanders

WANDERERS AND ISLANDERS

LEGENDS OF THE LAND: BOOK ONE

STEVE COCKAYNE

www.orbitbooks.co.uk

An *Orbit* Book

First published in Great Britain by Orbit 2002
This edition published by Orbit 2002

Copyright © MetaVentures 2002

The moral right of the author has been asserted.

A CIP catalogue record for this book is available from the British Library.

ISBN 1 84149 120 9

Typeset in Bembo by
Palimpsest Book Production Limited, Polmont, Stirlingshire
Printed and bound in Great Britain by
Clays Ltd, St Ives plc

Orbit
An imprint of
Time Warner Books UK
Brettenham House
Lancaster Place
London WC2E 7EN

With sincere thanks to everyone who helped me, knowingly or unknowingly, in the writing of *Wanderers and Islanders*, with various permutations of help, advice and inspiration.

In particular, I would like to mention Eimer Gallagher, Chris Shaw, Ann Hunter, Jenny Wood, Jon Balley, Joy Balley, Martin Dow, Liz Manners, Neeleigh Sparks, Suzy Frith, Simon Frith, Andrew Taylor, Wendy Tury, Anne Dewe and, of course, Pauline Cockayne.

Without them, it would have been a very different book.

S.V.C.

Contents

One:
OBJECTS OF DESIRE

Lee is my name, and this is my house, and in my house I await you. For long years you have been away, and for long years I have waited. But I wait patiently, for I know that in time you must return.

Perhaps you do not know me, but I know you well indeed. I know you better than anyone alive, for on the day you were born, so too was I born, and from that day to this I have watched you, and I have waited.

I watched you as you emerged unwillingly into the world from your place of safety, and I watched you as you grieved for all that you left behind you. And your grief was your first gift to me, and for your grief I cared well.

As you began to grow, so too did I grow, and always I was at your shoulder. I watched you as you made your first faltering steps on life's journey, and I watched you as you found joy, and I watched you as you found delight. But at other times too I was watching. I watched you as you found sorrow, and I watched you as you found anger, and I watched you as you found pain. And when you found these things, you turned to me. You turned to me and you offered me your sorrow, and you offered me your anger, and you offered me your pain, and you charged me with their care. And these gifts too I embraced, and for these gifts too I cared well.

I watched you at each crossroads, and I watched you as you followed the path of your choosing. But for each path chosen, another path is spurned, and for the paths you spurned, you knew regret, and for the things that were no longer within your grasp, you knew regret, and for the things that once might have been but now no longer could be, you knew regret. And you offered me your regret, and for that too I cared well.

And on your regret I grew strong, and on your grief I grew swift, and on your anger I grew lithe, and on your sorrow I grew bold.

So now, in my house, I wait. In my attic, or in my cellar, or in some forgotten corner, I wait. For year upon year, there has been little for me to do but wait. Sometimes at night, when none but the stars can see me, I might run in the garden, glorying in its overgrown state. Sometimes at dawn I might walk down to the shore, and there offer my form to the grateful waters. Sometimes at dusk I might stand at my mirror, perfecting my dreaming postures, admiring the play of the sidelong light on my supple form, the smooth perfection of my limbs, the soft contour of my cheekbone.

But more than all else, I love to dance. To my secret, dark music, I love to dance. Silently tracing my endless pattern, spinning my web of arabesques, balancing, hanging, somersaulting, springing, diving, topsy-turvy, earth above me, feet in air – I dance the dance of the shadow.

And soon, the time will come when you must know me once again. Soon the time will come when you must push ajar the door, the door that protects you from all of those things that you would love to forget. Soon the time will come when you must push ajar the door of this house. And soon the time will come when you must face me.

For I am your shadow, but I am your protector too. You fear me, but you need me, for your fear is your protection, your fear is your defence. Yes, the walls of this house are built from fear, and the walls of this house are built strong. Strong to protect you from all that you need but dare not name, strong to protect you from all that you seek but dare not discover, strong to protect you from all that you desire but dare not embrace.

For this house is my realm, and in this house, alone with your grief and your sorrow and your pain and your anger, I grow strong. I grow strong, and I grow swift, and I grow bold, and I grow supple, and I grow ready for what is to come.

★   ★   ★

From the Journal of Victor Lazarus

Friday 23rd January

This winter has been an exceptionally bitter one, and my miserable existence in this wretched little room is driving me gradually to despair. My funds have dwindled almost to nothing, so that I can no longer permit myself the least amusement, and I am forced to subsist upon the plainest of provisions. I cannot even afford to keep a fire burning during the day, and so, around noon, I habitually take an hour's brisk walk. On days when the weather is too wet for walking, I am left with no choice but to retire to bed for the afternoon, wrapping myself in blankets and eiderdowns against the cold.

When first I left the service of the King, I estimated that my gratuity would be sufficient to sustain me for approximately five months, but regrettably I failed in my calculations to foresee the length of time that might be required to secure any remunerative employment. Therefore, as the months passed, and as one disappointment followed another, I found myself obliged to move into more and more squalid accommodation, each room smaller and meaner than the one before. Sometimes I find myself wishing that I had elected after all to remain in the service, but I am forced in all honesty to admit that the army is no longer the place for a man of my years.

However, basic disciplines must still be observed, and I have therefore instigated certain routines from which I do not permit myself to deviate. Each morning, without fail, I scan the advertisement columns. I take careful note of every opportunity that seems to offer any promise, no matter how remote. I write the letters of application, and I read and file whatever replies the morning delivery might have brought. Sadly, there have been few replies thus far. And if I am to be truthful, I have to admit that the undemanding, middle-ranking position in which I spent so many years has left me but poorly equipped to make my way in this unfamiliar world beyond the walls of the garrison.

Today, for example, I have written seven letters. The morning delivery, however, has brought just two replies. One of these contains an undertaking to retain my particulars on file until such time as my services may be required – how many times have I read those words! – and the other contains an outright rejection. The majority of my letters receive no reply at all.

At least the weather is dry today. As soon as I have completed this entry, I shall set out on my usual walk to the courier's office at the end of the street. After that I shall visit the market. My staple diet nowadays consists of stewed root vegetables, but, in an effort to cheer myself through the lonely weekends, I still permit myself the occasional luxury of a cheap cut of meat.

Monday 26th January

The courier's man brought nothing for me this morning, but later in the day there came an unexpected tap at my bedroom door. I was surprised to discover there the keeper of the lodging house. She is a stout woman who is normally reluctant to climb the stairs and prefers to remain downstairs in her kitchen with her dogs. However, on this occasion she had made the ascent, and was holding in her hand a long white envelope, sealed with scarlet wax and bearing my name in an untidy, crabbed hand. This document, she told me, had been delivered to the house earlier in the day. The messenger had apparently been an elderly lady who had been wearing a long frock of the old-fashioned kind. She had clearly not been an employee of the Courier's Office! I hurried at once to the window, but no sign of her remained.

As soon as my hostess had returned to her quarters, I broke the seal on the envelope with trembling hands, and unfolded the single sheet of parchment that I found within. With mounting astonishment, I found myself reading what I could only take to be an offer of employment! I could not at once call to mind the vacancy to which the letter referred, but a search of my files revealed the following advertisement:

Assistance required with Restoration

My house, which is a large one, has fallen into neglect, and much work is required in order to render it fit for habitation. I would greatly welcome any assistance from reliable and hard-working persons. If you feel that you are suitably qualified, please apply in writing to . . .

The signature was indecipherable. In recent months I have replied to many such advertisements, so perhaps it is not surprising that I could summon up no recollection of this particular short paragraph. I suppose that among a large number of similar items, it must simply have slipped my mind. I tried to imagine the application that I might have written. I would have been at pains to emphasise my orderly mind, my ability to command men, my talent for managing accounts, and my long record of organising complex tasks with speed and efficiency.

I directed my attention towards the letter. The writer invited me to call as soon as convenient at an address on the outskirts of the town. The name of the road was familiar to me, although, try as I might, I could not recall noticing any private houses there, dilapidated or otherwise.

At any rate, before setting out, I shall need to polish my boots, trim my moustache, and brush down my good uniform. I am determined to present my most favourable aspect to my future employer.

Rusty Brown and his Mother

'Pull your socks up, Michael. I'm not having you going to school looking like that.'

Rusty Brown paused at the front gate. Leaning on the gatepost, his heavy satchel swinging awkwardly in front of him, he carefully balanced himself, first on one leg, then on the other, pulling up the prickly grey socks. He could still hear his mother calling to him from inside the house.

'And don't forget to shut the gate after you.' She sounded cross. 'We need to keep those leaves out of the flower bed. And after school you're to come straight home. I won't have you hanging about on the green with those Hopkins boys.'

Sighing, Rusty pulled the gate shut and shoved his satchel to his side. Then he headed off along the lane towards the corner where it joined the main street of the village.

The boy lived alone with his mother. He had been baptised Michael Brown, but because of his freckled face and his unruly mop of red hair, everyone in the village called him Rusty. Everyone, that was, except his mother and, of course, Granny Hopkins. His mother didn't like nicknames. In fact, there were quite a lot of things that Rusty's mother didn't like. For instance, she didn't like washing sheets and pillow slips. This was strange, because she seemed to spend nearly all her time wash-ing them, except when she was doing her work at the village church. She told Rusty that she had to wash things for other people because she had to earn a living, and that sometimes people had to do things they didn't want to do. The house always smelled of soap and starch and scorched linen. Sometimes the ladies from the big houses would call at the back door to collect their laundry, but more often Mrs Brown had to walk up the main street to deliver it to them.

Nor did Mrs Brown like it when Rusty asked her about his father. All she would ever say was that his father had had to go away a long time ago, and would not be coming back. When Rusty tried to ask more questions, she would start to get cross, and after a while he found that he couldn't pluck up the courage to ask again.

They didn't have many new things in the cottage. The table was old and scratched, the saucepans were dented, and the stuff-ing was coming out of the armchairs. When Mrs Brown wasn't busy with the laundry, she would sit by the stove in the little parlour, knitting or darning or mending clothes.

'The schoolmaster spoke to me today,' said Mrs Brown one evening. She was in her usual place by the stove, sewing a patch on Rusty's second-best trousers. 'He said you've been doing very well at your lessons.' Rusty started to fidget. 'No, listen. He told me that if you work hard, you might be able to go on to the high school when you're older. And later on, you might even be able to get a place at one of the academies. Do you think you'd like that?'

Rusty nodded. He liked school, but he had never really thought about what might come afterwards.

'Then you might go to live in the city. Study for one of the professions.' Rusty noticed that she was looking up into the corner of the room as she spoke. She seemed almost to be talking to herself. 'You could keep me in my old age. I shan't want to go on washing sheets for ever.' She looked down at him again. 'You'd have to work hard, of course. But I don't suppose you'd mind that, would you?'

The village where they lived was a small one, situated in a remote and uncharted corner of the land. There was only one town within reach, and the royal highways and the city were even further away. Few people passed through, everybody knew everybody else, and everybody seemed to know everybody else's business. The village was just large enough to have its own school, but there was just one schoolroom and one schoolmaster, a man whose ancient tweed jacket always carried the scent of tobacco smoke. The only other grown-up who came to the school was Granny Hopkins, who must have been well over eighty. She was a bad-tempered old woman who came in each morning to sweep the schoolroom floor and to stoke up the big cast-iron stove in the corner.

Granny Hopkins was making her way out through the

school gates just as Rusty arrived. She met his gaze briefly.

'Hurry up, Michael,' the old woman grunted. 'It won't do to be late.'

Rusty stood at the edge of the schoolyard and looked around him. Eileen Gilbert and some of the other girls were playing a singing game, and a group of boys were kicking a ball about. In the far corner of the yard, Colin Hopkins and his brother Sammy were hauling themselves clumsily to the top of the climbing frame. Rusty watched them, but he did not join in any of the games. He was happy playing on his own. Or, at any rate, he wasn't exactly unhappy.

It was hot in the schoolroom that morning, and Rusty's socks had begun to feel prickly around his legs. Quietly, using his feet, he pushed the socks down to his ankles. He knew that he must remember to pull them up again before going home to his mother, but he also knew that the schoolmaster didn't much mind about things like this.

Rusty looked around the room at the other children. They were sitting in pairs at double desks, and only Rusty sat alone. The others all had newer clothes than he did, and he remembered that they all had fathers too. Just for a moment, he felt lonely.

But then the schoolmaster caught his gaze and Rusty quickly turned his attention back to the column of division sums in front of him. The first one came out easily, and gradually he felt himself becoming absorbed in the comfortable world of numbers. He didn't notice when the schoolmaster left the room, and he didn't really notice when the rest of the class started to make a noise. When a paper dart landed on the desk in front of him, he brushed it away, still engrossed in his work. And he remained engrossed until he felt a light touch on his shoulder. The schoolmaster had come back into the room and was standing beside Rusty's desk. And at his side was a strange little girl.

'This is Laurel,' said the schoolmaster. 'Laurel, you'd better sit here. This is Michael Brown. People usually call him Rusty, you can probably guess why. Brown, Laurel's family have just arrived in the village. I'd like you to keep an eye on Laurel, make sure she finds her way about, all that sort of thing.'

The first thing Rusty noticed about Laurel was that her clothes were old and frayed and patched, just like his own. Her hair was long and thick and black and rather untidy-looking, and it hung loose, not in plaits or bunches. Her cheeks were a pale, yellowish-brown colour, and the big, dark eyes, looking straight at him, seemed to shine with a life of their own. She had a restless air about her, and her movements were quick and lively. Next to her, the other children seemed suddenly slow and dull. Rusty couldn't help himself from staring as she took her seat next to him.

'Rusty's got a girlfriend!'

The gruff voice from the back of the room belonged to one of the Hopkins brothers. There was some laughter at the remark, but the outbreak of disorder was swiftly quelled by the schoolmaster's beady stare.

To begin with, Rusty felt shy with Laurel. The other children, suspicious of anyone new or strange, kept a wary distance, so, by accident or design, the two were thrown together. At playtime, he took her around all the school buildings, and the yard, and the small muddy field at the end of the yard. Rusty soon found that Laurel needed his help with her school work. He supposed that she must have been doing different kinds of lessons at her last school.

In the weeks that followed, the two children started to become friends. When the weather was fine, they would some-times sit together on the climbing frame, dangling their feet from the second-highest platform. Laurel could wriggle her way between the bars like a cat, grinning down at Rusty as he hauled himself laboriously after her. When it rained, they would sit in the small shelter at the top of the field, the splintery bench scratching the backs of their legs.

'Your socks have fallen down,' Laurel teased him one day.

'I don't care,' replied Rusty. 'My mum's always going on about it, though.'

'I don't care either,' said Laurel. Suddenly, she leaned towards him and whispered in his ear, 'Anyway, you've got nice legs.'

Rusty felt a blush racing up his neck and face. But at that moment, in the distance, the schoolmaster started ringing his bell, and the boy was spared the embarrassment of a reply.

'Hello, Laurel,' said Mrs Brown, emerging from the tiny kitchen with a tray of jam tarts and two glasses of milk. 'Michael has been telling me all about you. In fact, he hasn't talked about anything else for days. Why don't you go and sit down at the table?'

Rusty's mother had been anxious to meet his new friend and had finally persuaded Rusty to invite her to the house. Now she stood at the kitchen door, watching while the two children helped themselves to food.

'Look what I've got,' said Laurel when they had finished eating. From an inner pocket of her smock she drew out a funny little leather purse, from which she emptied a dusty pile of coins onto the tablecloth. Rusty stared at them.

'The littlest coin from every country in the world,' she explained. 'Great-Grandmother gave me them. She collected them everywhere she went.'

Spellbound, Rusty sifted through the collection, fascinated by the strange shapes and colours. Some of the coins had holes in the middle, there was one made of bone, one shaped like a star . . . He picked out a tiny six-sided silver coin, turned it over in his hand. On one side was a picture of a woman's head, perhaps the queen of some strange country, and on the other side was a picture of a little animal that might have been a dog.

'Now, where did that one come from?' said Laurel. 'Great-Grandmother did tell me, but I forget now. We gave them all names, though. We used to call that one the puppy-penny. Do you like it?'

Rusty nodded silently.

'You can have it if you want,' said Laurel carelessly. 'I've got lots more.'

Still silent, Rusty slipped the coin into his pocket. And at that moment, he thought he could see something stirring restlessly behind Laurel's dark eyes. But a moment later it was gone. As Laurel started to gather up the remaining coins, Mrs Brown appeared from the kitchen. She glanced down at the table, and Rusty could not miss the sharp expression that crossed her face.

After Laurel had gone, Mrs Brown talked for a while of other things, of the ladies at the church, and of the old King in his palace in the city. She did a little darning, folded some sheets, polished her silver candlesticks. She did not mention Laurel, and she did not suggest inviting her again. Rusty felt that somehow the visit had not been a success, so he did not say anything either.

'Watch this,' said Laurel.

They were in a corner of the yard the next morning. Laurel stood facing the wall. She slowly extended her arms in the air above her head and pointed one toe forwards. Rusty watched her, puzzled, wondering what was going to happen. For a long moment, Laurel just stood there. Then she made a little skipping movement, and before Rusty could work out what was happening she was swinging her arms down in front of her, flicking her legs up behind her, and suddenly she had tipped herself upside down against the wall. The locks of her black hair swayed to and fro between her outstretched arms, her ragged skirt hung down across her face, and her pale brown legs stretched straight up, the heels of her battered sandals resting lightly against the wall. Rusty was speechless. He had never seen anything like this before. He could feel his stomach turning over and his heart seemed to be pounding in his throat. And then, suddenly, in a windmill of arms and legs, Laurel was right side up again, flushed and giggling, clapping the dust of the yard from her hands and brushing her long hair away from her face.

'I bet *you* can't do that.'

Rusty was feeling quite breathless and his clothes seemed tighter than usual.

'I wish I could,' he managed finally. 'Will you show me?'

Laurel looked at him. Slowly her eyebrows went up. Then she broke into a grin.

'All right.' She was laughing now. 'But first you'll have to catch me.' And she darted away across the yard.

The Theatre of Magic

The bells at the Institute of Calibration were sounding their morning peal across the city as the man in the wide-brimmed hat passed through the West Gate and strode purposefully along the broad tree-lined avenue that cut through the heart of the commercial district. The magician's robe with its gold-and-scarlet emblem billowed out around him, and the heavy tread of his stout boots warned bystanders to stand well clear of his path. He had trodden the same route, from his living quarters in the Western Suburb across the city to his workshop in the King's palace, every morning for the past twenty years, and the sights and sounds around him no longer impinged on his attention. Passing swiftly through the bustling market place, ignoring the jangling of carriage bells as he ploughed his undeviating furrow across busy thoroughfares, his gaze was directed at the ground and he seemed oblivious to all around him. He looked up just once, as the palace came into view, to scan the billowing line of signal kites that strained at their moorings on the gatehouse of the palace.

The fighting in the border campaign continued . . . the King would be in residence all week . . . sixteen criminals arrested by the militia . . . another brutal killing by the Wolf Boys . . . In other words, nothing out of the ordinary was taking place. Nodding to himself, he made his way through the front gates into the palace courtyard, briefly acknowledging the aged sentry who had occupied the same post for almost as long as he could remember. On the far side of the courtyard, he passed through an inconspicuous doorway set in a high stone wall, walked quickly up a narrow flight of steps, turned left, turned right, and emerged into a long straight corridor. Still staring at the floor, he continued briskly on his way, his boots echoing on the stone flags. Finally he halted at a heavy oak door that bore the following legend:

> *THEATRE OF MAGIC:*
> *LEONARDO PEGASUS,*
> *CHIEF MAGICIAN TO THE KING*
> *Please Ring for Attention*

Muttering to himself, he fumbled inside his robe, eventually locating a massive iron key that he inserted into the lock. After more fumbling, and some protesting noises from the lock, and considerably more muttering, he managed to turn the key, shoved open the creaking door, carefully wiped his feet on the worn doormat, and bent down to pick up several items of mail. He glanced vaguely around the antechamber, taking in the familiar dusty clutter of battered furniture, tottering stacks of papers, disordered shelves of books and discarded pieces of apparatus. The room was lit dimly through one small lattice window, but he needed no additional light to find his way around. He looked absently at the bundle of letters in his hand. Most of them he tossed dismissively onto a small writing desk, raising a medium-sized cloud of dust, but one letter bore the royal seal and this one, he knew, could not wait. He broke the seal, unrolled the parchment and glanced through the list of memoranda that it contained, scribbling the occasional note with a pencil stub which he retrieved from his waistcoat pocket.

He was interrupted in his concentration by the sudden harsh jangle of the doorbell, and the next few irritable minutes were spent dealing with two carrier's men who seemed to have called at the wrong address. It was a great relief to remind himself that his new assistant would shortly be joining him. It would certainly be useful to have some help about the place again, but on the other hand . . .

In his mind, he ran briefly through the familiar arguments for and against employing an assistant, then he packed the thoughts away and put them safely aside for later consideration. Removing his robe and hat and draping them untidily across a side table, he picked his way through the clutter towards a small doorway framed by a pair of old and faded velvet curtains, which had once been deep crimson but were now almost colourless. These he drew aside to reveal a low door that opened easily at the turn of a small shining key and, stooping slightly, he stepped through the doorway and down the three steps into the realm within.

After a moment's groping in the dark, his fingers located a panel of heavy electrical circuit-breakers. (At that time, only a few parts of the palace had been wired for electricity, but the special nature of the magician's work required access to the most up-to-date technology.) He threw a switch and the cavernous vaulted space of the Theatre of Magic blazed into life. His nostrils flared reflexively at the familiar smell of scorched dust mingled with paint, glue and ozone. Leonardo Pegasus paused to draw breath. Then he stepped onto the main stage of his theatre and set to work.

The main stage was at that time entirely taken up by a huge relief model of the border territory at the southern extremity of the kingdom. The King had been waging a military campaign there for the past eighteen months, and the magician's model replicated the state of that campaign in minute detail. Every feature of the terrain was accurately represented. Tiny scaled-down models of fighting units and war engines dotted the landscape, some of them puny and feeble, others sturdy and bursting with energy. Each unit was accurately calibrated for levels of training and equipment and quality of leadership. In places the opposing armies were partially obscured by movable translucent patches of various sizes and colours representing the transient effects of light and darkness, cloud and rain. The magician studied the sheaf of notes that he still held in his hand and made a few adjustments to bring the model up to date. Satisfied at last, he made his way to the far corner of the theatre to a caged area where his special equipment was stored. From here he carefully wheeled the Empathy Engine into position.

The Empathy Engine was housed in a mahogany cabinet about the size of a large chest of drawers, with a padded leather seat, attached by sturdy cast-iron brackets, on which the magician could sit facing the controls. A sloping panel on the top surface bore several ranks of dials and switches, and at the front and sides were mounted assorted brass levers, handles, cranks and pedals. At the back was a trapdoor that opened to reveal coils of multi-coloured cable with various mechanical attachments. Leonardo unrolled two of these cables and carefully attached them to the small figure of the enemy commander at the head of the oppos-ing forces. He attached a second set of wires to the forward command post of the King's army. He then pulled out a pair of solidly built Bakelite headphones that he clamped over his ears. Seating himself and grunting, he reached into a recess on the control panel from which he pulled out a shaded pair of eye-pieces attached to the machine by a long, wobbly set of lazy tongs. Peering into the eyepieces, he began to make adjustments to his controls. His concentration was unrelenting and he worked in silence. He had only a few hours before the King's next visit.

As well as the main stage on which Leonardo was working, the Theatre of Magic had a number of side stages housing other proj-ects at varying stages of development. One such project con-cerned the forthcoming reorganisation in the Herald's Department. The model on the stage represented the departmen-tal offices, and little people could be moved from desk to desk in an effort to find an arrangement that was acceptable to everyone. On another stage were the preliminary sketches for an ambitious project to predict the effects of some new tax legislation due to come before Council in the autumn. At the far end of the room was a large table covered with a jumble of scrolls, books, notes, diagrams and sheaves of plans, all cloaked in a thick layer of dust.

And tucked away behind a curtain in an obscure corner, safe

from prying eyes, the inquisitive visitor might have been surprised to discover another small model stage. On this stage
stood a model of Leonardo's own workshop. At the centre of it
stood the miniature figure of Leonardo. And beside the figure
of Leonardo stood another figure. It was the figure of a thin,
pale, fair-haired young woman.

Laurel's Secret

For several days it had rained hard in the village and the children had been made to stay indoors, restlessly confined to the
schoolroom. At the first sign of a break in the clouds, the
schoolmaster sent them outside to dispel some of their energy.
Rusty dug down into the games box, through layers of musty-
smelling beanbags and skipping ropes, and picked out his
favourite set of quoits.

He was not a good shot with the quoits. However hard he
tried, he found that the flaking rubber hoops somehow kept
missing the peg, but still he liked to keep trying. Sometimes he
tried different ways of pitching, hoping that one day he might
hit on the perfect action, but today he was doing even worse
than usual. He was collecting his hoops from the puddles in
which they always seemed to land when, to his astonishment,
three other hoops skimmed briskly past him, dropped onto the
peg, and spiralled one after another to the bottom. Turning, he
saw Laurel standing at his shoulder.

'Can't you shut your mouth?' she giggled. 'You look stupid
like that.'

'How did you do that?' asked Rusty.

'I don't know,' came the reply. 'I just sort of found I could do
it. I . . . well, I imagine them being there, and then there they
are. Go on, you try. I'll help you.'

Rusty wasn't sure exactly what Laurel was doing to help him,
but when he tried concentrating on the target, he discovered
to his surprise that he was suddenly doing better.

'I had a dream about you last night,' said Laurel, throwing another hoop. 'You were in a big old house. I think you were waiting for someone.'

'I had a funny dream too,' said Rusty. 'I was with an old man in a rowing boat. He had a moustache. And he was dressed like a soldier. And then the boat got stuck on some rocks, and I dived into the water and I swam across to an island. And—'

'Can you swim?' Laurel interrupted him.

'A bit,' said Rusty. 'My mother sometimes lets me go in the river. Can you?'

'Like an otter,' came the reply. 'And I can dive. Have you ever swum in the sea?'

At that moment heavy drops of rain began to spatter the ground again. The two children gathered up the quoits and ran across the field to the shelter, jumping in puddles, splashing one another and shouting excitedly.

They collapsed on the bench together, both giggling uncontrollably, their raincoats soaked. The air in the shelter smelled of wet gaberdine.

'I know a secret,' said Laurel.

'I know heaps of secrets,' said Rusty. 'I bet I know more than you.'

'Maybe you do,' said Laurel, 'but I bet my secret's the biggest.' She paused, looked down, then looked up again. 'The biggest, and the most dangerous. I'll tell you if you like. Only you mustn't tell anyone else.'

Suddenly the laughter had stopped. Rusty felt Laurel's touch on his shoulder, and he felt the dark eyes beckoning, and he felt something behind the eyes reaching out towards him. For a long moment time hung suspended, and Rusty felt almost as if his heart had stopped beating. Slowly, reluctantly, he could feel his head turning towards the girl. And, far away, deep behind the dark eyes, he caught a glimpse of hard fires burning. And then Laurel leaned towards him and he could feel her warm breath on his cheek as she whispered to him.

★　★　★

The next morning, Laurel did not arrive at the school. At play-time, she still hadn't arrived, and Rusty noticed that there were several other empty places in the schoolroom. Loitering around the yard, he overheard a scrap of conversation from a group of girls.

'Janet's mum says she's caught the scarlet fever, and their Tommy's staying away from school too.'

Rusty was frightened by this news, but eventually he plucked up courage to speak to the schoolmaster. The man took his pipe from his mouth and fiddled with it for a moment before answering.

'Yes, young Brown, there is an epidemic,' he said finally. 'But don't worry. It happens every few years, and the ones who are sick mostly get better after a few weeks.'

'What about Laurel?'

'Yes, I'm sure she'll be back.' The man looked vague for a moment. 'You seem to be getting on well with Laurel.'

'She's nice. A bit . . . strange, though.'

'Well, that's good, isn't it?' replied the master. He gave Rusty an odd look. 'We can often learn things from strange people. Perhaps you'll learn something from her. I have to say, you seem to be getting a little bit bored with my lessons.'

'Sometimes it seems too easy,' replied the boy. 'I keep want-ing the next bit.'

The schoolmaster looked at him thoughtfully, still fingering his pipe.

'Time to get back to work,' he said finally. 'Where's my bell?'

Across the yard, the children had already started to form themselves into a line.

The Herald's Office

Halfway through the morning, the magician paused in his work, stepped into the antechamber, and put the kettle on the stove. He shuddered at the astringent taste of the instant coffee, then remembered that Alice would be arriving the following Monday. Alice was the young woman whose image Leonardo kept so carefully hidden from visitors. He wondered whether she would be able to make a decent cup of coffee.

It was on one of his routine weekly visits to the Herald's Office that Leonardo had first met Alice. The Herald was the official responsible for promulgating royal decrees, issuing the minutes of Council meetings, and informing the public of any other items likely to be of interest. Her office was housed in a ramshackle half-timbered building situated on a narrow lane that ran behind the main thoroughfare leading downhill from the palace. Many people at that time were still unable to read, so the promulgations had to be carried out by teams of criers. These iron-throated individuals were employed to shout the news from a number of strategically situated pitches in the city's squares, markets and places of recreation. Anybody who wished an item of news to be inserted into the weekly bulletins would bring the relevant documentation along to the office, where, on payment of the correct fee, the item would be registered by one of the intake clerks. The material would then be sorted into categories, transcribed, and finally pasted up onto the unwieldy lengths of parchment known as master scrolls. From these, the clerks would eventually copy the weekly prompt scrolls that each crier carried to her pitch. There, she would beat her drum until a crowd began to gather, at which point she would ceremonially break the seal on the prompt scroll and begin shouting the news. A good crier did not just read out the bare facts that were written on the scroll. A good crier had the gift of weaving the facts into a real story, a colourful, spellbinding narrative that drew listeners in large numbers, kindled their imagination, and held them in thrall right up to the climax, after which they would applaud enthusiastically, sometimes throwing money on especially good days. And after the final roll on the drum, they would disperse and go about their business in a state of near-rapturous enlightenment. A good crier working a prestigious circuit could become a celebrity in her own right, sometimes even employing her own musicians to beat her drums for her. Shouting the news could be a rewarding career indeed.

Leonardo had met Alice on a Friday. Most of the work on the prompt scrolls was carried out over the weekend, so on a Friday morning the Herald's office was generally reckoned to be a good place for bumping into influential people with a story to tell.

The intake area of the office was long and narrow, the ancient stone-flagged floor comfortably uneven, and the space broken up at random intervals by tottering columns that seemed barely to support the yellowed ceiling. The room was utterly ill-suited for accommodating the dense crowds of people who milled around the intake desks, but it had been the same for generations and nobody would have dreamed of suggesting any alteration. The excited chatter, the clerks' exasperated cries of 'Who's next, please?', and the occasional roars of derision, which occurred when someone who should have known better was found standing in the wrong queue, combined to create an almost unbearable, never-ending cacophony. And since most of the incumbents of official positions at that time still wore the traditional garb of their brotherhoods, complete with armorial emblazonments, the crowd presented a spectacle of clashing colours that assaulted the eyes just as the noise assaulted the ears.

So, on the Friday in question, the magician's colourful figure had attracted no special attention. He dived into the throng and joined the cheerful, noisy fight for places in the queues for the various intake desks. Eventually finding what he hoped was the right queue, Leonardo was momentarily taken aback to hear a harsh, grating voice coming from somewhere around the level of his waist.

'Well, if it isn't Wiz the wise magician! We've got to stop meeting like this.'

Leonardo winced at the disrespectful nickname. The owner of the gruff voice was Veronique, a long-standing acquaintance who occupied one of the Senior Clown positions in the Jester's department.

'How's business, Vero?'

'Never better, sweetheart,' bragged Veronique. 'Busy department, always will be busy. I've said it often enough. Everyone needs to laugh, especially in times like these. What have I been telling you all these years? In hard times a magician will get thin, but a clown will always stay fat.' She slapped her round belly and then poked Leonardo in the ribs by way of comparison.

Leonardo looked down with irritation at the short, tubby figure in her motley costume and grotesque make-up. He found Veronique an insensitive companion, was sometimes infuriated by her, but knew that he would always forgive her abrasiveness because in times of trouble she had been a loyal friend.

'These queues seem to get longer every week,' observed Leonardo.

'Long on Entertainment, at any rate. Not so long on Magic,' came the caustic reply. 'Hello, there's a funny-looking girl on your desk. Haven't seen her before. Bit skinny for my taste.'

Leonardo caught a brief glimpse of a thin, serious-looking young woman with pale, austerely sculpted features and straight fair hair. Then, before he could study her further, the queue for Entertainment surged forward as a second intake clerk joined the one at the desk, and Leonardo found himself temporarily marooned behind a column, his view obscured, pondering yet again on the inconveniences of working as a one-man team.

Eventually he reached the front of the queue. The young woman smiled briefly in acknowledgement as he handed over his documents. He noted with approval her air of calm concentration as she swiftly scanned the text, attached an official cover form, and guided him through the routine questions concerning content, urgency and likely popularity of the item. She looked up at him with polite expectancy while he rummaged through his pockets for the fee. Her eyes were an unusual shade of blue.

'I haven't seen you before, have I?' ventured Leonardo.

'I've only just started,' she replied. Something about her softly accented voice told him that she was not city-born. He paused briefly in his rummaging.

'Have you come from far away?'

'Quite far, yes.'

Obviously a woman of few words. Judging by her accent, Leonardo reckoned that she probably hailed from the north-east corner of the kingdom, possibly one of the outer isles.

'Here we are.' He had finally found the right change. 'I hope you're settling in all right down here.'

'Oh yes, I seem to be, thank you.' She started to make out the receipt. 'It's different, though.'

'Thank you. No, keep it, I never know what to do with all those little scraps of parchment.'

Another brief smile lit up her face.

'Anyway, I'd better get on, you've got other people waiting. I'll doubtless see you again. What's your name, by the way?'

'Alice.'

'Well, goodbye, Alice. I'm sure you'll enjoy the city once you get the hang of it. Oh, by the way, people sometimes call me Wiz. But my proper name is Leonardo Pegasus. And my formal title is Master Pegasus.'

'Ah yes.' The girl paused. 'Master Pegasus. I think I've heard a bit about you. Well, goodbye, then.'

'Goodbye.'

She treated him to another brief smile as he made his way towards the exit, and then she was out of his sight.

After that chance meeting, the magician had started to think seriously about employing an assistant once more. He swallowed the last shuddering gulp of coffee. And he wondered again what Alice's coffee would be like.

★   ★   ★

Dusty

The holiday fortnight and the annual fair were approaching, and there was a growing sense of excitement in the village. The fair was the event to which everybody looked forward eagerly all year, and which everybody talked about for months afterwards, for here could be found goods too exotic to be offered at the weekly market, too varied to be carried by the wandering pedlars. Here could be found traders offering merchandise from every corner of the world: bolts of fabric in every imaginable colour, wines and spirits in massive casks, complicated-looking household appliances, packhorses and racehorses and stud-horses. And accompanying the traders would be an extraordinary variety of entertainers: mummers, dancers, jugglers and puppeteers, wandering criers bringing news from city and town, as well as mysterious people who performed in closed tents to which children were not admitted. Little wonder, in this inward-looking rural backwater, that the fortnight of the fair was anticipated with longing for months beforehand.

But somehow, this year, as the time approached, Rusty Brown found himself unable to work up any excitement. He couldn't forget about the scarlet fever, and he was frightened for Laurel, and he felt that nothing could make him happy until he knew that she was well again. He thought about going round to her house to see her, but he realised that he did not know where she lived, and somehow he could not pluck up the courage to ask anyone. At playtimes he moped around the yard on his own. Once or twice he tried to turn himself upside down the way Laurel had done, but he achieved nothing more than a grazed knee and a bump on his head.

As the days passed, the absent children returned one by one to school, and by the start of the holiday fortnight, everyone except Laurel had been back for over a week. Rusty felt sick and anxious. He ate his meals with difficulty, but somehow he knew that he had to hide his unhappiness from his mother.

★   ★   ★

At last the holiday began. Rusty walked slowly up the lane, along the main street, and past the church to the fairground. It was a hot, dry day, and he dragged his battered sandals in the dirt, wiping them from time to time on his socks, which had as usual collapsed in untidy folds around his ankles. Somehow the fair felt flat and dull compared with other years. The flags hung limply in the still air, the goods on the stalls looked faded and sad, and the animals sat wearily in their pens, scratching themselves. The music that he heard would not have been out of place at a funeral, and the sword-swallowers and fire-eaters seemed to be suffering from indigestion. Rusty wandered from stall to stall, ignoring the patter of the barkers, until unexpectedly his eye was caught by a shabby, inconspicuous hoopla stall. It was set slightly back from the main thoroughfare.

'Throw a hoop and win a prize, young sir! Every hoop over the pole wins a prize! Three hoops over wins a special prize! Roll up and try your luck, young Rusty!'

Rusty was startled at the use of his name, as he was sure he had not met the sallow-faced man before. Probably it was just a lucky guess, not so hard, really . . .

Before he knew it, he was feeling in his pocket for a coin. His fingers found nothing but fluff, a piece of string with a fish-hook attached, an unpleasantly soft piece of toffee . . . but then he felt something small and flat and six-sided, wriggling its way out of the corner where it had been hiding, wriggling its way into his fingers. It was Laurel's puppy-penny. Uncertain of its value, he held it out to the man. The man looked at it sharply, then he nodded, plucked it quickly away, and handed the boy three battered wooden hoops.

For a moment Rusty thought he caught a faraway flicker behind the man's eyes. But an instant later it was forgotten, suddenly eclipsed by a sharp, vivid sequence of images, of the three hoops rattling down against the chipped paint to settle one on top of another on the board, the three hoops encircling the wooden pole, the three hoops skimming briskly through the air. And then his wrist seemed to be flicking the hoops one after another straight onto their target and all the people were cheering.

'Well done, young sir, well done indeed!' shouted the man. 'The winner of a very special prize!'

He reached under the counter and produced a light brown, lively-looking puppy with pricked-up ears, a black patch on one side of his face, and a thin, energetically wagging tail.

'Every boy needs a dog, young sir. His name is Dusty. Take good care of him now.'

Rusty wandered around the fair in a daze, dragging the small dog behind him on a length of rough hairy string that the man had given him. He wasn't really sure whether he wanted a puppy, but he was quite certain that his mother would be cross with him for bringing it home. Eventually he made up his mind to return it to the man. But, try as he might, he could not find the stall again. And so the boy headed back up the lane towards home, the string chafing the palm of his hand as the dog made constant detours to inspect invisible objects at the roadside.

When he finally got home, his mother's words came as a pleasant surprise.

'I can't think how we can afford to feed him,' she said. 'But look under the stairs, and I think you'll find an old basket. That would do for him to sleep in. We'll have to put it up in your bedroom, though – I can't have him down here messing up the clean sheets.'

'You mean I can keep him?'

For a moment she didn't say anything.

'I suppose so.' Her voice had a kinder sound than usual. 'He might cheer you up a bit. You really seem to have been down in the dumps since . . .' She paused again, then seemed to make up her mind. 'Is it to do with Laurel?'

'Oh. Oh yes, where is she?' Suddenly, Rusty could feel the tears pricking the backs of his eyes.

'I'm sorry, Michael,' said Mrs Brown slowly. 'You'll have to understand this sometime. You see . . . Laurel won't be coming back again.'

'What, not ever?'

'No, not ever.'

Now the tears were running down Rusty's freckled cheeks. He hugged the little dog tightly to him. Against his chest, he could feel the small heart beating.

Alice

During the later period of his reign, the King had amassed a large number of personal counsellors, of whom Leonardo Pegasus was the senior specialist in those techniques of the will that were at that time collectively refered to as Magic. Leonardo's position entitled him to a number of privileges. His living quarters were located outside the city walls on the prestigious slopes of the Western Suburb, he was paid a generous stipend, and his work was stimulating but rarely overtaxing. He was also entitled to employ an assistant.

Most of Leonardo's peers employed one or more assistants. Each year, cohorts of eager girls and boys graduated from the various academies, and many more made their way to the city from all corners of the kingdom. Each one of them hoped to find a position in which they could start picking up the basics of one craft or another, and from which they could subsequently lay the foundations of a successful career. To begin with, of course, they would be expected to carry out all the more mundane tasks that were essential to the running of a busy department, but this was a small price to pay for the rewards that lay in store. A position with one of the King's counsellors was naturally one of the most sought after, and the counsellors could therefore afford to be very particular indeed in their choice of assistant. There was much undeclared competition between them as to who could acquire the most personable, talented and attractive assistant, but nevertheless this was one privilege that Leonardo, almost alone among his peers, had for a long time been reluctant to take up. From his limited experience of working with others, he knew himself to be a poor delegator, finding that explaining a task to someone else always seemed to take up far more time than simply doing it for himself. And he had also observed, from the experiences of some of his less fortunate or more careless peers, that employing an assistant, especially a young and attractive assistant, had its own special dangers.

For, in those days, alongside the privileges of rank came certain constraints. The King's counsellors were forbidden to marry, and they were forbidden to engage in any form of sexual liaison. Only single persons with an unblemished record were accepted as counsellors, and every counsellor was required to swear a solemn oath, stating, among other things, that he or she would remain in a state of chastity for as long as he or she held office. Of course, in reality the King's counsellors suffered the same appetites as any other group of men and women, and although these things were seldom spoken of in public, it was widely believed that many of their relationships with their assistants went some way beyond what was required for strictly professional purposes.

Naturally, these liaisons (assuming, of course, that they existed at all) were carried out with the utmost discretion, and it was only through accidental discovery, perhaps combined with the threat of blackmail, that any of them ever became exposed to public scrutiny. But, through one mischance or another, it happened that a number of Leonardo's professional associates had in recent times been unlucky enough to come to grief in just such a way. The Chief Actuary, for example, who had long been indulging a weakness for dark-skinned boys, was unfortunate enough to leave open the blinds of his top-floor office on the very day of the year when the windows were to be cleaned. And who would ever forget the embarrassing detour from the straight and narrow path suffered by the Assistant Head of

Palace Security at the hands of those long-legged, sure-footed twins from the mountain district? Both worthies had been hastily banished to remote outposts, and neither would be seen again in the city, at least not for the duration of the present reign.

Returning to his workshop from the Herald's Office, Leonardo shuddered at the prospect. But then his mind turned towards coffee, and a more reassuring thought introduced itself. The magician reached for his abacus and started to calculate how much time he was wasting by having personally to carry out the many mundane tasks of his office. He reached for a quill and some ink, and a sheet of parchment on which to make a list. He estimated the hours spent each week on opening mail, answering the door, delivering messages . . . and, of course, making coffee. It would certainly be useful to have a second pair of hands about the place. He could employ someone sensible, someone efficient, someone with a decorous, professional approach. It would enable him to concentrate his attention on the more important work, and in addition . . . it would give him more time to develop a certain project that he had had in mind for many years . . .

The pale, serious face of the girl at the Herald's Office formed itself into a vision on the blank parchment at which he was still staring.

Over the next few months, Leonardo came to look forward to his visits to the Herald's Office. His conversations with Alice were always brief, and she revealed little about herself, but somehow Leonardo began to find himself captivated by the very brevity of their exchanges, punctuated as they were by the warmth of her occasional smiles, the unruffled gaze of her unusually blue eyes. He came to believe that he could detect some indefinable rapport or affinity between them. And gradually his visits started to become more frequent. On one occasion, he even forgot to take with him the documents that had been the pretext for his journey.

The girl was constantly in his thoughts. She even began to make appearances in his dreams. He realised that he was going to have to do something.

And so it came about that in his spare hours Leonardo Pegasus started to build the model on the small stage that he kept hidden behind the curtain in his workshop. He reconstructed the face and the form of the girl in as much detail as he could recall, he dressed the miniature figure in the livery of the Brotherhood of Magicians, and he positioned it on the model stage side by side with his own small-scale likeness. He coupled up the empathy engine, and through it he scrutinised the two little people through each other's ears and eyes, he experienced their thoughts and their feelings, and he succeeded in convincing himself that the future he was constructing could hold nothing but good for him. He examined every detail of his design and he satisfied himself on every question. Or rather, he satisfied himself on every question except one, and that one he somehow forgot to ask.

Because somehow, despite his years of education and training, despite his position as the leading magician in the kingdom, Leonardo had oh-so-conveniently allowed himself to forget one vital clause of the Code of Conduct of the Brotherhood of Magicians, the Code that he had spent so many long nights learning by heart for his final examinations at the Academy of Magic. And the clause in question ran thus:

8.14: Use of the Arbitrator.
When the Magician has a personal presence as a Participant in the Segment of Future that he is constructing, that Segment cannot be considered Well Constructed until it has been subject to the thorough scrutiny of an independent Arbitrator who has no personal concern in the matter.
The penalty for an infringement of this Regulation is automatic Banishment to an Outpost.

In reality, of course, this rule was ignored by the majority of practitioners. It was just so convenient to use one's magical craft, now and then, to bring about the fulfilment of run-of-the-mill personal wishes, that few could resist the temptation to do so. And surely the Code had only ever been intended to prevent gross or dangerous abuses of the craft, not to place pointless obstacles in the way of a little trivial corner-cutting? And besides, the risk of discovery was really very slight. Leonardo, with an arrogance common to many of his seniority, had by now convinced himself that he could arbitrate on his own future in a totally objective way, and he had therefore decided that he would be quite justified in pressing ahead to construct the future that he had designed in miniature.

And, by a happy chance, the reorganisation of the Herald's Office happened to be on Leonardo's current list of projects. He knew that most of the incumbents of junior positions there would be under at least a three-year indenture, but he knew equally that such indentures were routinely broken by those in senior positions when they found it convenient to do so. He frowned down at the model. After a moment's consideration, he rolled back his wide coat-sleeves, reached down into the corner that represented the paste-up shop, and picked up two neighbouring work tables. He scrutinised them through his spectacles, turned them this way and that, and then he set them back down, but now they were pushed together to form a single larger table . . . Perhaps in this way three people could do the work of four . . . Now, the chief pastemaster could in no circumstances be expected to work in the same room as a certain female copyist . . . but here was a position in the copying studio which would certainly prosper in the hands of someone suitably talented . . .

He worked on into the night, making finer and finer adjustments and from time to time connecting up the Empathy Engine to experience for himself the new state of affairs. And eventually he began to understand what had to be done.

★　　★　　★

In due course, the pieces of Leonardo's plan fell into place. The reorganisation at the Herald's Office was announced, and the Herald personally congratulated Leonardo on his ingenuity. She declared herself well satisfied with the new organisational structure, while conveniently glossing over the distasteful fact that, in the course of its implementation, a number of unfortunate individuals would inevitably be displaced from their positions.

As it happened, one of these displaced persons was a young intake clerk named Alice. Although Alice had been employed at the Herald's Office for a much shorter time than any of her colleagues, the Herald was relieved to be able to inform her that a new position awaited her as Personal Assistant to one of the King's senior counsellors.

On the day of Alice's transfer to her new position, there occurred a mass escape of lobsters in the fish market, and Leonardo therefore suffered an unwelcome delay to his morning journey. He was made to wait in a frustrated group of pedestrians until the fishmongers had rounded up their stock. When he was finally permitted to proceed, he continued on his way with an even quicker tread than usual. Rounding the final corner of the corridor a few minutes late, he was relieved to discover the slight figure of Alice awaiting him patiently at his doorway. At the sound of his boots on the flagstones, she turned to face him.

Leonardo looked her up and down with approval. Alice had already kitted herself out with the appropriate costume. She wore a new ceremonial cap and tunic bearing the intricate scarlet-and-gold emblem of the Brotherhood of Magicians, and with her neat black hose and her pointed black boots and her pale face and her pale hair, she looked more than anything like a character from a pack of playing cards.

Favourably impressed, Leonardo showed her into the outer office and started to explain to her where things were kept. She asked few questions, but he soon realised that she was taking in everything he said, and seeking additional information only when necessary. The magician began to relax, sensing that the partnership was indeed destined to be a propitious one.

Alice learned the job quickly and within a few days was effort-lessly dealing with correspondence, fielding visitors, and imposing order on the piles of clutter that had threatened to overwhelm the antechamber. She carried out every task with calm efficiency, and Leonardo never had to repeat an instruc-tion to her. Yet somehow Alice seemed to impose nothing of her own personality on the workshop. Every morning, she was at her post at precisely the appointed hour. During the work-ing day, her dedication to the task in hand was total. And at the end of the day, she was gone. Strangely, Leonardo could not recall ever seeing her arrive or leave. He began to be aware of an insubstantial, almost weightless quality about her. She made no noise, created no fuss, introduced no personal possessions into her workspace, and moved about the room only when necessary, scarcely disturbing the air around her when she did so. Sometimes it seemed to Leonardo that he could only have dreamed her into existence.

Yet, after a very short time, he found himself wondering how he had ever managed without her.

From the Journal of Victor Lazarus

Monday 26th January (continued)

Although the road was familiar to me, I could not immediately locate the address I was seeking. I walked up and down several times before I eventually discovered what must once have been an imposing entrance. The wrought-iron gates, almost buried in a tall, overgrown hedge of thorn bushes, were thick with rust. One of them hung askew by a single twisted hinge, but between the gates there was a gap just wide enough to admit a man and, after an unexpected moment of apprehension, I managed to squeeze myself through. Pausing to brush down my uniform, I could at last see what lay within.

For a moment, I stood frozen in awe. High above me, at the top of a sloping patch of ground, loomed the house. It was a tall, imposing structure, very much in the gothic style, thickly encrusted with mullioned windows, gables, turrets, chimney pots, weathervanes and gargoyles. The lower storeys were encircled by a dense jungle of unpruned shrubs and undergrowth that excluded all light from the windows, and from this untamed mass the twisting tendrils of creepers made wild sorties, snaking up the drainpipes and choking the guttering. Yet more unruly vegetation overwhelmed the garden, overgrowing the paths, intertwining with the tall hedge and even with the gates through which I had so recently passed. Above me towered tall trees whose gloomy shadows blotted out whatever patches of light might have remained. I could form no notion of how far the garden extended behind the house or what might lie concealed in the dank undergrowth. Perhaps it was only my imagination, but the air seemed colder and damper inside the gates. In a daze, I moved forward.

Before me, the front path ascended in a series of uneven stone terraces. Carefully I picked my way between the huge thistles that had forced their way up between the flagstones, until eventually I arrived at a steeper flight of cracked steps that led me between crumbling pillars to the imposing front porch. Facing me stood a tall pair of entrance doors, from which the paint had long ago peeled away to reveal grey weathered oak. I tugged at the rusty bell pull, but could hear no sound from within. For a minute I waited, but there came no response, so finally I gave the right-hand door a cautious push. To my surprise, it creaked open.

I found myself in a high-ceilinged hall. Above me hung the ruins of a massive chandelier, now thick with dust and cobwebs. To my right rose a heavy mahogany staircase that drew the gaze upwards into the half-light of the upper storeys. Before me stood another pair of double doors. Into each of these doors was set a narrow pane of tarnished glass. Standing on my toes to peer through, I caught a glimpse of a long, dusty corridor in whose panelled walls closed doors stood at regular intervals. Finally, to my left, I discovered a kind of waiting area. Some attempt had clearly been made to render this presentable. The floor had been swept and the sills dusted. On a low table at the centre of the room was arranged a battered chess set. Against the walls stood three long, wooden benches that might at one time have been church pews. Seated on the benches were two men.

Nodding to them, I sat down, carefully pulling up my breeches at the knee to avoid spoiling the creases. There followed a short silence, during which I started to pass the time by studying my two companions. The first was a thin, elderly man with a balding head and small gold-rimmed spectacles. He sat with a forward stoop, and was dressed in the old-fashioned formal style in black coat and waistcoat, highly polished black shoes, striped grey trousers with turn-ups, and a stiff high collar and cravat. A gold watch-chain bisected the front of his waistcoat, and from his pocket he periodically drew a heavy gold watch on which he checked the time, giving sniffs of increasing disapproval. The second man was younger and more heavily built. He was clad in the rough overalls and heavy boots of a manual labourer. The sleeves of his thick, collarless shirt were rolled up above the elbow, disclosing muscular arms which he constantly folded and refolded. It occurred to me that all three of us might well be in competition for the same position.

There followed another long interval. Eventually I decided to break the silence by inquiring of the others how they came to be there. The older man, who was named Harold, told me that until his retirement he had been a librarian. He said that he was looking for a little part-time employment with which to supplement his pension, and that he had replied to an advertisement that he had found displayed on the noticeboard at the local pensioners' club. The younger man was named Sam. He said that he was a jobbing handyman and had recently arrived from the country. He was engaged to be married to a young girl from his home village, and was seeking regular work in order to build up some savings to give them a start in life. He had heard of the position by word of mouth from a drinking companion. Each man had applied in writing, and each had received a reply identical to my own. Since arriving at the house, neither had seen anyone.

None of us was much gifted in the art of conversation, and so another silence ensued. I stared down at the low table in front of me. After a little while, my eyes lighted upon the chess board. As I gazed at it, it gradually dawned on me that it was not of the ordinary kind. Instead of the customary squares, the field of play consisted of a labyrinthine array of interlocking radial lines and concentric circles. And instead of the usual red and white, the chessmen were in three colours: black, white and grey. I had just started to notice that the chessmen were not even of the usual shapes when I became aware of what appeared to be the corner of an envelope protruding from beneath the board. I reached down and drew it towards me. The envelope bore two lines of script in a familiar spidery hand:

> *To the guests in my house.*
> *Please open and read.*

The others must have noticed it at the same instant, for when I looked up I could see the same unspoken question in both pairs of eyes. I looked back at them with raised eyebrows. The young man replied with an immediate nod of the head and, after a brief pause for consideration, the older man replied in the same fashion. Breaking the seal on the envelope, I read aloud to them:

> *Dear friends and helpers,*
> *I am currently living in temporary accommodation, but I am hoping that I shall one day be able to return to my house. I would*

therefore be most grateful if you could kindly put things back in order for me. Feel free to do whatever you consider necessary. You will find a chequebook, which should give you access to adequate funds. Would a year be enough time for you to get everything ready? Please let me know if not. I look forward to meeting you on my return. Good luck.

The signature was once again indecipherable.

I looked at my companions and they looked at me. And then the three of us arose as one man, stepped towards the double doors, and passed through into the main part of the house.

Two:
FEAR OF THE DANCER

At the topmost place in my house, I have a favourite spot in which I can watch and I can wait. At the top of a narrow spiral stair stands a tall turret, a turret in which there is but a single six-sided chamber, a chamber bare of all furnishings, a chamber with one tall window to each aspect. Above the windows, a beam spans the roof space, and from this beam, for hour after hour, I hang inverted by my knees, and I watch the landscape that spreads out beneath me. And from here, with just a little concentration, I can see everything I wish to see.

In a village at the foot of the hills, I see a boy and his dog, journeying together through the adventure of childhood. Today they have waded across a stream to the little island where they love to play for hours unending. I watch them as they climb trees, fish for sticklebacks or swim in the water, I watch them as they play at outlaws or pirates or smugglers. I know that the boy has few friends of his own kind, and I know that his love for the dog conceals a great hurt in his own young life. I watch the boy and on his loneliness I grow strong.

In another direction, in a great city at the heart of the land, I see a man of awesome powers, a counsellor, a magician. I shiver as I watch him, for he draws on hidden forces to ensnare an innocent girl, a girl by whose grace he has become enchanted. Perhaps the man does not yet understand the path down which he travels, perhaps he does not yet fully comprehend the true nature of his actions, but I know that he too once nursed a wound in his heart, and I know that he seeks now to heal it by whatever means he can command. I grow strong as I watch him, for I thrive on his torment and on his pain and on his hunger.

And as I survey the landscape beneath me, I can follow the journey of each one of you. I watch you as you hesitate at each crossroads, I watch you as you puzzle over the signs, I watch you as you take your first faltering steps along one road or another. And I watch you as you trace out all your interlocking pathways, sometimes turning to greet one another, sometimes uniting in happiness and joy, but more often spurning the other's path, foregoing all hope of union, grieving later at your loss. I study with curiosity the roads you follow, but my deepest love, my darkest passion, is for the roads you spurn, for by these roads I shall one day return to possess you.

I could stay here for ever, for I love to watch the patterns you weave, but today I awoke with the certain knowledge that visitors are on their way. And that means that there will soon be work for me to do.

For I know that soon you will be returning to my house. For years you have spurned me, for years you have convinced yourself that your life's destination lies in your hands alone, but soon you must return. For you have neglected me, Lazarus, for too long you have stayed away from my house, and now there is a price to be paid. You must take heed of me now. You must take heed before it is too late.

From my high place, I watch patiently as you and your companions cross the threshold of my house to brave the realm within.

From the Journal of Victor Lazarus

Monday 26th January (continued)

As we passed one by one through the double doors, we scarcely dared draw breath. Every sound was muffled by the dust of years, and the silence and the gloom of the house enveloped us utterly. Above us loomed bulky items of furniture and rolls of carpet, their outlines softened by dust sheets and obscured by cobwebs. Blankets of dust cloaked the chandeliers and choked the cast-iron radiators. Countless motes of dust swam in the half-light, dislodged by the draught of our passing. Thick drifts of dust carpeted the very boards on which we stepped. A tentative triple trail of footprints marked our progress as we passed softly from room to room.

The stillness of the house seemed inviolate until, abruptly, Harold was seized by a fit of coughing. After copious apologies, he was obliged eventually to proceed with a large pocket handkerchief held over his mouth and nose. Sam and I elected to follow his example before we resumed our exploration.

As we threw open door after door, we discovered chambers containing locked cabinets, chambers containing packages neatly wrapped and stacked, and chambers containing objects strewn around with reckless abandon. When we ascended to the upper storeys, we passed through a further succession of rooms that appeared only to have been used for storage, rooms where tottering piles of books and albums and documents spread out across the floors and towered higher than a man could reach. Finally we arrived at the very top of the house, which we approached by means of a narrow spiral staircase. This led to a tiny six-sided turret room that appeared quite empty. I did not linger here, as I thought I could detect an unpleasant chill in the air.

Having now inspected every room, we turned around and began the descent. By the time we reached the ground floor, the daylight had long since turned to dusk. We therefore agreed to return to our homes and to meet again early on the morrow.

Back once more in the chilly security of my lodgings, I attempted to place my thoughts in order. I cannot claim to be the most imaginative of men, but during the exploration of the house I had more than once felt a sharp sense of unease that amounted almost to fear.

Alone for a moment in an empty room, I caught from the corner of my eye a fleeting movement that might have been a fluttering curtain or might have been a passing shadow. But, when I turned around to look, I found nothing. I had no wish to appear foolish, and I therefore decided to say nothing about the matter to Harold or to Sam.

But my most alarming discovery was in the final corridor, which led to the turret room. By the time I had rounded the last corner, I had put myself some distance ahead of the others, and as I made my way towards the spiral staircase, I took good care to kick aside the dust as I walked. For in that dust, starting nowhere and ending nowhere, I had seen a wavering line of prints, whether human, animal or demon I could not tell.

Some of the prints appeared to have been made by naked feet, but some of them could only have been the prints of hands. My mind cannot conceive of the sort of creature that might have left such a trail.

No Such Things as Witches

Rusty Brown's breath was coming in fierce gasps as he pedalled the last few yards to the top of the hill. Then, as the familiar view of the valley unfolded before him, he slipped into top gear, and relaxed back into the saddle to freewheel down the long, gentle slope into the village. He was tired from the long ride, and the mud from the football field had begun to harden uncomfortably on his legs. He pictured the large kettle that would be simmering on the stove. It would be good to get home and clean up.

Rusty had been attending the high school in the neighbouring town for nearly two years. When the roads were dry, he liked to make the eight-mile journey by cycle, but during the winter, the only way to traverse the deep ruts and thick mud was by hitching a bumpy ride in the carrier's waggon. He was relieved that spring had come. The light wind ruffled his red-brown hair as he coasted past the old schoolhouse and splashed through the ford, sending half a dozen ducks quacking furiously in all directions. Opposite The Plough he took a sharp right turn to cut along the footpath that bisected the village green, emerging seconds later in the back lane that led to home. He crested the humpback bridge, was airborne for one exhilarating moment, then bumped back to earth, veered sharp right again and skidded sharply to a halt in the yard behind the cottages. Alerted by the sound of brakes, Dusty came bounding downstairs and burst out of the back door to greet his master.

Mrs Brown was looking on through the kitchen window as her son propped his bicycle up in the little lean-to at the back of the house, while the dog circled excitedly round him, barking and wagging his tail. She glanced at the stove. The kettle was just coming to the boil, and, while Rusty kicked off his plimsolls and hung his blazer and kitbag on the hook by the back door, she lifted the kettle from the stove and carefully poured the boiling water into the chipped enamel basin in the sink, added just the right amount from the cold tap, then arranged the soap and sponge on the draining board. As Rusty stood at the door pulling his colourfully hooped jersey inside out over his head, she could not resist a rueful glance at his football socks, which had as usual collapsed around his ankles. Over the years, Rusty's socks had become a joke between them. The boy caught his mother's look and grinned. She countered with her customary enquiry.

'Good game?'

'Oh, you know. Usual thing.'

Mrs Brown smiled to herself. Her son would never excel on the sports field. He had no competitive instinct to speak of, but he had plenty of youthful energy, and seemed to enjoy the sheer physical exertion of the game She squeezed past him into the parlour, leaving him to get cleaned up, while Dusty busily chased the abandoned football jersey around the kitchen floor.

Kneeling at the grate to build up the fire in the little stove, Mrs Brown found herself watching the boy through the kitchen door. He was standing at the sink in his faded blue shorts and woollen socks, one foot up on the draining board, sponging the mud from his knee with an air of quiet concentration. She was touched by the graceful, unselfconscious poise with which he went about the simple task. He was almost as tall as she was now, and his spare frame was beginning to fill out. As she watched, he paused for a moment, his attention caught by something in the distant fields outside the window. She caught his profile, silhouetted against the late-afternoon sun, and noticed for the first time that his features were beginning to acquire the sharpening that comes with adolescence. The boy brushed his straying fringe away from his eyes, and the gesture reminded her for a moment of his father. It dawned on her then that in a short while he would no longer be a child. There were things that she would have to tell him soon – but not yet, not just yet. A sudden pang of sadness pricked at the backs of her eyes, and for a moment she weakened, enjoying the sensation rather than pushing it away. Then a sudden commotion jolted her back to the present.

'Mum, Dusty's chewing my jersey again!'

She hurried through to rescue the garment before the dog destroyed it.

'Sorry, Mum. He just seems to like the smell of it.'

She sniffed it briefly, wrinkled her nose.

'I really can't think why.'

A little later, they were seated in the dilapidated armchairs on either side of the stove, mugs of tea cradled in their hands. Dusty, in temporary disgrace, had been exiled to the yard, where he was pursuing his favourite occupation of burying things and digging them up again. Rusty, relaxed after an energetic afternoon, could feel the warmth of the fire and the hot, sweet tea seeping through him. He was becoming drowsy, and was not paying full attention to what his mother was saying. He gathered vaguely that Mrs Brown had been doing her work in the church that morning, taking her weekly turn with the cleaning or the flowers.

Rusty was faintly puzzled by his mother's devotion to the church. Although it occupied the greater part of her free time, she seemed to approach it with a sense of resignation that displayed nothing of religious conviction or even of enthusiasm. When he had been younger, she had taken him with her to the Sunday services, but as he had failed to show any sort of interest, she had not insisted on his continuing. He wondered what, if anything, his mother found there. At any rate, she certainly found her cleaning mornings a fruitful source of news and gossip.

Lulled by the stream of words, Rusty was almost ready to fall asleep when a chance phrase jolted him back to the here and now.

'. . . and I really could have smacked that stupid old Mrs Hopkins. Do you know, she actually expects us to believe that someone has put a curse on the village?'

'Someone has done what?' This was sufficiently out of the ordinary to claim the boy's attention.

'Why can't you ever listen to me? I was saying that some of the women at the church, the smallholders' wives, they've been saying that there's a curse on the village. People still remember that terrible harvest last year, and this year, well, nobody seems to be able to grow anything at all except a few crocuses. Then Mrs Evans said that nearly all their lambs were stillborn and . . . well, it just seems to have frightened people. Some of the women are muttering about witchcraft, and the men . . . well, most of them are just sitting outside the inn all day, not going near the fields . . . and now people have started saying that it all began when that bell fell in the river.'

Rusty remembered the odd events of the previous summer. There had been some repair work taking place on the church tower. The men working on their scaffolding had had to unhang the bell, and in the course of getting it down, part of the scaffolding had collapsed and the bell had fallen from the scaffold, tumbled down the sloping patch of ground beside the church, and ended up in the river, where it had somehow become tightly wedged between two rocks. So far, nobody had managed to shift it, and for nearly a year there had been no bell to call the faithful to prayer.

'What's it got to do with the bell?' asked Rusty, his brow wrinkling in perplexity.

'Well, I think it's just a lot of silly superstition,' replied his mother briskly. 'But some of the people round here still believe the old stories. Old Mrs Hopkins, you know, Colin and Sammy's gran, she must be nearly ninety by now, she says it's a witch's curse, and the luck won't come back to the village until the bell is put back in its place. But honestly, what nonsense. Things have moved on. We've got cities and highways and machines. There aren't any witches any more. It's just silly superstition, that's all.'

Rusty swallowed the last of his tea, lukewarm now.

'Were there witches in the old days, then? Were they—'

His mother interrupted him quickly.

'No, of course not, I told you, it's all just stories. And I would have thought you'd have more important things to think about, what with your exams coming up and everything else. Which reminds me, it's about time you got on with your homework.'

'But, Mum . . .'

'No buts. Upstairs with you.'

The Magician and the Prince

At Alice's suggestion, the magician had purchased and installed in the antechamber a small power-driven engine designed for the grinding and infusing of coffee, and, also at Alice's suggestion, he had instigated the routine of preparing a fresh infusion each day, usually around the middle of the morning. When the infusion was ready, Alice would fill up the two blue-and-white-striped china mugs that they kept for private use, and would call Leonardo in from his work in the theatre. Then they would sit down together in the antechamber, drink the coffee, and discuss any current business that might need discussing.

Over the past few months, Alice had transformed the

antechamber into a rather elegant-looking reception area. The magician's clutter had been cleared away into a storeroom, and the visitor was now confronted with a dramatic sweep of space, sparsely furnished with angular armchairs, a low coffee table, and a selection of medium-sized shrubs growing in ornamental pots. There was also a fretwork rack on which were stacked a number of the monthly digest scrolls that the Herald's Office had recently taken to issuing. Leonardo had been keen for the scrolls to be placed on display, but he was not too sure about the shrubs. However, Alice seemed to enjoy looking after them, and he was happy to see her making productive use of her spare moments.

During today's coffee period, there was just one matter for Leonardo and Alice to discuss. The young Prince, heir to his father's throne, was due to visit the workshop in just a few hours' time. Leonardo was nervously fingering a note that had arrived the previous week. The note was written in the ornate hand of the King's senior scribe on a square of the King's personal vellum.

> *Dear Pegasus,*
>
> *It is my wish that my son the Prince should, as part of his continuing education, receive instruction in matters of Government, which will include Statecraft, Warfare, Politicking, Heraldry, Jesting, Jousting and Sorcery.*
>
> *With reference to the last item, it is my wish that you shall make available some time in your calendar to offer him brief instruction in the basic principles of Magic. I trust that it will be convenient for him to call at your premises directly after the midday rest period on Thursday of next week.*
>
> *I would be most grateful for your indulgence in this small matter.*

The royal seal was appended. A hastily pencilled note had been added in the King's own hand:

P.S. Just the basic principles, spare him the detail. I don't suppose he'll ever need to practise magic personally, but he will certainly have to employ people who practise it. Perhaps even yourself, if you're still around when he succeeds me! It's about time he started understanding all this dull grown-up stuff, he will certainly have to use it in earnest one day.

P.P.S. He is very fond of iced buns. Please oblige.

Leonardo was checking Alice's list of final preparations.

'We'll need somewhere to sit down,' he mused. 'I've cleared a side stage in the theatre and dressed it with a rug and two armchairs and a small table. Better have some ink and parchment ready in case he wants to make notes.'

'It's already there.'

'And I've got the blackboard and chalks in case I feel the urge to draw one of my diagrams. We've practised the correct form of address—'

'We could do it on our heads if we had to.' She surprised him with one of her rare laughs, but Leonardo was too nervous for humour.

'Quite. Now, have you sorted out that piece of red carpet for the outer office?'

'It's over there in the corner, still rolled up. We can put it down right at the last moment.'

'Good idea. And then it's just the buns.'

'They're ordered. I'll just need to nip down to the bakery in the rest period.'

Leonardo was very impressed indeed. Alice normally insisted on a full hour to herself at the middle of the day, during which time, by unspoken agreement, Leonardo granted and respected her privacy. Leonardo himself generally spent an extended period in one of the taverns that dotted the main thoroughfare, sometimes enjoying a solitary drink, sometimes sharing a flask of ale with the clown Veronique, or whoever else he might bump into. As far as he could tell, Alice remained in the office during this time. He sometimes wondered what she did there.

'Yes, buns.' He collected himself. 'From the bakery. Very good. And I think that's all. Are you nervous?'

She laughed again.

'No, of course not – he's just another visitor, isn't he?' A frown of concern creased her pale brow for a moment. 'Why then, are you?'

Momentarily taken aback at this gesture of concern, Leonardo found himself having to resist a sudden urge to touch Alice on the forearm.

'Yes, I suppose I am a bit. After all, he will be King some day. It's very important that I make just the right impression on him.'

She smiled, and her momentary warmth gave him heart. 'I'm sure you'll get it exactly right. Now I don't want you worrying.'

'Well, yes, I suppose I've survived worse. Anyway, I'd better go and finish getting the theatre ready.' He paused, seemingly in deep thought. 'And then I think I'll take an early lunch.'

'Just you make sure and get back on time.'

'His Royal Highness the Prince Matthew.' Alice kept a perfectly straight face as she made the formal announcement in her softly accented voice, retiring with a courtly bow as the Prince swept down the short staircase into the Theatre of Magic. Leonardo bowed as deeply as his creaking back would allow, carefully straightened up again, then raised his head to take a closer look at his royal guest.

It was some years since he had last encountered the King's son, and he realised that he had vaguely been expecting to see the twelve-year-old schoolboy of their previous meeting. He was therefore somewhat taken aback to be faced with the well-built, self-possessed, lightly bearded young man who now stood before him. He was also surprised to notice that the Prince was wearing the semi-formal daytime dress of cap, hose and tunic rather than the full Court dress that one would traditionally expect on an official visit.

'Most deeply honoured to be in your Highness's presence.' The practice sessions with Alice had been time well spent. The Prince glanced over his shoulder to check that Alice had closed the door behind her. Then he pulled off his cap and stuffed it in his pouch.

'Let's cut out the medieval claptrap now that we're alone.' His demeanour had suddenly shifted from stiff formality to businesslike briskness. 'All this mumbo-jumbo is going out of the window as soon as I'm on the throne.'

'As your Highness pleases,' intoned Leonardo, unsure now of his mode of speech. The Prince pulled a wry face. 'I mean, certainly, no problem at all. What would your – I mean – what would you like to see first?'

'Well, I've visited most of my father's counsellors over the past few weeks – you know, geomancers, soothsayers, crystal-gazers, accountants, mesmerists, cartographers, clairvoyants and that other sort that I can never remember. Perhaps you can just explain to me what you do that is different from what all the others do.' The Prince had been poking around among the side-stages, and had made his way over to Leonardo's planning table, immaculately dusted and tidied by Alice. He picked up a sheaf of tattered documents.

'What's this?'

'That, your – er – is a project currently under development. I call it the Multiple Empathy Engine.' Leonardo decided that it was time to steer the Prince back towards the seating area. 'But why don't you come and have a seat over here, your – er . . .'

'You'd better call me Matt. Now, about your magic?'

They made themselves comfortable. Leonardo cleared his throat.

'Well, all the other types of sorcerer try in different ways to look into the future, to help your father the King discover what lies ahead of him in time. The geomancers and crystal-gazers look into stones of various types, the mesmerists and clairvoyants look into people's minds or souls, and the sooth-sayers – well, I'm not actually too certain where they look, but of course—'

'Yes, yes,' interrupted the Prince, with a trace of impatience. 'I've met all of them. Today I want to know what *you* do.'

Leonardo paused for thought. He was not often asked to explain his art to the uninitiated, and, when he had managed to collect his ideas, he started speaking with some hesitation.

'I actually help to bring the future into being,' he explained finally. 'Once your father the King has consulted with all of the other counsellors, looked into all the possibilities, as it were . . . he can then start to decide what future he actually wants. So eventually he chooses a future, and then . . . before he constructs it, he calls me in and I . . . well, I help him to test it.'

'And how exactly do you do that?'

'Well, Matt –' it was a struggle for Leonardo to employ the informal mode of address '– I build it. In miniature, of course.' With a vague gesture of his arm, the magician indicated the various model stages dotted around the large room. 'When your father the King has begun to formulate his ideas, he grants me an audience and discloses to me what he has in mind. And I am permitted to ask him a number of questions.'

'You are permitted to question the King?' The young man seemed genuinely surprised.

'Indeed, your – er, Matt – the purpose of these questions is to enable your father the King to apprehend with greater clarity the vision which he has begun to construct. In other words –' he caught the Prince's quizzical look '– to ensure that whatever it is that he is proposing can actually be made to work in practice.'

The Prince considered this for a few moments, perhaps recalling some of his father's more intemperate dinner-table fantasies.

'Very sensible, I should think,' he finally concluded in a matter-of-fact way. 'What questions do you ask, exactly?'

Leonardo assumed an air of haughty dignity.

'That, your Highness, is the first mystery of my craft.'

The Prince made a note on a scrap of the parchment that Alice had thoughtfully provided. 'So where do all your toys and puppets come into it?'

Inwardly, Leonardo was most offended to hear the cunningly designed tools of his trade described in this flippant way, but he made a supreme effort to contain his feelings. However, sensing that the conversation was not going well, he had unconsciously begun to retreat into the old-fashioned formality.

'Perhaps I have not explained with sufficient clarity to your Highness. Your father the King specifies his chosen future for me in exhaustive detail. He explains to me how it might be achieved in practice. And then I construct it for him in miniature.'

'So how does that assist my father in bringing the future about?'

'By the use –' Leonardo paused for dramatic effect '– of my Empathy Engine, your Highness. The second mystery of my craft. By means of the Empathy Engine, your father the King is able actually to see and hear and live and breathe the very future that he has in mind. And not just through his own eyes and ears.' Leonardo had begun to warm to his subject. 'He can experience his chosen future . . . as if it were through the eyes and ears of another person. Any person, in fact, who is enmeshed in it. Anyone he chooses. Come over here.' He led the way across the room to the main stage, and drew back the threadbare velvet cloth that covered it.

'This model represents the military campaign that is at present being waged on the borders. Without leaving this spot, your father the King can experience every possible future course of action, just as though it were actually happening to him at this very moment. If he so desired, I might connect the Engine thus –' he swiftly connected the leads '– and he can then experience all the sensations of battle from the viewpoint of the enemy commander, or from the viewpoint of this private soldier in the ranks, or from the viewpoint of the peasants in this village. Thus he can be certain that his chosen course of action will produce exactly the effect he requires upon every person who is enmeshed in it.'

Aware that he was being carried away by his enthusiasm, Leonardo made a conscious effort to rein himself back. The Prince, meanwhile, seemed sunk in bewildered thought. After a long interval, he slowly formulated a question.

'But where does such a thing end? A campaign on this scale would surely have some sort of effect on every person in the kingdom. Not just on my father and his army, but on the counsellors, the administrators, the merchants – and, yes, even the peasants in the fields and the wanderers on the trackways ... To experience every possible future from the point of view of every person in the kingdom ... well, it would surely take for ever. And anyway, how can anyone decide where to draw the distinction between those who matter and those who do not?'

'That, your Highness –' the Prince winced '– is the third and deepest mystery of my craft.' Leonardo started to draw the cover back over the model. 'If your Highness would now permit me to conclude my exposition?'

They returned to the seating area. 'When your father the King has seen and heard and breathed his future from every appropriate point of view –' the Prince raised an eyebrow '– he will begin to gain an understanding as to whether his notion of the future is well constructed. If it is not well constructed, he will dictate that the necessary adjustments be made, and then in due course he will return to the Empathy Engine to experience the future again, and so on until he is satisfied. And when he is finally satisfied that the future is well-constructed . . .' Here Leonardo paused again, before dramatically concluding his delivery. 'Then the Empathy Engine will offer him a vision of the future of such compelling power that every detail of it will be imprinted for ever upon his heart and upon his will. And the power of that vision will be such that the future willed by the

King will simply come in to being. There will be no need for any further exertion on his part.'

'Oh?' puzzled the Prince. 'So what actually happens to bring it about?'

'Well – your father simply issues instructions to his military people, or to his administrators, or whoever it might be, and they go away and carry out his orders.'

The Prince had been sketching a diagram on his parchment. He looked up thoughtfully.

'So, to put it briefly, my father has an idea. He tests it. With your help, of course. He adjusts it. And then he carries it out. Is that about it?'

Leonardo had not expected to hear the complexities of his craft reduced to such a curt formula.

'Well, I suppose in a nutshell . . . leaving aside the intricacies of the three levels of mystery . . . and taking for granted the wisdom accumulated by those of my calling and passed from generation to generation . . . Yes, I suppose that *is* about it.'

'I see.' The Prince seemed sunk in thought again. 'And how many counsellors does my father employ?'

'I am unsure of the exact number, your – Matt. Several hundred, at any rate.'

For several moments more, the silence resumed. It was broken by the sharp click of the door latch. Bowing deeply, Alice re-entered the room, carrying a tray of coffee and iced buns. 'May it be drawn to your Royal Highness's attention that refreshments are now served?' she intoned with impeccable pomp. The Prince inspected the gaily decorated buns and made another wry face.

The Schoolmaster's Book

On Thursdays, Rusty usually stopped off on his way home to have a cup of tea with the schoolmaster. He was the only pupil from the village school ever to have gone on to the high school,

and the schoolmaster was always eager to keep up to date with
what was happening in the towns and cities. Most of Rusty's
village schoolmates were by now starting to learn their family
trade, or earning a wage in the fields.

Pausing on the front path with its neatly tended borders,
Rusty could hear the master playing his peculiar music on the
battered old upright piano in his study. His left hand traced out
a regular, repetitive rhythm, while the fingers of his right hand
danced nimbly over the keys, weaving fantastic patterns around
the beat. Rusty waited for a suitable break in the performance
before tapping on the window.

'Welcome to my house, Michael Brown,' came the usual
greeting. 'Come inside, the kettle's on.'

Soon they were seated beside the fire in the tobacco-scent-
ed study, toasting teacakes on long brass forks.

'So what's been happening to young Brown this week?'

'Nothing much really, sir. Oh yes, my mum said a strange
thing. She said that some of the old people believe the village
has been cursed. By a witch.'

'A witch?' said the master sharply. 'Do people really still
believe in witches?'

'Well, Mum says it's all nonsense.'

The boy paused to take a large bite from his teacake. A
trickle of melted butter ran down his chin, and he hurriedly
wiped it away with the back of his wrist.

'Do you believe in them, sir?'

The schoolmaster did not reply straight away. He had started
to assemble the various components of his pipe, and continued
in an unhurried way until he was satisfied with the result. Then
he put it down unlit.

'Well, all these old stories must have come from somewhere,'
he began thoughtfully. 'I think, perhaps a long time ago, before
our people settled the land, there may have been others living
here, people perhaps with different ways, people who worshipped gods different from the god we worship today. Older
gods than ours.' He spoke slowly, seeming to choose his words

carefully. 'And then when our people arrived, the worshippers of the old gods would have retreated into the far corners of the land, into remote places where they could still follow the old religion. And perhaps in time people might have come to fear them. People always seem to fear things that are different.' He was silent for a moment. 'They might even have invented alarming names for them, to scare their grandchildren.'

'Witches?' pondered the boy. 'I don't remember any of this from your lessons.'

'None of this is in the history books. But I've made a bit of a study of the ancient legends. I've got one or two books, if you're interested. Not in this room.' Suddenly, he rose to his feet. 'Leave your tea here.'

A strange look had come over the schoolmaster's face, a look of urgency that Rusty had not seen there before. Stooping, he drew aside a curtain and led the way through a low doorway. They found themselves in a dark, cluttered little back room. The schoolmaster lit a candle, and in the small pool of light, Rusty's gaze was drawn to a low, glass-fronted bookcase. The master produced a key from his waistcoat pocket and unlocked it. A musty smell seeped from inside. Squinting in the faltering light, Rusty could make out several uneven rows of ancient-looking books. Many of the authors' names had a foreign sound to them, and some bore titles in languages that he could not recognise. Quickly the schoolmaster located an octavo-sized leather-bound volume that bore the title *Legends of the Forgotten Age*.

'You can borrow this if you like,' said the schoolmaster, and Rusty noticed that he had dropped his voice to a whisper. 'You may find some interesting things in here. Bring it back next time you come. And –' he looked uneasy for a moment '– best not show it to your mother.'

That night, Rusty managed to smuggle a short length of candle and some matches up to his narrow room. When he judged that his mother had retired, he pulled the schoolmaster's book out from under his pillow and started to flick through its pages, hunting for a story that would catch his imagination. For a moment he was distracted by Dusty, who had sensed that something unusual was happening and was sniffing inquisitively around the bed.

'Quiet, Dusty, good boy,' he soothed the dog. 'I'm just reading. Go to sleep.'

So Dusty slept and Rusty browsed. And this was what he read.

The Legend of the Wanderers and the Islanders

At the beginning, the Great Being breathed life into the Land, and into the mountains and into the rivers and into the trees of the Land. And then the Great Being breathed life into the people of the Land, and a fragment of the Great Being was lodged for ever in the heart of every woman and the heart of every man.

Now at that time the Land was a harsh and inhospitable place, overgrown with impenetrable forest and infested with savage beasts. One place alone was safe for the men and the women, and that place was a certain island. This island was separated from the mainland by a perilous stretch of water, and it was protected against marauders by jagged rocks and cliffs. But behind the rocky coastline lay tranquil grasslands and gentle hills, and at the very heart of the island lay a sacred place that was dear to the heart of the Great Being. But, beautiful as it was, the island was too small to support the whole community of people, and so the Great Being decreed that the men and women should be divided into two clans, the clan of the Wanderers and the clan of the Islanders, and that the two clans should work together in covenant to manage the affairs of the Land. And this was the way in which they were to divide their tasks.

The Wanderers were to travel abroad, hunting for food and gathering fuel and listening for news. And the Wanderers were to share their food and their fuel with the Islanders, and were to make known freely to them the information that they gathered on their wanderings. The Islanders, meanwhile, were to remain on the Island, and were to attend to the cooking and the weaving and the cleaning. And, in addition, the Islanders were to attend to the upkeep of the sacred place, for at that place the wise ones of the clan could attend to the wishes of the Great Being and so could ensure that all things were properly done. And the Islanders were to offer a welcome to the Wanderers and were to make known freely to them the wishes of the Great Being.

And so, as the years went by, the Wanderers came to know every path and every hedgerow and every stream of the Land, and the Islanders tended the homestead and the sacred place and remained in daily communion with the Great Being. And the secrets of the Wanderers and the secrets of the Islanders were passed on from generation to generation.

And the Great Being was glad, and so the Great Being saw fit to bestow upon the people a special talent. And so it came about that each of the Wanderers learned how to look into the eye of another, and to see there all the pathways of her life, twisting and turning, both backward to the day of her birth and forward to the day of her departure. And those who bore this talent were said to bear the Gift. And it likewise came about that each of the Islanders learned how to view the whole of the Land in one glimpse, as if through the eyes of a bird of prey hovering at great height, and so they learned to understand the ways in which the lives of all the men and women were woven together to form a never-ending seamless web. And those who bore this talent were said to see the Land through the Eye of the Kestrel.

But in time the covenant of the clans began to break down. The Wanderers took to wandering further and further afield, their visits to the homestead occurring at longer and longer intervals. The Islanders for their part remained hemmed in by the protective walls of the homestead, venturing abroad only for their visits to the sacred place. And so the Wanderers began to look upon the

Islanders with envy, because they led a comfortable life and faced no dangers or difficulties. And the Islanders in their turn began to look upon the Wanderers with envy, because they were able to see new landscapes each day and to explore the whole of the Land with all its excitements and surprises.

So the Wanderers' visits to the island became more and more perfunctory. They became mistrustful, and they grew tight-lipped with the news that they gathered. The Islanders in their turn found themselves lacking the will and the spirit to maintain the Wanderers' homes or to replenish their supplies, and they eventually became secretive even about the wishes of the Great Being. So all the plans that the Islanders made were founded on information that was out of date, while all the expeditions upon which the Wanderers ventured were misdirected and unplanned and ended in confusion. And in time a deep rift developed between the clans. Finally, the Wanderers ceased altogether to visit the Island, and all communication came to an end.

So the Wanderers were cut adrift from the Great Being, and they turned their attention to other gods, wild spirits who lived in the hedgerows and rivers and mountains of the Land. And meanwhile, the Islanders remained on their island, forgotten by all but a few.

Now of course life could not continue in this way because each clan could achieve nothing without the aid of the other. But it so happened that around this time, the Wounded Ones began to arrive in the Land. Clever folk they were, skilled in the use of tongues, knowledgeable in many crafts, persuasive and fleet of foot. Quickly the Wounded Ones built their own towns and cities, constructed their own roads and set up their own system of trade, manufacturing and service industries, rejecting the ancient ways and worshipping instead their own colourless god. So the Wanderers were relegated to the ditches and the byways, and the Islanders were marooned on their island. And the Wounded Ones took over the day-to-day running of the Land, and grew powerful and prosperous and complacent.

And the Great Being observed this and wept, for the Wanderers continued to follow the eternal cycles and loops of their great march without knowing their destination, while the Islanders continued in lonely communion with the Great Spirit but lost all knowledge of the world beyond the shores of their island. And the Wounded Ones managed the world with grey efficiency.

'I think I liked the story,' said Rusty on his next visit to the schoolmaster. 'But the ending was a bit funny.'

The schoolmaster was examining the remains of a plum cake and did not reply straight away.

'Funny in what way?' he finally asked.

'Well, wouldn't the Great Being have done something to put things right?'

'I don't suppose there was anything much that could be done,' mused the schoolmaster, measuring a slice of cake with his protractor. 'And actually, if you think about it, the world remains pretty much the same way today.'

'Another thing,' said the boy, 'I'm still not sure where the witches fit in.'

Finally satisfied with the division of the cake, the school-master looked up at him.

'Well, if you read between the lines, the story tells you quite a lot about the witches. You see, there are still a fair number of wandering folk about, once you start to look out for them. Pedlars, tinkers, carriers, knife-grinders, entertainers – they all go by the small roads, they all travel around, and it's quite likely that many of them may share a common ancestry. And they certainly have some rather peculiar talents. Some of them, the pure-blooded ones, are even said still to bear the Gift. It's in the story. How does it go, now? *A bearer of the Gift can look into the eyes of another and see the whole pathway of her life mapped out before her in all its twists and turns.* Something like that, anyway.'

The schoolmaster's eyes seemed to be focused on distant

horizons. After a while he looked down and noticed the boy again.

'So you see, it's quite likely that ignorant folk might have mistaken the Wanderers for witches. People certainly don't trust them. People call them thieves, and liars, and worse. And people who want to be thought of as respectable –' Rusty was surprised to detect a sharp note of distaste in the word '– prefer not to speak of them at all.'

Rusty thought about his mother. He threw a plum stone into the fire.

'And the Islanders?'

The master looked at him strangely.

'Perhaps they still live on their island, although no one seems quite sure exactly where it is. I believe one or two may even have visited the mainland on odd occasions. But there are really very few of them about, very few indeed.' He seemed to want to change the subject. 'Now, the Wanderers – well, they pass through here all the time. Don't you remember that funny little girl, the one that used to sit next to you – what was her name – Laurel?'

Rusty's heart took a long pause between beats.

'Laurel was a Wanderer?' The walls of the study seemed to ripple before his eyes.

'Certainly she was. Her family were camped near the village for a few weeks, long enough to put her into the school, in any case. I think they were tinkers – or perhaps they were road-menders. Yes, that's it. Roadmenders. And then one day they left in a great hurry. It would probably have been around the time of the scarlet fever.'

'But I thought . . .' Rusty had to make an effort to speak the words. 'Didn't Laurel die in the epidemic?'

'Die? No, I don't think so. No, I'm sure she was up and about by the time they left.'

'So she could still be alive somewhere?'

'Undoubtedly. But you'll have your work cut out finding her. Those Wanderers never pass the same way twice.'

★　　★　　★

From the Journal of Victor Lazarus

Tuesday 3rd February

My colleagues and I are now embarked upon the massive task of putting our employer's house in order, and therefore for the past week I have been too much occupied to keep a daily record. However, I now find myself with an hour to spare, and so I shall attempt to give an account of the events that have taken place to date.

On the morning of the second day we met again as we had arranged, and, at my suggestion, we began by compiling an inventory of tasks to be carried out. It ran as follows:

A) Interior
1 Clean interior of house
2 Inspect interior of house and catalogue repairs required
3 Catalogue contents of house
4 Engage workmen to carry out repairs and redecoration
5 Refurnish house and rearrange contents.

B) Exterior
1 Cut down undergrowth in garden
2 Inspect exterior of house and list repairs required
3 Engage workmen to carry out repairs
4 Replant garden

In the days that followed, a suitable method of working quickly emerged. With my long experience of commanding men, I have been accepted as the leader and organiser of the unit. Harold, in his long career as a librarian, has developed some very clear ideas about how objects should be classified and ordered, and these ideas he is now starting to apply to the many objects in the house. Sam is of a practical turn of mind and is ingenious and strong, so that he seems best suited to carrrying out the heavy work.

As we set about examining the house and grounds in more detail, Harold produced from his portmanteau a ponderous ledger and began to make notes in a small, neat shorthand. Sam in the meantime carried out an investigation of the cellar, where he succeeded in locating the boiler room and the generators, and soon we had light and heat to aid us in our task. Next, while Harold and I continued our examination of the contents of the house, Sam made a sortie into the town where he engaged a gang of workmen whose first task was to cut down and burn the undergrowth that choked the garden. As dusk approached, Harold and I continued to make our way through room after room, our progress illuminated from above by faltering pools of yellow electric light, and from either side by the flickering red of bonfires. Standing or squatting on bare floorboards, Harold continued to make his endless lists, and I watched and I wondered, astonished by the extraordinary variety of the items that we were encountering.

We discovered a collection of books that encompassed a comprehensive range of interests both practical and academic. We discovered volume after volume of personal journals that described the life of a scholar, a traveller, a man of affairs, an athlete. There were cases of fossils, cases of butterflies, stacks of oil paintings, albums of watercolours, albums of photographs, cabinets of musical instruments, piles of musical manuscripts, scientific equipment, culinary equipment, hunting trophies, sporting trophies and countless other objects that we have yet to catalogue.

It appears that the owner's living quarters occupied only a few rooms. The remainder of the house has more the appearance of a museum.

★   ★   ★

Rusty and Dusty go to the Circus

Rusty could not understand why his mother had not told him the truth about Laurel, and, after the schoolmaster's warning, he did not feel able to ask her outright. Indeed, for some time after that conversation, he felt nervous and uncertain in her presence, and Dusty, catching something of his mood, took to spending long periods upstairs in Rusty's bedroom, engaged in his favourite solitary pursuit of chewing football jerseys. Then something happened that provided a welcome diversion.

It was a Saturday in early summer. Feeling the need to work off some surplus energy, Rusty and Dusty had left the house early in the morning for a run on the village green. As they crossed the humpback bridge, Dusty's ears pricked up, and a moment later Rusty too realised that something out of the ordinary was happening. In the distance he could hear music.

In the ordinary run of things, not much music was heard in the village. The schoolmaster's eccentric piano-playing was familiar to everyone who had been through the school. The churchgoers had learned to tolerate the mournful chords that tall, dour Doctor Gilbert coaxed from the wheezing harmonium, perhaps finding them in keeping with the nature of the misanthropic god they worshipped there. And, around the time of the annual fair, occasional bands of wandering musicians would pass through the village, entertaining the villagers with simple, rustic melodies sketched out on mandolin or concertina. But none of these could compete with the rich, dark, romping sound that they could now hear dancing towards them from the direction of the village green.

As Rusty and Dusty rounded the bend in the lane and the main part of the village came into view, an extraordinary sight met their eyes. Six or seven musicians in red-and-gold uniforms, with trumpets, drums, and other instruments that Rusty could not name, were marching up the main street. They were closely followed by two huge, lumbering animals that Rusty tentatively identified as elephants and were attended by a motley company of people in colourful costumes and bizarre wigs, their faces painted in extraordinary patterns. Around the village green stood straggling rows of waggons and trailers, while, at the centre of it all, a gang of tough-looking men were in the process of erecting a huge tent.

Rusty had read about circuses, but had never actually seen one. The first posters had appeared in the village the previous week, and he had hardly been able to contain his excitement. And now, at last, the circus had arrived. He stood open-mouthed until he was accosted by one of the clowns. Despite the gaudy make-up and wig, the man spoke in quite an ordinary voice.

'Want to see the show, son?' Rusty nodded dumbly. 'Then how about delivering some handbills for us? One to each house in the village. Here's a ticket for you, and, oh yes, the dog gets in free as long as he behaves himself.'

And he was gone, leaving Rusty with a handful of colourful bills and a pale green, smudgily printed ticket with a thin perforated line scored down the middle. He set off at once for the nearest letter box, Dusty bounding along excitedly at his heels.

Making his way from house to house, Rusty noticed that many of the other local children had been pressed into service by the visitors. Some of them were giving out more handbills in the street, and two of his former schoolfellows had been supplied with a bucket of paste, and were busy plastering every wall and tree with posters. On the green itself, some of the girls were helping to unload armfuls of costumes from one of the waggons, and Colin Hopkins and his brother Sammy had climbed a tree and were making fast the end of a long, tattered line of flags.

Returning home rather later than he had planned, Rusty found his mother as usual hanging out sheets in the backyard. As he had expected, she did not share his enthusiasm for the coming spectacle. She studied the handbill with a sour face while Rusty and Dusty looked on apprehensively.

'All right, I suppose you can go,' she said at last. 'But you're to come straight home afterwards. I don't want you loafing around on the green. And these travelling shows have a lot of bad characters hanging about them, so you're not to go talking to anyone you don't know.'

'No, Mum. Can I go tonight?'

Still suspicious, she examined the handbill again.

'I don't want you staying out after dark. You can go in the afternoon, the evening show is too late. By the way . . .' Rusty had started to sidle away. 'No, wait, I haven't finished yet. What did you think you were doing, delivering those handbills? Those people shouldn't be getting children to do their work for them. Now, will you stop fidgeting and help me with the sheets?'

'But, Mum—'

'The sheets. Come on.'

So, that afternoon, Rusty and Dusty joined the queue that had started to form at the entrance to the circus tent, eventually filing in to take their places on the tiers of wooden benches that surrounded the ring. The tent was alive with chatter, and in the background could be discerned a low humming sound, which Rusty realised must come from the generator that powered the electric lights for the show. High up above him, almost hidden by the dazzle of the lights, he could make out a mysterious, intricate web of ropes and wires and pulleys. Screwing up his eyes, he followed the maze of lines, trying to work out how they connected up. Meanwhile, Dusty's sensitive nose had picked up the scent of strange animals, laced with the sharp tang of oranges that a couple of the clowns were offering to the waiting crowd.

Just then, a spotlight fell on the band, the other lights faded jerkily down to nothing, the conductor tapped on his music stand with his stick, the crowd fell silent and the fierce, startling chords of the opening fanfare eclipsed all the other noises. Rusty's pulse quickened. He tightened his grip on Dusty's collar. The show had begun.

The small crowd was captivated by the spectacle that followed, but afterwards Rusty felt that somehow it had not been quite what he had expected. Later, when his mother encouraged him to put his thoughts into words, he finally found himself saying that he had found the experience rather frightening. True, he had been spellbound for the duration of the show, but somehow the whole performance had possessed an edge of cruelty that had unsettled the boy. The animals had borne the marks of the whip, and they had snarled viciously as their trainers taunted them. Then there were the acrobats, two men and a young girl, in tight black costumes that displayed every sinew of their bodies and sinister black masks that concealed their faces. They performed every balance, every breathtaking turn, with a chilling air of indifference. At one moment, passing close to where Rusty sat, the girl happened to meet his gaze and shot him a look of such sullen hatred that he felt his blood run cold and could scarcely bear to watch the rest of the act. The music that accompanied the show was discordant in its harmonies, jagged in its rhythm and acidic in its flavour. The jugglers juggled with wickedly curved knives, and the clowns seemed to find their humour only by inflicting injuries upon one another in more and more inventive ways. For the finale of the show, as the music rose to its climax, the entire company came together for a grand tableau and, on the final chord of music, a sudden deafening explosion erupted in their midst. When the smoke cleared, Rusty was startled to see the performers lying inert on the ground, their costumes drenched in blood. Then the lights were abruptly extinguished, and when they came up again, the ring was empty except for a number of sinister red patches on the sawdust. There was a shocked silence before the audience broke into timid applause. There were no curtain calls.

The crowd straggled out confusedly into the fading daylight, the mud and the drizzle heralding a welcome return to normality. On the far side of the green, Rusty could make out the stooping form of Granny Hopkins, slowly making her way across the grass, picking up pieces of litter.

'Straight home, Michael,' she called to him in her ancient cracked voice. 'You're not to go getting into trouble.'

And with Dusty trotting silently behind him, Rusty headed for home.

From the Journal of Victor Lazarus

Wednesday 4th March

I am glad to report that our work is progressing in an orderly and steady fashion, with no serious obstacles in our path. Harold has recruited a unit of clerical staff to assist him in the sorting and cataloguing of objects. Sam, meanwhile, has engaged further gangs of workmen to attend to the necessary repair work on the fabric of the building. In the corridors, the floorboards have been pulled up for an inspection of the electrical wiring. Plans have been drawn for the building of shelves and cabinets, galleries are being prepared for the many pieces of art and sculpture, and a platoon of gardeners has been engaged to attend to the landscaping of the grounds.

I note with some pleasure that, under my guidance, the men have formed themselves into a highly effective working unit. As the weeks pass, I am beginning to gain a better understanding of the strengths and weaknesses of my colleagues. Harold has an admirably precise notion of how things should be ordered, although at times he can display a tendency towards inflexibility. As an example of this, he has insisted on classifying all the works of biography in the library as fiction! Sam has proved to be exceptionally hard-working and good-hearted, although at times he can perhaps be a little careless. On one or two occasions his men have dropped and broken pieces of porcelain, and on one occasion a cigarette end nearly started a fire in a pile of manuscripts. But, given the excellent rate of progress overall, these minor lapses are easily overlooked.

As for myself, I have set up a command post and orderly room in a strategic position on the first floor of the house, from which I can oversee all operations and attend to the accounting and administration. Harold's neatly presented columns of figures convince me that everything is well under control, and I am confident that we shall have the house restored to its former condition in ample time for the return of the owner.

There remains only one other matter to note. Thankfully, there have been no more footprints, or indeed hand prints, but as the corridors are now swept at frequent intervals, perhaps I should not be too surprised at this. I have to admit, however, that from time to time I continue to experience the unsettling sensation of being under observation. However, I continue to remind myself that there is no cause for alarm, as there are, of course, large numbers of people constantly at work in every part of the house. Nowadays I am very seldom left on my own.

The Circus at Night

Mrs Brown could tell that Rusty had been unsettled by his visit to the circus, and when she suggested an early night, for once he did not argue. It had been some years since she had last brought him hot milk and biscuits at bedtime, but the long-dormant ritual, prompted by reawakened needs, took the opportunity quietly to reassert itself. The boy drank the milk quickly and was soon asleep.

Rusty slept badly, dreaming fitfully, turning this way and that in his narrow bed. His dreams began, as they often did begin, with the journey across the water, the waves lapping against the side of the boat, the stolid old ferryman pulling evenly at the oars. Then came the juddering lurch as the boat became grounded.

'It's no good, youngster,' said the ferryman finally. 'I can't get you any further. From now on, you're on your own.'

And then the plunge into the black water. For a moment the blackness enveloped him utterly. Then, one by one, images from the circus swam up from the dark to confront him: the scarred and snarling beasts, the mocking faces of the clowns in their grotesque make-up, the derisive sneers on the lips of the acrobats. A juggler plucked a long-bladed knife from the air and, spinning abruptly to face him, hurled it with swift and deadly precision to impale him through the heart. Rusty awoke with a cry of terror to feel two heavy paws on his chest. Dusty's anxious face was hovering inches away from his own.

'Just a dream, Dusty, just a bad dream. Go back to sleep.'

His mother must have been asleep in the big bedroom, Rusty thought, otherwise she would surely have come running to his bedside. For a long while, he lay awake, constantly turning over, unable to make himself comfortable. He could hear, faintly, the distant music of the circus band, followed by muffled applause. The evening show must have just reached its finale. As the images of the performers drifted again before his eyes, waves of conflicting feelings broke across him. For a moment he knew again the dread, the chill of the circus, and wanted only to find a place of safety, far away from it. Then a moment later he felt himself drawn back towards the big tent, as though bewitched by its mystery. The circus was beckoning, and within him, for a moment, he felt something stir. Something tightly bundled and enclosed and folded, something that cowered behind dark protective walls of fear. But from behind those walls, he could recognise a small answering voice, the voice of something that yearned to open out and be.

And so the dread and the enchantment ebbed and flowed through him as he lay there, each dissolving in turn into its opposite. And at length, bit by bit, the waves of dread began slowly to recede, and as the waves of enchantment swelled through him, the boy might have been glimpsed slipping silently from his bed, dressing himself swiftly in the dark, descending the stair softly, on tiptoe, stealthily drawing back the bolts on the kitchen door. As he skirted around the yard, clinging instinctively to the shadows, a faint patter from behind told him that Dusty had decided to join the midnight expedition.

The moon cast two long, sharp shadows as they slipped out into the lane. On the village green, all was silent. The show was over, the public had departed, and the circus folk had retired to their living waggons for the night. Drawn onward, the boy and the dog crept silently around the big tent, around the still-warm generator van, along the straggling rows of living waggons.

But all was not quite still. From between the curtains of one waggon, a flickering light was showing and, as Rusty drew nearer, he could hear voices. Drawn now by curiosity, he clambered on top of a barrel and peered between the curtains. Two women were inside, one a young girl, the other old and wrinkled. They were both smoking clay pipes, which gave off a tantalising aroma. Through the thick glass, he caught a scrap of their conversation.

'Why won't you let me throw the knives, Madame?' the girl was pleading. 'I hate the rest of it. It's only the knives I want.'

'You're still too young,' growled the old woman. 'Besides, in this circus, the knives is man's work. Now hold your tongue. I want to hear no more of it.'

Although Rusty did not have a full view of the girl from his precarious position, he was certain that she was the sulky performer who had cast him a look of such withering hatred from the circus ring. So she had had enough of being an acrobat . . . He wondered whether the older woman might be her grandmother. Fascinated by the drama that was unfolding, he craned forward to get a better view, tipping the barrel at a precarious angle. Then a sudden sharp bark from Dusty warned him, rather too late, that he had outstayed his welcome.

After that, everything seemed to happen at once. Rusty lost his balance and the barrel overturned, tipping boy and dog onto the ground and bumping loudly against the side of the waggon. Sharp cries came from within, and at the same moment two young men suddenly rounded the corner, halting abruptly as they caught sight of Rusty. It passed through his mind that they might be the other two members of the acrobatic act – the girl's brothers, perhaps. And then they were upon him.

'Spying on our women, were you? Well, we don't like that, do we, Charlie?'

Angry hands grabbed at Rusty's elbows, but he managed somehow to wriggle free. Before he knew what he was doing, he had rolled under the waggon and out the other side, scrambled to his feet, and started to run. Behind him he could hear Dusty barking and snapping furiously at the men. As he flew along the rows of waggons, he could feel the heavy tread of his pursuers, close behind him and gaining on him. They were bigger than him and stronger than him and faster than him. He had only one advantage. He was on his home ground.

Without conscious thought, he zigzagged his way between the waggons to the far side of the green, where the river flowed silver in the moonlight. Crouching low behind the bank, he moved quickly along the towpath. A stitch had begun to tear at his side, and as he stumbled onwards, gasping for breath, he knew that he could not run much further. But luck was with him. Underneath the little humpback bridge, he knew a hiding place.

Crouching in the dark, he struggled to regain his breath, desperately hoping that the chase had been abandoned. Gradually his breathing slowed, and he allowed his body to relax. It was a warm night, and it was dry and snug under the bridge. He settled himself on a patch of soft grass, leaned back against the brickwork, closed his eyes for a moment . . . With luck, in a few minutes' time he would be able to slip away. He was just beginning to wonder how he could get back to his room without waking his mother when the silence was broken by approaching footsteps. His heart sank as he realised that the men were approaching along the bank, and he felt a fresh surge of panic as he remembered that the path under the bridge finished in a dead end. There was no way up on to the road. Unless . . . Hastily he pulled off his heavy clothing and stuffed it out of sight behind a patch of brambles. Then he slipped silently into the river.

The water did not feel cold, and the current was not too strong, but, tired as he was, he found himself struggling to make progress as he swam upstream. He drew some comfort from the thought that the two men would surely give up their chase now. He swam on, his slow strokes scarcely disturbing the surface of the water. It was strange – the water seemed deeper than he remembered. And then, on the river bottom, illuminated in a shaft of moonlight, he saw the bell.

There could be no doubt that it was the bell that had fallen from the church tower. It had settled almost upright, wedged between rocks, just as his mother had described. Seeing it there, he felt an unexpected wave of calm permeating gently through him. He took a gulp of air, then dived down and swam towards the bell in long, deliberate strokes. He could reach out and touch it now.

His fingertips tingled at the contact. Then his whole arm tingled, and suddenly his entire body came alive, as if charged with electricity. The bell seemed to shift a little. He pushed with both hands and kicked with his legs and it shifted again, and he felt that with just a little more effort he might be able to dislodge it . . .

But then his lungs cried out suddenly for air, and he twisted swiftly around and broke the surface, gasping for breath, wet hair streaking his forehead. As he prepared to dive once more, the moon disappeared behind a cloud, and the bell was lost from sight. He headed for shallower water. Shivering now, he stepped ashore.

He had lost his bearings, and it took him a few confused moments to understand that he had landed on the rocky midstream island, the island where in days gone by he had played. He spun around in confusion, trying to work out in which direction home lay. Then, from a dark cleft between two rocks, he heard a voice calling to him.

'Come into the cave, Rusty Brown.'

The voice was soft and musical . . . But surely, he thought, if there had been a cave on the island he would have known about it . . . it must be the witch who had put the curse on the village . . . she would be angry with him for disturbing the bell . . .

Mesmerised, as if drawn by some unseen force, he found himself turning slowly around towards the cleft, sliding effortlessly in between the rocks . . .

'Come deeper inside, Rusty Brown.'

It was damp in the cave, but it was warmer than he expected, and the walls were moist and slippery. At first he seemed to be in total darkness, but then he began to discern a soft patch of light ahead of him.

'Come deeper in, Rusty.'

Gripped by fear but drawn onwards by some power he could not comprehend, he felt himself pulled inexorably forward. Now he could see her ahead of him as she sang her enchantment. Surely it was the girl from the circus! Her lithe figure danced before him, her sleek black costume betraying every contour of her body, her narrow black mask concealing her eyes. As she came closer, he realised that she was younger than he had imagined, almost young enough to be in school, young enough to be sitting beside him.

'Laurel?' he gasped. 'Laurel, is it you?'

He still could not see her eyes, but her lips were smiling now. Slender hips were circling before him, sinuous arms reaching out towards him. One horrified thought burst into his head.

'I'm not ready for this.'

He was trying to struggle, but he was no longer in control of his movements. He could feel the supple limbs encircling him like tentacles, and then the eyes behind the mask were blazing into his, dark, furious eyes behind which burned hard fires . . .

And then, with a sudden eruption of splashing and barking, Dusty was on the scene. With a harsh scream, the girl recoiled from his attack, and for an instant Rusty could see her in her true shape, twisted and ugly and malicious, and suddenly the enchantment was broken and he was wrenching himself free, slithering down the bank, tumbling over rocks. Then he lost his balance and he was falling through space and his head hit something hard and the black waters closed over him.

The Mystery of Alice

In the days when the old King was still on the throne, the Congress of Counsellors used to convene regularly on the second Thursday afternoon of each month. The purpose of this meeting was to coordinate policy between the various counselling departments, and to give the representatives of those departments the opportunity to compare notes on matters of mutual concern. With purposeful chairmanship, the routine business of the meeting could probably have been transacted in around fifteen minutes, but in practice, the members, privileged men and women who were seldom pressed for time, were quite happy to take advantage of the social opportunities afforded by the occcasion. It provided them with a pleasant afternoon in which gossip could be exchanged, blame attributed, rivalries exercised, scores settled, absent colleagues abused, the young berated and the price of coffee discussed at length. As a result, the meeting generally continued into the early evening, and Leonardo, whose attendance was regular but not very enthusiastic, had got into the habit of travelling straight home afterwards without calling in again at his workshop.

Although Leonardo prided himself on being able to remember his appointments without recourse to a diary, this pride was in fact utterly ill-founded. Leonardo's management of his timetable was chaotic, but so far he had resisted Alice's attempts to take control of it. Fortunately the monthly Congress was always signalled by the signal kites for three days before the event, so Leonardo at least had the security of an early-morning reminder as he strode his customary route up the main thoroughfare towards the palace.

'I shall be heading off for an early lunch,' he told Alice just after midday. 'I'll go straight on from there to Congress. I'm sure you can take care of things for the afternoon.'

Alice looked up briefly from the memorandum she was drafting.

'I'm sure I can. Just you be certain and leave the tavern in plenty of time.' The briefest glimpse of a smile, and then she was immersed in her work again.

'And I'll go straight home afterwards. See you tomorrow, then.'

She nodded absently, not looking up.

Pausing at the palace gates, Leonardo allowed himself to enjoy the panoramic view of the southern part of the city that extended before him. It was a clear day, and the wind was steady. To his left, the dull square buildings of the administrative area gave way to the jagged ruins and crumbling tenements of the Undertown, currently blighted by another plague of Wolf Boy killings. In a couple of places, columns of smoke were rising diagonally from derelict lots. Leonardo wondered whether the fires had been started deliberately or accidentally. At any rate, the wind was favourable today. When it blew from the east, the stench of the Undertown was unbearable.

To Leonardo's right spread the orderly streets of the commercial district, each establishment flying its individually liveried kite. Above the market area, the air was choked almost solid with the jostling multicoloured shapes. Collisions between kites, line tangles and disputes over airspace provided a steady supply of short news items for the Criers, and were a regular source of lucrative business for the Advocates of the Lesser Assizes. Wondering idly when the next kite-related murder would be committed, Leonardo turned his gaze back towards the main thoroughfare, which extended downhill a steeply sloping couple of miles to the main gate of the city. He could just discern the distant gatehouse, its castellations giving it the look of a toy fort. A lone kite fluttered from it, spelling out the message of the day for visitors to the City, but from his vantage point at the palace gates it was too distant for Leonardo to read. Beyond the gatehouse gleamed the wide silver stripe of the river, bearing its constant flow of traffic to and from the docks. Beyond the river he could make out nothing. Whatever lay out there was lost in haze.

Dodging a couple of small power-driven vehicles as he crossed over a side turning, Leonardo passed through the familiar pair of double doors into the noisy, smoky atmosphere of The Crier's Rest. Despite the early hour, the crush booths had already filled up with lunchers. Leonardo scanned the room in irritation, eventually spotting Veronique seated at the far end of one of the long benches that extended alongside the communal table. He collected a flask of ale and joined his friend.

'How-do, Wizzy-boy!' came the familiar croak. 'Seems like Wizzy's too busy to come down the Herald's these days!'

'Hardly that.' Leonardo smiled briefly as he seated himself. 'Alice takes the copy along most weeks. It makes life easier for me.'

'Oh, yes, the gorgeous Alice. Shaping up nicely, is she?' The clown managed to extract every possible nuance of lewdness from the innocent words. Leonardo winced.

'She's adjusting to the routine very well, if that's what you mean. In fact, she has brought about a complete transformation. I don't know how I managed before. She does all the administrative work, and that leaves me free to concentrate on my magic. Not that it's really a full-time job at the moment.'

Veronique nodded glumly. The King had been out of sorts lately, and had been making fewer calls on the services of his counselling departments. The magician and the clown took long draughts of ale and fell into silent reflection, until the arrival of a fresh wave of drinkers forced them to squeeze up along the benches to make room.

'Lot of changes down there,' said Veronique finally. 'They've changed the queueing system. It's quicker now. And they've changed all the paperwork. That's got them all chasing their tails. And then there's that new woman on Sorcery. Bit of a dragon she looks.' The clown seemed lost in thought for a moment. 'Good figure, though,' she continued after a moment. 'What I'd call a real woman. Why not put her in your antechamber? Now she really would look the part.'

She paused to light one of her small, foul-smelling cigars, then abruptly changed the subject.

'Have you heard, those Wolf Boys have been up to their monkey business again?'

Through the haze of smoke and the sour reek of ale and the coarse banter of his companion, Leonardo listened with half an ear to the distant chiming of bells from the Institute of Calibration, anxious not to be late for Congress. Hearing the third quarter, he began adjusting his robe in readiness to leave.

'Hang about, you've got time for another flask,' said Veronique. 'Come on. My shout.'

Leonardo was about to relent when, feeling in the inside pocket of his robe, he realised with a start that something was missing.

'How silly of me. I've come without my notes.' He started to become flustered. 'I'll have to run back to the workshop for them. Sorry, Vero, I'd better go straight away.' He rose hastily and, bidding his friend goodbye, strode back up the hill towards the palace.

As he fumbled with his key in the outer door, Leonardo had temporarily forgotten that Alice would be taking her rest period. He was therefore surprised when he entered to see her cap and tunic arranged neatly on the chair by the door, with her long, pointed boots placed carefully side by side underneath. Then he saw Alice. Stripped down to her black hose and singlet, Alice was dancing.

She was dancing in silence, but as Leonardo watched her, he could sense with some unknown part of himself the rhythm and the harmony that she was creating. She seemed to inhabit the whole of the wide expanse of flagstones in the middle of the anteroom, and as she curved and dived and leaped, she delineated that space with geometric precision, spinning with her fingertips and with the points of her toes an interlocking web of broad circles and shapely ellipses and sweeping hyperbolas. Arching and vaulting and spanning the space, gliding and dissolving from one attitude to the next, she created in her wake an unseen moving sculpture, sketching out with her spare form a harmonic progression of arabesques, minarets and finials that spoke with terrifying sharpness to the magician in a language that his intellect could not begin to interpret. Now she appeared as a leaping tiger, now as a swooping crane, now as a scorpion poised to strike. And at last, after a spiralling cadence of turns that left Leonardo breathless, her movement resolved itself with dramatic suddenness into equilibrium, the delicate tracery of invisible architecture still suspended in the air around her, slowly fragmenting into a multitude of pinpoints, gently drifting to rest in intricate mosaic, softly dissolving into blackness. A sidelong shaft from the window highlighted the graceful line of her collarbone, her shoulder, her knee. Breathing evenly, her features tranquil, she stood lightly, facing the magician, still as a tree.

His hand still clutching the doorknob, Leonardo felt suddenly clumsy and rude, as though he had intruded into something delicate, something private. He coughed as delicately as he could.

'I – I'm sorry – I—'

Alice seemed to notice him for the first time. She looked at him, unruffled and unembarrassed.

'It's quite all right, nothing to worry about.' Her soft tone soothed him. A moment's silence passed, then she came to herself. 'I have to get dressed now.'

With a quick movement she gathered up her things and disappeared into the cloakroom, leaving a flustered Leonardo to hunt for his missing notes. From the Institute of Calibration, a distant bell started chiming the hour.

★   ★   ★

A Special Place of Safety

Mrs Brown was awoken by Rusty's distant cries and Dusty's terrified barking. She sprang from her bed, swiftly checked her son's room and found it empty. By the time she had descended the stair to check the other rooms, boy and dog had arrived at the back door.

'You're soaked!' exclaimed Mrs Brown. 'Look at the state of you! You're dripping all over my clean floor! What on earth have you been doing?'

He stared at her blankly for a moment before marshalling his thoughts.

'It must have been a dream. I suppose I walked in my sleep. Because when I woke up, I was in the water. And Dusty was trying to pull me out. I'm frightened, Mum.'

Suddenly he burst into tears. In a moment, his mother's arms were around him, rubbing his bony shoulder blades, stroking his dripping hair.

'It's years since you've done that. But when you were very little, you used to do it all the time.'

Rusty's wildly beating heart began gradually to slow, and his sobs came to a halt. His mother wiped his face.

'So what did you dream about?'

'It was all about the circus,' he recalled haltingly. 'It seemed so real. And the witch was in it, the one who stole the bell, or was it the acrobat girl from the circus? She was in the dream too. And, Mum –' he hesitated fearfully '– she had Laurel's eyes. Could it have been Laurel in the circus?'

His mother did not reply at once.

'Poor boy,' she said finally. Her face was lined with anxiety. There was a long silence before she spoke her next word.

'Laurel.'

The name hung in the air between them, the name that neither of them had spoken for so many years, a massive knotty obstruction waiting to be negotiated. When Mrs Brown continued, there was anguish in her voice.

'If only that girl had never come here. And if only you could just have forgotten her when she went. I thought you had, to begin with, I really thought you had. And then you started having the nightmares and walking in your sleep. I don't know what you dreamed about, but you used to wake up screaming, really screaming. Sometimes I'd find you in the yard. Once you even got as far as the green. But that was all over years ago. I really thought you'd put it behind you. But I should have known she'd come back.' She collected herself a little.

'How much can you remember about her?'

Rusty frowned in concentration as he gathered the scatttered fragments of his thoughts.

'Well, I remember sitting with her in that shelter in the schoolyard. And I remember her coming here once. You didn't seem to like her, I never knew why. And then I thought she'd died, in the scarlet-fever epidemic. But now I'm not sure any more. I talked to the schoolmaster, and he told me that her people were wandering folk and they'd taken her away. So now I don't know what to believe. What did happen, Mum?'

His voice had a jagged edge of desperation, and Mrs Brown finally knew that the time had come when she must tell her son the truth about the events that had taken place so many years before.

'Upstairs and get your dressing gown. I'll light the fire. Let's start getting you dry.'

Later, Rusty was curled up on the hearthrug at his mother's feet with his head on her knee, just as he had done when he'd been a little boy. Dusty was curled up too, his head on Rusty's knee, looking up at him with troubled eyes. Mrs Brown began hesitantly.

'Yes, Laurel's people were Wanderers, that's true enough. And she lived through the fever, that's true too. She was a tough one, all right. And after that, they moved away and, well, I suppose it was wrong of me, but I just sort of let you believe that she'd died. Oh, I don't know, I didn't really mean to deceive you . . .

but I did want you to forget her, and, well . . . it just seemed to be for the best. You see, something else happened. Something you've forgotten.'

She was talking faster now. The words were coming in a rush, as though she were unable to stop them.

'The day they went, her grandmother came here to see me. I opened the front door and she walked straight into the house . . .' Abruptly she seemed to change the subject. 'Do you remember any of the things that Laurel said to you? Secret things, perhaps?'

Rusty shook his head. Dimly, he could picture that wet afternoon in the little shelter at the top of the school field, the puddles on the ground, the smell of wet raincoats, but not one word of the conversation remained with him. He felt a dull, slow ache, as though something irreplaceable had been lost.

'Well, her grandmother said . . . that Laurel had told you a secret, one of the most terrible secrets of the Wandering Folk.' Faintly, behind his mother's voice, Rusty began to hear another voice calling to him across the years, and he knew straightaway that he had heard these words once before. His mother was still speaking, carried away now by her narrative.

'They have a law, apparently, that says that no stranger is ever to be entrusted with such things, only one of their own kind. And she said that if you were allowed to hear this secret – I can still hear her words, just as if it had happened today – the consequences for you and for all of our people would be too dreadful to contemplate.' She paused for breath. 'And then she told me that she had a spell, an enchantment that would help you to forget. Well, I didn't know what to believe. It seemed so far-fetched – but she had such a way of looking at me . . . And I was so frightened, I didn't know what to do. So in the end I agreed to let her say the enchantment.'

Rusty was looking up at her, transfixed.

'Then she took you to a private place, and she did what she had to do.'

As he heard these words, the scene seemed to come to life in miniature in front of Rusty's eyes, as if acted out by tiny characters on a puppet stage. He watched as the old woman led the boy out of the back door of the house to the tumbledown privy at the end of the yard, while his mother paced anxiously indoors. He watched as, behind the rough-planed door, with its bolt with the chipped black paint, the old woman started to weave around him a maze of obscurity and forgetting, and he watched as she gathered up Laurel's secret and rolled it like a snowball along the dust-muffled corridors of that maze, gathering size until it grew huge with layer upon layer of silence, and rounding corner after corner until it was hidden by the overlapping angles of the walls and was locked away in a safe place and was utterly lost to him.

His mother was still speaking.

'She said that the secret would be locked away in a special place and that it would be safe there until—'

'Until?'

'Until the day your life depended on it. She knew that you would grieve at the loss of the girl, so in return she granted you one act of kindness. She said that the secret would be safely hidden until the day your life depended on it.' She was lost in thought for a moment.

'I still don't know whether I did the right thing or not.' Her voice sounded bitter. 'And, even now, I don't know whether she was telling the truth. I just wish none of it had ever happened. Oh, those Wanderers, they bring nothing but misery. I wish it hadn't all been stirred up again. I just want to forget it for ever.'

Rusty was calmer now.

'Mum?'

'Yes?'

'Do all the Wanderers have eyes like Laurel's?'

'Eyes? You know, I don't think I ever noticed her eyes.' She was stroking his head, the familiar accent of her voice gently soothing him. 'I do remember her hair, though. It was black, very long and very thick . . . And I remember all those strange coins she had in that funny little purse . . . And I remember the way she looked at my candlesticks . . . Are you ready to go back to bed now?'

But the boy had already fallen asleep at his mother's knee.

The next day, the circus had gone from the village. And the next night Rusty Brown slept soundly again. But a few days later, on his way home from school, he was surprised to hear the church bell ringing out once more across the green.

'When did they put the bell back?' he asked his mother.

'Oh, didn't you know? Somebody had a word with the circus people. They did it before they went. And you'll never guess how they did it, I wish I'd seen it, apparently they got one of their elephants to pull it out of the river, and the men hung it back in the tower today. Were there any elephants in your dream?'

Three:
ORIENTATION AND DISORIENTATION

Concealed amongst the high beams, I make certain that you do not notice me when you burst in upon my vantage point. You will notice me soon enough, Lazarus, as soon as you discover where to look. In the meantime, I amuse myself by scattering clues to tantalise you, clues to perplex you. Small clues at present, clues that could be interpreted as nothing but accidents, random, insignificant acts of carelessness. But I warn you now, if you fail to read their message, I shall have no choice but to leave larger clues, and then larger clues still, until at last you can ignore me no longer. And of one thing you can be certain. I shall do whatever I must do until you are forced to take heed of me. For you must take heed of me, Lazarus. You have no choice but to take heed.

For the time being, though, while you and your people hack and burn and count and sort, I am content to remain here, at the top of the house, hanging from my beam, and seeing what there is to be seen in the folds of the distant landscape.

Around the magician, dark clouds are gathering. Clouds that he cannot see, cannot name, cannot comprehend. For in the face and form of the girl Alice, he dimly recognises something, something that disturbs him, something that touches him in some fashion that his intellect cannot encompass.

And I know what it is that he recognises. It is something that he once fleetingly knew, something that has long lain buried. I know that in the girl, the magician recognises something of me. For in just such a crossing of the ways might the touch of my hand be felt, in just such an encounter might the shadow of my presence betray itself. The magician apprehends the feeling but dimly, and with only the bluntest of his faculties. Is it a simple attraction that he feels, or is it the grip of the chill hand of dread? He does not know. Perhaps his feeling has something of both. He struggles to assert his mastery, but it is a struggle that he is doomed to lose.

The boy, meanwhile, has recovered from his nightmares and is enjoying an interlude of happiness, forgetting for a while the secrets and the terrors of the dark. As his village shakes off the harsh bonds of blight, the boy too seems once again to thrive. Entering the summer of his sixteenth year, he meets a girl from the same village, and together they find themselves doing the things that young people love to do. I watch them in the far distance, as they roam through the woods and over the hills, as they swim in the river, as they lie in the long grass watching a lone bird of prey, which hovers in the air far above them. And I also watch the dog Dusty, the guardian whose anxious presence weaves a fragile web of protection about them.

Sometimes on their rambles they might exchange a few words of greeting with a band of tinkers or knife-grinders whom they meet in the lanes. Sometimes they might sit down with them to smoke a tentative pipe or to share a simple meal. And at times such as these, it seems almost as though the boy might be searching for something. But perhaps this is just my fancy. Probably he is simply taking innocent pleasure in a passing interlude. And it is an interlude that will be all too short, for the people in the village are not broad-minded people, and they do not hold the wandering folk in high regard.

I turn my attention back to what is happening in my house. Work continues at a brisk pace, and soon there will be life in the old place again. You are doing well, Lazarus. How methodically you go about your business, you and your lieutenants. I watch them for a moment. The old one, Harold, is rigid and set in his ways, and I can make little use of him, but the young one, Sam, is more open, more biddable. Good-hearted he is, and faithful, and not too intelligent. And how willingly he carries out his duties, be they on your instruction or on mine. Oh yes, I can make much use of Sam, for sometimes Sam can be clumsy, and now at last you too are beginning to notice his clumsiness. A trivial accident here, an unimportant breakage there, perhaps not *always by Sam's own hand, but always when Sam is nearby. Soon you must face him, and when you face him, you face me also.*

Yes, Lazarus, you must face me soon, for these practical jokes begin to tire me. Soon our real business must begin. And soon the time will come when you must take heed of me. I need be patient for only a little while longer.

From the Journal of Victor Lazarus

Wednesday 18th March

Over the past few days, the garden at the front of the house has finally been cleared of undergrowth. As a result, the house is now in full view from the road, and I have begun from time to time to notice the curious faces of onlookers peering between the railings. Until today, this has not impeded our progress, but this afternoon, a new development occurred.

I was conferring with Harold in the sculpture gallery, in an attempt to finalise the arrangement of exhibits, when I was surprised to hear a firm knock at the front door. I instructed Harold to continue with his work alone, and made my way downstairs to investigate. Upon opening the front door, I discovered in the porch a stout lady in late middle age. She wore on her head an elaborate hat decorated with feathers, and she carried under her arm a bulky handbag. She introduced herself to me as the chairman of the local historical association, and, to my astonishment, enquired whether she might be permitted to inspect the contents of the house. It struck me that it would be prudent to discuss such a matter with my colleagues, and I therefore avoided giving an immediate response, suggesting to her instead that she return on the following day.

★   ★   ★

Thursday 19th March

Another breakage occurred this morning. Sam and one of his men were engaged in hanging a painting, rather a pleasant little landscape painted in watercolour and mounted in an ornate gilt frame. As they were hoisting it into position, it somehow slipped from their grasp and fell to the floor. The frame was badly damaged, the glass was smashed, and, worst of all, a long shard pierced the painting itself. I have made up my mind that if this carelessness continues, I shall have to have some stern words with Sam.

The stout lady returned this afternoon. (I had in the meantime discussed her request with my colleagues, and we had come to the conclusion that she should be permitted – under strict supervision, of course – to make an inspection of the contents of the house.) I myself conducted her on the tour. At the conclusion of our business, I invited her into the kitchen for refreshment before her return to the town. She was clearly impressed by what she had seen, and, in the course of our conversation, she enquired whether it might be possible for the rank-and-file members of her association also to come on a visit. Apparently a former owner of the house had been a well-regarded local man who had subsequently made a distinguished career in the world. The lady mentioned his name, but it was not a familiar one to me. I acceded to her request, albeit with some misgivings, and a date was arranged.

Friday 3rd April

Despite my earlier doubts, the visit by the historical association has passed without incident. I am, however, beginning to regret having been so accommodating, as a number of other individuals and organisations have now made contact with me to enquire about possible visits. Now that I have acceded to one such request, I am finding it no easy matter to refuse others. The local artists' circle, for example, wishes to examine the collection of paintings. Various musicians and composers have expressed an interest in the rooms of instruments and manuscripts. One very old man, bent almost double, wishes to scrutinise the garden for certain rare herbs that he believes were once grown here. The list shows every sign of becoming endless.

Naturally, I am attempting to indulge everybody's enthusiasms as best I can, but I am finding that dealing with such enquiries has begun to occupy a substantial proportion of my time.

There has been yet another accident today. This time a piece of sculpture was knocked from its plinth, with much resultant damage. I still find myself strangely reluctant to confront Sam about these mishaps. I really must steel myself to have a talk with him.

Wednesday 8th April

Work continues to proceed at a good pace. The front garden is currently in the process of being replanted, although much work remains to be done at the rear of the house. Indoors, meanwhile, the majority of the downstairs rooms have now been put in satisfactory decorative order, and the main bulk of the book collection has been catalogued and arranged. The restoration of the art gallery is nearing completion, and a piano-tuner is currently on site, attending to the collection of instruments.

As it happens, it was during one of the tuner's visits that I decided to hold an extraordinary meeting with Harold and Sam in my orderly room. The purpose of this gathering was to discuss the issue of visitors and how they might best be accommodated. Our discussion took place against the background noise of plonking and twanging.

The single question to which we were addressing ourselves was this: should any further visitors be admitted to the house? I requested that my colleagues express their points of view on the matter. Harold's opinion was that a precedent had now been set by the admission of the historical society, and that the people of the town had in any case a moral entitlement to view the collection, which is apparently considered to possess considerable historical interest and artistic merit. Sam was even more forthright. He made the point that the house had more the character of a museum than of a place of residence, and that it should therefore be operated as a museum and an admission fee charged to visitors. For my own part, I remained uneasy, as I was quite certain in my own mind that the owner's original correspondence had made no reference to public access. In answer to my challenge, however, it emerged that my companions had quite different recollections concerning the contents of the documents in question. Confident of my ground, I secured agreement that a search should be made for the original papers, but, to my perplexity, they were nowhere to be found.

Given that the vital evidence could not be located, I had no alternative but to accede, albeit reluctantly, to the will of the majority. It was decided that the public was to be welcomed. Harold was to publish a table of opening times, and Sam was to arrange for a sign to be erected at the front gate. As the meeting broke up and we emerged from the room to go about our various business, our ears were assaulted by the abrupt dissonance of a snapping piano string.

Thursday 21st May

Events here are continuing to develop in unforeseen directions. The number of visitors to the house is such that I have been obliged to recruit several additional administrative staff to oversee them. Harold has organised the printing of admission tickets, has set up a procedure for their sale, and is currently engaged in the writing and editing of a visitors' guidebook. Sam's men have built a cloakroom adjacent to the admission area, and plans are currently afoot for the construction of a refreshment room next to the kitchen. Mrs Proudfoot, the lady from the historical society, has declared an interest in the position of catering manageress. And, much to my surprise, I myself have, by default, taken on the role of curator in what has become, in effect, the town's combined library, museum, concert hall and art gallery. An uneasy sensation is growing within me that I am no longer in full control of this venture!

Amongst the crowds, I have become aware of a number of regular visitors. There is an elderly lady who wears a long, old-fashioned type of costume. She has located a comfortable armchair in an upstairs room where the collection of fossils is stored, and she can usually be found dozing there in the afternoon. One of these days we shall forget about her and lock her in there at night! There are a group of musicians who spend their days performing long, extemporised ensembles on the keyboard instruments. They produce sounds quite unlike any music I have ever known, but many of the visitors seem to appreciate their efforts.

There have also been a few children, and it has been decided, in the interests of education, that they should be admitted to the premises free of charge. Several of them can regularly be found disporting themselves in the rooms of toys, and one small red-headed boy has discovered a collection of comics among the periodicals. He spends day after day stretched out on the floor among them, utterly engrossed in their tales of adventure and wonder, while his pet dog disappears on long expeditions around the garden.

It occurs to me that one of the reasons for my initial reluctance to admit visitors was that the number of breakages and accidents seemed certain to increase. To my great relief, this has not been the case. However, of the few accidents that have taken place, every one seems in some way to be connected with Sam. I find that I continue to put off speaking to him. I really must make the time as soon as possible.

★   ★   ★

A Night with the Wanderers

'That tickles!'

Rusty plucked the blade of grass from Eileen's fingers and tossed it away. Eileen looked at him with mock pity, then broke into laughter.

'That won't help you. There's lots more where that came from!'

They were lying side by side in the long grass, up in the hills above the village, basking lazily in the early summer warmth. A little way away, Dusty was chasing a butterfly, batting at the fluttering wings with soft paws. High above them, a lone kestrel hovered. And from the valley, they could faintly hear the church bell chiming the hour.

'Was that three o'clock or four?' Rusty murmured, half to himself.

'I'm not sure. Anyway, there's plenty of time. Come here!'

The kestrel veered away, and for a few minutes all was quiet again, until Dusty suddenly broke in upon the pair with a series of short questioning barks. Reluctantly, Rusty and Eileen heaved themselves upright.

'Silly dog.' Eileen started to rearrange the tangled locks of her brown hair. 'Can't he see we're busy?'

But Rusty's attention had been caught by a thin column of smoke rising from a distant clump of trees beside a lane.

'See that? What do you think it is?'

'I bet it's Wanderers,' said Eileen. Suddenly she was on her feet, straightening her dress. 'Come on, let's go and have a look.'

And she was away down the hill. Dusty ran after her, barking excitedly. Shrugging, Rusty followed at his own pace.

Rounding the corner of the lane, they came upon the Wanderers' encampment in a small clearing at the roadside. There was just one waggon, painted a plain dark green and unexpectedly functional in appearance. Directly in front of them, a ragged young man was sitting beside a fire, sharpening a knife that had a long, oddly shaped blade. A lean, grey horse was grazing a little way away, and somewhere they could hear a baby crying. At the sound of their arrival, the man looked up. He was dark-haired and sallow-skinned, and his eyes were black and intense. His smooth face and sparse moustache indicated that he was only a few years older than Rusty.

'Welcome, strangers.' The greeting was unexpectedly formal. 'My name is Gideon Blackwood, hedge-layer by trade. My home is your home.' He held out his hands to them in greeting.

Rusty hesitated for a moment, but Eileen was less inhibited. Half-pulling him by the forearm, she stepped forward.

'Hello, Gideon,' she said. 'I'm Eileen, and this is Rusty. Oh, and the dog's around somewhere. He's called Dusty. Dusty, come away from there!'

During these introductions, a woman had emerged from the waggon. She too was very young, and was dark-haired and dark-eyed like the man. The baby, now sleeping soundly, was cradled in her arms. She smiled lopsidedly as she approached them.

'I'm Peg,' she said. 'Will you stay and eat with us?'

Rusty was uncertain.

'I think my mother—' he began.

'We'd love to,' Eileen interrupted. 'What a beautiful baby. What's her name?'

'She hasn't a name yet,' replied Peg. 'Among our people, a child does not choose her name until her first birthday. It takes a little time for her to find out who she is.'

'Can I hold her for a minute?'

'You're welcome. Why don't you come inside with me? You can talk to her while I get on with the supper.'

An hour later, Gideon and Rusty were sprawled beside the fire, sharing a flask of thick, dark red wine. Gideon's hedge-laying tools were spread out on the ground, and Rusty, having recovered from his initial shyness, was bombarding him with questions about his trade and about the practicalities of the wandering life.

'How do you find your way from place to place?' asked the boy. Gideon looked puzzled.

'We don't have to find our way,' he replied after a moment. 'The way finds us.'

Rusty in his turn was puzzled by this, but before he could ask any more questions, Peg announced that the meal was ready. Rusty had been expecting an exotic hotchpotch of hedgerow plants and the flesh of wild animals, so he was rather disappointed to receive a plateful of quite ordinary food, which had obviously come mostly from tins. However, at the end of a long day any food was very welcome, especially with another flask of wine to accompany it.

Afterwards, Gideon stuffed a pipe with aromatic herbs, lit it with a spill, and, after taking several long puffs, passed it to Rusty.

'Sometimes we tell stories in the evening,' he said after a pause. 'Do you know any good ones?'

'Do you know the one about the Islanders?' asked Rusty.

It grew late. Peg lit a couple of lamps, Gideon brought out a mandolin, and, in the fading light, the music and the wine and the smoke started slowly to weave and loop around them in lazy rings of enchantment. Eileen curled up at Rusty's right side, her head heavy on his shoulder. Dusty lay down at Rusty's left side, his tail flicking now and again as he settled into a doze. Slowly the sounds of the fire and the music and the voices merged into a soothing background hum until everyone's eyelids began to droop.

'We ought to go home soon,' murmured Eileen.

'It's dark,' yawned Peg. 'You'll never find your way. Sleep now. We'll put you on the road in the morning.'

And, one by one, they fell asleep at the fireside.

Early the next day, Granny Hopkins was making her way across the village green, stooping now and then to retrieve a piece of litter. She was on her way to The Plough, where she worked for an hour or two each morning, sweeping out the taproom, unblocking the sink, and generally making the place presentable for the day's trade. Granny Hopkins must have been at least ninety, but her eyes were still sharp, and she was quick to notice the three dishevelled figures, two human and one canine, who were emerging, just uphill from the church, into the main street of the village. She had no difficulty recognising them. There was Margaret Brown's boy Michael, with his nasty little dog. And surely the girl was Eileen Gilbert, the doctor's daughter. She certainly ought to know better. Granny Hopkins gave a loud sniff of disapproval before continuing on her way. Had they spent the whole night up in the hills? In her day, young people had not been encouraged to behave in such a fashion.

Certainly none of the three was looking their best. Rusty's mop of red hair was garnished with a mixed salad of leaves, grass and other vegetation, and the buttons of his shirt were not all connected to the right buttonholes. Eileen had lost the buckle from one sandal, her summer dress was torn and her shin was grazed from scrambling through barbed wire. Even Dusty, padding along beside them, presented a dissolute figure, with mud on his paws and different parts of his coat pointing in different directions. Eileen was fiddling with her hair as she walked, vainly trying to make it presentable.

'Why couldn't you have taken me home last night?' she was complaining. 'Daddy will have a fit. What am I going to say to him?'

'Maybe he won't be up yet.' Rusty tried to reassure her. 'He might think you're asleep in your room.' He gave her hand a hopeful squeeze.

Eileen stopped walking and turned to face him. A hair slide sprang apart, releasing a long untidy lock of hair across her face.

'You don't know him, Rusty. You don't know what he's like. He'll have been waiting up all night for me.' She was beginning to sob.

Sure enough, as they arrived at the house, they could see that the door was standing open, framing Doctor Gilbert's angular figure. He was clad in pyjamas and dressing gown and his face was red. Taking absolutely no notice of Rusty, he concentrated his glare on the girl. When he spoke, his voice had an edge of menace.

'Inside.'

Her head bowed, Eileen entered the house without saying a word. Silently, the doctor closed the door, leaving Rusty and Dusty standing foolishly at the gate. Dusty pricked up his ears. From the open window of the downstairs study, the man's voice could be heard.

'I can't imagine what your mother would have thought.' His anger was barely under control. 'Heaven knows, I've tried to bring you up respectably. And now you tell me that you've been spending your nights with the washerwoman's son. In a tinkers' camp. Smoking their disgusting herbs as well, judging by the smell of you. Is there anything else you want to tell me?'

The girl's reply, punctuated by sobs and sniffs, was indecipherable. As the doctor continued his tirade, Rusty decided that he was unlikely to contribute anything further by his presence. He attached Dusty's lead to his collar and the two of them slunk away, trying hard not to imagine the reception from Mrs Brown that would be awaiting them.

The Congress of Counsellors

Lulled into a trancelike state by the monotonous drone of the Senior Counsellor's voice, Leonardo Pegasus sat in his usual place at the long mahogany table, scanning the faces of his peers. The man opposite him looked insufferably smug, the one next to him maddeningly pompous, the woman at the far end anxious to the point of paranoia. Leonardo sighed heavily. He was weary of their company and longed to be back in his workshop with Alice. He stared at a blank piece of wall, allowing his thoughts to drift. Against the neutral background of the wall, the slim figure of Alice seemed once again to dance before him.

Dancing was an activity that had not previously occupied a position of any significance in Leonardo's world, but Alice's graceful performance had awoken something in him, some dull, reluctant beast that had until now slumbered peacefully in its corner. It seemed to Leonardo that her dance had spoken to him in some indefinable way, perhaps not in the language of words, but in some unknown code, a code of great, strange-textured, oddly shaped forms, forms that he could neither name nor comprehend. They circled slowly around him as he watched them, weaving, as they circled, a knotted web of strange and unfamiliar thoughts, ensnaring him, confusing him, confounding him.

As a man of science, Leonardo lived in a world of words and numbers and precisely defined concepts. He had little experience of these strange new things that inhabited this strange new world. He wondered whether they might be feelings. Yes, feelings, that must be it. He couldn't work out how to make them go away, but it occurred to him that he might try to achieve some kind of control over them. He would start by identifying them and naming them. What was named could be understood, could be manipulated.

Leonardo reached across the table for a quill and ink, and started to make a list on the parchment in front of him. Admiration, that was easy, perhaps even envy. And wonder. And . . . yes, that one must be guilt. As if he had intruded uninvited upon something delicate and private. And then, he was forced to admit, just a trace of, well, perhaps he might call it aesthetic appreciation. After all, what man could remain indifferent to the economical curves of that slender form? But even that was not all. There was something else, something for which he could not find a word. He struggled to untangle what was left of the knot, his hands unconsciously grappling with each other on the table top. Yes. He had it. It was something that was a little like humility . . . and also a little like fear. The magician shivered.

At that moment, the voice of the Senior Counsellor broke in upon his thoughts.

'And what would be the view of the King's Chief Magician?'

Slowly, Leonardo looked up. He did not reply straight away. He furrowed his brow, as though pondering on grave and weighty matters. He scanned the expectant row of faces. Finally, with practised ease, he spoke.

'I am more than content to add my voice to those of my honoured sisters and brothers.'

When Leonardo finally got to his bed that night, he felt weighed down by a great burden of tiredness. Congress had continued until very late. Although the coffee had, as usual, tasted like disinfectant, the rest of the refreshments had been acceptable, and he had eaten enough sandwiches to escape the irksome task of preparing an evening meal for himself. But when he finally arrived at his apartment building, he discovered that one of the elevator captain's ponies had been lamed.

'Sorry, guv'nor, but without a full team I can't get you beyond the third floor. Perhaps the walk will do you good.'

With an irritable grunt, Leonardo declined further help and climbed the full eight storeys to his apartment.

In the workshop the next day, neither Leonardo nor Alice referred to what had taken place. And as the days went by, Leonardo began to feel an awkwardness that he did not know how to dispel. In his idle moments, he found himself watching Alice closely as she went about her business, and now he was seeing her through new eyes. He realised that the poise and command she brought to her dancing were present in her every trivial movement. To her work, as to her dance, she brought total concentration. She carried herself with an air of unself-conscious composure that led Leonardo to believe she was guided by some unknown force, some mysterious congruence that shaped her life in weird, offbeat, unguessable ways. And she retained her air of mystery. She volunteered only the minimum of information about herself or about her life outside the palace. It was as though she kept a part of herself sealed away in a secret place, behind a boundary fence that was invisible but rigorously patrolled. Leonardo started to think of her as an alien life form, perhaps a visitor from another planet. And he found himself wanting, desperately, to know more about her.

But if Alice felt anything of the kind in return, she certainly gave no indication of it. So, on the surface, business between them continued more or less as normal.

At the beginning of the summer, Alice requested a leave of absence to visit her family, who, she informed Leonardo, lived on one of the islands off the north-east coast of the kingdom. This was not a request that Leonardo could reasonably refuse, and he was therefore thrown back on his own resources for a few weeks.

One Friday morning, for the first time in months, he found himself at the Herald's Office. As Veronique had told him, the queues were now moving forward much more quickly, and the intake area was therefore quite sparsely populated. A gang of painters was at work on the walls, and Leonardo noticed that the floor had been relaid with black and white chequered tiles, and was now disconcertingly level. He was soon at the front of his queue.

'Yes, please?'

The brisk voice belonged to a well-built woman on the verge of middle age. Armorial garb was evidently no longer required by the Herald, for she was wearing a waist-length black leather jacket with a bewildering number of pockets, decorated in an intricate pattern with small brass studs. Her hair was cropped short, except for an untidy fringe that hung in her eyes. She wore an official-looking badge that told Leonardo her name was Nina. He introduced himself.

'Leonardo Pegasus, magician.'

She raised an eyebrow. 'Pegasus? Oh yes. Yes, I've heard about you. You're Alice's new boss, aren't you? Really upset the applecart, that did, her leaving bang in the middle of the reorganisation. So of course muggins just gets dumped here. I never asked to work on intake, you know. Not my sort of thing at all. Anyway, what do you want?'

Taken aback by this outburst, Leonardo fumbled in his pockets, trying to locate his parchment. The woman sighed.

'Get on with it. There's little enough time these days, what with the numbers being cut and everything. And these forms! I'm not allowed to use the old ones any more, I've got to use these, all five of them, and they just take for ever. Never seem to be enough copies, either. I'd like to get my hands on whoever came up with this system. Oh, found it at last, have you?'

Leonardo came away feeling like an unwelcome intruder. Why couldn't the woman be like Alice? He realised that he was missing Alice badly. He wondered if she would send him a postcard.

In The Crier's Rest that evening, Leonardo tried to explain some of the complexities of his feelings to Veronique. Leonardo greatly valued the little clown's advice, because Veronique had a unique and refreshing ability to put complicated matters into perspective.

'Do you fancy her?' she asked with her croaking laugh. 'You do, don't you? What d'you reckon she's like in bed, then?'

The Brotherhood of Cartographers

One afternoon, after a stiff climb, Rusty and Dusty found themselves at a favourite spot, a grassy bluff overlooking the village. It had taken several weeks for Mrs Brown to calm down fully after Rusty and Eileen's night with the Wanderers, and during this time, Rusty had been forced to find what comfort he could in the quiet of the hills and the undemanding companionship of his dog. Now, stretched out drowsily on his back, he could feel the reassuring weight of Dusty's head on his chest. Ruffling the wiry fur at the back of the dog's neck, he gazed up at the clouds, brooding on the narrow-mindedness of adults.

On his return from his misadventure, his mother had marched him straight to the forbidding house of the village priest, where he had been given a long, harsh lecture on the wickedness of the young and the terrifying nature of retribution. And Eileen, after some extremely severe words from her father, had been confined to her room until further notice. Dawdling in the lane outside her house, Rusty had seen her standing forlorn at her window, but when he called up to her, she had drawn the curtains hastily.

Sighing in bewilderment at the injustice of it all, Rusty allowed his thoughts to drift back over their adventures that summer. He remembered an earlier afternoon in the hills, when they had lain side by side in the long grass, watching a kestrel hovering high above them. Snatches of their conversation came back to him.

'What do you think the world looks like to her?' Eileen had mused.

'How do you know it's a her?' he had teased, and she had responded with a playful poke in the ribs.

'I just know. Now button yourself up, it's getting cold.'

Rusty made an effort to thrust aside his memories of the girl and concentrated instead on the kestrel, trying to imagine her aerial view of the landscape. The kestrel would be able to see how all the lanes and streams and hills were connected together. If she could talk, she could explain how to find the way from one place to the next. Perhaps, he thought suddenly, she could even tell the Wanderers the way to the next village.

For in his conversation with Gideon Blackwood, Rusty had stumbled upon something that puzzled him greatly. He had been trying to find out how the Wanderers were able to make their way from place to place across the land, how they managed to arrive at the right time for the annual fairs and other regular gatherings. But Gideon, although prepared to talk quite freely on every other matter, had on this point been surprisingly evasive. From his monosyllabic responses, Rusty had pieced together the information that the Wanderers did not exchange directional information by word of mouth, that they kept no form of written record, and that they did not use any form of chart.

On this last point, Rusty was particularly intrigued. He had been learning about the work of the Brotherhood of Cartographers in his geography lessons at the high school, and the master had mentioned in passing the extraordinary diagrams that the members of the Brotherhood were said to produce. Charts, they called them.

Rusty became immediately fascinated by the notion that these charts could indicate, to those initiates who were able to interpret them, how the different parts of the land were connected together, how city was linked to town and town was linked to village by road and river and trackway and highway. But when he asked the geography master whether he could borrow some charts to study, he was told that the work produced by the Brotherhood was kept under lock and key, and that their charts were available only to a privileged few. And although the master had no wish to discourage the boy, he was unable to help him further.

Cycling home that afternoon, it occurred to Rusty that if one master could not help him, there might well be another who could. Accordingly, he decided to pay a call on his old schoolmaster in the village. Skidding to a halt just before he reached the ford, he propped his machine against the old man's gatepost and made his way up the front path. He could hear no music, but the front door stood ajar as usual. Rusty discovered the master seated at his parlour table with several dozen components from the inside of his piano spread out in front of him.

'It's not working properly,' explained the schoolmaster, without looking up. 'I'm just taking it to pieces and putting it back together again. That usually seems to do the trick.'

Rusty came straight to the point.

'Sir, do you know anything about the Brotherhood of Cartographers?'

The old man looked up at him with an expression some-where between amusement and reproach

'It seems to me that young Brown is becoming rather too fond of mysteries,' he said after a long pause. 'Perhaps a little too fond for his own good. I think we definitely ought to have a cup of tea before we talk about cartography. Just let me go and put the kettle on.' His voice grew fainter as he retreated to the kitchen. 'By the way, I believe I may have the tail-end of a Battenberg cake in the pantry. I'm not sure why. I could never tolerate marzipan.'

Eventually, after several cups of tea, they paid a visit to the glass-fronted cupboard in the back room, and the boy came away with an armful of dusty books and documents that he smuggled upstairs to his room while his mother was out delivering laundry.

That night, by the light of a flickering candle, he spread the books out on his bed. It was not long before he discovered that the Brotherhood had already drawn charts for the chief cities of the land and for much of the coastline. These charts, he read, were all locked away securely in the vaults of the Brotherhood. He read next that further work was in progress on the charting of the Royal Highways and adjoining areas, but he was intrigued to discover that no work had so far been done on the charting of the less-frequented rural areas, still less of the inhospitable mountain regions or the outlying islands. And he also discovered that the principles of cartography were protected by Charter Ancient and Inviolable, and that no chart was to be made known to anyone outside the Brotherhood. Meanwhile Dusty, who had by now become accustomed to Rusty's nocturnal habits, slumbered peacefully in his basket.

The next morning Rusty searched the chest of drawers in his small room, digging amongst old golliwogs and shapeless lumps of plasticine and pieces of kites and lead soldiers until he unearthed the flat tin box of watercolour paints that had been given to him one long-ago birthday, briefly tried, then abandoned. Downstairs, he seated himself at the table, bringing with him a clean sheet of lining paper and a chipped cup half filled with water. The paintbox lay open in front of him, the brush resting expectant in its central channel. Dusty sniffed curiously at his side.

'What are you up to?' Mrs Brown, up to her elbows in wet sheets, called out to him from the kitchen.

'Trying to paint the village as a kestrel would see it from the air.'

His words were addressed more to himself than to his mother. Frowning in concentration, he dipped the brush into the water, wiped it against the rim of the cup to squeeze out the surplus water, circled it foamingly around the untouched perfect square of aquamarine pigment, then paused, trying to picture the curve of the river.

'Just remember, dinner's in an hour, and I'll want that table clearing.'

Absorbed in his task, the boy did not reply. Mrs Brown heaved the washtub across the yard to where the mangle stood. These days, she didn't know what Rusty was getting up to half the time, but whatever it was, she hoped it would keep him out of mischief. He had been moping over that girl for long enough.

After that first tentative effort, Rusty began to spend much of his spare time painting charts. He tried several versions of the village, and when he was satisfied with them, he turned his attention to the surrounding countryside. Sometimes he would spend whole days in the hills, imagining himself hovering with the kestrel, discovering how the lanes and streams and woods were connected together, recording his visions in watercolour paint on a thick pad of buckling cartridge paper. Sometimes he asked Dusty to carry his paintbox, but the dog seemed more interested in retrieving the screwed-up balls of paper that represented his master's less successful efforts.

As time went on, Mrs Brown became accustomed to seeing

the colourful rows of charts spreading out along her son's bedroom wall, and when he told her, a year later, that he wanted
to study for a degree at the Academy of Cartography, she was
happy to give her assent. She did not understand anything of
these strange new sciences, but felt in an obscure way that
what he was doing might have some sort of practical value.
And she knew that in the cities there was a need for young
people with such qualifications. She pictured her son gaining
his degree, making a distinguished career, caring for her in her
old age.

Laurel's Last Show

'Five minutes, Laurel. The clowns are on.'

   'Nearly ready, Madame.'

   Craning forward in the dim light of the living waggon,
Laurel squinted at her reflection in the tarnished mirror as she
put the final touches to her black lipstick. Satisfied, she pulled
her mask down across her eyes, smoothed out a wrinkle in her
tights, and carefully adjusted the folds of her cloak around her
shoulders. She didn't turn to look at Madame Constanzas, but
she knew well enough when the wrinkled old face had with-
drawn from the doorway. Alone, Laurel allowed herself to relax
slightly. She had never stopped feeling the tightness in her
abdomen that came before every show, but tonight she carried
an additional burden that she could not share with anyone else.
This performance was to be her last. It was the eve of Laurel's
seventeenth birthday, and at the end of tonight's show she
would walk away from the circus ring and nobody would be
able to bring her back.

Although the circus had been her whole life for nearly ten
years, Laurel still had clear memories of the time before. Like all
the circus people, she was a Wanderer by birth, but unlike most
of the others, she had not been born into the circus. Her father's

people had been roadmenders, and her mother had explained to her that the family was forced to travel because the roads always needed mending right across the land. At any rate, for as long as Laurel could remember, the scene that greeted her through the window of the waggon had never been the same from one month to the next.

But, roadmender or no, her father had believed in the importance of schooling, and, whenever they were staying anywhere for more than a few days, Laurel would be installed in the local school where, time after time, she would try to pick up the threads of her lessons. Naturally, Laurel's mother and grandmother had warned her always to keep her distance from the other children, the village-dwellers, and never, never to pass on to them any of the special knowledge of the wandering people. And Laurel had kept her word faithfully – or at least she had done so until the day she met the little red-headed boy.

For he was the one who had been the cause of all the trouble. It had been early autumn, and Laurel's family had been encamped just outside a village at the edge of the hill country. Laurel's father had said that he had several weeks' steady work ahead of him, and the girl had therefore been put into school. At first, it had seemed no different from the many other schools she had attended, but on her first morning there she had met a boy named Michael Brown, a boy who seemed somehow unlike the other children of the village-dwellers. Like Laurel, this boy seemed to keep his distance from the others, and, like Laurel, he was dressed in clothes that were old and patched and frayed. Wary at first, the two children had gradually won each other's trust, had gradually begun to whisper secret things to each other, had gradually become friends. Eventually, Laurel had even been invited to visit the boy at his mother's house. The mother had given her things to eat and drink, but despite this generosity she had seemed to Laurel a cold, unhappy woman. She regarded the girl warily, and the invitation had not been repeated.

But Laurel had continued to feel drawn towards the boy in a way she did not fully understand, and soon afterwards, one wet afternoon in the schoolyard, she had felt a sudden prompting to do the thing that her grandmother had warned her never, never to do. It had not felt like anything much at the time, but later, when her family had discovered what had happened, Laurel had immediately been taken out of the school and kept inside the waggon until the time came for them to move on again. She shivered at the memory of the beating her father had given her, of the tears her mother had shed, of the anger and bewilderment on her grandmother's face.

Soon after that came the beginning of Laurel's time at the circus. Arriving at the compound, she was placed under the guardianship of Madame Constanzas, a tiny, wrinkled old lady who hobbled painfully about with the aid of a thick, knobbly walking stick. Madame ran the circus with one of her sons. As well as looking after the paybox, she was responsible for the training and education of the circus children.

'I was not always as you see me now,' said Madame on Laurel's first day. 'In my day I was a great rope-walker. The world was at my feet. Until this.' And she knocked twice with her stick on the floor of the waggon.

Every morning was spent in training. At first, Laurel revelled in the novelty of it. She showed a natural talent for the work of the circus and quickly mastered the basic moves of juggling, tumbling and rope-walking. Before she had been in the circus for three months, she had made her first appearance in the ring. But when she heard the terrifying hubbub of the crowd, the roaring and the stamping and the whistling, she began to develop a fear that never left her. Before long, all of her early joy had deserted her and she felt nothing but dread for the ring, and nothing but hatred and contempt for the crowds who stared at her. Despite her growing skill in her craft, Laurel began to perform with a sullen indifference that drove Madame Constanzas to despair.

'Why must you be like this?' demanded the old lady one morning.

'I hate the ring,' wept Laurel. 'I want to go back to my mother.'

'You know you cannot,' growled Madame. 'Your father has signed your indentures. You are bound to this life until you attain your majority. Now, stop that weeping and show me your somersault again.'

In some way that she did not fully understand, Laurel connected her unhappiness with the red-headed boy to whom she had whispered the secret. Puzzled by this, one day she plucked up the courage to ask Madame Constanzas about it. The old lady listened carefully.

'Put it from your mind, child,' she said finally. 'Things unravel themselves in time. For now you must work hard and be patient.'

Laurel was not satisfied by this reply, but she was not by nature an introspective girl and soon she found other things to occupy herself. For as she grew older, Laurel noticed that some of the boys in the villages were becoming interested in her in a new sort of way. They were strange awkward creatures, full of sidelong looks and mumbled words, seemingly unable to say plainly what they meant. But their attention unsettled Laurel, and she was unsure at first how to deal with it. Finally it came to her that, if only she had not made friends with the red-headed boy, none of these troubles would be plaguing her. So Laurel made up her mind that she would never allow such a thing to happen to her again. Whatever it was that these boys wanted, she would give them nothing. In time, she learned from the other girls in the circus how to single out a boy from the crowd, how to tempt him with looks and promises, how to lead him to a frenzy of anticipation. And then she learned how to cheat him, how to steal from him, how to humiliate him in a hundred ways. And, always, she knew that the next day the circus would move on, and he would be gone from her life for ever. So even if she never saw the red-headed one again, she would have her revenge on the rest of his kind.

But it was not until Laurel learned how to throw knives that she found a way in which she could give full vent to her rage. She had been working with two young men in a trapeze act when the old knife-thrower had been trampled by an elephant and was forced to retire from the ring.

Laurel had long admired the old man's skill with the knives, and she begged Madame to be allowed to take over the act. Initially reluctant, the old lady eventually relented, and, after some weeks of rehearsal, Laurel began to develop the tired routine into something that was truly her own. As time went on, she found that she could incorporate more and more of her fury and resentment and hate into her performance, and, as she continued to grow into a woman, she developed a style and attack that gripped and mesmerised every man in the crowd. She revelled in this new-found power over them, sometimes even believing that she could enter their dreams to taunt them as their indifferent wives snored beside them. But if ever a man or boy ventured to cross the boundary that separated the performer from the spectator, he would be met with a hostility and contempt that left him in no doubt as to his transgression.

Madame Constanzas and her son, alarmed at first by these open displays of viciousness, were soon surprised and gratified to register a sharp increase in takings. They offered Laurel star billing and a handsome salary, but she had no interest in these things, for her grievance continued to smoulder in her heart as angrily as ever. And Laurel understood that she was bound to the circus only until she should attain her majority. She knew that on that day, she would be free again to go where she pleased. On that day, her sentence would come to an end.

After a cursory bow to the crowd, Laurel snatched up her cloak and, before the applause had died, she was out of the ring, away from the tent, and quickly picking her way between puddles to the living waggon she shared with Madame. Madame, she knew, would be in the paybox, counting the takings. For a few minutes, Laurel could count on being alone. She checked that the curtains were drawn tight, then peeled off her costume for the last time, tossing it as always on the floor of the waggon for Madame to tidy away. Then, without stopping to wash or remove her make-up, she scrambled into her travelling clothes. Reaching under the dressing table, she drew out the bag that she had hidden before the show, tucked in her set of throwing knives, and headed swiftly for the back gate of the compound.

Keeping to the shadows, she stole along the row of waggons and rounded the corner at the end. Then, just as she came in sight of the gate, she found her way abruptly barred by the tiny form of Madame Constanzas.

'Madame, I was just . . .' she faltered, but the old lady interrupted her.

'I know, child, I know. Say no more. Tomorrow you will be seventeen, and the circus can no longer hold you. In my heart, I had hoped that you might decide to stay with us, for you have a great gift for the ring, but, in truth, you have always been your own mistress.'

She gazed unflinchingly at the girl. Suddenly Laurel found herself close to tears.

'Oh Madame, I never wanted it to be like this. But I've never been happy here, it's not as if I hadn't told you, and—'

'Hush, child, hush. You must do what is right for you. You know you will always have a home here if you wish to return, but tonight, and for many nights to come, you have a long road ahead of you. So go now, quickly, before you change your mind. And may good luck go with you.'

And without another word, the old lady turned around and hobbled away about her business.

For a moment, Laurel hesitated. She looked back towards the familiar lights of the circus compound, then she looked forward at the hard road climbing steeply into the hills. Perhaps there would be wild animals there. Perhaps there would be bandits. She reached into her bag, fingered the curved blade of a knife, felt a quick surge of warmth in her belly. The knives would be her friends in the days to come. She would need no other.

Then, sniffing back her tears, Laurel drew her cloak around her and strode forward into the night.

The Black Kites

Following his usual morning route across the city, Leonardo Pegasus was once again lost in thought. His thoughts were not, of course, focused on his immediate surroundings, but on the serious task of attempting to recall the exact shape of Alice's left kneecap. The kneecap had caught the magician's attention during the previous morning's coffee break, when Alice had been sitting with one foot on her chair, her knee pressed up against her shoulder. However, even with such weighty matters on his mind, Leonardo could not avoid noticing that the pulse of city life was subdued. There was little traffic on the roads, few people on the pavements, and no trade was taking place in the market. A suspicion started to form in his mind, and when he rounded the corner into the main thoroughfare, he knew that he had been right. Fluttering from the roof of the palace gatehouse was a sombre line of black kites. The King was dead.

A brief conversation with the sentry provided the final confirmation.

'Time for me to call it a day, I reckon,' mused the ancient warrior. 'Can't cope with any more of these changes. Just hope my Bessie and me can live on the gratuity.'

At the workshop, Alice was opening the morning delivery of scrolls.

'That Prince Matt seems a smart young fellow, all right,' she said brightly. 'It might do a bit of good, having him there on the throne.'

Leonardo was not so sure. He pottered aimlessly around the Theatre of Magic. Gloomily, he gazed at the model stages, their characters motionless and forlorn. He recalled that the Prince had been quite dismissive of the paraphernalia of his craft. 'Toys and puppets' – that had been the expression he had used. Leonardo picked up a miniature cavalryman from the main stage and turned it around in his hand. Its pinhead eyes stared stupidly back at him. He wondered whether the new King would bother to continue with the campaign on the borders. He wondered whether he would keep up any of the old traditions.

Leonardo considered sitting down for a mug of coffee with Alice, but decided that Alice's naive optimism was not what he needed at that moment. An early lunch was called for. He launched himself in the direction of the tavern, leaving Alice gaping at the empty doorway.

The Crier's Rest seemed to be the only place where there was any activity in the city that day. The narrow taproom was already thronged with customers, and everyone was anxious to air their views concerning the changes that the new King seemed likely to introduce. Leonardo caught snatches of conversation as he elbowed his way through the crowd.

'Whatever happens, people will need to be told what's going on in the kingdom . . .'

'He seemed very interested in my crystals when he visited the laboratory . . .'

'I can't see him wanting a lot of heraldic apparel. You should see the designs for the new court dress . . .'

'They say he wants to burn the Undertown to the ground . . .'

In the confused tangle of exchanges, Leonardo could discern threads of concern, complacency, paranoia, bravado, and simple terror.

'You'll be laughing at any rate, Wizbang,' croaked a familiar voice at his elbow. 'There's one thing he's bound to be doing.'

Leonardo looked blank.

'Making plans for the future.'

Two hours later, Leonardo and Veronique were slumped face to face across the long table in the back room.

'What I'm trying to get into your skull — ' Veronique was slurring her words ' — is that this new Prince . . . King, I suppose, now . . . this new King . . . is a Miserable. Little. Git.' She accented each word by banging her flask down on the table, spilling quite a lot of ale in the process. 'Anything that's funny . . . or silly . . . or funny . . . or . . .'

'Serves no practical purpose?' suggested Leonardo, who when drunk was better at summarising other people's thoughts than he was at composing his own.

'Spot on, my old Wizard, spot on. Serves no practical purpose. I like that. Couldn't have put it better. Yes. Serves no practical purpose. Yes . . . Yes . . . What was I saying?'

'That the new King has an underdeveloped sense of fun.'

'That's right. Spot on again. He's a Miserable. Little. Git.' Veronique repeated her performance with the flask, losing the last of her drink in the process. 'He won't want jesters. Won't want clowns. Our lot will get shut down, just like that. You'll see.'

'Another drink?' suggested Leonardo, becoming even more concise.

'Hang on a minute. What was I saying?'

'That your department will be closed down.'

'Closed down, shut down. Yes. You'll be all right, though, you magicians. He's serious, see, that's what's the matter with him. The future, that's important to him. He'll want lots of people like you. You'll all be sitting pretty. And you'll be about the only ones who are.'

The clown seemed to find this very funny, and repeated it several times between cackles of hoarse laughter. Her tears formed wavering tracks down the thick, white make-up on her cheeks.

'I'm not so sure,' said Leonardo finally. 'When he came to see me, he didn't seem too impressed with my set-up.'

'That's just his way.' Veronique was wiping her eyes. 'Miserable git. Doesn't let on much. Doesn't wear his heart on his sleeve.'

'He certainly doesn't do that,' Leonardo agreed. 'My shout, I think.'

Once the old King had been buried and an appropriate period of mourning observed, King Matt let it be known, by means of the Criers, that important changes could soon be expected in the way the city was governed and organised. New departments would be created, and old departments would be closed down. There would be new roles for certain senior people. And certain other senior people would no longer have any role. One by one, in alphabetical order, the counsellors were summoned to the throne room to be informed of their fate. A few of them emerged with smirks of triumph on their faces, but those few kept to themselves and seemed reluctant to disclose what had been said to them. Many more emerged looking unhappy or angry or confused.

The Congress of Counsellors that month was therefore a gloomy occasion. Many of those present were making farewell speeches, a few were being artfully evasive, and those whose names fell near the end of the alphabet, Leonardo among them, remained silent, as they had yet to learn their fate. After the meeting, the traditional refreshment period continued far into the night and was an unusually emotional affair.

When Leonardo finally arrived home, he discovered that the elevator ponies were still in mourning for the old King, and that he would once again have to walk up the stairs.

'Got to show respect, guv'nor,' said the Elevator Captain gloomily. 'Wouldn't be right otherwise.'

The Expedition to the Mountains

The rules of the Academy of Cartography strictly forbade the keeping of animals in the undergraduate wing, so when Rusty had heaved his cabin trunk down from the carrier's waggon that autumn, his first task was to search the town for an accom-modating landlord who would take a lenient attitude towards Dusty's presence. This was a wearisome task for Rusty, who had to drag his trunk with him from door to door, and also for Dusty, who was no longer a young dog and did not enjoy long walks as much as he once had. However, they managed eventu-ally to locate Mrs Roberts, a large, good-natured woman with a feather duster permanently in her hand. Mrs Roberts kept a houseful of dogs and was quite happy to accommodate an extra one. Unfortunately, the house was situated rather a long way from the lecture halls of the Academy, and although Rusty was happy to begin each day with a walk, it was not long before Dusty began to wish that his master did not have to attend quite so many lectures.

Rusty enjoyed his new life, worked hard and soon came to know a number of like-minded young men and women. With Dusty accompanying him everywhere he went, he quickly became a well-known figure among the students. He wrote to his mother every week, entrusting his letters to the intricate network of carriers and Wanderers who at that time formed the only channel of communication between town and country and city.

At the end of his first year, a vacation assignment was set for the students at the Academy. Working in small teams, they were expected to travel to an uncharted part of the country, to explore a specified area and to produce an original chart show-ing roads, hills, villages and rivers. Most of the students aimed to work with a group of their friends, and in this way their expedition could serve as a holiday as well as a study assign-ment. Rusty eventually found some acceptable company for himself, and learned shortly afterwards that the group was to travel to the foothills of a remote mountainous area, where they would be required to explore and chart the southern slopes of one of the smaller peaks. Rusty checked with the others: they were content for Dusty to join them on the trip.

★   ★   ★

'You got yourself into a bit of a state last night!'

Tom Slater, as usual, was first down for breakfast, and Rusty found him determinedly attacking a large plateful of fried food, his long legs protruding awkwardly from beneath the small table. Rusty, somewhat tousled, was dubiously scrutinising the contents of the buffet table, wondering whether Dusty would enjoy devilled kidneys. During the previous few evenings, the four students had been conducting extensive and thorough investigations into the quality and strength of the local ales, and the night before, towards the end of the session, a rather competitive edge had started to develop.

'Didn't give up early like some,' countered Rusty. Eventually deciding on porridge for himself and bacon for Dusty, he joined his friend at the table.

'Any sign of Charles and Sally?'

Tom gave a sidelong glance in the direction of the bedrooms.

'I don't reckon we'll see them for a couple of hours yet. Did you hear them in the night? At least you don't keep me awake.'

Rusty felt slightly irritated at the prospect of another late start, but said nothing. Perhaps he took his work more seriously than his fellow students did. Anyway, the task was fairly simple, and there was plenty of time to complete it. He poured himself more coffee.

Across the room, the innkeeper was watching the two young men with mild curiosity. The mountains seemed to attract all kinds of people. In his time, he'd played host to militiamen on the trail of bandits, bandits on the run from militiamen, wide-eyed folk seeking enlightenment in the rarefied air, earnest people studying weeds, sharp-faced people studying vermin, people just scaling peak after peak for no apparent reason at all . . . and now these four kids, wandering off each day and coming back with those peculiar diagrams that they tried so hard to keep hidden. Charts, they called them. He shrugged. Couldn't see the attraction of the mountains himself. Cold, inhospitable, dangerous places. What was wrong with a comfortable fireside?

Later, Dusty dozed in the morning sunshine while Rusty sat in the porch of the inn, adjusting the straps of his pack. It was his turn to carry the cartographical machinery that day, and he had already spent some time manhandling the heavy octants and triangulation engines through the narrow neck of the canvas bag. Finally satisfied, he eased his feet into his clumsy hiking boots, then rolled down his thick grey socks over the tops of the boots. As he did this he thought briefly of his mother, smiling faintly as he remembered all the times she had scolded him for allowing his socks to fall down. Ready at last, he looked up.

A panoramic view of the mountains fanned out before him. In the foreground, undulating green uplands, not unlike the hills of his home country. And further away, the jagged peaks, extending upwards into the mist. He could just make out the small peak that was their object of study for the week. The fresh, unfamiliar tang of the mountain air tickled his nostrils.

Eventually, around mid-morning, they were on the road. They had a long climb ahead of them before they could start work. Tom led the way up the steep track, loping ahead in long, springing strides. Charles and Sally, full of energy even after the previous night's exertions, followed side by side, not far behind him. Rusty brought up the rear, slowed down by Dusty, who had already started to regret his decision to join the excursion. As the others reached the first bend, Sally turned around and called back to him.

'We'll wait at the bridge just after the fork, if you need to catch up.'

They climbed steadily for an hour until the grassy uplands gave way to more rugged terrain. Dusty was insisting on more and more frequent rests, with the result that Rusty had long ago lost sight of his other companions. Reaching the place where the road forked, he unhitched his pack and sat down on top of it, looking each way, uncertain which path to take. He tried to remember the conversation of the previous night. He was sure that Sally had told him to turn right, but the right-hand path seemed to be descending, which must be wrong. He hesitated, until Dusty, finding his second wind, set off briskly along the left-hand path. Rusty knew that Dusty had a good instinct for these things, and had learned to trust him. He shouldered his pack again and followed the dog.

As they climbed higher, Rusty began to feel a damp chill in the air. He paused for a moment, buttoning his windcheater tightly around him. It was getting misty ahead, but as long as he stayed on the path he would be safe. The others would be waiting for him at the bridge . . .

The mist was growing thicker now, and he could no longer make out the outline of the hills on either side of him. He realised that he had been on this path for too long. He should have reached the bridge about five minutes after the fork in the road. He must have allowed Dusty to lead him the wrong way. Apprehensive now, he turned slowly around. In front of him, half-obscured by the mist, loomed a tall figure.

'Tom?'

There was no reply. He spun round again, only to glimpse another figure behind him, then others to left and right. He realised that he was surrounded. He tried to swallow, found his throat dry. He reached for Dusty's collar. The dog was trembling and his hair was bristling fiercely.

'Sally? Charles?'

The circle was tightening around him. His heart started to race as the figures stepped silently forward. Now he could see that their faces were hidden behind scarves and kerchiefs. His gaze caught a curving glint of bronze and he realised with alarm that they were carrying unsheathed knives. Bandits! He started to shiver. He had heard stories about the bandits who roamed the mountains, bands of desperate characters who would kill first and steal second. Boy and dog froze in terror as the bandit leader advanced menacingly towards them. A curved blade winked. Hard eyes glittered behind a black mask.

And then Dusty stepped forward into the silence, raised his head and howled. Startled, the bandit leader looked down at the small dog, looked up at Rusty, looked down at the dog again. And in that moment something passed between the three of them, something that Rusty could not understand or name or control. But something passed . . . and then, at a single harsh word of command from their leader, the whole band turned on their heels and vanished into the mist. And Rusty, confused and dazed, knew that his life had been spared.

And he knew also that the leader of the bandits had been not a man, but a woman, a young woman of about his own age. A young woman with large, dark eyes, eyes behind which burned hard fires.

Rusty's three companions, who were actually not far away, were alerted by Dusty's howling and raced back to offer whatever help was needed. Tom, with his long legs, was first on the scene. He found Rusty rooted to the spot, unable to speak. And at his feet lay Dusty, motionless and limp.

The innkeeper had seen many people leave for the mountains, and quite a few of them, if they came back, had come back changed in some way or another. It was therefore no great surprise to him when the four students who were making charts came back earlier than expected that day, looking confused and frightened. The red-headed boy with the dog seemed to have come off the worst. His eyes were wild and his clothing was in disarray. He was holding the dog in his arms, clutching it tightly to his chest, but otherwise he seemed to have no strength, and the other two lads were struggling to keep him upright, while the girl gabbled an incoherent account of what had happened. The innkeeper did not get excited. He was happy to arrange for some soup to be sent up to the room, happy to send for the local doctor, happy for the boy to stop in bed as long as he kept paying his board. He had seen them come back worse.

Rusty lay in a fever for three days. He did not eat, his sleep was disturbed, he raved incoherently and he seemed unable to comprehend anything that was said to him. The doctor advised his friends to give him time, to wait until he was well enough to be taken home. So they gave him time. And Rusty dreamed.

The water was lapping against the side of the boat.

'It's no good, youngster,' said the ferryman finally. 'I can't get you any further. From now on, you're on your own.'

And so he plunged into the black water. For a moment he could see nothing, but now something was coming towards him through the darkness. As it came nearer, he could see that there were two objects, side by side. They looked like . . . two eyes. The eyes behind the mask. And something from behind those eyes had passed, first to the dog, then to himself, then back through those eyes, through those eyes with the hard fires burning deep behind them. The eyes behind the mask. Laurel's eyes.

Something had passed that had somehow linked the three of them together. Something like a pathway, something like a web, something perhaps like a network . . . And somewhere, enmeshed at the heart of that network, something was hidden from him, an empty space, a dark absence, a mystery . . . a secret, that was it. The secret at the heart of the maze. Laurel's secret, dwelling at the heart of that dark secret place, entangled in the network of paths that somehow linked the girl and the dog and himself . . . He could feel the heaviness of the dark place all around him . . . dark folds of heavy fabric, a cloak, perhaps, or curtains . . . yes, curtains that masked the stage of a puppet theatre, a marionette show . . . If he could only draw those curtains aside . . .

Groping his way in the blackness, above and below and around that dark place, he could sense the form of the secret, could hear the rustle of its folds, breathe the musty scent . . . The scent of something long buried, buried as Dusty might have buried a bone . . . Dusty, the guardian of the bone for so many years . . . and the secret as only Dusty could know it, the shape, the scent . . . nothing that he could see clearly or put into words . . . if only those curtains would part . . .

That labyrinth of secret pathways extended in every direction, invisibly connecting the three of them, reaching out beyond, reaching out to others nearby, spreading and branching and spanning beyond to many more, the invisible background throng all linked by the unending filigree network of threads . . . He could feel the threads, seize a handful of them, grasp and pull . . . and as he pulled, the curtains on the puppet stage parted for an instant . . . a glimpse of two figures, a dark-haired man, his arm around the shoulders of a fair-haired girl . . . The man was a stranger to him, but the girl had a face that he knew, spoke with a soft voice, a voice that he seemed to have known all his life, a voice that soothed and reassured, a voice—

And then the curtains closed again and he was in darkness, a hot hammering darkness, a darkness dense with an intermeshing warp and weft of dancing connections, jagged harsh pulsing threads that scratched and tore and burned like hard fires . . . like hard fires behind the dark eyes of a black-haired girl, a girl with a secret to tell, a secret that had slumbered for so long in the heart of a little dog, a secret that finally was Rusty Brown's alone.

And he remembered a question he had once asked his mother.

'Do all the Wanderers have eyes like Laurel's?'

And his mother had replied:

'I don't think I ever noticed her eyes.'

Days of Confusion

Eventually, Leonardo Pegasus received his summons to King Matt's throne room. He decided, given the gravity of the occasion, that it would be appropriate to present himself in the full armorial garb of the Brotherhood of Magicians, including the full-length quilted ceremonial robe, long-toed boots and extra-wide hat. He had considered asking Alice to attend him as train-bearer, but had finally decided that it would be more fitting for him to attend unaccompanied. It was not until he was finally ushered into the throne room, resplendent in his finery, that he realised that he had misjudged the situation.

The young King was not wearing court dress. He was not even wearing semi-formal attire. He was clad in a plain, dark grey coat and trousers, with a white, stiff-collared blouse and a discreetly patterned necktie. His hair and beard had been trimmed short and he was bare-headed. Glancing around in confusion, Leonardo saw that the room had been refurnished. The heavy ornate curtains had been replaced with plain slatted blinds. The ancient murals, depicting scenes from the lives of generations of Kings, had been obliterated with a coat of paint in a dull off-white colour. The priceless chandeliers had been abandoned in favour of a stark row of ugly and unflattering power-driven illumination engines. Even the throne and its dais had been removed. Instead, the King was seated on a contemporary-looking high-backed chair behind a large, modern and very tidy desk. He did not look up from the memorandum he was studying.

'Good morning, Master Pegasus. I won't detain you for long. Please take a seat.'

Leonardo had not expected to be invited to sit in the presence of the King, and had some difficulty squeezing his bulky ceremonial attire into the narrow chair. He tried to settle himself. He felt uncomfortable and hot.

'As you know, my late father retained a very large number of specialised counsellors.'

The King spoke rapidly, as if reciting a carefully prepared speech for the hundredth time. 'I have decided to manage my affairs along rather different lines.' He looked at Leonardo for the first time. 'In particular, I shall be taking my advice about the future in a quite different form.' In answer to Leonardo's unspoken question, the King turned his head towards a side doorway and called out a name.

'Kevin?'

After a short delay, there appeared a sallow-faced young man with dark, curly hair. He was wearing an outfit very similar to the King's, and he had a smug expression on his narrow face. Tucked under his arm was something that looked like a small flat attaché case. He placed this on the desk and opened the lid. In the base of the case were several rows of sliding multi-coloured round beads, rather like the abacuses used by the traders in the market. In the lid of the case was a glass surface that bulged slightly at its middle. With fingers that trembled very slightly, the young man shifted a few of the beads from side to side, and a glowing abstract pattern appeared somewhere behind the glass. As Leonardo watched, he pushed another bead and the pattern started to change. The magician stared in perplexity as a series of geometric shapes appeared, shifted, jostled with each other, changed colour and form. Leonardo's heart began to race. His throat felt dry. Before he could find words, the King had continued with his speech.

'It is called the Counselling Engine,' said the King. 'It will be my soothsayer, my accountant, my magician, my herald . . . even my jester, if I should ever feel the need for such a thing. Kevin and his associates have been working on it for some time. Thank you, Kevin.'

With the faintest narrowing of his eyes, the young man closed the lid of the machine, tucked it under his arm, and withdrew. The King waited until the door had closed. His gaze was fixed on the surface of his desk while he spoke.

'As I am sure you will realise, I shall no longer be requiring your assistance. In fact, bearing in mind that the transition to the new system of government is likely to be a testing period for all of us, it is my view that your very presence in the city will be an unhelpful factor in the process. You will therefore pack up whatever belongings you need and vacate your working accommodation and your living quarters within one month. You will receive a monetary settlement to assist you in this process. Have you any questions?'

There were many questions that Leonardo probably should have asked, but, overcome as he was by shock and confusion, only one thing came to mind.

'What will happen to Alice?'

'Alice? Your assistant?' The King looked uncomfortable for a moment. 'Alice is a talented young woman. I shall be needing people of her type. I intend to offer her a position within the new administrative structure. She can look forward to a rewarding future. Now, have you anything else to ask?'

Leonardo could think of nothing. In his elaborate costume, he felt cumbersome and old-fashioned and ridiculous. He shook his head dumbly.

In a daze, he wandered slowly back to his laboratory, wondering how to break the news to Alice. Entering the antechamber, he noticed her tunic on the chair by the door and realised that he had again intruded upon her rest period. He looked up.

This time, Alice was not dancing. Positioned at the exact centre of the room, she appeared to be balanced, impossibly, in an upside-down position, her toes pointing uncompromisingly at the ceiling, her inverted features staring at him blankly. Leonardo felt a sudden vertiginous rush of apprehension. He found himself clutching at the doorpost.

Alice remained inverted and motionless, even her breathing barely perceptible.

'Alice?' gasped the magician. 'Alice?'

But such was the concentration required for her feat that she seemed quite unable to hear him. Terrified and confused, Leonardo spun around in the doorway and fled. He did not stop running until he reached The Crier's Rest.

The next day, Leonardo arrived at his workshop rather late in the morning to find a note in Alice's familiar round handwriting.

Have been called over to the royal apartments to help get the new offices ready. Hope this is all right. Will come in tomorrow and open the mail. A.

A faint trace of her scent clung to the parchment. Leonardo sniffed it, then sniffed again, inhaling deeply. He closed his eyes, and for a moment he found himself adrift in a tranquil world of long grass, of clover, of the sea. Then the vision faded, and he opened his eyes again and glanced around the antechamber. He noticed that faint traces of dust were already becoming visible on the horizontal surfaces. Some of the shrubs were in need of watering. Unopened mail was strewn untidily across the doormat.

In the Theatre of Magic, the Empathy Engine stood neglected in a corner, its cover awry. Leonardo remembered that it was temporarily out of action, awaiting the delivery of a replacement part. For a moment, it appeared to him as nothing but an ill-conceived carcass of scrap metal. He surrendered to a sudden impulse to kick it. A brass handle fell off and rattled derisively across the floor.

Over the days that followed, Alice's appearances at the workshop grew fewer, and Leonardo's appearances at The Crier's Rest grew more frequent. One day, staring at the thickening dust on the table tops in his antechamber, Leonardo was puzzled to see a circular dust-free patch. Looking around the room, he noticed other such patches here and there. For a moment he did not understand. Then he realised. The potted shrubs had gone. Alice would not be coming back.

'If only she was still here, if only she was still here . . .'

Leonardo and Veronique were at their usual places in the tavern. The King had decreed that the Jester's department was to stay in business, albeit in reduced form. Veronique still did not know whether she would be among those seeking new employment, but she seemed unconcerned about her immediate future. It was late, and the rough wooden surface of the table was strewn with empty flasks. Leonardo was in a state of voluble self-pity.

'If only she was still here, it wouldn't be so bad. I don't care about the workshop or any of the stupid junk in it, or the poky little apartment, or the Elevator Captain's useless ponies, or the position, or the money . . . I suppose I can go somewhere and find something to do . . . but why did he have to take Alice away from me?'

'Oh, leave off. What good is the girl to you now? I never knew what you saw in her, anyway. Skinny little guttersnipe.' The clown sucked noisily at her short cigar. A mischievous look appeared on her face. 'Do you reckon she liked you, then?'

'I suppose so. I don't know. How can I tell?' Leonardo drained his glass.

'Easy. Go and see her. Ask her to have supper with you. She can only say no. And who knows?' Veronique winked lewdly. 'You might strike lucky.'

Leonardo groaned loudly.

'Vero, I can't believe I'm hearing you sometimes. You don't understand at all. I don't want to – to "strike lucky", as you put it. Not everybody's motives are as base as your own. I admire Alice. She is a very special young woman. She has many . . . unique qualities.' For a few moments he struggled with his thoughts. Finally, an idea came to him. 'Anyway, what would I do if she did say no? I just want . . . I just want . . . Oh, I don't know what I want,' he concluded in exasperation.

'More drink?'

'That'll do to be getting on with.'

From the Journal of Victor Lazarus

Tuesday 2nd June

This house seems plagued by ill fortune. This morning a terrible accident occurred, by far the worst to date. A gang of men was at work on the main staircase, hoisting into place a large statue that I had discovered hidden under a tarpaulin in an out-building. It was a handsome life-size bronze depicting a young man in heroic pose with a sleek, watchful dog at his side, and Harold had suggested that it might present an impressive sight if positioned on the main landing at the head of the staircase.

Under Sam's command, the men were hoisting the massive piece the last few inches into its final resting place when suddenly one of the ropes gave way, sending it crashing down to the bottom of the staircase. The statue was badly buckled and dented, the banisters demolished, the stair carpet ripped, and several floorboards splintered. But, worse still, when it came to rest in the entrance hall, one of the men was trapped beneath it.

Everyone within earshot rushed to free him, and, when once we had managed to lift the ruined statue, we discovered that he was still alive, although terribly crushed by the weight. I fear, however, that in addition to his bodily injuries, the shock must have caused his mind to give way, for, when he recovered consciousness, he began jabbering and screaming about what he referred to as a 'creature of the dark'. As far as I could make out, he claimed to have glimpsed this horrifying apparition gnawing through the rope with its teeth just a moment before the accident occurred.

We lost no time in summoning medical assistance, and the man was quickly removed to the infirmary, where he hovers even now between life and death. Meanwhile, much remedial work will be required to make good the damage to the house. Tomorrow I must definitely speak to Sam. I have delayed it for far too long.

Wednesday 3rd June

At last I have had my talk with Sam, but I find that it has left me more perplexed than ever. This morning I called the man into my orderly room, and, without inviting him to be seated, presented to him a catalogue of the unfortunate incidents that have occurred in his vicinity since the commencement of our task. As I read, I became aware of an expression of horror on his face, an expression that intensified from moment to moment as I progressed through my list. Upon reaching my conclusion, I demanded to know what explanation he could offer me. For several moments he remained speechless, but finally, after repeated prompting on my part, he haltingly began an incoherent account of the events that had occurred. To begin with, I could make no sense of his ravings, but eventually I started to gather that he believed himself no longer to be in command of his own actions, and in some way to have surrendered himself into the control of some unknown agency.

Having once hinted at this, he seemed for a moment too frightened to say more. I sensed that a different approach was likely to be more productive, and therefore invited him to be seated. After much coaxing, he was able to continue his account. On every occasion on which an accident had occurred (he told me), he had experienced an eerie sensation of detatchment from his body. It was, apparently, as though he were observing events that were taking place far away beneath him, as though everything were happening to some other person and he himself were merely an observer stationed at a remote vantage point somewhere in the roof of the house. My incredulity was doubling by the minute as he continued to explain that, at the conclusion of each incident, he would find himself back again inhabiting his own body in the ordinary way.

I was scarcely able to restrain my anger at this ludicrous fabrication, and was all set to dismiss the man's entire account as fanciful nonsense when I caught sight of something that chilled the very blood in my veins. As he tried pathetically to form his next sentence, Sam's jaw dropped slackly open, a vacant look came into his eyes, and just for a moment, crouched behind his trembling form, I caught a glimpse of another, darker shape, a narrow shape that resembled a human being only in the fashion that a caricature resembles its subject. It was present for no more than a split second, and then it was gone, and once again I could see only the familiar form of Sam. He appeared white and shaken, but he could at any rate clearly be identified as Sam.

In the normal course of things, I am a man of even temperament, some might even say that I am stolid, but on this occasion I was utterly unnerved by what I had seen. When I had managed to collect my wits, I could only suggest to Sam that he might have been working too hard and that his imagination had become overactive. I proposed that he take a few days' rest and return to the house only when he felt more steady. To this he readily assented, and, thanking me, turned to leave.

As he did so, again I glimpsed for an instant the insubstantial figure that followed in his wake. This time I detected something in its bearing, something perhaps in the way it carried its shoulders, which gave me the irresistible impression that it was laughing at me!

But once again, no sooner had my eyes started to register the jeering image than it was gone. Reeling with shock, I hurriedly closed the door and turned the key in the lock. I sat at my desk and hastily committed to paper every detail of the foregoing events.

(Later)

When once I had completed my account, I sat with my head in my hands and started desperately to rack my brains for an explanation. I thought long and hard about the terrible and extraordinary events of the past few days, I examined some of the earlier entries in this journal, and at last I began to see how certain incidents might be fitted together to form a sinister pattern.

I recalled, for example, that uncanny sensation on my very first day here of being under observation. I read again my account of the vague form that I had glimpsed for an instant, of the disturbing prints of feet and hands in the dust. I re-examined my record of the whole sequence of accidents, and of other glimpses of shadowy figures. And I came at last to the following, profoundly unsettling, conclusion.

Concealed within this house lies an intruder, a sinister, unearthly being bent on making deadly mischief against myself and my companions, a being who seeks perhaps to endanger our entire enterprise.

The hour is late now, but tomorrow I must inaugurate a full hue and cry. The wrongdoer must at all costs be hunted down.

(Midnight)

A message has been delivered from the infirmary. The injured man has died.

Thursday 4th June

At the start of the day I called together, in the main hall, all of my workers. There I described to them what I had seen, and explained to them what had to be done. A thorough search of the house, from cellar to attic, was to be carried out. The men were to arm themselves with whatever weapons came to hand, and were to search systematically from room to room, looking in every cupboard and behind every cabinet and under every table. I could not help noticing one or two sceptical glances between one man and another, but they went about their task willingly enough.

As the search proceeded, I walked among them, ensuring that full vigilance was being maintained. In my excited and fanciful state, I more than once experienced the feeling that some-one was again watching me, someone perhaps with a malignant eye. But on each occasion, when I turned around, there was nobody to be seen but my own men.

Eventually the search was complete and the party reassembled.

Questioning the men thoroughly, I confirmed that every room and corridor and outbuilding had been inspected. However, despite our best endeavours, the intruder had managed somehow to escape detection. I was bitterly disappointed at this, but concluded that nothing further could be accomplished at that time. I therefore thanked the men for their efforts and ordered them to return to their normal duties, with a final reminder to remain constantly on the alert. My ears detected some further mutterings of discontent, and I was conscious of receiving one or two pitying looks, but in a short time everyone was back at his duties. Dissatisfied with the failure of my search and unable to settle to anything, I continued to roam the house looking for clues, but could discover nothing further.

Wednesday 10th June

Yesterday I granted myself a half-day's leave to attend the funeral of the man who had been killed. Among the mourners was Sam, who I was glad to see looked much more like his old self. When I enquired after his health, he told me that he was feeling much steadier and was intending to return to his duties the following week. I shall be most grateful to have him back.

I note with relief that there have been no further incidents at the house, and I am now beginning to suspect that my own imagination has been as overactive as Sam's, very probably also as the result of overwork.

Remembering Alice

Leonardo tore up the list he had been writing, swept the pieces onto the floor of the antechamber, and stared gloomily around at the stacks of scrolls and books on his shelves. He knew that before long he would have to start packing up the contents of his workshop, and he knew also that he would have to start making decisions about what to take with him, what to give

away, and what to throw away. At that moment, he felt inclined
to throw away everything and to walk out of the city empty-
handed, but, during his more rational interludes, he knew that
he would need books and scrolls and materials and equipment
in order to carry on his trade in the future. He was finding it
very hard, however, to decide exactly what things he was going
to need, and this was because he had very little idea exactly
what his future occupation was likely to be. Was there any
demand for magicians elsewhere in the kingdom? He did not
know, and he did not know how to find out. He pictured himself wandering the highways of the land, presenting himself at
every castle, demonstrating the Empathy Engine to every
tuppenny-ha'penny baron and earl and squire. Sighing, he
reached for another sheet of parchment and, not for the first
time, wrote across the top *Essential Items*. He underlined the
two words and paused for thought.

But before he could continue with his task, his ears caught
the chiming of bells from the Institute of Calibration. He
considered making an adjournment to The Crier's Rest, then
sternly told himself that it was too early in the day. Instead, he
decided to make himself some coffee. Struggling with the
coffee engine, he caught himself wishing that Alice was there to
do it for him. He sighed again. No matter how he tried to
divert himself, his thoughts kept returning to Alice. He crossed
the room to where a large sheet of parchment was tacked
crookedly to the wall. On the parchment were drawn the horizontal and vertical axes of a graph. Within the space defined by
the axes was a scatter of small crosses. He reached for a quill,
dipped it in a large jug of sable ink, and drew a fresh cross.

Leonardo had had the idea of drawing the graph four days
previously, on the day following the disappearance of the
shrubs. He had decided that each time he thought about Alice,
he would mark a cross on the graph. Recording his thoughts in
this way, he believed, would somehow help him to understand
them, perhaps even help him to regain some kind of control
over them. The graph indicated that, since the disappearance of

the shrubs, he had thought of Alice at least six times every hour, sometimes as often as once a minute. He stared at the crosses, hoping to see some kind of pattern. Densely marked expanses of black were interspersed haphazardly with more thinly scattered areas. The little crosses seemed to perform a mocking dance, teasingly forming indistinct figures that cartwheeled and pirouetted before his eyes before abruptly dissolving again into meaningless scribbles. He continued to stare at them, until his thoughts were interrupted by the bubbling hiss of escaping steam and spurting liquid from the coffee engine. Muttering to himself, he rummaged vaguely around for a cloth.

Eventually, he was able to sit down with a passable mug of coffee. Again he thought about Alice. Sometimes Leonardo sustained himself with the hope that Alice might call in unannounced at the workshop, but so far she had not done so. He wondered whether he could find the courage to follow Veronique's suggestion of paying her a call in her new quarters. He tried rehearsing a selection of introductory remarks.

'Hello, Alice, what a surprise. I'd quite forgotten that you were working over here these days.' No, too casual.

'Hello, Alice. I just happened to be passing. Thought I'd see how you were.' That wasn't bad. Perhaps a little too paternal?

'I've been missing you, Alice. Would you care to have supper one night?' Bold, but it might just do the trick. He tried to imagine all her possible responses to these overtures. Chilling indifference? Violent rejection? Artful evasion? Or perhaps eager compliance? Drawing on his professional skill, Leonardo dwelt for a while on the last option, trying out a selection of provisional futures. He even considered reconnecting the Empathy Engine. The spare part had been delivered that morning. He had just begun to hunt for his screwdriver when he recalled that the power supply to his workshop had, by royal decree, been disconnected.

He reached out to adjust the coffee engine, burned a finger, sucked it in annoyance. He poured himself another mug of coffee. It was no good. Every time he seriously considered

Veronique's suggestion, he came up against one large insurmountable obstacle. The thought of seeing Alice in her new
surroundings, serving her new master, was more than he could
bear. He knew that she would no longer be wearing the livery
of the Brotherhood of Magicians, for, prowling the corridors of
the palace the previous morning, he had chanced to run across
her. She had been wearing the neat, efficient-looking grey
tracksuit that was now the required form of dress for the workers in the King's administrative department. She had smiled
briefly, had even paused to exchange a few words, and, despite
her horrible costume, the brief moment of rapport had cheered
Leonardo for the rest of the morning. He had sat for an hour at
his planning table, pondering over the couple of sentences she
had spoken to him, dissecting them for hidden meanings, looking ahead to the next encounter, planning what he might say.
Later that day, outside the palace bakery, he had seen her again
but that time she had passed on her way without noticing him.
This plunged him into depression for the rest of the afternoon,
and during these lonely hours he had augmented his graph
with a whole boiling, furious column of crosses.

Leonardo took another gulp of his coffee, which was still just
warm enough to be drinkable. Glumly he pictured Alice in her
new setting, Alice taking memoranda from the humourless new
King, Alice laughing with her new colleagues, Alice making
coffee on some silent new miniature engine. Then his thoughts
turned back to Alice as he had known her, Alice in her page's
outfit, Alice ushering in a visitor, Alice drafting a memorandum,
Alice sitting with her foot on her chair, Alice with a mug of
coffee cradled in her hands, Alice with her chin resting on her
knee, Alice dancing, Alice upside down. Alice.

Leonardo shivered. He reached for his coffee mug and was
surprised to discover that the murky liquid was now completely
cold. Another bell chimed. The Crier's Rest would soon be
open.

*   *   *

Sally is Worried

'Are you sure you're going to be all right?'

Sally's kindly face was twisted with concern as she helped Rusty down from the carrier's waggon outside his lodgings. Rusty stared at her vaguely for a moment. Then, apparently with some considerable effort, he managed to stutter a few words.

'Yes, I guess so. Don't worry.'

Clutching Dusty tightly in his arms, he turned away from the girl and entered the house without looking back. In the narrow hallway, he pushed his way past Charles, who was unloading his baggage for him, and headed straight up the stairs towards his room. From the kitchen he could hear the muffled barking of Mrs Roberts's dogs. On the first landing, he found his way barred by the substantial form of Mrs Roberts herself, the usual feather duster firmly gripped in her meaty hand.

'Good trip, Mister Brown?' she enquired brightly. Shaking his head grimly, Rusty squeezed past her without a word and disappeared up the second flight of stairs. Shrugging, the land-lady continued with her dusting.

'Students!' she muttered to herself.

Outside, Charles and Sally were clambering back into the waggon.

'Are you sure it's safe to leave him?' asked a worried Sally. 'He seems to have had a terrible shock, and he isn't getting any better.'

Charles took a more relaxed attitude.

'Give him time to settle,' he said firmly. 'We'll call on him again in a day or two.'

Sally was still uneasy.

'I suppose Mrs Roberts will know what to do,' she said finally. 'And she knows about dogs. So she can help him with Dusty.'

Alone at last in his shabby room, Rusty laid Dusty carefully in his basket and arranged his tattered old blanket around him.

Then he threw himself face downwards on the narrow iron bed, pulled the counterpane across his shoulders and fell into a troubled sleep. The door, which he had left open, was quietly closed by Mrs Roberts when she came up later to check on him.

An Offer from Veronique

'I'm fed up with your whining,' snapped Veronique. 'What are you dithering about? You know exactly where you can find her. If you want to see her, just go to where she works and see her. Aren't you supposed to be a magician? Sometimes I think you're completely useless.' She drained her flask and squinted meaningfully into its vacant depths.

'You make it sound so easy,' moaned Leonardo drunkenly. 'What shall I say to her? And what shall I do if she doesn't want to talk to me?'

'Call yourself a man?' The clown had lost her patience. 'Invite her to supper. Somewhere sexy. Give her the works. Pink tablecloths. Candles. A dish of sweetbreads. And if she still says no, well, that'll just have to be the end of it.' She spat the stub of her cigar across the room.

'But I couldn't bear it if she said no. What could I do? It would be so – so final. She would never be mine.'

'She isn't yours now,' shouted the clown. 'In fact, she's never been yours. But, if you make her the offer, she just might agree to it. But first, you've got to ask her. She's not going to come running to you on her own. Now, are you going to get us both a drink?'

In the crush of the taproom, Leonardo, who was no longer in full control of his reflexes, trod heavily on somebody's foot, causing the spillage of a moderate amount of liquor, and bringing about a not-very-pleasant altercation. When he eventually returned to his place, Veronique, having seemingly recovered her good spirits, was intent on introducing a new topic.

'Have you heard the Criers lately?' she croaked with relish. 'It's all happening in the Undertown. Those little Wolf Boys have been at it again. Beat up a couple of women last night.' She frowned. 'Didn't rape them, though. Didn't touch their money, either.'

The Wolf Boy attacks, as they had become known, had been going on intermittently for some years now, and the pattern was always the same. The victim would be surrounded by several assailants, chased through the dark lanes of the Undertown, and trapped in a corner or at the end of an alleyway, where they would then be set upon and beaten to death. Regarding the precise details of the manner of death, and of the state in which the bodies were left, the militiamen and the Criers had so far maintained a tactful silence. As a result of this reticence, an extravagance of choice rumours had been circulating in the city. It was said that the attackers were degenerate creatures who had once been human, but who had now been reduced to living the life of wild beasts. It was said that they slept on derelict sites, fed on garbage, ran on all fours, hunted in packs. It was said that the victims were horribly mutilated, although never robbed of their money or otherwise interfered with. Making creative use of these scraps of material, one of the more inventive Criers had come up with the fanciful name by which the killers were now generally known.

'I wonder why they do it?' pondered Leonardo.

'I could tell you a thing or two.' The clown was employing her most gleefully sinister tone. She leaned close to Leonardo to maximise the dramatic effect. 'They kill with their bare hands. Tear the flesh with their nails. Drink the blood. And sometimes,' she paused, 'they eat bits.'

'For heaven's sake, Vero, you do come out with some nonsense. Things like that don't happen in this day and age. Where do you get these stories from?'

'It's not just stories.' Veronique was becoming unusually excited. 'I've actually seen them. I know where to go. You can come with me one night if you don't believe me. Watch them in action'

For a long moment Leonardo was speechless.

'You're mad,' he said finally. 'I don't believe even you could be so stupid. Nobody with any sense would go into the Undertown at night.'

'Oh, it's all right if you know your way about,' responded his friend airily. 'Lots of people go there. Your precious little Alice goes there every single night.'

'What?'

'Alice. She goes there. Goes through, at any rate. She lives in the North Estates. Walks through the Undertown on her way home.'

'How do you know that?' Leonardo was aghast.

'Oh, I don't know,' said Veronique vaguely. 'You hear these things.'

That night, the magician dreamed of Alice in the Undertown, Alice in rags, Alice barefoot, Alice with filthy matted hair, Alice running on all fours at the head of a ravening pack of wolves. He dreamed of Alice straddling his prostrate form, fierce and lean and unforgiving, head flung back, spine arched, pincer-like thighs squeezing his ribcage, cracking the bones, forcing the breath from his lungs. He dreamed of Alice with hooked claws and pointed fangs, savagely tearing strips from his flesh. He dreamed of Alice with blood dribbling from her mouth, streaking her pale chin, her throat, her breasts. And he dreamed of Alice yelping in wordless triumph over his mutilated corpse.

When he awoke, his mouth and throat were acrid with the salty taste of blood.

A Surprise for Mrs Roberts

Night had fallen when Rusty awoke, and the room was illumin-ated through the open curtains by the harsh, flint-coloured street lighting that had recently been installed in the town. He sat upright on the bed, shivering and hugging his knees against the cold.

Blankly, he scanned the contents of the cramped little room. The objects that surrounded him no longer seemed to have any purpose. Irregular stacks of books, already gathering dust. Charts of unrecognisable locations, spread across the rickety table, rolled up in stacks, tacked to the faded floral wallpaper, their corners curling up where the drawing pins had fallen out. A sad-looking jumper lay drooping over the single hard chair, a pair of moth-eaten woollen socks lay crumpled in two opposite corners of the room. All of it seemed nothing more than litter, the useless clutter of a meaningless life. In the dressing-table mirror he glimpsed a figure that at first he did not recognise as himself. The blank, tear-streaked face that stared wildly out at him might have belonged to a stranger.

Only Dusty, asleep in his basket, could offer him any comfort. Rusty jerked himself upright, stumbled across the room, dropped heavily to his knees by the basket, hugged the dog to his chest again. He didn't want to be here, among all these useless things. He wanted to be far away.

And then, kneeling on the worn carpet with his face to the wall, hugging the dog to him, he began faintly to feel something pulling him. Something at the hidden core of his being, something that cowered neglected behind a dull wall of fear, yet something that at the same time yearned to open out and be. And, fanning out around him, radiating out from his centre, he began again to sense the network of pathways that led from this place to every other place, spreading out across the land, interweaving and branching and leading him . . .

Leading him where? He didn't know. Perhaps anywhere would do.

'Come on, Dusty. Time to go.'

He heaved himself unsteadily to his feet, blundered heavily onto the landing and down the two flights of stairs, threw open the front door and staggered out into the night.

Aroused from her doze by the commotion, Mrs Roberts abandoned her cocoa, shuffled to the door in her slippers and called out after her lodger.

'Have a nice evening, Mister Brown. See you tomorrow. Breakfast at eight?'

But there was no reply. Mrs Roberts shrugged her heavy shoulders. He had been such a nice young man when he'd first arrived. Now he seemed to have become completely inconsiderate. He hadn't even closed the front door behind him.

With a sigh, Mrs Roberts bolted the door and made her way back to the warmth of her kitchen.

From the Journal of Victor Lazarus

Thursday 11th June

I have been tragically premature in relaxing my vigilance. Today there has been a fire that has caused untold damage, and, today also, I have seen the face of my foe. I shall try to recount the sequence of events with as much detachment as I can muster.

It began towards the end of the afternoon. The last of the day's visitors were making their way out of the building, and the handful of staff who remained on duty were putting things in order for the morrow. I was left alone in my orderly room attending to some administrative tasks. Engrossed in the columns of figures before me, I did not at first notice the smell that had begun to penetrate the room. When eventually I detected the whiff of burned sugar, I dismissed it from my mind as unimportant, thinking that Mrs Proudfoot had perhaps left some gingerbread too long in the oven. It was only when the smell became stronger that my attention was finally wrested from my accounts, at which point I was startled to see wisps of smoke curling under the door.

Abandoning my papers, I dashed from the room, only to run

headlong into a thick black cloud that seemed to be issuing from the downstairs part of the house. I clapped a pocket handkerchief over my mouth and nose and hurled myself down the stairs, seeking the place where the smoke was thickest. As I had initially suspected, it seemed to emanate from the refreshment area. I threw open the kitchen door, only to find myself recoiling from a blast of scorching air. The room was ablaze!

For a moment I was stunned into indecision and stood staring helplessly into the flames, desperately attempting to calculate the odds against my saving the house. Then I came to my senses and slammed the door shut, hoping thereby to contain the blaze for a few precious moments. I cried out for help, and, thankfully, help at once arrived. Someone in the town must already have noticed the smoke, for at that moment the men of the fire company burst in upon the scene with their axes and hoses, and eventually the flames were extinguished.

When things had quietened down, I made an inspection of the devastated areas. The damage to the house was extensive, and I began to doubt whether the mischief wrought by flame and smoke and water could be made good in time for the return of the owner.

But perhaps the fabric of the house is the least of my concerns. For during that moment when I stared transfixed into the flames, I saw a sight for which nothing on earth could have prepared me. At the centre of the blaze, capering and leaping and shrieking with unholy glee, danced a dark, spindly, crooked figure, surely the same figure that I had glimpsed on the day of my interview with Sam. As the creature whirled around on its hooked toes, for a moment its gaze met mine. Then the flames sprang up anew, and the twisted shape was lost to my sight.

So on one matter my mind is firmly made up. From now on, I will remain in this house night and day until the evildoer is brought to book. For now that I have glimpsed the face of my foe, I know that this creature will continue to lurk in wait for me, and I know that until I have sought it out and destroyed it,

I can know no rest. For at the final instant before the creature vanished back into the flames, it spoke to me. It spoke in a voice that I lack the power to describe, a voice that was somehow at the same time both loud and soft, both rough and smooth, both masculine and feminine. And that voice spoke words that will remain etched in my memory until the end of my days.

'*Take heed of me, Lazarus. Take heed of your Shadow.*'

Four:
TALES FROM THE UNDERTOWN

From time to time I still spare a thought for the ones far away, the student and the magician. The student has at last uncovered the thing that slumbers at the dark heart of his maze, but, facing it in its nakedness, he faces something that his intellect is not yet equipped to comprehend, his will not yet trained to control. For a while, perhaps, he will have no choice but to abandon himself to it. And, hard as it might be, I shall have no choice but to watch him, and to wait.

The magician too is losing control of his will, surrendering it in a haze of self-pity and sour ale to the mischievous promptings of the clown Veronique. In his distraction he has ceased utterly to care for his worldly position, and he dwells instead on the loss of the girl Alice, the girl whose image now invades his waking hours, whose shadow stalks his dreams, who lures him inexorably and unknowingly towards his hour of reckoning. But the magician deludes himself, for the girl was never to be his. Alice is dedicated to the service of a different master altogether.

And now, at the black heart of the city, the Undertown is calling its children home. Home to face the thing you fear, home to face the hidden aspect of your being, home to face that for which you yearn, that for which you yearn but dare not name. Yes, the cry of the Undertown is a deep cry indeed, and at one time or another it cries out to each one of you.

And in your house, Lazarus? In your house, you have caught a glimpse of me at last, for as I lingered to exult in my handiwork, your eyes met my eyes through the flames. And I knew then that I had been

*your enemy for too long and that you had suffered too much, and so I
begged you take heed of me. I revealed to you my true self, Lazarus,
could you but have seen it, but in your fear you heard only what you
wanted to hear, saw only what you wanted to see. In your fear you
closed the door that had opened between us.*

*So now the yearning is upon me to reach out again to you, to draw
you back to the dark heart of my house, to restore to you all of those
things from which I have been protecting you. And now I must seek a
way in which to draw you back. I must seek a way to reach out to you,
and you in your turn must seek a way to reach out to me. I beg you,
Lazarus, you have but to seek me out, you have but to extend your
hand. Then, at the meeting of our hands, you will know at last what
must be done.*

Beggars' Row

On the morning following the monthly congress, Leonardo
Pegasus set off as usual for his workshop, not because he had any
work to do, but because he knew that, bereft of the sustaining
structure of routine, madness would leap exultantly into the
void and take command. The elevator in the apartment building descended with terrifying speed, bumping alarmingly when
it hit bottom.

'Sorry, guv'nor,' the Elevator Captain apologised. 'New pony
joined the team. Still a bit frisky. Take a month or two to break
her in.'

'In a month or two, I shall no longer be here,' replied
Leonardo.

'Going anywhere nice?'

The reply was fortunately inaudible.

Arriving at the front entrance to the palace, Leonardo decided on impulse to make a detour. Instead of following his usual
route through the front gates, he turned to his right, heading
along the upper ring road that girdled the palace wall on three
sides. If anyone had asked him why he was doing this, he would

have said that it was just for a change of scene, but this was only partially true. For at the rear of the palace stood the service gate through which deliveries were made, and through which the more humble members of the palace staff made their daily entrances and exits. Leading from the service gate down to the ring road was a steeply sloping cobbled street named Beggars' Row, which was, as its name implied, one of the few locations in the city where unlicensed begging was still tolerated. The Row was, as usual, peopled with a haphazard row of ragged, skulking, vaguely human forms. Leonardo stationed himself at the entrance to the Row, leaning nonchalantly against a wall.

The view from here was very different from the one to which he was accustomed. Below him, to his left, stood the drab blocks of the industrial area, flying the unattractive corporate kites of the various manufacturing and service industries that had their headquarters there. Beyond these, Leonardo could make out the gilded rooftops of the Western Suburb where, for the next few weeks at any rate, he still had his living quarters. In the far distance were the docks, their position indicated by the soaring masts and rigging of the tall vessels at anchor there. In front of him a long street of drab shops and run-down businesses led northwards to the ruins of the Third Gate and the derelict section of the city walls. And in front of him too lay the jagged, stinking expanse of the Undertown, allowing him a clear view across to the massive rectangular blocks of the North Estates. He knew now that Alice lived there. If he waited here, she would surely pass him on her way to work.

Leonardo waited for over an hour, during which time large numbers of palace employees passed through the service gate, some of them throwing coins to the beggars, but Alice was not among them. After the bulk of the people had made their entrance, Leonardo came to the reluctant conclusion that he was not going to see Alice that day. He decided to make his way to his workshop and spend a little time bringing his graph up to date.

Turning along Beggars' Row, he walked slowly up towards

the service gate, casting his gaze along the forlorn line of hunched shapes that leaned or crouched or lay against the wall. He briefly pictured himself taking his place among them, his finery reduced to rags, his expensive boots gaping open. An old man with a wooden leg rattled a tin cup at him. A blind woman sat silent on the ground, her legs extended straight in front of her like a doll. Leonardo was not normally a charitable man, but occasionally he liked to amuse himself by performing a random act of kindness. He felt in his pockets for a coin.

The beggar he singled out for his generosity was younger than the others, scarcely more than a boy, probably not even out of his teens. He sat dejected on the ground, knees hunched under his chin, arms wrapped around his shins, face almost hidden under a ragged mop of red hair. He did not have a cup or a hat for money, did not even make the effort to retrieve the few coins that lay scattered around him. And at his feet, curled up among the coins, lay a small brown dog.

The dog was what had caught the magician's attention. He was quite fond of dogs, had even owned one himself at one time. Still fingering his coin, Leonardo stooped down to stroke the animal. Like the boy, it did not respond. He looked more closely at it. It did not look healthy. Its fur was matted and filthy, it felt cold to his touch, and surely there was something unnatural in the way it was lying? With a shock, Leonardo belatedly recognised the stink of decay. Hastily dropping his coin, he turned and hurried away, choking back the rising flux of vomit.

Fang and Gash

It is twilight. Hugging the shadows, two lean ragged creatures swiftly pick their furtive way through the devastation of the Undertown. Until nightfall, they keep always in the shadows, for in the shadows they can pass unnoticed by the daytime folk. But in truth, even in the shadows they do not feel comfortable – not, at least, until night has fallen. Daylight makes them edgy,

and they prefer to keep their edge for the hours of darkness.
Then they can roam abroad unchallenged, and then they can do
what they love to do. They can scent out a quarry, pursue it,
close on it, bring it down. Sometimes the militiamen give
chase, but they are mostly middle-aged and stout, and the creatures can easily outrun them. And mostly they do not even need
to run. They know every alleyway, every sewer, every culvert,
every catwalk of their domain. When they have to disappear,
they can disappear. And when it is time to return, they will
return, silent on their bare feet, unforgiving, lethal.

Fang and Gash have fed well these last few nights, and so this
night they have decided to slip away from the pack. Sometimes
they like to have a little fun on their own, and tonight they have
scented something special in the air, something that tells them
that fun is on offer. Somebody very much out of the ordinary
has come to the city, someone clever and special and gorgeous
and tempting. So, as the darkness gathers, they stretch themselves, tiptoe away from the slumbering pack, slink across thoroughfares, scale walls, drop silently into yards, thread their way
through the tangled skein of alleys. Always they avoid the
crowds, avoid the traffic, keeping only to the secret trackways of
the nighttime folk. Soon the walls of the palace loom above
them. They slip across the ring road, and, hugging the wall,
come to the place where the beggars wait.

Usually they avoid the beggars. They are poor sport, scrawny
and lacking in spirit, but tonight they sense that there is one
among them who is different. They slip into a dark place, and wait
and watch. And, as the last flickerings of daylight expire, one by
one the beggars haul themselves to their feet and limp away. Soon
only one remains on the row, hunched apathetically, staring at the
ground. Fang and Gash wait a little longer, until they are sure that
the coast is clear. Then they emerge from their hiding place and
steal softly up Beggars' Row towards the solitary figure. It is him,
sure enough. A beautiful, delicious red-headed boy.

They squat down in front of him. He does not look up. His
attention seems focused on a brown dog that lies motionless on

the cobbles in front of him. The rank, maggoty stench of the dog tells them that it has been dead for too long to be of any interest to them. Fang and Gash exchange looks. Then Fang feels around among the cobbles, picks up a coin from the small number that are scattered there, toys with it, drops it again. Aroused by the faint sound, the boy looks up slowly. His vacant, grimy, freckled face shows no emotion. Now Gash picks up another coin, spins it directly in front of the boy's face. The blank eyes register nothing. Now Fang scoops up the coins in a handful, hurls them in the air, allows them to scatter over a wide area. The boy's cracked lips part a fraction, but he shows no other response. Now Gash reaches down, seizes hold of the dog's tail. Slowly, he begins to drag the carcass towards him.

A sudden look of panic crosses the boy's face. Slowly, Gash rises to his feet, dangling the dog by its tail. And, slowly, the boy rises too. He has started to breathe faster and suddenly there are tears in his eyes. Still holding the dog, Gash starts to back away, grinning mockingly. And then the boy flies at him, screaming and clawing like a mad thing. Yelping with delight, Gash spins around towards the bottom end of the Row and begins to run, the boy hot on his heels. Then, in an instant, Fang has launched himself at the boy in a flying tackle that brings both of them rolling to the ground in a fierce confusion of bodies. A moment later they are back on their feet and all three are running.

They race through the Undertown, zigzagging their way through the maze of alleys, Fang and Gash tossing the dog one to another, each time allowing the boy almost to catch up with them before making the next pass. Once they think they have lost him, but a moment later he is diving down upon them from the top of a wall, screaming and dashing them both to the ground, and then they are up and upon him with claws bared, and now he has the dog and it is his turn to run from them, and he streaks away down one twisting path after another, always eluding them, always knowing somehow which way to turn, and they know with hungry admiration that they have met their match. Now he is cornered and they have the dog again, and so they let him chase them, and soon all three are chasing each other in circles, now upright, now on all fours, until all hostility is forgotten and they no longer know who is hunter and who is quarry. The narrow courts of the Undertown echo with their reckless laughter as they dive and leapfrog and cart-wheel through the night, until at last the jagged breaths come tearing at their lungs and they know that they can run no more and they somersault heavily over a wall and roll wearily down a bank and tumble together into a friendly rubbish heap.

And there, wrapped around each other in a warm tangle of limbs, with rotting vegetables for a blanket and a dead dog for a pillow, they sleep.

The scent wakes him. The cold, grey half-light tells him that it is either dawn or twilight, he cannot be certain which. As his eyes adjust themselves, he can see that the place where he has slept is now sparsely dotted with more of the ragged creatures. They squat on their haunches, keeping their distance, biding their time, regarding him with wary respect. His two new friends from the night before are crouching close to him. One of them, the one called Fang, is holding something out, thrust-ing it under his nostrils. It is a ragged, bloody hunk of raw meat. The scent is rich, fresh, appetising. His nostrils flare and he begins to salivate. The one called Gash leans towards him.

'Join us,' he whispers. 'Join us.'

The scent of the meat is more than the boy can bear. Without thought, he snatches and tears and gnaws and swal-lows, blood and saliva running down his chin. And when the meat is gone, he reaches out hungrily for more.

A Summons to a Celebration

After the episode of the dead dog, Leonardo abandoned his notion of waiting for Alice at the service gate. A couple of mornings later, making his usual way up the main thoroughfare, he took his habitual glance at the line of signal kites that fluttered from the gatehouse. There were routine messages about the latest Wolf Boys murder, and about an epidemic that was striking down the city's elevator ponies. Then Leonardo read that the King's newly refurbished administrative area would shortly be opening for business, and that a day of celebration was to be held in the new office extension the following week. Leonardo grunted in disapproval. As he made his way through the gate, the aged sentry greeted him.

'Good morning, Master Pegasus. I expect you'll be attending the celebration?'

'I don't imagine they'll want too many of my kind there,' grumbled Leonardo. 'We remind them of everything they want to forget. If they do ask me, it will only be out of guilt. And even then I won't go. I know when I'm not wanted.'

'Well, that's up to you of course, Master. Anyway, I shan't be going either. I finish here at the end of the week.'

Leonardo felt a sudden, unexpected surge of grief. He was surprised to find himself seizing the old man by the hand.

'I'll miss you,' he exclaimed fervently, and he could feel tears pricking at his eyes. 'It won't be the same without you.' He realised that he had never even known the old man's name. 'Have they chosen your replacement?'

'Oh no, Master, there won't be any replacement,' replied the sentry with surprising cheerfulness. 'They're getting some sort of security engine. Admissions controller, they call it. You have to put a sort of token in a slot.'

Arriving at his workshop, Leonardo was not surprised to find only one item of correspondence awaiting him on the doormat. Since the dissolution of his office, few people had been inclined to get in touch with him. Stooping, he picked up the small scroll, squinted at it in the gloom, then walked over to the lattice window, which was now the only source of light in the room. Scrutinising the parchment, he was surprised to recognise the emblem of the King's administrative offices, but when he saw the neat, rounded handwriting of the address, he felt as if his heart had, for a moment, ceased to beat. Then he broke the seal. It was a summons to attend the celebration. The bulk of the text bore the impersonal character imposed by the mechanical writing engines that were just then coming into use, but the short postscript at the bottom, like the address, was written in Alice's familiar hand:

Hope you can come. A.

This changed everything. Leonardo looked at the calendar, counted the days. For a while, he was so happy that he forgot to mark up his graph.

Life with the Wolf Boys

I love to watch them. By day they sleep, in sewers or in derelict buildings or in rubbish heaps. But by night they run, moving and thinking and acting as one, and then I love to run with them.

At twilight they awaken, scratch themselves, stretch themselves. They sniff the wind, alert for the scent of fresh quarry. At each scenting they exchange glances, signalling yes or no with a claw, with an eyebrow, until they catch a scent that they know is good, and then together they arise, silently they fan out across the secret network of paths, gently they ease themselves into measured pursuit, carefully holding back, keeping downwind of the quarry until all are spread out and ready. Then one or two will slip quietly ahead, position themselves upwind, give the quarry sight and scent of the leader . . .

And then the pack catches the sharp tang of fear, and the chase is on, the quarry driven away from the thoroughfares into the tangle of smaller and smaller paths, the pack skilfully navigating the unseen network, breath soaring, heart pounding. The runners on the wings start to pull together, closing the circle, tightening the noose, until the quarry stands surrounded, cowering, whimpering . . .

And then they are upon it, grip of iron restraining the thrashing limbs, fangs and claws tearing at the distended veins, fierce tongues lapping the hot rich blood as it wells and spurts and gushes into the hungry throats, the body twitching feebly until at last it gives up its life. And now the claws tear deep into the soft flesh, the fangs rip chunks from the lifeless form. The flesh tastes rich, tastes moist, tastes good.

And then, hunger sated, one by one they turn, slinking away, abandoning the ruined corpse to the rats, creeping on all fours back to the sleeping place, huddling against the cold, hugging and stroking and giggling and dribbling over each other in a rank confusion of exhausted bodies.

And the next night, they will be hungry again.

The Celebration

The new administrative area at the palace consisted of a single very large room, housed in a newly constructed six-sided penthouse situated at the highest point of the palace. It had large windows to every aspect, windows that would have offered a spectacular panoramic view of the city had not the architect had the foresight to equip them with lockable iron blinds, intended, presumably, to prevent the staff becoming distracted from their duties.

Arriving on the roof of the palace, Leonardo picked his way among chimney pots and ventilator shafts towards the row of large, new grey kites that fluttered from the penthouse in the late afternoon breeze. Inside, Leonardo cast his gaze around. The room was drab and unattractive. The floor was covered with some sort of scratchy grey artificial fabric, the furniture was of grey-painted metal, and the various administrative engines hummed and chirped and flashed and winked with sinister smugness. As a concession to the uniqueness of the occasion, a few bunches of colourless balloons had been attached here and there to the walls and ceiling.

The celebration had seemingly been in progress for some

hours already. The majority of the company were clad in the dreary grey of the new order, the humbler folk in tracksuits, the more exalted in stiff, formal outfits of tailored cloth. Everyone was chattering frenetically. Standing out in the expanse of grey, Leonardo noticed a few colourful figures who still wore the old armorial garb, members like himself of the previous generation of courtiers, now looking out of place and old-fashioned. The furniture had been pulled back to the edges of the room, a power-driven music engine was grinding its way through mechanical arrangements of unrecognisable tunes, and a number of people were awkwardly jerking and shuffling about. Leonardo peered into the throng, wondering whether Alice were among them, but before he could find an answer to this question, he felt a hand at his elbow. Turning, he recognised the dark young man named Kevin who had demonstrated the counselling engine to him. He was consulting a scroll bearing a long list of names. Leonardo noticed that his hands were still trembling.

'Welcome, er, Master Pegasus.' Kevin's tone was ingratiating. 'We are so glad to see you, delighted that you are exploiting the opportunity to maintain our professional contact.'

'I was watching the dancing,' said Leonardo, not sure what was expected of him.

'Matt is very keen to encourage dancing,' said Kevin. 'He feels passionately that his staff should be empowered to express themselves.'

Leonardo could not find a suitable reply to this. To his eyes, none of the dancers seemed to be expressing anything other than embarrassment or discomfiture.

'Anyway, enjoy,' Kevin continued smoothly. 'I'll maybe catch you later.'

He vanished into the crowd, leaving Leonardo momentarily disorientated.

'Refreshment?' said a female voice. Leonardo found himself confronted by a wary-looking woman in a grey catering apron. She was carrying a large tray bearing an elaborate geometric arrangement of what appeared to be small squares of dry bread. Leonardo picked out a light brown square and nibbled it cautiously. It turned out to be just what it seemed: brown bread, and not particularly fresh. Noticing that he was finding it difficult to swallow, the woman took pity on him.

'There's water on the big table,' she said. 'Plain or salted. It might help.' Then she too was gone.

Leonardo elbowed his way confusedly through the crowd. These people baffled him. Their dancing seemed graceless, their chatter stilted, their food inedible. He looked around for someone he knew. In the distance he recognised Nina, the sharp-tongued woman from the Herald's Office, still wearing her studded leather jacket. She was leaning against a column, talking animatedly to a tall middle-aged man. In another corner Leonardo caught a glimpse of Veronique, disconcertingly clad in a new grey outfit, her wig and make-up considerably toned down. Leonardo started pushing his way across the room to greet his friend. But before he got there, he saw Alice.

She was among a group of young people clustered around the music engine. The others were dancing with degrees of competence that varied from mediocrity to utter hopelessness, but Alice danced with grace, with energy, with passion. To Leonardo's eyes, she blazed like a comet among them, and he could not understand why the others paid her so little heed. Spellbound, he gazed, until finally she noticed him.

'Master Pegasus! You came!'

She abandoned her dancing, excused herself, ran to greet him.

'Hello, Alice. How are you getting on?' Leonardo enquired.

'Oh, not too bad, not too bad at all. I'm starting to get the hang of it. Why don't you come and dance?'

'I would if I could dance like you.' Leonardo was taken aback by his own candour.

'But it's easy. Anyone can do it. I could teach you, if you want.'

'Yes, I'd like that. I'd like that very much.' Leonardo eyed the dance floor apprehensively. He felt a sudden yearning to join the dancers, but at the same time, his feet seemed shackled to massive, immovable weights. He shifted uncertainly, first one way, then the other. There was an awkward pause, during which Alice tilted her head to one side, then tilted it back again. Finally she broke the silence.

'Well, I'd better get back to the others,' she said brightly. 'I expect I'll see you later on.' She patted him on the forearm and was gone.

Perplexed, Leonardo stared after her as she vanished back into the crowd. She had been so quick to greet him, and then so quick to abandon him. He had just started to analyse their brief exchange when a familiar gruff voice interrupted his thoughts.

'You're well in there, Wizbang,' croaked Veronique with lascivious relish. 'That was a come-on if ever I heard one. Keep your eye on that one. Make sure you know when she's leaving.'

'Oh, leave off, Veronique,' groaned Leonardo. 'Right now I need a drink. Is there any proper drink at this celebration? I think I need something stronger than salted water.'

'Stick with old Vero,' croaked the clown. 'I've sorted out a few bits for us.' She reached inside her costume and produced a small, transparent, promising-looking flask.

Leonardo spent the next couple of hours in the company of a small group of malcontents who had also sniffed out Veronique's private supply of drink. Periodically, he glanced over his shoulder to check on Alice's movements. After a little while, the drink began to work its magic, and Leonardo had almost started to enjoy himself when the clown leaned across to whisper to him.

'She's leaving,' she hissed, blowing a cloud of rancid cigar smoke in the magician's face. 'Get in there. Attaboy.'

It might have been the effect of the drink, or perhaps it was a trick of the light, but for a moment it seemed to Leonardo that he could make out a dark, shadowy form stirring behind the familiar silhouette of his friend. However, there was no time for him to dwell on this. Rough hands were dragging him to his feet. Coarse voices were cheering him on. And on the far side of the room, Alice was disappearing through the exit. Staggering and breathing heavily, Leonardo launched himself in pursuit. Behind him he could hear Veronique's faint cry of encouragement.

'Give her one from me!'

It was twilight, and a thin rain had begun to fall as the two figures passed through the service gate of the palace and made their individual ways along the unevenly cobbled, twisting stretch of Beggars' Row, now deserted for the night. First came the girl, swift, sure-footed, straight-backed, her fair hair streaming behind her, her rain-cape billowing gracefully around her narrow shoulders. Some distance behind lurched the magician, stumbling on the irregular surface, his hat awry, his robe flapping damply around him, his eyes blurred, his breath dull with drink. The slender figure at the centre of his field of vision commanded his total attention, the buildings on either side of her seeming to sway and stretch and crumble and dissolve in the acrid city drizzle.

Dodging across the ring road, he caught a glimpse of her as she turned into the North Way, but by the time he reached the junction, she was no longer in sight. Panting, he paused. Would she stay on the thoroughfare or would she, as Veronique had suggested, take a short cut through the perilous maze of the Undertown? Perhaps he had already lost her. Unsure of the best tactic, Leonardo hesitated. Then his eye was attracted by a cheerfully illuminated brown-and-cream kite, flying from the awning of a coffee stall. Seeing this, some last surviving rational part of him decided, reluctantly, that it would be wisest to call off the hunt and take a little sustenance. Resigned, he stepped under the awning, picked his way among half a dozen tables to the counter, paid for some coffee, seated himself, looked around. And then his heart stopped.

Alice was there, seated at a corner table. To one side of her stood a mug of coffee. In front of her was a surprisingly substantial-looking pastry that she was in the process of dissecting with knife and fork. His own mug halfway to his lips, Leonardo watched her, marvelling at the concentrated precision with which she carried out her task. Transported, he felt his fingers begin to relax, and he realised, too late, that the mug was slipping from his grasp. An instant later, he was on his feet, leaping and howling with pain as the scalding liquid soaked through his shirt and breeches. Alice looked up, startled. It took her a moment to recognise the lurching, shrieking, demented figure.

'Alice!' cried the magician, piteously extending his hands towards her.

She gave a little gasp, and he saw her pale face turn dead white. Then she quickly laid down her utensils, sprang to her feet, dodged around the table and was gone. It took Leonardo a moment longer to collect what remained of his wits, then he too launched himself out into the night.

From the Journal of Victor Lazarus

Friday 12th June

On the morning following the fire, I made an inspection of those parts of the house that were worst damaged and ordered them to be sealed off until such time as they could be made safe.

By a great stroke of good fortune, the majority of the areas accessible to the public have been spared. This means that all necessary repair work can proceed without undue hindrance to our daily influx of visitors. A team of men have been at work since first light, but they go about their duties in a desultory fashion and make little progress. I sense that for some reason their hearts are not in the task. I shall be relieved when Sam

returns, as he seems to have a knack of engaging their commitment in a way that somehow eludes me.

Meanwhile, I have ordered a camp bed to be set up in my
orderly room. It is my intention to remain in this house night
and day, until the fiend that calls itself my shadow has finally
been run to ground.

Three nights ago, I returned for the last time to my lodgings
in order to collect certain necessary items. Foremost among
these was my service revolver, which I have made up my mind
to carry with me at all times. Upon the stroke of each hour, I
patrol the house, armed and alert. Thus have I prepared myself
to meet whatever eventuality may arise.

In the course of my tours of inspection, I have started to
become aware of more grumblings of discontent among the
men. Thus far, there has been no outright challenge to my
authority, but if things continue in this way, I may be forced to
consider increasing their wages in order to retain their loyalty.
This morning, I even overheard two of them referring to me as
'Mad Lazarus'! However, I must not allow these things to sway
me in my purpose. The men have their work to do, and I have
mine.

Thursday 18th June

At last Sam has returned. At my request, he has resumed immediate command of all the repairs and building work, while
Harold continues to look after the exhibits and the visitors. I
cannot sufficiently express my relief at being unburdened of the
day-to-day responsibilities of command. I am at liberty now to
concentrate all of my strength, all of my vigilance, on the pursuit of the fiend who seeks to destroy me, the shadow who
stalks these corridors by day, and who stalks my dreams by
night.

I cannot help but notice that my men now shy away from
me and avert their eyes when I approach them. It seems that
they have started to fear me, although I fail to understand the

reason for this. It has never been never my wish to rule by fear, for my sole intention is to destroy the fiend who haunts me. Why should anyone concern themselves with my private business, so long as they continue to be paid for their work?

Thursday 25th June

Sam has had the notion of renewing the electrical wiring throughout the house. He visited me in my orderly room today and put his case to me with great conviction. In his opinion, the fire in the kitchen most probably had its cause in the over-heating of some old cables, and he believes that, in the interests of safety, the entire installation should be stripped out and replaced with newer and more reliable equipment. In giving my assent, I could scarcely make the effort to glance at the plans he had produced, and merely agreed that he should do whatever he considered best. He was plainly taken aback by my apparent lack of concern.

In the course of my patrol this afternoon, I was heartened to observe that, in various parts of the house, floorboards have already been pulled up to expose the old cables and make way for the new. I took the opportunity to make a brief inspection of the wiring. Indeed it did look most unsafe. The insulation, I noticed, was of the old-fashioned canvas kind, and in places had been quite eaten away by mice.

No further trace of the fiend these past few days.

Alice in the Undertown

He shakes away the last scraps of sleep and squats on his haunches, sniffing the wind. The scent that he catches excites him in a way that is somehow new, somehow unfamiliar. Not a city scent, not a scent that figures in the gamy lexicon of the Undertown. The scent of a lonely place, a place far away from here . . . He detects sharp, clean air, a whiff of ozone, the scent of the sea . . . the fragrance of long grass, a faint

starring of clover . . . And there is something else. Maybe a little ice-
blue dash of fear . . . and also, perhaps, just a whiff of coffee?

He turns expectantly towards the others. Fang responds with nar-
rowed eye. Gash twitches a claw. Fang and Gash are his friends, they
know that he is special, they know that he is different. From the others,
no response. Whatever it is that catches his attention, it means nothing
to the rest of them. Disappointed, for now he disengages himself, turns
his attention elsewhere.

Ah, yes, here is another scent. This one has coffee in it too, but this
time interwoven with coarser, ranker strands. There is sweat, both fresh
and stale, strong poisonous drink, and there, at the centre of the skein,
something damaged, something wounded, something that might once
have been arrogance or pride, but that now carries the sour yellowish
tang of bitterness, the dark crimson of frustration . . . and the black reek
of rage. He looks around at the others. This time there is no question.
Here is a quarry to be reckoned with. They arise as one, spread out,
vanish into the branching maze of pathways.

As Leonardo emerged into the North Way, Alice was some distance ahead of him, nimbly threading her way among the few
desperate-looking characters who were still abroad on the
streets. He walked hurriedly after her, elbowing people aside,
ignoring their startled cries. Then he saw her dart down a side
turning next to an apothecary's flyblown shop. As he rounded
the corner she was still in sight, but a moment later she had
vanished down an even narrower lane. Leonardo shoved his way
past more bystanders, this time drawing glances that offered
menace as well as surprise, and a moment later found himself
pursuing the girl down a winding street of boarded-up door-
ways and crumbling brickwork.

Behind a shattered wall on a derelict plot, silent eyes registered his passing, and a moment later, a barefoot figure stole out
into the lane.

Ignoring all danger, Leonardo was intent only on his pursuit
of the slender figure that seemed to hurtle ahead of him down
a shifting, narrowing tunnel. If he registered his surroundings at

all, it was simply as a series of featureless obstacles to be negotiated, and he paid no attention to the incidental details of
cracked concrete, rusty shutters, burned-out vehicles, peeling
posters, overflowing rubbish bins and seeping drains. The shadowy form that slunk along a short distance behind him evaded
his notice entirely. And when another form appeared, darting
along the top of a wall to his right, his attention remained concentrated only on his own quarry. One by one, other forms
tagged along, behind him, beside him, above him, even in the
sewers beneath his pounding feet. Within minutes, Leonardo
was unwittingly isolated at the centre of a silent, contracting
ring of hungry predators.

Running now, the girl dodged down an alleyway alongside a
garishly lit, vulgar place of entertainment. Still following her,
the magician found himself abruptly dazzled by the flashing
lights of the multicoloured display kites, stumbled on a loose
cobblestone, and, by the time he had righted himself, realised
that she was lost from his sight.

'Alice,' he called feebly. 'Alice. Come back.'

Then, with a start, he found his way barred by two ragged
figures. He became aware of his accelerated breathing, of the
furious pounding of his heart.

'Excuse me. Please let me pass.'

Moving as one, they advanced a step closer. Beginning to
panic, Leonardo spun clumsily around. Three more shapes cut
off his retreat. Then, on his left, two more dropped silently
down from the top of a wall. Clumsily, he fumbled in the folds
of his robe for his purse.

'Here. I've got money. Is that what you want?'

There was no response. He had hardly a moment to catch his
breath before they closed in another step, tightening the circle.
Highlighted in lime, then in magenta, then in cobalt by the
flashing kites, their sharp adolescent faces were hungry and piti-
less and gleeful. In lime, in magenta, in cobalt, he registered a
narrowed eye, the twitch of a neck muscle, the thin dribble of
saliva from parted lips. Then, fangs and claws bared, they were

upon him, their rancid stench bruising his nostrils, their naked feet silent on the wet cobbles. The magician crumpled to the ground, numb to their blows, feeling only relief as the black tide swept up and engulfed him.

From the Journal of Victor Lazarus

Tuesday 30th June

Today, for the first time in weeks, I caught a glimpse of my shadow, but the fiend eluded me! I was making a patrol of an upstairs landing, when I saw the creature as clear as daylight. It was hanging by its knees from a banister rail, leering at me insolently with its inverted features. I reached at once for my revolver, stepping forward as I did so for a steadier aim, and suddenly found myself tumbling headlong! I had caught my foot in one of the holes in the floor where the boards had been removed by Sam's men. As I struggled to right myself, the creature dropped silently onto its hands, balanced there with its legs cocked in the air, squinting at me for a moment longer, then somersaulted away down a corridor. By the time I had recovered my composure, there was no further sign of it. No matter: if I can only maintain my vigilance, I will sooner or later hunt it down.

An Unexpected Rescuer

The blackness was pierced abruptly by a long, shrill, warbling noise. Leonardo was dimly aware of the sounds of shouting voices and running feet, and then he became aware of something prodding him. His consciousness began to return. He was being prodded in the shoulder, rhythmically, inquisitively. His body shifted slightly on the damp cobbles, and stabs of pain in various places alerted him to the whereabouts of his assorted bruises, grazes and contusions.

'All right,' he found himself mumbling thickly. 'I'm awake now.'

Cautiously he opened his eyes. He could see a pair of heavy, black, scuffed boots. One of them was planted firmly on the ground in front of his face. The other, which had apparently being doing the prodding, was withdrawing from his shoulder to join its companion. Painfully, Leonardo craned his neck to look upwards. From the tops of the boots protruded a pair of sturdy female legs clad in fishnet stockings. The legs disappeared inside a short, tight, black skirt, which in its turn disappeared inside a black, heavily studded leather jacket.

'Oh,' said a familiar curt voice, 'it's you.'

The owner of the boots, legs, stockings, skirt and jacket brushed her fringe from her eyes. Leonardo recognised the woman from the Herald's Office. She was twirling a small silver whistle in her hand.

'It's Nina, isn't it?' said Leonardo. 'What are you doing here?'

'I was on my way home,' replied Nina. 'I live here. Just as well for you I do.'

She squatted down to get a better look at him.

'Anything broken?'

Behind her brusque manner, Leonardo could detect a faint note of concern. He shifted himself experimentally.

'I don't think so,' he said finally. 'Quite a few sore spots, though.'

She gave a small nod.

'Can you stand?'

He allowed her to help him to his feet. Then, warily, he looked around him, his eyes confused by the multicoloured flashing of the overhead kites. But, so far as he could tell, there was no sign of his attackers. He shivered. The rain was getting heavier. Nina looked up at him for a moment, seeming to consider her options. Then she came to a decision.

'All right. Let's get you indoors. You won't have far to walk.'

Leonardo walked slowly, allowing Nina to support him. Looking rather like a lopsided entry for a three-legged race, the ill-matched pair hobbled along another alley or two, crossed over a thoroughfare that was unfamiliar to Leonardo, and ducked into a grim labyrinth of run-down tenements. There were apparently no elevators, pony-driven or otherwise, in this part of the city, for there followed a painful climb up several flights of steps. Eventually Leonardo found himself slumped in a sagging armchair in front of a spluttering gas fire in the front parlour of Nina's cramped little flat. He stared around him at the jumble of battered furniture and untidy heaps of books and scrolls, all entwined in the unruly foliage of numerous potted plants. A large cat scrutinised him suspiciously, circled around the chair, and finally jumped up to settle on his lap.

'That's quite an honour,' said Nina, appearing from the kitchen with two steaming mugs of punch. 'Malkin doesn't take kindly to visitors. Now, are you going to tell me what brought you to the Undertown?'

Leonardo stroked the cat thoughtfully. It was difficult to answer the question succinctly.

'I was following someone,' he said after a long pause. 'Alice. I was following Alice. And then I was attacked. They looked like wild animals. Do you think they were the Wolf Boys?'

'Probably,' said Nina. 'We get a few of them round here. The rent is very cheap, of course, but there are drawbacks. So how did you come to be on the trail of our little Alice?'

Bit by bit, Leonardo's story emerged. Soothed by the cat's regular breathing, and lulled by the warming glow of the punch, he told Nina of his early fascination with the girl at the Herald's Office, of his scheme to lure her into his own workshop, of the dissolution of his office, of his uncontrollable grief at her departure, even of the graph he had started to draw. The only thing he did not mention was the occasion on which he had entered the antechamber during the rest period and found Alice dancing her secret dance. Somehow, this still seemed too private to share with anyone else.

As Leonardo talked, he discovered that he could contain his sorrow no longer, and gratefully he allowed the tears to roll down his cheeks. Kneeling at his feet, Nina listened attentively, interrupted little, passed him a handerchief when he needed it, replenished their mugs occasionally.

'So how do you feel about Alice after all that?' she asked finally.

'It's strange.' Leonardo's knuckles were suddenly white as he gripped the arms of the chair. 'It's almost as if she led me into it. And Veronique. She encouraged me too. And even the King. If it hadn't been for him, none of this would have happened.'

Nina gave him a look that was half concerned, half reproachful.

'Let's get this right. Are you saying it was because of the King that you got beaten up?'

Leonardo's anger subsided.

'Yes . . . No . . . No, of course not. Oh, I don't know.' He stifled a yawn. He found that he had run out of things to say. He noticed that Nina was yawning too. He had no idea what time it was. He yawned again.

'Oh, I'm sorry. I think I need to go to sleep now.'

'I'm sure you do,' replied Nina. He noticed that she was stroking his wrist. 'It must have been a hell of a day for you. Thing is, darling, I've only got the one bed. It's quite a big one, though.'

She had started to unbutton Leonardo's shirt.

From the Journal of Victor Lazarus

I leave this entry undated, for I begin to lose all sense of time. By night and by day the fiend haunts me, and I scarcely know any longer whether I am waking or sleeping. I can bring myself neither to drink nor to eat, and I grow weak and thin, and I despair of ever running my foe to earth. Visitors and staff scatter before me as I prowl the corridors, their faces white with terror. At night I turn this way and that in my narrow bed, too terrified to surrender myself to sleep, lest I should begin again to dream. For in my dreams the dark one stalks me in a thousand forms, one night as a ravening wolf, the next as a cloaked assassin, the next perhaps as the faceless and implacable agent of terror, sometimes huge and threatening, sometimes elusive and insubstantial.

Last night I dreamed (at least, I pray that it was but a dream) that the house itself was destroyed. Tiles slithered one by one from the roof, the noise building in a mighty crescendo, until I found myself deafened by the thunderous avalanche of slate. Massive sections of brickwork bowed outwards and disintegrated in clouds of choking dust and shards of splintering glass. The floors, the ceilings, the staircases, the very timbers of the roof, groaned and cracked and splintered, and suddenly, to the echoing cacophony of demoniacal laughter, the house was reduced to a wasteland of rubble.

All was darkness. I staggered amongst the wreckage, crying out feebly for help. At first it seemed that all had deserted me, but at length my ears detected the faint answering tones of Harold and Sam. Never was I so glad to hear another human voice! By the first faint glint of dawn they appeared, first Sam in his overalls, hammer in hand, then Harold, still clutching his ledger as though his life depended on it, which perhaps it did. Encircled by the jagged outlines of the ruins, we built a fire and huddled around it, awaiting the light of day. It was bitterly cold. Sam built a rough shelter from pieces of wreckage. We sat inside it and we waited. I became aware of a sense of expectation, as though we were awaiting a visitor.

When I awoke, I found myself lying on hard ground, encompassed by the skeletal forms of charred timbers. For a moment it seemed that the nightmare continued, until belatedly I recognised my surroundings. I was lying in the fire-blackened kitchen of the house. I must have wandered there in a daze and fallen senseless to the ground. My ears continued to echo with faint, mocking laughter, but once again the fiend was nowhere to be seen. I despair of enduring this madness for much longer.

So you have grown to fear me, Lazarus. You patrol the corridors of the house with your revolver, vengefully you swear to destroy me when we meet. And I too in my turn have grown fearful, hiding my face even as I try to show myself to you, fleeing in terror when you approach me too near. Once you saw me in a corridor, but, betrayed by your own clumsiness, you caught your foot and tumbled headlong, and by the time you had righted yourself, my strength of will had deserted me, and I could show myself to you no longer.

So then I determined to visit you in your dreams. As a pure and graceful girl I came to you, dancing the dance of the Great Being itself, and I watched as you fretted and moaned and reached out in your sleep for your revolver, and then I knew that even in your dreams you could see me only as the agent of terror, clutching at your heart with bony claws.

And now I have tried to reach out to you in so many ways, and I have exhausted myself in the trying. So I grieve and I grow thin and I grow weak and I despair of ever finding you.

But deep within my house there dwells another, another who understands all that takes place here. In a far corner, remote and neglected by all, an old lady slumbers in her chair, and she it is who extends to me the hand of comfort, she it is who understands what I must do when all seems lost.

And now I too know what I must do.

The Magician Seeks a Market

He could feel a heavy weight pressing down on his chest, forcing him to the ground, crushing the breath from him. Leonardo opened his eyes with a start, to be met by the impassive gaze of the cat Malkin. Relieved, he looked around him.

He was alone. The bed in which he was lying occupied almost all of the tiny room at the back of the flat. The walls were of bare, cracked plaster, and the room was foggily illuminated through a grimy skylight. It was raining outside. Leonardo watched the drops of water trickling down the slanting glass. He had just started to wonder what had become of Nina when she appeared in the doorway, wrapped in a faded dressing gown and bearing a large tray of hot scones and coffee.

'Are you coming back to bed?' asked Leonardo. 'It's been a long time since anyone brought me breakfast.'

They wrapped themselves in the thick, slightly prickly, paisley-patterned eiderdown and ate in companionable silence. Malkin helped them with some of the raisins from the scones.

'So how's life at the Herald's Office?' asked Leonardo eventually.

'Don't ask.' Nina scowled. 'To tell you the truth, I'm totally fed up with it. Ever since that stupid reorganisation, the rot's really started to set in. Everything's up in the air. New regulations, new paperwork, new procedures. It's all totally haywire and . . . and somehow utterly boring at the same time.' She stared down at the eiderdown for a moment, then her face broke into a smile. 'Listen, that's enough about me. What are you going to do with yourself?'

'I'm not sure,' replied Leonardo. 'I've got all my scrolls and equipment, and the King has given me a bit of a gratuity. I suppose I shall go somewhere else and set myself up as a magician again. There must be work for magicians.' He paused. 'But I've really no idea where to start.'

Nina looked at him thoughtfully for a moment.

'I might just be able to help you,' she mused. 'If you want me to, that is. There's one good thing about my sort of work, I do get to find out what's going on. I can come up with all kinds of stuff if I keep my ears open, you know, contacts, opportunities and whatnot. Do you think that might be any help?'

'Yes. Yes, I think it might,' said Leonardo. 'Thank you, Nina, that would really be helpful.'

'No problem. And, look, if I can do anything else, you know, packing and so on . . .'

Leonardo was reaching out to replace his mug on the tray when he felt a sudden stab of pain. He winced. Nina looked at him, concerned.

'I think I'd better lie down again for a bit.'

She helped him to rearrange his pillows, eased him into a comfortable position, put the tray on the floor, shooed away the cat.

'There, that's better.' She leaned across the bed towards him. 'Okay if I join you?'

It was some time since Leonardo had walked with a spring in his step, but with a little encouragement, his feet were happy to oblige. The next day, he entered the palace through the main gate, dodged around the admissions engine, which was not yet working properly, and made his way to his workshop. He now had only a few days in which to pack up his belongings, so Nina's offer of help had been welcome. He was staring at one of his many tall stacks of scrolls, wondering where to start, when he heard the sound of her footsteps at the outer door.

'So this is where it all happens.' Nina gazed around the room for a few moments, then tossed her leather jacket onto a chair and joined Leonardo in examining the scrolls.

'*Fundamentals of Empathy* . . . *Breathing as Others Breathe* . . . *Construction of Provisional Futures* . . . Hey, you've got some pretty amazing stuff here.'

Leonardo watched her as she skimmed along the racks of scrolls and books, glanced at the wreckage of the model stages, flicked through the papers on his planning table.

'*Proposals for the Multiple Empathy Engine.* What's that?'

'Oh, that old thing.' Leonardo did not seem very interested. 'An idea I had a while ago. I never got around to developing it. It's rather complicated to explain.'

She looked at him curiously.

'Try me.'

'Well, I'd have to start by explaining the basic principles of constructing a provisional future.'

'Fundamentals of Magic?' An impish grin appeared on her face. 'No problem. I've been to the lectures.'

Leonardo's eyebrows rose in astonishment.

'At the Academy. When I was doing my degree. I majored in Dispatches, of course, but there was a choice of – what d'you call them? – lesser options in the final year. So I had a crack at this twelve-week Magic course.' Her eyebrows hunched together for a moment. 'I guess education must have changed since your time.'

'So it would seem. You'll understand future construction, then?'

She nodded impatiently.

'Empathy?'

She nodded again.

'So I suppose you will have come across the Empathy Engine, or something similar at any rate. I started using it when I was a young magician, and I still do things more or less the same way today.' Leonardo settled himself. 'Well, as you know, every provisional future has to be tested before it can be brought into being, and the Empathy Engine was designed as a test device. Once I had tested a provisional future from every appropriate viewpoint, I could then be confident that it was well constructed.' Nina nodded. 'Well, after I'd been doing that for a few years, I started to find the whole process extremely time-consuming. I had to test out every possible provisional future from the whole sequence of viewpoints, one after an-other. It was what you might call a linear process, and it just seemed to go on for ever. So I began to wonder if I could cut a few corners. Would you like some coffee, by the way?'

Nina shook her head.

'Perhaps later? What was I saying? Oh yes, Multiple Empathy. Well, I reckoned it would be much quicker if I could somehow test out all the different viewpoints simultaneously, rather than sequentially. Get them all out of the way in one go, so to speak. That was the fundamental concept behind Multiple Empathy. I think I might even have drawn up some plans for the engine. But somehow I never found the time to build it.'

Nina did not speak for several minutes. Leonardo started to say more, but she waved him impatiently into silence. Finally she shook her head slowly.

'Quite amazing,' she said at last. 'I was just trying to think what your Engine reminded me of. And now I've got it. There's an old story my gran used to tell me when I was a little girl. You've probably heard it. About the Great Being who made the world? *A fragment of the Great Being was lodged in the heart of every woman and the heart of every man . . .* I think that's how it went. Just a story, of course. But your Multiple Empathy Engine . . . it would be like . . . like . . . being the Great Being. Having a fragment of yourself in every woman and every man. Sort of being everybody in the world. All at once.' She laughed uneasily. 'Don't you understand what you've got here?'

'I suppose you could think of it that way,' said Leonardo doubtfully. 'But it's rather a fanciful interpretation for my taste.'

'You don't get it, do you? Can't you see you're sitting on an absolute gold mine?' exclaimed Nina, waving her arms about in exasperation. 'There are people crying out for this kind of stuff! You could market it commercially. Make some real money. Give it a fancy name . . . like Instant Enlightenment . . . or Spiritual Submersion . . . or even Multiple Empathy, although maybe that sounds a bit too scientific. All you need is to identify the market.'

'I suppose it could be quite a powerful experience,' mused Leonardo. 'But there's a snag, you see. I just don't know anything at all about any of this marketing, or unique selling points, or customer profiles or any of these funny words people keep using. I like to think I know my craft, I'm a good magician, at least I think I am, but I'd need . . .what do you call it?'

'An agent?' Nina suggested.

'An agent. Exactly,' agreed Leonardo. 'And where will I find one of those?'

Nina seemed to be weighing things up.

'Darling, let me make you a proposal,' she said finally. 'I'll be your agent. You've got the technical know-how. I can provide the contacts, sort out the marketing. We go into partnership. Hit the road and market Multiple Empathy. It can't fail. What do you say?'

Leonardo was aware that time was running out. This was the best offer he was likely to get.

'Where do we start?' he said quickly.

Nina looked around the workshop.

'We start by sorting out this lot.'

Nina scorned Leonardo's habit of writing lists, and suggested a more direct approach to the task.

'Look at all this stuff you've got.' She waved her arm around vaguely. 'You'll need to take some of it, of course, but most of it, you probably won't ever look at it again. So let's begin here, by the door. Just pick up one thing at a time. Look at it. And decide. If you want it, it stays here, in this room. If you don't, it goes in there, in the theatre.' She paused, seemingly doing some mental arithmetic. 'I reckon it'll take us about four days to get through it all. Then we just have to pack up what's in here.'

Leonardo was uncertain.

'What about all the things I can't decide about?' he worried.

'We'll have to decide sooner or later. So let's decide sooner. Okay, so we might make a few mistakes, but we'll just have to live with them. We'd still make mistakes even if we spent the rest of our lives deciding. So why don't we just get on with it?'

So they began. Leonardo would have liked to stop occasionally for coffee, but somehow the coffee engine seemed to have been examined and dealt with in the early stages of the process and Nina would not allow him to waste time looking for it. For the next few days, they did little except sort and sleep, but eventually their task was done. Exhausted, they slumped to the floor and watched the dust settling back around them. In the antechamber towered a compact stack of useful items: boxes of scrolls, all labelled, pieces of magical equipment of various sizes, useful lengths of timber, small items of furniture, and, presumably, the coffee engine. In the theatre sprawled a much larger heap of disintegrating scrolls, broken equipment, random lengths of timber, abandoned furniture, half-empty tins of paint, a two-thirds-empty tin of treacle, several chipped mugs and numerous other items that Leonardo could neither identify nor remember. He picked up something that might have been the remains of the ill-fated Abacus of Equilibrium, or might have been a toy abandoned by the former Prince. He threw it back on the pile.

'What are we going to do with all this?' With a vague sweep of his arm, he indicated the detritus of his working life.

Nina, ever practical, considered.

'Well, we can hardly have a bonfire,' she said at last. 'It wouldn't be too smart to burn the palace down. So let's just leave it here. Shut the door. Let someone else cart it away.' She walked around the pile, taking a last look. Her eye was caught by a sheaf of yellowing parchment, protruding from underneath the wreckage of the main stage.

'What's that?'

Leonardo pulled it out and unfolded it. They both looked. It was the plans for the Multiple Empathy Engine. Not for the first time that week, Nina lost her temper.

'Did you put this here?' she stormed. 'What on earth do you think you were doing?'

'I'm sorry, Nina,' said Leonardo sheepishly. 'I don't know what I could have been thinking of.' After a tense pause, he made another attempt at mitigation. 'You did say we might make a few mistakes.'

Nina held out her hand.

'You'd better let me look after it,' she said firmly.

'Good idea,' Leonardo agreed meekly.

Thrusting the plans into an inner pocket of her jacket, Nina strode back into the outer office.

'What about the paint?' moaned Leonardo, still staring at the pile. 'It might come in handy for something.'

She rolled her eyes.

'Come out here and shut the door. Now.'

That night, they had a little free time to relax in one of the private booths at The Crier's Rest. Nina was keen to discuss their next move.

'What we need now is a waggon,' she was saying. 'Not a power-driven one. Too many places where you can't refuel them. An old-fashioned waggon with horses. We can pack all the stuff in that. Go anywhere we want. Locate our market.'

'Have we got enough money for a waggon?'

'Yes, I've worked it out, and we have, just about. We've got your gratuity and my savings, and if we pool it all, we can just about manage. It'll be a good investment. Oh yes, something else. I know someone down at the mews. I can borrow a coach house for a few days. We can keep the waggon there.'

Leonardo, feeling drowsy after several days' hard work and several flasks of ale, was paying little attention to Nina's enthusiastic stream of words. He let his eyes wander around the noisy, smoky room. A lively group of young palace employees, clad in the functional grey, had occupied one of the booths on the opposite side of the room. With a start, he recognised Alice among them. Their eyes met for a moment, then she looked quickly away.

Leonardo enjoyed a brief moment of mean-spirited satisfaction. He was glad that Alice had seen him with Nina. He reflected upon his experiences with the two women. They were so different from each other. Nina, despite her occasional irritability, had turned out to be warm-hearted, kind, helpful . . . Alice, with her bright, professional mask, had ultimately revealed herself to be cold, ruthless, self-absorbed. He wondered what he had seen in her.

Perhaps she had been too young to understand his need, too immature to respond to it. He studied her angular figure, mentally contrasting it with Nina's more womanly form. Then he felt someone poking him in the forearm.

'You haven't been listening, have you?' Nina interrupted his stream of thought. 'Stop staring at her, she's history now. I was saying, we'll have to carry everything down the back stairs to the service gate, so it'll probably take us about two days to load the waggon. But I reckon we can still be on the road first thing Friday. Bang on schedule.'

Leonardo considered this.

'Could we make it a bit later on in the day?' he suggested tentatively. 'I might need to see a few people in the palace, make my official goodbyes, all that sort of thing.'

Nina appeared irritated for a moment, then changed her mind.

'No problem,' she said quickly. 'I'll need a bit of time to secure the load, put Malkin in her basket, harness up the horses and whatnot – I don't suppose you'll be much use for any of that. I can meet you at the service gate just before the rest period.'

'Perfect,' replied Leonardo. 'You think of everything.' He yawned. 'Can we go to bed soon?'

She laughed.

'Come on, then. Drink up.'

By Friday, the weather had improved, and the sun was shining as Leonardo made his way to the foot of Beggars' Row to wait for Nina. Even the beggars looked cleaner and more cheerful than usual. Leonardo leaned on the wall and cast his gaze over the city, taking in the nautical kites fluttering merrily over the docks, and the Undertown, free for once of smoke and placid in the midday sunshine. Just to his right, across the ring road, he could see the narrow carriageway leading down to the palace mews where he knew Nina would be putting the final touches to their carefully laden waggon.

From the Institute of Calibration, the bells chimed for the rest period. A few people emerged from the service gate, drawn by the sunshine to take their recreation out of doors. Leonardo watched them, smiling indulgently.

An hour later, slightly more anxiously, he watched the same people returning to the palace for the afternoon. He started to wonder what had happened to Nina. Another bell chimed. He waited another hour. Still she did not appear.

Leonardo was becoming very anxious now. He wondered whether some misfortune had befallen Nina. He pictured her lying in the infirmary with a broken leg, pictured her crushed by falling masonry, pictured her set upon by the Wolf Boys. The sun continued to shine, but Leonardo was no longer feeling warm. A horrible suspicion had begun to develop in his mind. Nina was not going to come. Shivering, he tried vainly to push the thought away, but each time he tried, it would return, more powerful and more stubborn than before. Leonardo sighed wearily. He tried to formulate a plan, but could come up with nothing. Finally, he concluded that his only sensible option was to wait on the same spot until the end of the afternoon. If Nina appeared after all, he did not want to miss her.

So he waited. Eventually, small groups of people began to emerge again from the rear of the palace. They were smiling and laughing, preparing themselves for a pleasant weekend away from their toil. Leonardo slumped against the wall and closed his eyes.

'Master Pegasus? Are you all right?'

The familiar soft accent brought him to his senses. Opening his eyes, he recognised the slight form of Alice standing in front of him, her weight on one straight leg, her pale face lined with concern.

'Yes, quite all right, thank you, Alice. I was just waiting for someone. Maybe you've seen her. Nina, from the Herald's Office?'

Alice tilted her head to one side and gave him a very strange look indeed.

'Well, yes, I think I did see her. But it was first thing today. I was on my way in. She was driving a waggon and horses, heading up the North Way. Seemed to be in quite a hurry. She nearly ran me down, actually.' Alice must have noticed Leonardo's look of desolation, for her expression softened. 'I'm sorry. Should I give her a message if I see her?'

'No,' groaned Leonardo. 'No message.'

Alice looked at him for a long moment.

'Well, I'd best be going. Are you're sure you're all right? It's my exercise class tonight. I mustn't be late.'

'Run along, then,' said Leonardo. 'And have a nice weekend.'

'You too.' She smiled, touched him lightly on the arm, then turned and was gone.

Leonardo stared up the North Way after Alice until she was lost from his sight. Then, with a heavy tread, he started to make his way clockwise along the ring road, with no idea in his head what he should do. Nina had cheated him out of everything. He was almost penniless. He did not even have the plans for the Multiple Empathy Engine, on which so many of his hopes had rested.

Arriving at the front gate of the palace, he paused. The admissions engine was working properly now. He watched as people arrived, posted their entry tokens, passed through the barrier. With no token to his name, the palace was now a world sealed off from him. He paused a moment to collect what remained of his energy, adjusted his robe, and took a final look at the view that he knew so well, the commercial and administrative areas, the descending slope of the main thoroughfare, the distant gatehouse, the river.

Then, for the first time, he allowed his gaze to focus on the countryside and the distant landscape that lay beyond the river. He wondered what he would find there. And then, without a backward glance, he strode away down the hill.

★   ★   ★

From the Journal of Victor Lazarus

(Undated)

I was awoken in the night by a faint, intermittent noise that seemed to originate from some distant part of the house. It sounded at first like the same demoniacal laughter I had heard in my dream, but, after listening carefully for a few moments, I began to think that the sound was more akin to the sobbing of a grieving child. Impelled by curiosity, I arose from my camp bed and, still in my nightshirt, stepped cautiously from my chamber into the corridor.

It happened to be the night of the full moon, and the passage ahead of me was illuminated by pale shafts of broken light that slanted down from the tall lattice windows. Outside my room, I could hear the sobbing more clearly, although I was still unable to discern from what direction it originated. Cautiously I set out to investigate, opening each door and examining each room in turn. Once, as I passed along the main landing where the statue stood, I fancied I heard a soft footfall. I turned quickly around, but there was nobody to be seen. As I moved onwards, the sobbing continued as clearly as ever.

I arrived eventually at the room of fossils, the final room of my tour. Here, I noticed that the noise seemed to be, not louder, but somehow clearer, more distinct. I opened the door. The leather armchairs stood as usual with their backs towards me. Silently I reached out to flick on the electric switch, but no light came. I recalled that Sam had lately been working on the wiring installation in this part of the house.

Cautiously, I tiptoed around to the far side of the room. As my eyes slowly adjusted themselves to the gloom, I saw that one of the chairs was occupied by a diminutive figure. I edged closer, until I was able to discern its features. To my utter bewilderment, I recognised before me, not the acrobatic demon of my nightmares, but an old lady. It was the same old lady who was the customary daytime occupant of that chair. As usual, she was fast asleep.

I could only draw the conclusion that Harold had neglected to awaken her when he had made his final tour of inspection the previous evening. I hesitated, unsure what to do for the best. As I did so, I noticed that the sobbing noise continued uninterrupted, and it slowly dawned upon me that it was not coming from the old lady. I was about to turn around again when the old lady opened her eyes.

I must have presented a grotesque figure. I was unshaven, my moustache was doubtless awry, and I was clad only in my flapping nightshirt and a pair of carpet slippers. But if the old lady was alarmed, she gave no indication of it. She gazed at me through calm, ancient eyes, eyes set in a small face that in the half-light appeared as soft as a child's. And then she spoke.

'Your shadow is weeping, Victor,' she said. 'Take heed now, and do what you have to do.'

For a long moment she gazed at me. Then the lines of tiredness and age stole back across her face, and in another moment she had closed her eyes and was sleeping again.

I became aware then that the sobbing had ceased, leaving behind it a heavy silence that seemed almost like a physical presence. Warily, I reached for my revolver, then realised, my heart sinking, that I had left it under my pillow. Every nerve tingling, I turned slowly around. There, at the centre of the room, silhouetted in a shaft of moonlight, stood a thin, dark, unsteady shape. It peered at me through luminous eyes. At long last I was face to face with my shadow.

Clenching my fists, I stepped forward cautiously, and as I did so, the shadowy form stepped forward also. Step by step we approached each other, until at last I had it in full view.

At first, I was quite unable to believe what I saw. The shadow was not the tall, threatening form of my nightmares. Before me stood a hunched, skinny, pathetic figure, clad in a ragged, ill-fitting jerkin and threadbare hose that gaped open at the knees. Straggling hair hung limply across its face, and its grimy cheeks were streaked with tears. It appeared very young, no more than thirteen or fourteen years of age, and seemed quite defenceless. Was this weeping child the creature that had held me in such terror for so many months? Such was my relief that I was forced to restrain myself from laughing aloud.

At that moment, the creature took another hesitant step towards me, caught its foot in one of Sam's loose floorboards, stumbled and fell headlong to the floor. It made a feeble attempt to stand, but lacked even the strength required to do that. Then it gave a loud sniff and began to cry again. For once, I was at a complete loss. Eventually I concluded that my only viable course of action was to place the creature under lock and key for the remainder of the night, and to consider the matter further in the morning.

The Special Task

As the bells started chiming for the end of the afternoon work period, Alice disconnected the administrative engine on her desk, carefully locked her cabinet, slipped her few belongings into her small satchel, and then headed straight for the door. Alice had been trained to carry out her duties with cheerfulness and efficiency, but her dedication did not extend beyond the end of her allotted hours. Her duties in King Matt's administrative area were quite interesting, her colleagues were pleasant enough, but tonight was the night of her exercise class, and she did not feel inclined to linger.

The last of the daylight was starting to fade as she followed her usual route through the service gate at the rear of the palace and walked briskly down Beggars' Row. She felt sorry for the beggars and sometimes threw them a small coin, but today her mind was on other things.

That morning, one of her colleagues had been complaining to the overseer about the new automatic coffee engine. Overhearing, Alice had been able to suggest an alternative form of engine, and thoughts of coffee had led on to thoughts of her previous master, the eccentric magician Leonardo Pegasus. It had been some months since she had last seen him, and she realised that by now he would probably have left the city for good. She was sorry that she had not had the chance to say goodbye to him properly, for Alice believed in doing things properly, and despite the magician's odd ways, she realised that she had been quite fond of him. But she had seen little of him since leaving his employment, and the few times they had spoken, he had really behaved very strangely. It seemed somehow as if he wanted something from her, but, each time they met, she found him harder to understand, until finally she had come to dread his wild words and uncontrolled gestures. Perplexed, she shook her head.

The evening traffic had already begun to thin out, so that Alice was able to cross straight over the ring road without having to wait. Hurrying on past the coffee stall in the North Way, she was reminded of the night of the celebration. Master Pegasus had accosted her at the stall and had then followed her across the city, swaying erratically and mumbling incoherently to himself. She shivered at the memory. What had been happening to him? She wished that things could have worked out differently, but had no idea what she might have done to help him.

Alice continued her journey along the shabby sprawl of the North Way. She hated the city, hated its grime and its squalor and its uncaring people, and she found herself wishing, as she wished every day, that she had not been sent here. She pictured the island of her birth, with its sloping grasslands and rugged shores and vast echoing skies, and, poised at its silent heart, the sacred place that her people had tended for as long as anyone could remember. She pictured the calm, gentle folk of the island, her two sisters, her mother and father, and the quiet, serious man she had hoped one day to marry.

The island was situated in a grey stretch of water in a distant northern province of the kingdom, far away from the city. Life for the people there was hard, yet they bore it with strength and grace and fortitude.

As a child, Alice had been taught the history of her people, and she had learned that these qualities had been nurtured and developed over countless generations through the practice of certain intricate patterns of exercise and incantation, patterns that had been scrupulously followed through times of strife and times of peace alike. As she grew up, Alice in her turn had been taught the observances. Like many others, she had at first per- formed them haltingly and unsteadily, but in time she had grown in confidence, and they had slowly become the unshake- able foundation of her being. Among her people were wise ones who believed that the observances had been ordained by the Great Being at the very beginning of time itself, but Alice, along with the majority of the Islanders, simply followed them as she was bid, without concerning herself over such profound matters.

Sadly, the island was a small one, and its resources were suf- ficient to sustain only a limited number of people. Not every- one who was born there was permitted to stay. And, on the eve of her seventeenth birthday, Alice had been summoned before the council of wise ones. There she had been told, kindly but firmly, that there was a special task that the wise ones required her to carry out in the capital city of the kingdom, and that she must travel there at once, find lodgings, and secure employment for herself until further instructions could be sent to her.

'I am to live among the Wounded Ones?' she had asked, with dread.

'You are to live among the Wounded Ones,' the wise ones had agreed.

When she had asked more questions about the nature of her task, the wise ones had merely counselled patience, telling her that everything would become clear in due time. And with that, Alice had had to be content.

The bleak shuttered shopfronts of the North Way brought Alice back to the miseries of city life. In the early days of her posting, alone in her small room, the only thing that gave her the fortitude to endure her isolation had been the pattern of exercise that she had been taught when she was a little girl, and in which she now started to find fresh comfort. As soon as she eased herself into her sequence, the scents and sounds of her island home would begin to permeate slowly through her being, restoring to her all of that strength and grace and fortitude that she now needed more than ever. Later, when she succeeded in finding employment, she had fallen into the habit of working through her pattern during the midday rest period. More recently, she had joined an exercise class near her lodgings in the Northern Estates, at first just for one evening a week. But lately she had found that she wanted to attend even more often.

A scrap of memory drifted into her consciousness. A few months ago, during the rest period, she had been working her midday pattern as usual when Master Pegasus had entered the room unexpectedly. For a while, he had stood by the door watching her. He had not spoken, but she had noticed a strange look come over his face, a look rather like hunger, and also rather like fear. He had not subsequently referred to the incident – which, come to think of it, was rather odd in itself – and Alice now found herself wondering whether with some hidden faculty he had detected something in her private ritual, perhaps something that he needed, something that would help to heal the rift in his wounded soul. Sadly, she realised that it was probably too late.

His nostrils twitch. It is that special scent again, that intoxicating cocktail of sea and grass and wind and clover, encircled by a slow mantle of calm, that magical scent that excites him so much more than the stink of sweat or the tang of fear.

And this time he knows that the others will follow him. He is the leader now, and when he catches a scent, first Fang and then Gash will pick it up, then the rest of the pack will follow them. He casts his gaze around the circle of expectant faces, nods almost imperceptibly.

Within moments they are on the move, his lieutenants at the wings, the others fanned out between them. Independent of the rest of the pack, he slips silently ahead. This quarry is for him alone.

Alice turned down the side street that led to her usual short cut through the Undertown. When she had first told her colleagues that her daily journey took her through the area, they had reacted with surprise or shock, so lately she had given up mentioning it to them. But for Alice, the Undertown held no terrors. She felt sorry for the wretched creatures who roamed and scavenged there, and she sometimes wondered what had happened to bring them to such a sad state, but none of them had ever approached or threatened her. So when she rounded a corner and found herself face to face with a group of sharp-faced boys in ragged clothes, she thought little of it. Following her natural inclination, she smiled at them and kept walking, expecting them to stand aside. But this time they did not stand aside. Regarding her silently, they held their ground. Still unconcerned, Alice stepped lightly into the gutter, walked around them and continued on her way. A moment later, she realised, her heart sinking, that they had turned to follow her.

She started to remember some of the alarming stories with which her colleagues had tried to scare her. She began to walk faster and impulsively took a side turning down an unfamiliar lane, hoping to shake them off. But the soft footsteps continued to close on her. It was nearly dark now. She could not recognise the street she was in. With a growing sense of panic, it dawned on her that she was lost. Heart thumping, she darted down an alley, dodged around a pile of refuse, then found herself confronted with a high brick wall. With growing horror, Alice realised that she was trapped in a dead end.

She turned around slowly. Three gaunt, barefooted figures faced her, blocking the way, cutting off her escape. Further away, she could make out the dim shapes of others, dotted around the mouth of the alley, watching and waiting. Then the boy in the centre, the one she guessed to be the leader, stepped towards her, abruptly dominating the frame of her vision. He was lean and ragged, with a tangled mop of dirty red hair and a sharp, restless, freckled face that displayed an unpredictable succession of emotions. His clothes, or what remained of them, were filthy and torn, exposing a knee, a shoulder, a bony chest. Around his throat hung a necklace of bones. They looked like the bones of a small animal. Shreds of decaying flesh were still clinging to some of them.

Abruptly, as if in response to an unseen signal, his two companions moved swiftly forward, pinioning Alice by the arms, while the rest of the gang kept their distance, seemingly aware that this quarry was not for them. The red-haired boy took another soft step towards her. His mouth hung slightly open, exposing a jagged line of discoloured teeth, releasing a dribble of saliva. Warring emotions were chasing each other like storm clouds across his face, and his eyes were darting wildly here and there. Abruptly a scrawny arm snaked forward, the hand closing vicelike around her throat, shoving her back roughly against the wall. Averting her eyes, she could feel the pressure of his body against her, his breath hot on her face, his stench saturating her nostrils. Her heart pounded furiously against her ribcage. She tried to scream but produced only a choking gasp. The grip tightened around her neck. And then, struggling wildly, she managed to drag one hand free, raking at his cheek with her nails. She heard a muttered exclamation, felt the grip slacken. Imploringly, she looked up at him.

His face was streaked with blood now, along with the dirt and the spittle, but suddenly his eyes were still and wide, staring fixedly into hers. And in those eyes Alice was astonished to recognise something that she had never expected to see in this horrible city, something that she recognised, dimly but unmistakably, from the land of her birth.

And at the same moment he recognises something in her eyes. They are wide, blue eyes. There is fear in those eyes, and there is panic, but behind the fear and the panic there is something else, something that

terrifies him, and yet at the same time something from which he is pow-
erless to shield himself. For behind the eyes, just beyond the reach of his
arm, lies an impossible boundless ocean of everlasting calm.

And then, for an instant, his point of view shifts, and it seems that
he can make out the whole scene – the city, the alleyway, the boys, the
girl – from high in the air, as if through the eye of a kestrel.

His taut body began to relax. Mesmerised, he released his
hold on her throat, watched warily as she took a long ragged
gulp of breath, cautiously flexing her bruised neck, looking up
at him like a wounded animal. And slowly he began to understand what he had done. Confused, flustered, his heart pounding now in his throat, he stepped backwards unsteadily, away
from the girl. The others looked at him in bewilderment. When
he spoke, he could hardly find his voice.

'Not this one,' he gasped finally. 'Not now. Leave her.'

And then his features dissolved into anguish and with a cry
of pain he spun around and was gone. A moment later, the
others, leaderless now, turned tail and followed him.

Alice crumpled against the wall, her neck throbbing, her
breath coming in harsh, painful gasps, tears of relief streaking
her face. She stared after the boy in wonder. At last, Alice had
begun to understand the nature of her special task.

From the Journal of Victor Lazarus

Same night (continued)

My orderly room has a secure lock on the door, so I judged that
it would be safe to confine my prisoner there for the night. I
kneeled down to lift the small, inert body, and made the discovery that it was almost weightless. I carried it downstairs in
my arms, laid it carefully on my camp bed (having prudently
removed the revolver from its place under the pillow), and

paused to look down again at the small huddled form. Suddenly I was overcome by a sensation that I failed at first to recognise. I might perhaps have expected to be seized by anger or by righteous indignation, but it was neither of these things. After a moment it dawned upon me that I had permitted myself to succumb to something akin to compassion for my captive! I administered a stern rebuke to myself, together with a sharp reminder that this was a mischief-maker who needed to be kept under restraint and dealt with in the most severe fashion. I double-locked the door, then kneeled down to peer through the keyhole. The small figure lay motionless, and the sound of faint snoring was discernible. With a whispered 'Goodnight', I stole away, still perplexed at my own behaviour.

I was obliged to spend the remainder of the night in one of the armchairs in the room of fossils. To my further bewilderment, upon arriving there I discovered that the old lady was nowhere to be seen. Another unsettling event in a most unsettling night!

Five:
THE EYE OF THE KESTREL

So now you have seen me in my wretchedness, and at last you are moved to pity, and you lift me in your arms and you carry me like a child to a place of safety, and there you lay me on a soft bed, and at last I sleep. And as I sleep, I dream.

I dream of the boy, abandoning himself to the lure of the Undertown. For a time, with the misdirected energy of youth, he has run and hunted and killed with the savage things that live there, ravaging his body night after night, assaulting his mind, bludgeoning his spirit into oblivion. And once in a while, I am forced to admit, I cannot resist the call to run with him. But now, although he does not yet fully understand this, he has begun to know what it is that he seeks, has begun to sense that the time has come for him to move onwards towards it.

I dream of the magician, striding outward through the gates of the city, carrying nothing, owning nothing but the clothes he wears. He has been hunter, and he has been hunted, and finally he has been cheated of everything by the woman Nina, and yet he strides out with a lively step. For the city was his prison and the palace was his shackle, and it is only with the casting off of these things that he too can start to seek that which his being truly needs.

And I dream of the woman, setting out across the kingdom with the thing that she has stolen, the thing with which she believes she can make her fortune. And for a moment I am sad, for I know that the thing that she has stolen is too terrible for her to comprehend, too deadly for her to wield, too potent for her avaricious spirit to encompass. But a moment later I am glad again, because I know that there will be no easy way for her to learn the dangers of the path down which she travels.

But mostly I dream of growing and I dream of renewal and I dream of hope. I am glad, Victor, I am glad that you have found me and I am glad that you have cared for me. For now that I sleep in your bed, you and I can begin our real work, the work that I have waited for so long to start. I shall repay your kindness, Victor. You have shown me great tenderness, and now I shall be your friend. Now, you and I can begin to know each other.

On the Run

Once he had started to run, he didn't want to stop. Behind him he could hear the fading cries of his companions, the angry shouts and heavy boots of the militiamen, the occasional pistol shot. His pounding feet carried him through the lanes and alleys of the Undertown and onto the busy thoroughfare of the North Way, where he pushed his away between knots of startled bystanders, ignored the curses of shopkeepers, dodged out of the way of waggons and carriages.

When he reached the ruined gatehouse and the old city walls, he allowed himself to slow his pace, picking his way through the featureless sprawl of the North Estates, arriving at last on the south bank of the river, where he found a dry place to sleep among the tottering piles of the pier where the ferry docked. He had no money for the ferry, and the river was too wide and too swift for him to swim, so early the next day he made his perilous crossing clinging to one of the heavy rope fenders at the side of the boat, up to his chest in freezing, muddy water.

By midday, he had found his way to the northern edge of the city, where for the first time he could make out the silhouettes of distant hills. For a while he followed the Royal Highway, but he soon became exhausted by its hard, unforgiving surface and by the huge threatening power-driven vehicles with their deafening noise and choking clouds of soot. So, as soon as he was able, he found a side turning and vanished into the tangled network of byways that spanned the countryside and that he knew would lead him to his goal.

Later that day it rained, and he was forced to seek shelter in a remote abandoned house, almost hidden within an overgrown garden. In one empty room, a cracked mirror was still fastened to the wall. He examined his reflection, the reflection of the wretched creature he had somehow allowed himself to become. He was filthy, his feet were bare, and the last ragged shreds of clothing barely covered his body. His hair was long and matted, and his cheek was scarred by the bloody slashes from the girl's fingernails. One eye had swollen up and closed, and one shoulder seemed to hang lower than the other, so that his body had developed an irregular slouch. His gaze settled on the macabre necklace of bones that scraped against his chest. Shuddering, he tore it from his throat and hurled it at the wall, where it burst apart and scattered with a dry, mocking rattle.

That night, he slept in a small room at the top of the house, and he dreamed that a militiaman was stalking him from room to room with a revolver. The next day, hot with shame, he looked again at his reflection in the mirror and knew that he could not allow himself to be seen in daylight. So he remained in the house until nightfall, and then he stole out again into the slumbering countryside.

From then on he slept by day, in ruins or in hedgerows or in woods, and he moved by night. Hunger gnawed at him constantly, and he was forced to live on whatever food he could steal from field or from farmyard. Occasionally he met other nocturnal travellers on the road. Most would cross quickly to the other side, and one old woman even muttered what sounded like a curse, warding him off with a sinister gesture. One night a group of village lads found him skulking behind a tavern, and they chased him away with stones and knives as well as curses.

A few days later, at a village on the fringes of the hill country, he was driven by cold and hunger and desperation to seek shelter in a byre, where a patient cow allowed him to suck the comforting stream of thick, sweet milk from her teat. Content and replete, he threw himself onto a prickly pile of straw where he promptly fell asleep.

He was awoken by a metallic clattering noise. Cautiously, he opened his eyes. By a shaft of evening light slanting through the half-open doors, he could make out the homely figure of a young girl, bearing a yoke of milking pails and a three-legged stool. Half-buried in the straw, he watched as she went about her business, working her way methodically along the row of cattle, talking soothing nonsense words to them, crooning snatches of song. Cautiously, Rusty pulled himself into a sitting position. Marvelling at the girl's gentle absorption in her task, he wondered bleakly whether he could ever be part of the ordinary world again. He would have given anything to change places with the girl. He found himself choking back a sob.

At this unexpected noise, the girl turned around from her work. There was no hope of concealment. She saw him at once. Her mouth opened wide in a shriek of terror, and she ran from the shed, buckets clattering and splashing behind her, the cattle lowing in bewilderment. Rusty staggered to the door, where he halted unsteadily, momentarily dazzled by the red disc of the setting sun.

'It's all right,' he called feebly after her. 'I was just—'

But the girl must have sounded a general alarm, for the next moment burly figures were lurching towards him from all corners of the yard, shouting and brandishing billhooks and pitchforks. Frantically, he looked around him, seeking an unguarded exit, found one, and ran.

The lane from the farmyard led him out into the main street of the village, and as he raced towards open country with the farmer's men in pursuit, curious heads began to emerge from doors and windows. Before he had reached the end of the street, the whole village was at his heels.

But at least he knew how to run. That was one thing he had learned from the Wolf Boys. He raced ahead of the mob, vaulted over a gate into a field, dodged among a flock of startled sheep, dived through a hedge, then, spotting a sheltering wood ahead of him, turned abruptly uphill along a steep, narrow track, his bare feet fast and sure on the rocky surface. His heart was pounding furiously, and his breath sawed at his chest in jagged strokes, but he knew that he was outdistancing his pursuers. By the time he reached the safety of the wood, they were far behind him. He threaded his way between the trees, swung himself up into the branches of a tall oak, and watched with relief as the chase was abandoned and, one by one, the villagers returned to their homes. It was getting colder now, and the light had almost gone. Exhausted, he propped himself in the fork of a branch, drew his rags tightly around his body and promptly fell asleep again.

When he awoke, night had fallen. As he struggled into consciousness, his nostrils caught an unfamiliar smell, a sweet, sticky, smoky smell. He could hear men shouting and dogs barking. Quickly he hauled himself onto a higher branch and looked around him. Swaying pinpoints of light were strung out in distant procession along the track, and more were creeping around the sides of the wood. The villagers had returned in force.

He cursed himself for falling asleep. Frantically trying to ease the stiffness from his limbs, he scanned the horizon. The nearest edge of the wood, the edge furthest uphill, was not yet surrounded. That would offer him his best chance of escape. He was preparing to drop down from his branch when he heard voices from below and quickly checked himself, realising that there must already be people inside the wood. Beneath him, in the wavering circle of light cast by their lantern, he could make out two figures. One man, the lantern bearer, was restraining a large, savage-looking dog, which growled and tugged at its lead. The other was wearing priest's robes. He was holding open a large book and intoning words in an unknown tongue.

There was no time to lose. With a wild yell, the boy launched himself feet first from the branches. For an instant, two startled faces stared up at him, then his heels made contact with the shoulders of the priest, knocking him sideways against the other man and bringing the two of them heavily to the ground, entangled in a thick patch of brambles. The lantern spun away into the undergrowth, and he heard its glass shatter, caught a glimpse of the flames leaping up. Then, as he hauled himself to his feet, he saw the dog approaching him, its coat bristling, its fangs bared in a snarl. Holding his ground, he looked the dog in the eye and extended his hand. For a moment, he remembered the Wolf Boys. And then he remembered Dusty.

'Good boy. Nice dog.'

And the dog stopped growling and started to lick his hand. As it licked, he caught hold of its trailing lead, swiftly twisted it around a branch, kicked away one of the men, who was trying to make a grab for his ankle, spun around and made a dash for open country, brambles tearing at his shoulders, roots clutching at his ankles in the darkness. He could hear the men cursing and the dog howling frantically as the flames engulfed the wood.

And so he took to the hills. From the next summit, he paused to take in the sight of the blazing wood. To his relief, he could see no lantern bearers on his trail. He reckoned that the villagers would now be too busy fighting the fire to bother about one lone Wolf Boy, but nevertheless he decided to stay on the move all night.

He was limping now from his injuries, bleeding from his cuts, dragging himself on all fours when he could no longer walk, howling in pain at the moon, crawling through muddy ditches and over jagged rocks and through banks of thistles. Finally he could drag himself no further. He slumped to the ground, no longer knowing horizontal from vertical, lost his grip on the earth itself, rolled and skidded down a bank, bruised his ribs on rocks, struck his head a blinding, explosive blow. And then he knew no more.

From the Journal of Victor Lazarus

(Undated)

I returned at first light to my orderly room. Beneath the folds of the blanket I could make out the form of the creature. It lay motionless, but from the pattern of its breathing it was plain to me that it was awake. As I watched, the blanket twitched aside and a beady eye regarded me through an unruly tangle of hair. Beneath the covers, a thin, hoarse voice uttered a few faint syllables. I could not at first understand what it was trying to say, but after several repetitions reinforced by gestures it finally became apparent to me that the creature was demanding to be fed! Too astonished to argue, I made my way to the yard at the rear of the building, where Mrs Proudfoot had established a temporary kitchen in an old covered waggon. The hour was still early, and the good lady herself not yet in attendance, so I ignited my battered camping stove and warmed up a pan of milk, which I then poured into a bowl, and added some pieces of white bread and a little cinnamon and sugar. Before there was time for me to reflect upon the strangeness of my behaviour, I was on my way back to the orderly room, carrying the bowl in front of me.

As I rounded the last corner, I was horrified to see that I had left the door of the room standing wide open. I dashed inside, oblivious to the hot milk slopping down the front of my nightshirt. The bed was empty.

I looked wildly around until my attention was caught by a hesitant cough emanating from the direction of the window. The creature was sitting up on the sill, dangling its skinny legs.

It jumped down and skipped towards me, wrinkling its nostrils at the smell of the food.

'Hello, Victor,' (said the creature). 'My name is Lee.'

And Lee seized the bowl and started to lap greedily at the milk.

The Magician on the Road

Leonardo Pegasus had not ventured beyond the walls of the city for many years, and during his first few days of freedom, having no particular destination in mind, he made his way about more or less at random. He was more than content simply to enjoy the new sounds and sensations, the countryside and the hills and the rivers, the different smell of the air, the welcoming road wide open before him. Sometimes he walked, and sometimes he accepted the offer of a ride on a cart or waggon.

From time to time he fell in with other travellers. Many of these were wandering folk engaged in their various itinerant trades, but some, like himself, were people dispossessed, people in search of a new beginning. Sometimes he found a companion for a day or two, someone to share his journey by day and his lodgings by night. He discovered that, away from the city, board and lodgings were cheap, and the coins in his purse would easily sustain him until he could find a suitable position for himself.

When the weather became warmer, he joined a band of wanderers living in the open, roaming the lanes together, cooking and telling stories around the communal fire. Some of the stories he heard recounted the ancient legends of the land, and some of the stories related real events in the lives of the tellers. Sometimes he found it hard to know where the one ended and the other began.

One night, it occurred to Leonardo that there might be some scope in this new occupation for the deployment of his professional skill in the construction of futures. He suggested to his companions that, as an alternative to relating events of the past, it might make an interesting experiment if they were to attempt to devise some stories concerning things yet to come. This idea aroused considerable enthusiasm in the camp. Before long, the others found that, under Leonardo's guidance, they could easily bring to light their most secret dreams and weave fantastic yarns concerning the various futures that might lie in store for them.

Eventually, of course, it was Leonardo's turn.

'Tell us of your future, Leo,' clamoured his companions.

Leonardo stared into the flames for a long while.

'I am walking along a dusty road,' he began. 'It is noon. I am looking for something. I am not sure yet what it is.'

He was silent again. The others waited patiently.

'At the side of the road grows a tall hedge,' he continued eventually. 'A tall, overgrown hedge of thorn bushes. I come to a place in the hedge where I find what must once have been an entrance. It is a pair of tall, iron gates, thick with rust, almost buried among the thorns. The gates are chained and barred and padlocked. I cannot open them.'

Suddenly he slumped back, exhausted.

'Can you see anything between the bars?' queried a helpful voice.

'Be patient,' said the magician. 'Let me get my breath, then I'll have another look.' And he stared into the flames again.

Leonardo peered through a chink in the gates. At first, everything seemed obscure, but, as his eyes adjusted to the gloom, he realised that he was staring, not into darkness, but into a uniform, featureless grey void. Then, at the periphery of his vision, something began to move. Curling scraps of blackness started to dance in the corners of the void, converged on each other, separated again, then began to coalesce into a tentative image. Abruptly, the image crystallised, leaped out towards him, seemed to strike him a physical blow to the abdomen. It was the image of a girl, a pale, thin, fair-haired girl, a girl clad from head to toe in black, a girl dancing weightless in the void.

Leonardo sighed. He thought briefly of the real girl, remote and insulated in her grey city workplace, no more attainable to him now than the dream girl who danced in the void before him. Alice. He tried to summon an image of her face, but found that the pale hair framed only a blank oval.

'What is inside the gates?' His companions broke in upon his stream of thought.

'Nothing is inside. I can't go on at the moment.' Leonardo rose unsteadily to his feet and stalked off into the gloom. And at that stage, the party broke up for the night.

But for the next few days, wherever he looked, the apparition seemed to dance before Leonardo's eyes, mocking him, haunting him, possessing him, the whirling loops of choreography encircling him, sketching out tangled patterns of interlocking lines that ensnared him, enmeshed him, confounded him. Whichever way he turned, he found his way barred by the creature, lithe, pale, terrifying. And even when he awoke from his dreams, the laughter seemed still to echo around him.

From the Journal of Victor Lazarus

Thursday 15th October

With a massive effort of will, I have finally forced myself to direct my attention back towards the task in hand. The obsession by which I have been enslaved for so many weeks has at last begun to slacken its grip, and only now have I begun to comprehend how appallingly I have been neglecting my duties. While I have been squandering my time in pursuit of demons and shadows, Sam and Harold have been left to shoulder the overwhelming burden of the task. Three months from today, the owner of the house is due to return, and during those months, a very great deal remains to be accomplished. I have therefore resolved to make a fresh start. This morning, I have cleared the surface of my desk, sorted through my mail, and reviewed my calendar. I have come to the conclusion that a full inspection of the premises is long overdue.

Same day, later

To my overwhelming relief, much progress has been made since the time of my previous inspection. The bulk of the electrical and building work has been completed, and the interior decoration is mostly in good order. In the lower part of the house, the floorboards have been replaced, and in some places they have already been rubbed down and polished. The timbers that were charred in the fire have been stripped from the kitchen, the ruined plaster on the walls has been renewed, and the plumbers are due to start work shortly. Mrs Proudfoot has raised an order for some new and up-to-date kitchen equipment, a subject on which she apparently has strong views. The lady has equally strong views on the selection of tiles and wallpaper, and I fear that I have no option but to accede to her demands.

The garden at the front of the house is looking magnificent. The lawn has been mown in precise parallel stripes, the shrubs are neatly trimmed, and the railings have been given a fresh coat of paint. The garden at the rear remains in need of some major work, but I suspect that that task will not now be accomplished until the spring. Harold continues to issue tickets to a steady stream of visitors, and has engaged some additional staff to conduct guided tours and to look after the cloakroom.

On the subject of my captive, Lee, I remain in somewhat of a quandary. I find myself for some reason reluctant to disclose to my colleagues the bizarre events that took place on that night of the full moon. Only the old lady shares my secret, and her slumbers fortunately continue uninterrupted.

In the little turret room at the top of the house, I have arranged a camp bed and a table and chair for the prisoner, and although the door has a lock, I find that I continually forget to fasten it. However, Lee has shown no inclination to run away. I take food up to the turret at regular intervals, but otherwise I have been too much occupied to give the matter any further thought. Work is progressing at a furious pace, and as I patrol the premises I continually detect a sense of excitement, urgency and momentum that has not previously been in evidence.

The Keeper of the Ground

It was very cold and very damp when the boy awoke. He was lying curled on his side on a surface of smooth, bare stone. Carefully he eased himself into a sitting position, pulled his soaking rags more tightly around him, and massaged his aching limbs to restore the circulation. Then he looked around. The sky was just beginning to lighten, but he could make out nothing of the landscape. He waited, allowing his eyes to adjust. Slowly, in the grey light of dawn, he could begin to discern his surroundings. And there, directly ahead of him, wreathed in mist, loomed a tall, dark form.

Silently he sprang to his feet. Implacably, the figure barred his way. Swiftly he spun around, only to discover another figure behind him, tall, grim and motionless. And now he could make out more, to left and to right, silently waiting. Some were almost close enough for him to reach out and touch, others faintly discernible in the distance. He was surrounded, with no hope of escape. His pulse raced and his breath caught in his throat.

'What do you want?' he managed to gasp.

There was no reply. Frozen to the spot, he waited for the adversary to make a move. For what seemed like several minutes, nothing happened. Then a gap appeared in the clouds, a tentative shaft of sunlight pierced the gloom. The mist shifted a little, and, with a flood of relief, he could see that he was surrounded, not by human foes, but by a haphazard group of tall, silent carved forms. Whether they were carved from wood or from stone or from some other substance, he could not for the moment tell. Some were shaped with geometric precision, others were of more irregular outline. Some were smooth and blank-faced, others embellished with intricate patterns, but in the dim light, they had for a few moments taken on the appearance of human figures. He allowed a long, slow breath to escape his lungs.

The patch of ground on which the stones were arrayed was of smooth tessellated stone slabs, and with the beginnings of daylight he could see that it was engraved with a labyrinthine array of interlocking radial lines and concentric circles. Beneath his feet, apparently at the centre of the configuration, lay a six-sided slab that was larger than the others and slightly raised, and it was on this that he must have spent the night. In the distance, the mist still held sway and he could discern nothing.

With the shaft of sunlight had come a little more warmth. Beginning to relax, he yawned and stretched himself, started wondering where to look for food, which way to go next. The tension in his body ebbed away and with it the terrors of pursuit, so that when he felt the light touch of a hand on his shoulder it came not as a shock but a welcome surprise.

Turning, he found himself face to face with an old woman, tall and rather vague-looking. She was wearing a long robe that gave her a somewhat monastic appearance. Her long, grey plaits were wound behind her head in a loose bun, from which tendrils of hair were doing their best to escape. She gave him a long, curious look through her wire-rimmed spectacles.

'Hello,' she said finally. 'You managed to find us, then.'

The accent of her voice was soft, familiar, reassuring, and her tone was kindly. The boy could only nod dumbly.

'Well, you're very welcome here. You're not the first, and I dare say you won't be the last. No, no, don't try to talk just now. You don't have to tell me who you are, or what you've done, or anything else for that matter. I'm sure it will come out in good time anyway, it usually does. And I dare say too that you'll need a bit of time to sort yourself out – most of our guests do. We can probably find you a room, so you can stay as long as you want to, anyway. Oh, and by the way, they call me the Keeper of the Ground. That's my official title, I suppose. Sounds rather grand, doesn't it?'

It was a long, long time since anyone had spoken any word of kindness to Rusty. For a moment he was choked with tears and could not find his voice. When he finally spoke, he could manage just three words.

'Please help me.' Despite the warmth, he was shivering uncontrollably.

'Come along inside, then.'

She slipped her arm around his shoulders, enfolding him in her robe, guiding him between the tall shapes, away from the paved ground onto short, springy turf, and turning him around to face the landscape beyond. Now he could see the soft green hills, the gently winding path, the big welcoming house, the short flight of stone steps leading up to the double doors. And then the doors swung quietly open and she led him inside.

From the Journal of Victor Lazarus

Monday 26th October

I was making my way up to the turret this morning, carrying the usual bowl of bread and milk, when I was surprised to hear what sounded like music. As I mounted the stairs from the kitchen, my ears caught first of all a quick, sibilant rhythm, reminiscent of a snare drum played with brushes, in the style of a dance orchestra. As I drew nearer, I became aware in addition of a sinuous melody that wove in and out of the rhythmic pattern in a fashion that brought to mind a snake zigzagging through a thicket of bamboo. Rounding the corner, I was astonished to discover Lee, broom in hand, sweeping the floor in rhythmic strokes and humming a cheerful refrain. I stood silent and motionless, keeping my distance, watching in fascination. Rest and regular meals had certainly brought their measure of benefit for my captive. Lee had put on a little weight and seemed to be standing taller than before, and was skipping nimbly about, carrying out the task with confidence and grace. As I watched, an unfamiliar sensation stole over me, a sensation that I was unable immediately to identify. After a moment, however, I recognised it suddenly as the faint stirring of desire! Needless to say, I was considerably startled and embarrassed by this discovery, with the result that I was abruptly seized by a violent fit of sneezing. Alerted at last to my presence, my young captive turned around to face me. As I watched, a brief, secretive smile illuminated Lee's face. I quickly deposited the milk and hurried away in confusion.

Yes, you have cared well for me, Victor. It is wonderful what can be achieved with a little food, a little rest, a little kindness. I understand now that I have brought you much grief and much fear, but you have repaid the grief and the fear with nothing but love, and, by and by, it has dawned on me that I need to repay that love, I need to put back something into this house, this house that once I strove so hard and so foolishly to destroy. So I have found a broom and I have started to sweep.

The work exhausted me at first, and I could manage little more than the few bare boards of my own small room. But at length I ventured out into the corridors of the house, and as the days went by I found that, bit by by bit, I could do more. I enjoyed the work and I enjoyed the exertion, and now my strength is gradually returning to me, my limbs growing rounder, my outline sleeker, my posture more upright. And today, as I did my sweeping, I started to make my music again. So I did not hear your approach, and I did not run away and hide in my bed as once I might have done.

But as I swept, I knew by the smell of the food that you were

standing and watching. For a long moment you did not announce your-
self, but I knew that you were watching, and I knew also that you took
delight in what you saw. I want to make up for the harm I have done
you, Victor. I want to make you happy.

The Magician Dreams Again

Eventually, the summer came to an end, and Leonardo decided
temporarily to abandon the outdoor life for the comfort of a
warm bed. Bidding farewell to his new friends, he struck out
across country until he chanced upon one of the royal highways
that formed a rapidly growing network linking together many
of the principal towns of the kingdom. This led him before long
to a large, busy roadhouse, where for several days he found himself marooned by bad weather. The company here was not particularly congenial, so, for the first time in many weeks, he
found himself alone with his thoughts.

Seated at his solitary table, he stared through the window at
the grey sheets of rain. It occurred to him that he had been
enjoying his life lately, and had consequently had little time for
reflection, but now that he was alone there was suddenly little
else for him to do but reflect. He pondered over the period of
time he had spent with the Wanderers, over the stories around
the campfire, over his notion of inventing stories about the
future, over his failure to surmount the obstacles he had
encountered in his own story.

His mind drifted back to that awful night when his turn had
come to tell a story, when he had been unable to imagine any
sort of future for himself, when he had come up with nothing
but the terrifying images of the rusting gates, about which he
had spoken to his companions, and the demonic figure of Alice,
about which he had remained silent. Since that night, he had
avoided staring into fires. But now he decided that it was time
to try again. Across the room there was an unoccupied seat at
the fireside. Quickly, Leonardo repositioned himself. Taking a

draught of ale, he settled deeply into the chair, made himself comfortable, gazed reflectively into the flames. And slowly, he could feel his imagination beginning to work . . .

He was staring at the gates again, but this time they were not chained. This time, one of the gates hung askew on a single hinge, and between the gates was a gap just wide enough to admit a man. Before he knew what he was doing, he had squeezed through the gap. He was standing on a roughly paved surface. On either side of him grew tall shrubs and plants. And then, at the top of a sloping patch of ground, he saw the house.

It was a tall, imposing house, a house of many windows. The garden around it was overgrown, obscuring the lower storeys and choking the drainpipes and the gutters, but up above he could make out turrets and gables and chimney pots and gargoyles, all pointing jaggedly skywards. In front of him lay a path. Carefully he picked his way between the huge thistles that forced their way through the grey flags, until he arrived at a steeper flight of cracked steps that led him between crumbling pillars to the front porch. And now he found before him a pair of entrance doors, from which the paint had peeled away to reveal grey weathered oak. Uncertain of his next move, he waited.

Then something broke the silence, a faint sound coming from inside the house. Yes, inside the house something was moving. And now, at the touch of a finger, the doors swung open.

Without hesitation, the magician stepped inside. He found himself in a high-ceilinged entrance hall. Above him hung the ruins of a vast chandelier, thick with dust and cobwebs. To his right stood a heavy mahogany staircase that drew the eye upwards into the half-light of the upper storeys. Before him stood another pair of double doors, this time with a glazed panel set into each. He peered through the tarnished glass, and caught a glimpse of a long, dusty, panelled corridor from which opened many rooms. At the touch of a finger, the doors swung open.

Softly he tiptoed from room to room. Throwing open each door, he discovered chambers containing locked cabinets, chambers containing packages neatly wrapped and stacked, and chambers containing objects strewn around with careless abandon. He ascended to the upper storeys, only to find other rooms that seemed to have been used purely for storage, rooms where tottering piles of books and albums and documents covered the floors and towered higher than a man could reach. Everything was covered in thick layers of dust. Finally he reached the very top of the house, climbing a narrow spiral stair that led to a low doorway. The door was stiff, and it required some effort to force it open. The magician found himself standing in a tiny six-sided room.

The room appeared completely empty, but he felt in some way that he was not quite alone. Leonardo could not decide whether or not the other presence was friendly. Shivering, he quickly descended again to the main part of the house.

Back in the entrance hall, the magician considered his position. If this house truly represented his future, it would clearly require considerable attention before he could come to live in it. He regretted now that, despite his extensive learning and his wide experience in the magical arts, he had never made any serious attempt to construct a proper future for himself. In the protected atmosphere of the palace, it had not seemed necessary, but now he found himself wishing that he had thought of it sooner. Though, without his empathy engines and his model stages and his miniature figures, he suspected that he would find the difficulties insurmountable.

Suddenly it struck him that he might try to enlist some help. Perhaps he could advertise? It occurred to him that, in this dream world, anything was surely possible. Trying a few doors, he eventually managed to locate a small office, where he found a desk, relatively free of dust, and some parchment and ink. After pondering for a while, he drafted the following:

Assistance required with Restoration

My house, which is a large one, has fallen into neglect, and much work is required to render it fit for habitation. I would greatly welcome any assistance from reliable and hard-working persons. If you feel that you are suitably qualified, please apply in writing to . . .

At this point in his reverie, Leonardo became aware that his flask was empty. He realised with irritation that none of this daydreaming was going to achieve anything practical. On the other hand, it occurred to him, there might well be opportunities for remunerative employment in this neighbourhood. He decided to take some positive action. He would try what Nina might have called a sales pitch. The innkeeper would be as good a target as any for his first attempt. Mentally, he rehearsed what he would say. When he was ready, he crossed over to the bar with his flask, paid for more ale, then, when he was sure that he had the innkeeper's attention, cleared his throat and spoke his carefully prepared words.

'Do you happen to know of anyone in this neighbourhood who might require the services of an experienced magician?'

The innkeeper regarded his dishevelled-looking guest with careful politeness. Another lunatic, he supposed. Oh well, at least this one was paying for his own drink.

'No, sir,' he replied solemnly, 'not at present. But if I do hear tell of anything, I promise you that you'll be the first to know.'

Pleased with this, Leonardo returned to his table. Plans had started to form in his mind, and that night he slept well. The following day, the weather had at last started to improve, and he was able to continue on his journey.

The House of Rest

Dimly he was aware of gentle hands guiding him, of kindly voices welcoming him, of warmth and light and companionship.

Gratefully he slipped out of his filthy rags, gratefully he sank into hot fragrant water. Watching the water turn black around him, he laughed for the first time in ages. Eventually he was clean, and then they wrapped him in soft towels and guided him to a quiet place, and there he sank blissfully onto a welcome bed and slept.

For several days he did little but sleep, a deep sleep punctuated only by the occasional muffled ringing of bells. Sometimes when he awoke he would find food, and then he would eat a little, and then he would sleep again. And then one day, when he awoke, he started to feel curious.

He discovered that he was lying on his side, facing a roughly plastered wall. For a while, he stared at the wall, following the fine lines left by the plasterer's trowel, noticing how in some places they ran for long stretches in parallel, how in other places they curved and intersected and crossed over each other. After a while he turned onto his back, stared at the ceiling for an interval, then sat up and looked around him. He found that he was lying on an iron bed under four prickly grey blankets, their hems secured with regular rows of faded red stitching. The bed was positioned against one wall of a small white room. Next to the bed was a wooden upright chair, and above the chair was a high window. In the opposite wall stood a panelled oak door. It was open, and someone was standing in the doorway.

'Hello, stranger.' It was a woman's voice, brisk but not unfriendly. 'I've never known anyone sleep for so long. Are you about ready to return to the land of the living?'

'Yeah, I guess . . .'

She stepped into the room, leaving the door ajar, and seated herself at the foot of the bed. Rusty looked at her carefully. This was not the old woman who had spoken to him among the stones. This woman was younger. Not as young as he was, but probably younger than, say, his mother. She was sturdily built, her hair short and untidy, and was dressed in faded blue overalls. She was smiling.

'I'm called Helen,' she said, 'Well, probably not really, but that's the name they gave me when I came here. They've asked me to be your guide. You know, show you the ropes, help you settle in, all that stuff. If you want to stay, that is.'

'What is this place? And where's the old woman? The one who met me?'

'Hey, slow down! You must mean the Keeper. She's a pretty busy lady, but I expect you'll bump into her now and then. So, just for now, why don't you let me take care of you?'

At that moment, the peace was interrupted by the clatter of a handbell outside the room.

'Bells!' exclaimed Helen. 'This place runs on bells. Bells for getting up, bells for going to bed, bells for meals, bells for everything. They used to drive me nuts, but these days I'd feel quite lost without them.'

The sound of the bell continued, but it had gradually become quieter. Rusty guessed that the ringer must have progressed to another part of the house.

'How long have you been here?' he asked.

'Steady does it. You'll hear my story soon enough. Let's just concentrate on getting you sorted for now. That was the rising bell, by the way, so how about you getting your togs on, then we can go and find ourselves some breakfast.'

Indicating the bedside chair, she stepped tactfully outside. Rusty unfolded what turned out to be a tracksuit, faded and patched but clean and well-ironed. Under the chair were a pair of heavily darned woollen socks and a pair of battered plimsolls with fraying laces. He was unsteady on his feet, and rather out of practice at dressing himself, and it took him a little while to untangle the shoelaces, but eventually he was ready. He stepped outside into a corridor to find Helen leaning against the wall, her hands thrust into the side pockets of her overalls. From a distant part of the house he could hear the hum of conversation and the clatter of cutlery. The reassuring smell of frying bacon came drifting up towards him.

Entering the big, echoing, crowded refectory, Rusty felt

intimidated at first by the sheer number of people, by their noisy banter and their evident familiarity with one another. Helen found places for the two of them at one of the long deal tables and introduced him to a couple of her friends, a young man and woman of about Rusty's age, but, to his distress, he found himself unable to retain their names in his mind. Helen, quick to sense his discomfiture, patted his shoulder reassuringly, leaned close and whispered to him.

'It's all right, darling, we all feel a bit lost to begin with. I know I did – you should have seen me! But now I feel as if I'd been here all my life. And in a few days, so will you. Now, eat your porridge. No, don't argue. Is brown sugar all right?'

Later, they sat in two ancient armchairs in the common room, deserted during the day, comfortably surrounded by shelves of battered books, large, colourful paintings, an old upright piano, low tables bearing draughtboards and backgammon sets and other games less readily identifiable. A pair of French windows opened onto a broad flagged terrace.

'What happens here all day?' asked Rusty. 'I mean, what does everyone do?'

'Well, it really depends what state they're in when they turn up. Some of them want to make things, or grow things, or play music. Some of them want to look after animals – there's a farm, I can show you later if you want. Or there again, some of them want to talk, tell stories, that kind of thing, or maybe do exercise, go for walks in the hills. Not meaning to be rude, but I'd guess the Keeper would recommend some kind of exercise for you to start with. And maybe stories. Do you want to tell me about yourself? You haven't even told me your name yet.'

It took him a moment to remember.

'Michael,' he said finally. 'Michael Brown. Most people call me Rusty. Everyone, actually, except my mother.' He paused. A memory surfaced. 'And Granny Hopkins, of course. She must be over ninety by now. If she's still alive, that is.' He frowned.

Helen smiled encouragingly.

'You're doing fine. So how did Rusty Brown end up here?'

For a moment Rusty was nonplussed. Helen stood up and gestured towards the French windows.

'Come on. Let's take a stroll.'

He followed her outside, and they walked slowly across the terrace and then over the haphazard lawns of the unkempt garden. From time to time, through the foliage, he caught glimpses of distant vistas, the hills, a river, a lake.

'I used to have a dog,' said Rusty finally. 'His name was Dusty. I had him right from the time I was small. We went everywhere together. And then, when I grew up, he died. We were on holiday in the mountains. And then there was a lot of bad stuff. I did some terrible things.'

They had paused to rest on a lichen-covered granite bench overlooking the paved ground where the Keeper had found him. He could see now that it was set within a natural arena of gently sloping green. In the distance, a group of people bearing ropes and levers was engaged in repositioning one of the tall, sculpted stone forms on the wide geometric array of lines and curves. Wondering about the purpose of it all, he was lost in thought for several minutes. Helen did not interrupt him.

'I don't really understand what happened to me,' he continued eventually. 'But I guess I got into some pretty bad company. I suppose I liked it at first, but in the end I ran away. People chased me, but I could run faster than them.' His narrative had been gaining pace, but now it came to an abrupt halt. 'And I found myself here. I don't know how.'

'It's funny, isn't it?' said Helen. 'People always seem to find their way here. You did, and so did I. Now, are you going to tell me some more about Dusty?'

As he talked, they made their way around the grounds, Helen occasionally pointing out features of interest.

'That leads up to the farm . . .'

'If you fancy having a go at weaving, we could look in here . . .'

Friendly faces greeted him at each place, a bearded man in a fraying pullover, a middle-aged woman in a paint-stained smock, particles of clay speckling her hair. Eventually they found themselves in the main entrance hall of the house. On a side table stood a line of compact oblong packets neatly wrapped in crackly greaseproof paper.

'Sandwiches,' explained Helen. 'Some people like to take walks.'

Rusty gazed out at the sweep of hills, unfolding into the azure distance. Suddenly he felt tired.

'Soon,' he said. 'But not yet.'

A Wanderering Sorcerer

Panting slightly, Leonardo arrived at the top of the hill and paused to survey the landscape that revealed itself before him. He gave a grunt of satisfaction. The directions he had been given were good. The road led downhill, almost in a straight line, to the village huddled in the valley below. It had rained heavily during the morning, and the skirts of his robe were still damp, but his wide-brimmed hat had protected him from the worst of the weather, and his sturdy boots were standing up well to life on the road. For the first time, it occurred to him that the ceremonial garb of his brotherhood might well have had its origin as practical outdoor wear for the wandering sorcerer.

For a wandering sorcerer was what Leonardo Pegasus had become. To begin with, he had set his sights high and had tramped the kingdom seeking audience with the men and women of power in their offices and factories and fortresses. Most of them, awed by his rank, had received him with due deference, if not with cordiality. Most of them had listened patiently to what he thought of as his sales pitch, and then each of them had explained to him, politely but regretfully, that they already employed their own counsellors.

Leonardo had been permitted to meet some of these counsellors. They were mostly very young, probably only recently
graduated from the Academies, and all of them were using the
new miniature counselling engines and other, even smaller,
pieces of equipment that left Leonardo utterly perplexed. With
this apparatus, they were equipped to practise the newest, most
sophisticated, most powerful forms of magic yet devised.
Leonardo had begun sadly to realise that his own magic had
become out of date. For a while, he had entertained the notion
of teaching it to schoolchildren, but was shocked to discover that
it was considered too old-fashioned even for the kindergartens.

Sometimes, venturing into the more far-flung parts of the
kingdom, he had come across local barons and squires and
chieftains who did not employ any counsellors at all. Some of
them had not even heard of the magical arts. With these people,
Leonardo was at a loss. He had tried to explain the advantages
of creating empathy, of constructing a nested sequence of
futures, of conducting an arbitration. He was met with blank
stares and was asked to leave, not always very politely. On one
occasion he was forcibly ejected from a small castle by four
burly men-at-arms. After this incident, Leonardo had finally
concluded that his future employment prospects probably did
not after all lie with the wielders of power.

However, in some of the more isolated farms and villages, he
discovered that there was still an occasional demand for his skills.
He managed to earn a little income attending to the farmer who
suffered from bouts of melancholia, the housemaid crossed in
love, the recalcitrant cattle who would not stand in line to be
milked, the unruly stack of logs that was the despair of its owner.
From time to time, it occurred to him that none of these things
drew very much on his more sophisticated magical skills, but he
concluded that perhaps that was not so important, as long as he
could offer people a little help and earn himself a little income.
But even so, jobs of work were not plentiful, and he knew that
his funds were dwindling. Even the hospitality of simple country inns would soon be beyond his pocket.

A gust of wind whipped around the magician, tugging at his robe. He pulled his hat down firmly over his ears, extended a hand, felt the returning spots of rain. By now he had become quite used to sleeping in haystacks and barns, but a dry room would certainly be welcome tonight.

The sound of a rather out-of-tune piano interrupted the magician's train of thought. In a house directly to his right, a downstairs window had been left open and it was from here that the sound was emanating.

'Hello?' called Leonardo. The music broke off abruptly, and an elderly man appeared at the window. Clamped between his teeth was a large, rather complicated-looking pipe.

'Can I help?'

'I hope so,' said Leonardo. 'I'm looking for somewhere to stay. They tell me there's an inn in this village.'

'Indeed there is,' replied the man. 'Carry straight on, across the stepping stones, and it's on your left-hand side. You can't miss it. It's called The Plough.'

The Plough turned out to be a rambling old thatched building overlooking the green. Leonardo stepped inside, hung his hat and robe by the door, negotiated a room for the night, ordered a flask of ale and seated himself at the fireside. It was early, and he was the first customer.

Leonardo had discovered that in many of the more remote villages, a wandering sorcerer, although cautiously welcomed by some, would be looked upon with suspicion by most. He had therefore had to accustom himself to spending many of his evenings in his own company. Relaxing by the fire, he slipped off his boots and gazed into the flames. It occurred to him that, despite the hardships of the road, he was finding more contentment than he had expected in his new life. He wondered whether he would have fared any differently if he had retained ownership of his empathy engines, his scrolls, and all the other outdated paraphernalia with which Nina had absconded. At the time, it had seemed a terrible blow, but he realised now that in the end it had probably made little difference. For a moment he thought ruefully of Nina, wondered whether she had made her fortune with multiple empathy, wondered what she might be doing now, what name she might be using. He half-smiled and shook his head. Memories of Nina bothered him little these days.

Workers from the smallholdings had begun to cluster around the bar when Leonardo went to collect his next flask of ale. As he had expected, they kept their distance from him, and he returned unmolested to his place. Picking up his interrupted train of thought, he began again to consider his future. He was not keen to spend the coming winter on the roads, but could see no prospect of settled employment. It amused him that in all the years of the Theatre of Magic, all the countless hours he had spent constructing futures for other people, he had never attempted to construct a future for himself. Now he was getting quite good at it. Closing his eyes, he strode through the double gates and up the familiar path towards his house.

From the Journal of Victor Lazarus

Wednesday 28th October

Today I discovered Lee sweeping the floor again, this time in the downstairs part of the house. Various people were coming and going through the area, engaged upon one task or another, but, to my surprise, nobody paid the creature the slightest attention. I pondered on this for some time, until eventually it occurred to me that over the past few months the house has grown to be a busy and bustling place, in which all kinds of people are constantly going about their business. In these circumstances, I suppose that one extra person wielding a broom – even a person as remarkable as Lee – would in all likelihood go unnoticed.

★   ★   ★

Tuesday 17th November

Gradually, Lee is becoming an accepted member of the community, always willing to take on any small task that needs to be
done, seemingly eager to make reparation for all the damage
and distress that have been inflicted upon us. The cheerful
music that echoes through the corridors now forms a backdrop
to all our doings, and, bit by bit, Lee's good humour has begun
to infect the whole company. As I stroll around the house and
grounds and observe the staff at work and the visitors looking
on, I begin to detect an atmosphere of festivity that at times
amounts almost to hilarity. When we rest from our toil, Lee is
there to entertain us by sliding down the banisters, swinging
from the chandeliers, performing cartwheels and handsprings
and other feats of gymnastics. It is most refreshing to see the
gloom of this house dispelled, and to hear once again the sound
of laughter.

But, I am forced to add, we must not permit ourselves to
become carried away. The laughter and the hilarity must in no
circumstances divert us from the real task in hand.

The Captain and the Keeper

The next day, Rusty found his own way to the refectory,
collected some breakfast, and even found himself conducting
hesitant conversations with a couple of people. Helen arrived
just as he was finishing his meal. She was carrying a plate in
each hand and made no move to join him.

'Morning, Rusty. Sleep all right?' She continued hurriedly.
'Listen, I had a quick word with the Keeper and it's like I
thought. You're to start off on exercise group in the mornings,
and make your own choice for afternoons. Are you getting
yourself sorted out okay?'

'Yes, thanks, I think so. I seem to be managing.'

'Great stuff. See you later, then.'

She started on her way, then turned and called over her shoulder to him.

'Class starts on the next bell. Don't be late.'

Her tone was stern, but Rusty noticed the wink.

The exercise group met in the gymnasium, a bare, high-ceilinged room on the first floor. There were long mats on the floor, tall ladder-like contraptions attached to the walls, trapezes hanging from the beams. Rusty found himself in the company of some half-dozen people of various ages and shapes, supervised by a fierce-looking middle-aged man with a carefully trimmed moustache who introduced himself as Captain Lawson.

'Stand there,' ordered the Captain. He walked slowly around Rusty, looking him up and down, and eventually came to a halt facing him.

'What on earth have you been doing to yourself, youngster?' he asked finally. 'You look as if you've spent the last five years walking on all fours.'

Despite his forbidding appearance, Captain Lawson showed a great deal of patience and sympathy over the next few weeks. Bit by bit, he taught Rusty how to straighten his twisted limbs, how to hold his spine, how to spread his shoulders, how to regain control of his breathing. It was as though the boy were discovering for the first time how to stand and how to sit and how to walk and how to balance. Learning how to carry himself without pain, he began at last to understand how much pain he had been carrying with him.

He tried various activities in the afternoons and soon discovered that he felt most comfortable when he was helping with the running of the house. When he felt the need for the company of his new friends, he worked in the kitchen, chopping vegetables or stirring the huge pans of soup. In the laundry, helping to fold the sheets, he was reminded of his mother's house and found himself bathed in a security that he had not felt for many years. And when he wanted to be alone, he would find a broom and sweep the dust from the corridors.

In the evenings he usually joined the company in the common room, reading or playing games or trying to coax some sort of music from the cantankerous old piano. He became intrigued by a strange board game that was rather like chess, but was played by three people on a grid of interlocking lines and circles. Geoff, the man in the frayed pullover, had explained the rules to him, and they usually had a game in the evening. One night Helen joined them to make up a threesome. As usual, Geoff won an easy victory.

'It takes practice,' he said with a wistful smile. 'And I've had plenty of that.' He looked curiously at the two of them, then gave a shrug. 'Oh, well, it's getting late. I'll leave you young folk to it. Same time tomorrow?'

When he had left the room, Helen gave Rusty a speculative look.

'Fancy a stroll?' She indicated the French windows. It was a clear night, pleasantly cool. They walked out onto the terrace under the stars.

'You're looking good,' Helen started. 'Seems like the Captain's regime is agreeing with you. And they say you'll be ready for your attunement any time now.'

'Attunement?' The word meant nothing to Rusty.

'We're not really supposed to talk about it. Or at any rate, the Keeper sort of likes to explain it herself. But I suppose it's what we're all here for, really. The rest is, you know, really just preparation. Anyway, you'll find out soon enough.' She took his arm. 'How are you liking it?'

'It's wonderful.' Rusty was surprised by his own enthusiasm. 'It's like being on holiday. I haven't felt like this since . . .'

'Since . . . ?'

'Since Dusty, I suppose. By the way – ' he poked her playfully in the biceps, ' – you still haven't told me your story. Have you been – ' he hesitated over the unfamiliar word ' – attuned?'

'No.' She seemed downcast. 'Not yet. They say I'm not ready. It's taking me a long time.' For a moment she turned away from him, then she seemed to rally herself. 'Listen, there's really not much to say about me. You see, when I came here, I couldn't remember anything. Not anything at all, not even my name. They decided to call me Helen, I don't know why, but I still don't know who I am, not really. And I've still only managed to remember a few scraps of things . . . Are you sure you want to hear this?'

Rusty nodded. She drew him closer to her, then, slowly, she continued.

'Well, it seems I once took something, stole something maybe, something I shouldn't have had. I don't really know what it was, but something mysterious at any rate, maybe some kind of forbidden knowledge, a secret formula or something . . . and it seems I . . . I maybe tried to use it in the wrong way, a way it wasn't supposed to be used . . . I don't know. Anyway, whatever I did, it caused me some kind of damage, quite serious damage apparently, so it's going to take me a long time to recover. A long, long time.' She seemed closed in upon herself for a moment, then brightened. 'But they've been really good here. They let me help out, do all sorts of stuff. They say I've got a gift for helping people, even if I can't get my own act together.'

Rusty detected a sudden note of bitterness in her voice. For a few moments she was silent again.

'Anyway, that's enough about me.' She turned towards him, her face suddenly very close to his, her voice low. 'Listen, darling, would you like to come up to my room? You're a good-looking boy, you know, and I . . . well, a girl can get lonely some nights.'

Rusty was unprepared for this. He could not at once find a reply.

'I'm sorry,' he stammered at last. 'At any rate, not just yet.'

In the silence that followed, he could feel her gripping his arm more tightly, with a hand that trembled. Behind them, someone else emerged from the house, noticed them, tactfully withdrew.

'I'm sorry,' he said again.

'It's all right,' she said finally, releasing his arm. 'Forget I said it. You're a good lad. And thanks for listening.'

Side by side, they stared out at the infinite sweep of stars.

'Steady, now,' said Captain Lawson encouragingly. 'You're doing fine.'

Rusty could feel the reassuring grip of the Captain's hands around his ankles as he cautiously allowed his muscles and bones to adjust themselves to his upside-down position.

'You're working too hard, youngster. No need to screw your face up.'

The voice seemed to be coming from somewhere near Rusty's feet. He relaxed a little, started to enjoy the weightless feeling in his legs and hips.

'That's good. Ready for me to let go this time?'

Rusty managed a grunt. He felt the hands relax their hold and for a long, exhilarating moment he found himself in command of the delicate mechanism of interlocking forces that maintained his balance. He began to smile, feeling it could last for ever, then felt something start to slide out of his control, struggled to correct it, realised too late that he was pushing the wrong way, and collapsed sideways onto the mat in an ungainly, breathless skid of limbs. The Captain laughed in a friendly way.

'All right, son, you're getting there. Just sit still for a minute and we'll try again.'

At that moment, a visitor entered the gymnasium. It was the old lady. Rusty had not seen her since the morning of his arrival.

'How's our young Wolf Boy getting along?' she asked the Captain. He snapped to attention.

'Done all the basics, ma'am. Starting on the intermediate.'

'All right, Captain, stand easy, for goodness' sake.' She seemed amused for a moment, then turned to inspect Rusty, who was just coming to his feet.

'Show me how you stand.'

Her tone was suddenly brisker. Rusty adopted the standing posture he had been taught. She walked thoughtfully around him.

'Bend down. Go on, all the way. Legs straight, yes, that's good. Straighten up again.' She walked round him again. 'Now stretch right up.'

She seemed particularly interested in this posture and walked around him several times while he maintained it.

'All right. Now raise your right leg and balance on your left. Slowly. Yes, that's good. I can see you've done well. In fact, I think you're ready now.' She stopped in front of Rusty and looked him straight in the eyes.

'Very well, this afternoon, you may begin your attunement. I'll be down at the Ground straight after the bell. And please be punctual.' She turned to go.

'But I . . .'

'Oh, I'm sure Cook can find someone else to peel the parsnips. Now, I'll see you this afternoon.'

At the doorway she turned back.

'Just one other thing.'

'Yes, ma'am?'

'I think you should put your leg down now.'

Rusty could have sworn that he heard a trace of mischief in her voice.

From the Journal of Victor Lazarus

Saturday 19th December

There now remains but a short time before the return of the owner. I note with satisfaction that the bulk of the restoration work is complete, and that everyone continues in excellent spirits. Shortly I shall call the whole company together for a briefing session, so that everyone can be apprised of the final preparations.

I have lately been too much occupied to devote much thought to Lee, but today there occurred a curious incident that gave me much cause to ponder.

The kitchen has been restored to full working order, and Mrs Proudfoot has been kept very busy baking gingerbread and making sandwiches and other refreshments. This morning, around coffee time, I paid her a routine call in order to assess the quality of her bridge rolls. While I was sampling the fare, from the corner of my eye I caught sight of a slight figure, clad in a flower-patterned apron, who stood at the sink, washing dishes. It took me a moment to recognise Lee.

Mrs Proudfoot broke into a smile and patted me on the arm.

'Lee's been so helpful,' (she whispered confidentially). 'She's a lovely girl.'

I took this at the time for a joke, so that I was not at once struck by the full implication of the remark, but, during a quiet moment this afternoon, the good lady's words came back into my mind with renewed force. Mrs Proudfoot is clearly under the impression that Lee is of the female sex! I, on the other hand, have until now been making the opposite assumption, despite the admitted lack of any specific evidence to this effect. It occurred to me then that the slight figure and the husky voice, which I had taken to signify a half-grown lad, could equally well have belonged to a slender young woman. I strove to recapture in my imagination the creature's androgynous form, but still I was unable to make my mind up one way or the other. I strove then to picture the face, but found myself unable to summon up any image at all.

Sunday 20th December

Last night, I was haunted by dreams more disturbing than ever. It seemed that a dim form crept into my narrow bed beside me. I felt in the darkness the touch of a dry hand, the bloom of a soft cheek, a hot tangle of hair, a sharp caress of teeth. Sleek, hard limbs encircled me in fierce embrace . . .

I awoke with a cry of terror that must have echoed throughout the house. In the half-light, I could distinguish the form of
Lee, thankfully not in my bed, but poised at the threshold, smiling faintly, holding out a tray of tea.

I remind myself constantly not to attach too much importance to my dreams!

The midwinter festival begins in two days' time. I have decided
to close the house until the new year, in order to allow everyone to return to their families for a well-earned rest. For myself,
I shall be taking a short holiday in the mountain country, where
I look forward to exploring some of the ancient gaming
grounds and other archaeological remains. With luck, I shall
return refreshed and ready for whatever is to come.

Attunement

'All through our lives, we find ourselves subject to the pull of
certain forces.'

The Keeper of the Ground was conducting Rusty slowly
around the arena.

'Sometimes the forces augment one another, sometimes they
oppose one another. The art of living well lies in learning to
regulate the balance between the forces.'

'Sort of like learning to balance in the gymnasium?'

The old woman raised her eyebrows in approval.

'Just so. Captain Lawson has a most important job here. Yes,
nicely observed. Now, what was I saying? Oh yes, regulating the
balance of forces. That's where the Ground comes in. You see,
each one of the stone forms embodies one particular force.' As
they walked, she indicated the stones one by one. 'This one is
the Stone of Instinct. This is the Stone of Reason. That one
is the Stone of the Future and that one is the Stone of the Past.
And these are the Sky Stone and the Earth Stone. When I
found you, you were clinging to the Earth Stone, curled up just

like a baby.' She stopped walking and turned to face him, seemed to consider for a moment, then continued. 'Those should be enough for you to be going on with. And I think we've arranged them in the best configuration to start you off. If you do feel the need for any others, just mention it to one of the guides, and they'll sort it out for you. Well, good luck, then.'

She turned to leave. Confused, Rusty called after her.

'But what do I actually do?'

The Keeper sighed wearily.

'Didn't they tell you anything? I don't know, some of these guides are hopeless, quite hopeless. Oh well, it's quite simple, really. You see this six-sided slab where you're standing now . . .'

'The Earth Stone?'

'That's right. Well, as you can see, the Earth Stone lies at the centre of the Ground. You'll need to position yourself here to begin with. You can stand or sit or do whatever's comfortable. And then you just open yourself to the pull of the Earth.'

She waited while he eased himself into position.

'Yes, that'll do if it feels right. I should just stick with that to begin with. Later on, when you've got the hang of that, you can start trying the other Stones. One at a time to start with. Probably you'll find that some of them pull harder than others. So just remember that each Stone has its opposite. If you feel yourself pulled too hard by one Stone – the Stone of Reason, for example – all you have to do is open yourself to its opposite, which is obviously the Stone of Impulse. That one, over there. It's all quite logical, really. Oh, and if you find you need any of them moving, just speak to one of the guides. And that's really about it. Once you've got the hang of it, you'll discover that you can find a balance between the whole lot of them. And then you'll be done. Do you understand now? Well, if you've no more questions, I really am rather busy.'

And before he could open his mouth again, she was gone.

Rusty felt rather foolish, but there seemed no choice but to fol-low the old woman's instructions. After experimenting with various positions, he decided that he would feel most comfortable standing. Examining the Earth Stone, he found at its centre a shallow recess that neatly accommodated his feet. Carefully, he adjusted his body to the standing posture that Captain Lawson had so painstakingly taught him. Slowly he allowed himself to relax, felt his eyes closing.

He waited, uncertain what was supposed to happen next. A background chatter of random thoughts was impairing his concentration, until he remembered the Earth Stone and directed his attention downwards towards it. Gradually he started to get the sense of something massive and solid and heavy, and he realised that the Earth Stone extended a long way down into the soil beneath him, steadying him and anchoring him to the ground. Now the boundaries of his being started to extend outwards, merging into that huge reassuring mass. He let the heaviness of it draw him down deep into the black earth, until suddenly he plummeted—

Jolted by a sharp stab of alarm, he opened his eyes, startled at the swiftness and the intensity of the sensation. He looked around him. Expressionless, the Stones kept their various distances. At the edge of the arena he could see the house, its chimneys smoking. Distant figures were strolling in the garden. He exhaled slowly, realising that he had nothing to fear. After a moment, he closed his eyes again.

This time it was easier. As he allowed his defences to dissolve, he felt himself slipping into tune with the Stones, and then he began faintly to feel something pulling him to his left. The pull felt somehow unwelcome, and his first impulse was to resist it, but, as if sensing his reluctance, it grew suddenly more powerful, and all at once he found himself tugged violently back and forth across the Ground. At this, he panicked and fought, and the forces around him reared up angrily beyond his control and lifted him bodily from the ground and hurled him square against flat solid rock, dashing his breath from his body.

★　★　★

'I think that's probably enough for your first day.'

The Keeper of the Ground had returned to check on his progress.

'You seem to have encountered the Stone of the Future,' she observed. 'It can be rather daunting to begin with. Why don't you go for tea now and try again tomorrow? And let me offer you a word of advice. Leave that one alone until you've got the hang of the Stone of the Past.'

Over the next few weeks, Rusty continued to attend Captain Lawson's exercise class each morning, and returned to the Ground each afternoon. The old woman kept a close eye on him to begin with, but eventually decided that she could leave him to his own devices. Following her suggestion, he started by turning his attention to the Stone of the Past. When he examined it closely, he discovered that the surface of the Stone was covered in small pictures rather like the frames of a strip cartoon. He chose a picture at random.

It showed what seemed to be a house . . . no, not a house, it was a tent, a large tent, a circus tent. He peered closer, discovered that he could see inside the tent, could see a crowd of people watching the show, and in the middle of that crowd, a boy and his dog, staring open-mouthed at the performance of a young girl acrobat. For a while he was lost in the wonder of the scene, marvelling at the girl's agility, sharing all the excitement of the boy in the picture. Then the circus lights dimmed, and he knew that it was time to move on. He drew himself back and looked at the next picture.

It was raining. In a shelter, overlooking a schoolyard, sat the same boy, younger this time. Beside him sat a scruffy, dark-haired little girl. She seemed about to say something. He strained his ears but could not make out her words. So he tried another picture, this time caught a glimpse of a pale young woman, strangely familiar to his eyes, and at her shoulder, the shadowy figure of a dark-haired man. And then the image of the man seemed to fade, and the woman was left alone. Next he found himself staring in horrified fascination at a wild, deformed creature, living in a pack, hunting and killing and feasting on hot blood and raw flesh. And as he looked at more and more pictures, he felt himself drawn into the scenes, sometimes basking in their warmth, sometimes recoiling from them in shock. After a time, the pictures seemed to lose definition, their colours growing dimmer, their outlines becoming indecipherable, and then he knew that it was time to stop. And later on, he asked for the Stone to be moved further away.

Now he looked again at the Stone. From this distance, he could no longer decipher the individual images, but now for the first time he could discern the precise grid of perpendicular lines that divided each scene from its neighbours. And then he understood that he was becoming attuned with the Stone of Reason. It was a sharply rectangular, precisely defined stone. Staring at the bars of the grid, he was reminded suddenly of the climbing frame that had stood at the far end of the schoolyard, a tall geometric configuration of orthogonal metal tubes and horizontal wooden platforms. Dangling his legs from the second highest platform, he gazed down at the sturdy form of Sammy Hopkins, watching him as he heaved himself stolidly upwards, one bar at a time . . . Then, at the far corner of the frame, he glimpsed a lithe, dark creature twisting catlike through the grid of lines, weaving her own untamed pattern through the regimented structure—

—And now he felt the wild tug of the Stone of Impulse as one untamed voice was joined by many more, all threading in and out of each other in crazy polyphony that defied logic, defied rationality, yet created its own colour, its own texture, its anarchic motley tapestry of voices beckoning him this way and that—

   —And then it was as if the whole boiling pandemonium crystallised, and for an instant he could grasp the underpinning

structures of mathematical counterpoint that informed even
this perplexing world—

—And then from the tapestry emerged one voice, clearer than
the others, singing its own intricate melody, threading its way
towards him through the maze, twisting itself around him, spiralling into the air, carrying him headlong away from the chaos to
a place far away, a place of impossible boundless calm—

The Sky Stone was much taller than the other Stones. From
here, as if through the eye of a hovering kestrel, he could see the
landscape spread beneath him, the river, the distant hills, the sea,
the city, and the whole web of interconnecting paths that linked
them all, radiating outwards from the village of his birth,
spreading across the countryside, branching, intersecting, crossing unexpectedly with the paths of other travellers, the dark
young man and the pale young woman, the two children with
their wet raincoats, the little dog and the secret he carried, the
wild creatures of the night and their quarries and their pursuers, a wanderering magician tramping the roads, and, beyond
the distant shore, a boat grounded on rocks, the ferryman
watching patiently as his young passenger plunged into the
black water and began to swim . . .

And their paths forked and twisted and divided and united
once again in a never-ending, living network, and at last, dimly,
he could begin to discern where they led.

So now he was ready to attune himself again to the Stone of
the Future. Its form was still uncertain, its surface bare of detail.
It shimmered and it shifted and it spoke words to him that still
he could not translate. But at least he knew in which direction
it lay.

He started walking. He walked for a long, long time. But at
last, in the distance, he could see a house. Slowly, the house
grew larger, until, after a long, long time, he found himself
standing in front of a pair of tall iron gates. Cautiously, he

extended a hand. At the touch of his fingertip, the gates swung silently open. He passed through. Inside, a pathway led him uphill through a formal garden. At the top of the garden stood the house, a tall, solid, imposing, many-windowed, stone house. This, he knew, was his house, his place of safety, the place in which he could be anything he wanted to be. He walked up a short flight of stone steps to a columned porch, within which a pair of stout, freshly painted doors stood open and welcoming. In front of him, a corridor led to the lower parts of the house. To his right, there ascended a broad mahogany staircase. He decided to look upstairs first.

Inside the House

The first room he tried seemed to be some kind of office. It was a large room, dotted with untidy desks and large tables groaning beneath disordered piles of charts and scrolls and reports. The walls were adorned with more large charts and diagrams, pinned haphazardly, overlapping each other in places. In one corner, a larger desk was situated within a private enclosed area. It seemed that this was the place from which everything would be organised and coordinated. It seemed to be a room that was necessary but perhaps not very exciting. He stepped across the landing into the room opposite.

At first he thought that the room was in darkness, but gradually he became aware of faint, mysterious patches of light, patches that pulsed and glowed and slowly changed colour. Accompanying the lights were faint sounds, humming, hissing, faint rhythmic clickings and whirrings. He detected the scent of ozone mingled with scorched dust, and knew at once that this was a room where powerful forces of magic were present, magic that at the moment he did not understand but that he hoped some day he would conquer.

★   ★   ★

A third door led to an old-fashioned schoolroom. About thirty children were seated in rows of double desks, their small faces gazing up at him with hungry expectation. It seemed that he had something to say that would be of interest to them. He could not imagine what it might be.

Back on the landing, he noticed other doors. He guessed that they would lead him into bedrooms, bathrooms, lavatories, perhaps an airing cupboard. He decided to postpone the investigation of these to some later date. Then his attention was drawn to a narrow flight of stairs, leading upwards to a higher storey. Quickly he mounted the stairs. At the top he found a single small room, a narrow six-sided room with a tall window in each wall. And at the centre of the room stood a curious device that nevertheless had an air of familiarity about it. It was a polished mahogany cabinet, about the size of a chest of drawers. Attached to the cabinet were coiling lengths of cable, brass handles and levers, a pair of Bakelite headphones, and a binocular eyepiece with a long shade attached. He bent to peer through the eyepiece, then at the last moment changed his mind and looked instead through the windows. The room offered a panoramic view of the surrounding countryside. He concluded that it must be some sort of look-out post.

A Job for the Magician

A sudden thirst interrupted Leonardo's daydream. He reached for his flask and discovered that it was empty. Making his way across the taproom, which was now beginning to become crowded, he joined the ranks of impatient customers waiting at the bar. The landlord had temporarily vacated his post in order to make a round of the tables, emptying ashtrays and collecting flasks. When he returned, he seemed to Leonardo to be harassed and not particularly good-humoured.

Back in the house of his dreams, Leonardo descended again

to the ground floor, chose a door at random and opened it. This time he found a narrow flight of steps leading downwards. He decided to take a look at the cellar.

The hum of machinery and the smell of hot oil drifted upwards. In the gloom, he could make out boilers, generators and all the other mysterious engines that were required to keep the house running. He wondered whether he might engage a mechanically minded assistant to take care of this area, but concluded that he would probably end up doing most of the work himself.

Back on the ground floor, he made a reluctant mental note that he would need a broom cupboard and some sort of kitchen. He cared little for housework or cookery, although he had made an exhaustive study of the various technologies available for brewing coffee. He decided to try one final door before turning in for the night.

This room was a large one, extending the full depth of the house, and the ceiling was high. A huge log fire blazed in an inglenook fireplace, and the floor was of smoothly planed wooden boards, deeply polished and dotted with colourful rugs. In recesses around the walls he noticed shelves of leather-bound books, orderly racks of vellum scrolls, imposing pieces of sculpture, large abstract oil paintings, ornamental tubs in which flourished luxuriant tangles of house plants, their tendrils spreading out and twining around the books and statues. A few comfortable-looking leather armchairs were positioned around the fireplace and at one end of the room stood a beautifully polished grand piano. On a low table, a saxophone had been carelessly discarded. Leonardo strolled through a pair of French windows and found himself on a broad stone terrace decorated with several more pieces of classical-looking sculpture and a few carefully placed urns. A well-tended lawn sloped downwards towards dense shrubberies, beyond which Leonardo caught a glimpse of distant hills and water. He conjured up a deckchair, adjusted it to his preferred inclination, and seated himself.

Reflecting upon what he had found in the house, Leonardo had to admit that he was most impressed with the improvements that had been carried out on his behalf. But, even as he admired his surroundings, a sense of loneliness began to steal over the magician. Although the house had all the things he wanted, somehow it lacked life, lacked spirit. But even as the thought occurred to him, as if in answer to an unspoken call he sensed a faint tug of response. And the response came not from within himself but from some distant being, a being who perhaps dwelt in an unknown corner of the house.

There was only one place it could be. Laboriously, Leonardo mounted the narrow spiral stairs that led to the six-sided turret room. This time, the door opened easily. The room was still empty, but it seemed to the magician that it was larger and brighter than he had remembered. And he also noticed that the floor had been swept.

'Are these for me, sir?'

The brusque voice of the landlord catapulted Leonardo abruptly back to the here and now. The magician nodded vaguely as he watched the man making another collection of empties, deftly inserting a finger into the neck of each flask before carrying them away. Leonardo decided that he would allow himself one more flask of ale before turning in.

The room was crowded now, the villagers evidently wishing to take full advantage of the last hour of business. Leonardo elbowed his way to the bar, ordered his drink, felt in his purse. He swallowed. The purse was empty.

'I'm sorry,' he stuttered. The landlord was looking at him grimly. 'I seem to have run out of money. I can't pay.' But then a thought struck him. 'Could you by any chance make use of the services of a magician?'

'I only need one kind of magic just now, sir,' came the reply. 'Suppose you try and magic some of those empty flasks back to the bar?' He pointed towards the cluttered tables.

Leonardo thought about this.

'Does the work require any special qualifications?'

'No, sir. I think you'll be surprised how quickly you can get the hang of it.'

Leonardo considered his options, looked at the landlord again, stepped hesitantly across to the nearest table.

'Are these for me, sir?' he enquired experimentally.

'All yours, mate,' said a customer.

From behind the bar, the landlord nodded approvingly.

'There you are. You've got it already.'

Leonardo moved on to the next table.

Back on the Road Again

'—Ninety-eight, ninety-nine, a hundred! Well done!'

The members of Captain Lawson's class applauded as Rusty slowly lowered his legs to the floor and carefully resumed an upright position. Rejoining the others for the final sitting exercise, he felt exhilarated, triumphant, ready for anything. When the luncheon bell brought the class to a close, the Captain drew him aside.

'You can do it now, youngster,' he said. 'You can do it without thinking about it.'

'What happens next?' asked Rusty. The Captain looked wistful for a moment.

'I've taught you all I know,' he said finally. 'I can't get you any further. From now on, you're on your own.'

Rusty had begun to find that, as his control over his balance and posture became more precise, more delicate, he was able to attune himself simultaneously to all the stones of the Ground, holding himself in fine equilibrium while the intricate mechanism of opposing forces ebbed and flowed and played through him. And finally he discovered that he could balance every force precisely with its opposite, so that Instinct and Reason and Past and Future and Earth and Sky seemed to fuse into one and he drifted free at last, weightless in the boundless ocean of calm.

For a long, long time he remained there, dimly aware of the sun going down and the sun coming up and the sun going down again. And then the awesome mass of the Earth Stone slowly reasserted itself, drawing him back downwards to the very source, to the hidden centre of the world where beat the deep and aching pulse of the Life Force itself, offering him at last a glimpse of the dark realm that it commanded and of the hard fires that burned there.

And then, at the crux of his being, a gate swung open with a grateful sigh and all of the joy and all of the grief and all of the wonder swept into him and engulfed him. And in that moment, Rusty finally began to understand who he was.

'I found another Stone. Right at the end. A small one, away from the rest.'

Rusty was describing his experiences to the Keeper of the Ground.

'That would probably be the Stone of Compassion,' said the old woman. 'It often tips up at the last minute. You may well find that it gets bigger next time you visit us.'

'Next time?'

'Well, it seems to me that you've done just about everything you set out to do. You probably need to think about moving on.'

So, although he didn't move on straight away, he did begin to think about it. He spent a few more weeks helping in the kitchen and the laundry, he tried a little hoeing in the vegetable garden. Later, he lent his muscles to the working parties who from time to time were sent to the Ground to reposition the Stones for each attunement. He even spent some time as a guide for some of the frightened, confused folk who periodically arrived at the house. But he knew that the old woman was right. He needed to move on. It was just that he still wasn't sure where he wanted to move to.

But then one day he woke up and he knew. He knew that he wanted to go home.

'Leaving us already?' Helen had found Rusty clearing out his room. 'Listen, I've got something I want you to have. Can you come upstairs with me for a minute?' She caught his startled look. 'Don't worry, I'm not going to drag you into bed. But you'll need to keep warm on your journey.'

So she led him up several flights of stairs. Her room turned out to be a little six-sided turret at the top of the house, with a high, pointed roof and a tall window in each wall.

'It's a bit draughty.' She shrugged. 'But I love the view.'

Rusty was staring out of the window, taking in the whole sweep of the landscape. Momentarily transported, he missed Helen's next few words.

'You're miles away, you daft bugger. I was just saying, I had it with me when I came here, but I don't really like it any more. But it would look pretty good on you. You can have it if you want.'

With an effort, Rusty turned again to face her. She was pointing towards the back of the door. From the door pro-truded a nail. And hanging on the nail was a jacket. It was a leather jacket, black, well worn, and decorated in a dense, intri-cate pattern with hundreds of tiny brass studs.

'It's beautiful.' Rusty felt the texture of the leather. 'Are you sure you don't need it?'

Helen shrugged.

'Drop it back when you're passing. And, darling . . . take care of yourself. It's been nice knowing you.'

Her tone was casual, but he did not miss the look of sadness in her eyes.

Rusty paid a final call on the Keeper of the Ground, to thank her for all she had done for him. She gave him one of her vague looks.

'You've certainly made a bit of progress. I'm just thinking

back to when you arrived here! I must admit, I wasn't too hopeful to begin with.' She smiled faintly. 'Anyway, I'm going to ask you one thing in return. I want you to take what you have learned back out into the world with you. Offer it freely to those you meet, and you will have repaid me more than you know.'

She paused for a moment, as if uncertain whether to continue. Rusty hesitated, sensing that there was something else hovering in the air. She gave him a shrewd look.

'All right. Just before you go on your way, there is one other thing I want you to understand,' she said slowly. 'I do not say this to all my guests, but somehow I know that I can say it to you. It is this.' She paused again. 'The Ground and the Stones have no power of their own, none at all. Everything that has happened to you has happened within yourself. It has happened through the power of your own imagination and the force of your own will. Nothing else. The Ground is just pavement. And the Stones are just stones. Now go.'

So he went. He asked no directions and he consulted no chart, for he knew now exactly what path he had to follow. The day was raw, but with Helen's jacket around his shoulders, he felt protected from the worst of the weather. And when he reached the first bend in the road and turned to look back, the old woman and the house and the stones had vanished into the mist.

From the Journal of Victor Lazarus

Monday 4th January

This afternoon I called everybody together in the ballroom to discuss our final preparations for the return of the owner. Harold was in attendance with all his custodians and front-of-house staff, Sam stood at the French windows with the maintenance men and the gardeners, and Mrs Proudfoot and her kitchen helpers made up the full complement. I called the meeting to order, welcomed the company back from their holidays, then proceeded to deal with the main business of the day. I had come armed with an agenda of matters requiring attention, to which the others had contributed a number of additional items. Harold was concerned that a handful of perplexing objects continued to resist being accommodated within his scheme of classification. Sam was concerned that one of the boilers continued to display certain behavioural irregularities, and Mrs Proudfoot was unable to decide between liver sausage and luncheon meat for her sandwiches. For my part, I had yet to put the final touches to my accounts, which the owner would doubtless be intending to inspect in the course of his visit. Detailed minutes were taken of the discussions that ensued, and action points were agreed.

At the conclusion of business, as a matter of courtesy I asked the company at large if there were any final questions before the meeting was dismissed. I was not anticipating any response to this invitation, and was therefore taken somewhat by surprise when a husky voice spoke up from the back of the room.

'How about a welcoming ceremony?'

It was Lee. A murmur of excitement ran around the room. I sensed at once that a firm hand was required, briskly called the meeting to order, and explained patiently that our task had been first and foremost to put the house in order. Having made this point, I paused for a moment to collect my thoughts, at which moment it occurred to me that the owner might very well appreciate a modest display of welcome – of a suitable nature, of course. I put this to the company, with the suggestion that a few orderly lines of bunting or perhaps a short welcome address might be considered appropriate. I paused again. I had realised, rather too late, that someone would now have to be delegated to organise this. Almost every member of the company was already fully occupied. There remained only one person to ask.

'Lee,' I said, 'I give you the responsibility of organising the welcome.'

There was another murmur of excitement. I added quickly:

'But make sure you keep it within reason.'

'Thank you, Victor,' came the reply. 'You won't be disappointed.'

As the meeting dispersed, I noticed that Lee was smiling faintly. I went about my business with a strong sense of misgiving.

Six:
THE GIFT

Be still, Victor, be still. You have charged me with devising a welcome, and you are about to discover that I have truly excelled myself. For I shall offer you more than a welcome. I shall offer a festival, a carnival, a celebration. I promised you that you would not be disappointed, and that promise I reaffirm. Once, long ago, you feared me. In time you learned to tolerate me. Lately you have even learned to care for me. Today, at last, you shall learn to trust me.

But time runs short. Soon I must prepare myself for my own part in the celebration. In one of the attics of the house is a room of costumes, and to that room I go now, to search through the chests, to skim along the rails, to try on my fancy dress before the tall mirror, for today of all days I must appear to you just as you need me to appear. First, I try on the rags of the barefoot urchin, faded and patched and torn. Too humble, I feel. Next, I consider the livery of the page: tunic and hose and cap. Perhaps a little too formal. The garb of the athlete – running suit and canvas shoes? Too stark, too functional. Or the motley of the clown? The leotard of the acrobat? Or even the fur and fangs and claws of the wild beast? No, perhaps just a little too fearsome . . . But now at last I have it. This is the costume I have been seeking, the costume in which you and all of your people shall see me, the costume in which I can be as I truly am. Now I know how you shall see me on this day of days, Victor. Now I know.

★　　★　　★

From the Journal of Victor Lazarus

Tuesday 26th January

At last I have met the owner of the house, and I find myself now in a greater state of confusion than ever. To add to my perplexity, the nature of the welcoming ceremony devised by Lee has finally been revealed. Today, in short, has been the most extraordinary day of my life, and I find that until I have placed my thoughts in order, I shall be unable to sleep.

I was in my orderly room until well into the small hours of yesterday night, putting the final touches to the household accounts, but I was nevertheless awake again long before dawn, only too conscious of the pressure of business. For a time I lay in the darkness, then at first light I arose.

As I made my hasty toilet, I received my first inkling that events had started to accelerate beyond my control, for as I lathered up my shaving brush I started to become aware of distant strains of music. A sense of apprehension seized me. I swiftly donned my full dress uniform, which Lee had laid out for me the previous night, and set off to investigate. The sound, I discovered, was emanating from a brass band, which was strategically positioned on a prefabricated rostrum on the front lawn of the house.

Alarmed by this, and alerted now by other sounds from nearby, I decided to make a full patrol of the grounds. At the rear of the house, I was astonished to stumble upon a funfair and a circus, both of which were already plying a brisk trade. Before I could recover from these discoveries, I found myself drawn by the smell of cooking into the kitchen. Here I found Mrs Proudfoot roasting chickens by the score. Along the refectory tables, bottles of champagne were lined up in ranks of a dozen.

By this time, I was quivering with indignation. Concerning the identity of the culprit, there could be no doubt. This could

238 STEVE COCKAYNE

only have been the work of Lee. Glancing out of the window,
I could see that visitors were pouring through the front gates in
hordes. There were families with children, elderly people, even
visitors from foreign lands chattering in unknown tongues. I
knew then that it was too late to put matters right.

My heart sinking, I made my way to the entrance hall. Here
I discovered Harold, immaculately turned out in top hat and
tailcoat, distributing elaborately printed programmes to the visitors. I seized a copy from his hands and scanned the timetable
of events. There were to be musical recitals, poetry readings, relay
races, gymnastic displays, a treasure hunt, a three-sided chess
match, and, to round off the day, something called 'The Dance
of the Shadow'. My head began to reel. I set off determined to
corner the perpetrator, but no sign of Lee could I find.

It seemed now that my only hope was to intercept the owner
upon his arrival. I stationed myself at the front gates and read-
ied myself to present my apologies.

The New Potboy

'Are these for me, sir?'

'Yes, all yours, thank you, Leo.'

The magician deftly inserted a finger into the neck of each
of the flasks on the table and whisked them across the taproom
to the surface of the bar, whence they would be swiftly collected and transferred to the sink by the landlord. Without
pausing in his work, Leonardo glanced quickly at the sink.
There was room in it for about eight more flasks. As soon as the
sink was full, he would dry and put away the flasks that were at
present inverted on the draining board. Then he would rinse
out the flasks that were soaking in the sink, and then he would
invert those flasks and transfer them to the draining board. At
that point, the sink would be ready for the next consignment
of flasks. He glanced at the large clock over the fireplace. In
only an hour, the bar would be closing. It was wonderful how

quickly time passed when the mind was occupied.

It was several months since Leonardo Pegasus had taken up the position of resident potboy at The Plough, and the work was making stringent demands on his talents for tactical planning, strategic organisation and systemic conceptualising. The job required intense concentration, precise hand-to-eye coordination and highly developed interpersonal skills. In fact, it demanded total and utter dedication and commitment. Somehow, though, despite its demanding nature, it never seemed to keep him awake at night. Leonardo was sleeping well these days. He often dreamed of the house in which he hoped he might some day live, and very occasionally his slumbers were disturbed by a mildly erotic dream of Alice, but even these were now occurring at longer and longer intervals. At the end of the evening, when Leonardo had polished the last flask and returned it to its place on the shelf, he would retire to his pallet in the loft above the stables, giving not another thought to the problems of the working day until the start of his next shift. He was enjoying life tremendously.

The regular customers at The Plough had been uninquisitive about Leonardo's personal history, but nevertheless he had decided that, in order to avoid drawing undue attention to himself, he would adopt the shortened, familiar form of his name. The title of Master had been ceremonially packed in mothballs and hung up on a crooked six-inch nail hammered into a cross-beam in the loft, along with his ceremonial robe and hat. These days his preferred working garb was the long, tattered, colourless apron with which the landlord had thoughtfully provided him. An ancient pair of carpet slippers had replaced his heavy magician's boots. In this apparel, he could go about his tasks virtually unnoticed.

Only one customer had paid him any serious attention. This was an elderly, educated-looking man who visited the inn once a week and sat at a corner table, puffing at a complicated-looking pipe and taking infrequent draughts from a small flask, as if trying to eke out a slender pension. Leonardo recognised him as the helpful individual who had directed him towards the inn on the day of his arrival in the village. He noticed that the old man was in the habit of exchanging the occasional word with some of the younger drinkers who clustered around the bar. This gave Leonardo the impression that he had once known them well and was making an effort to keep track of their lives. Paying careful attention to these and other clues, Leonardo was eventually able to pigeonhole the man as a retired schoolmaster.

'You seem like an educated fellow. How did you come to find yourself here?' asked the schoolmaster one night.

'I came here from the city,' replied Leonardo. 'I used to be a magician.' He was momentarily surprised, not only by his own candour, but also by his use of the past tense. After that, the two of them developed a nodding acquaintance, and eventually the schoolmaster altered his drinking night to coincide with Leonardo's night off.

'I was always intrigued by the idea of teaching,' mused the magician on one such night. 'I used to employ assistants from time to time. I used to enjoy it, teaching them new things, explaining ideas to them, watching their young minds develop, all that sort of thing. I suppose it was one of the more reward-ing aspects of the job.'

'It has certainly had its rewards for me,' replied the school-master. 'But at times I wish that I could have had some experi-ence of the world of affairs, that mysterious place that people insist on calling the "real world". I have to say I envy you that. Sometimes it seems as though everything I have experienced in my life has been at second hand.'

'But experiencing things at second hand was exactly how I used to make my living,' countered the magician. 'I even devised a machine to assist me. I'm sure I must have told you about my experiments with the Empathy Engine.'

'I believe you may have.' The schoolmaster broke in hastily, anxious to head off another repetition of this story. 'Would you care for another flask?'

'Sounds like an excellent suggestion.'

Rusty Goes Home

The familiar view of the village unfolded below him as Rusty Brown arrived at the top of the hill and launched into the final weary mile of his journey. At the ford, he carefully negotiated the five stepping stones, noticing that the positions of the third and fourth ones had altered slightly since his previous visit. Opposite The Plough, he took his usual short cut across the village green, emerging into the side lane just before the hump-backed bridge.

And then, as he crossed the bridge, he saw the black waggon standing at the roadside in front of his home. With rising apprehension, he noticed that the parlour curtains were drawn. Heart in mouth, he approached the front door.

'Michael, I'm so sorry.' Granny Hopkins was emerging from the house, wringing her gnarled old hands in distraction. 'Nobody knew where you were. We've had to make all the arrangements. I expect you'll be wanting to go up?'

Inside, everything about the cottage seemed small and shrunken. Rusty noticed for the first time how low the ceilings were, how cramped the rooms, how narrow the stair. And when he apprehensively nudged open the door of his mother's room, the stiffly arranged figure on the bed seemed small and shrunken too. He stared numbly, not knowing what he was supposed to feel.

A light touch at his elbow interrupted his thoughts. With a start, he turned to see two spindly, black-clad figures hovering on the landing. For a moment, he failed to identify them.

His alarm must have shown on his face.

'Sorry, sir, didn't mean to startle you. All right if we take her now?'

Later, he sat for a long time on the narrow bed in his old room. The room had evidently remained unused, and all his childhood things had been left in place. A few of the charts he had drawn were still pinned haphazardly to the walls. A paintbox lay carelessly on top of the chest of drawers, as if discarded a moment earlier. He reached out for it, turned it over in his hand, stared at it blankly, started to remember the evenings he had spent at the table downstairs, painting his charts. Then, as he sat there, other, fainter voices began calling to him from more distant corners of his past. The kite . . . the ninepins . . . the golliwog . . .

And under the small table, in its old place, lay Dusty's basket, with his faded scrap of plaid rug still inside. At the sight and the scent of that rug, Rusty finally surrendered to his sorrow.

A Man Needs a Hobby

One particularly appealing feature of Leonardo's position at The Plough was that there was plenty of slack time between shifts. If a man had a hobby, here was an ideal opportunity to practise it. And, as it happened, Leonardo had started to develop a hobby. The hayloft where he slept was broad and spacious, well illuminated by skylights, and pleasantly ripe with the scent from the stables below. It was an ideal place in which, say, to construct something large and complicated and mechanical, and, bit by bit, Leonardo had in fact started to construct something large and complicated and mechanical, something that he had been meaning to get round to for years but for which he had somehow never quite found the time. Of course, he was no longer in possession of the original plans, and therefore had no choice but to proceed from memory, but he was confident that he could reproduce in fair detail what he had kept for so long at the back of his mind.

At first he had not been sure where he might obtain suitable materials. But he had retained all his powers of invention, and he soon discovered that the gutters and dustbins and spoil tips of the village afforded a rich source of supply. He built the framework of his device from fence posts and lengths of scrap timber and he built the housing from offcuts of corrugated iron

and sheet asbestos. Broken clocks and rusty bicycles and abandoned agricultural engines and old leather belts and shoelaces
provided the mechanical parts, and the remains of old tele-
scopes and spectacles were invaluable for the optical components. And in the darker recesses of the store cupboards at the
inn lurked countless mysterious bottles and jars that offered all
the necessary chemicals to power the batteries, lubricate the
moving parts and fuel the motors. And once in a while, when
he needed something of a more specialised nature, he might
take an afternoon trip into town on the carrier's cart. The town
was not a large one, and the savings from his wages were
meagre, but it was surprising what could be obtained from
some of the more enterprising backstreet dealers. It was a richly
rewarding hobby.

Of course, Leonardo had to remind himself from time to
time that his ideas would have been received with considerable
alarm by many of the inhabitants of this narrow-minded
backwater, so mostly he kept his thoughts to himself. Once
in a while, though, particularly in the course of an evening's
drinking, he could not resist dropping the odd hint to his
companion.

'Multiple Empathy?' pondered the schoolmaster. 'It seems to
me that the operator would require quite extraordinary mental
abilities in order to withstand it. Wouldn't it be like . . . like trying to be everybody in the world, all at the same time?' He
sucked ruminatively at his pipe.

'More or less,' agreed the magician. He stared for a moment
into the cloud of smoke that surrounded his friend. 'Yes, I've
been thinking a lot lately about the type of mind it would
require. The difficulty would lie in the need to reconcile all
those different viewpoints. There would be so many . . . so many
contradictions, inconsistencies, clashes of perspective. That
alone would require a mind of unique flexibility. And on top of
that, one would need the ability to . . . to sort of see the whole
picture spread out, if you know what I mean.' He gestured
broadly with his hands, knocking over a couple of empty flasks.

'But, of course, at the same time taking a totally objective view of it all.' He paused to draw breath. 'In the hands of the wrong person, there would be immense potential for doing harm. Immense. To others, as well as to oneself, come to think of it.'

The two companions were silent for a while, each wrapped in his own thoughts.

'Somehow it reminds me of something,' said the schoolmaster finally. 'At the moment, I can't quite put my finger on it. But I think I may have one or two books at home in my library. I'll have a rummage. And if I find anything, I'll try and remember to bring it in next week.'

'Sounds intriguing,' said the magician. 'How's your flask?'

At the Church and Afterwards

Helen's ornately studded leather jacket did not seem appropriate garb for a funeral, so Rusty was ransacking the wobbly, camphor-scented wardrobe in his mother's room, searching for an alternative. The formal suit that he had worn during his senior years at the high school was still hanging there, and although he found it rather tight across the shoulders and rather short in the leg, he decided that it would have to do. Among the belts and scarves on the narrow metal rail, he found a plain black tie that he did not recognise. He guessed that it must have belonged to his father. He could find no shoes, and was forced to make do with the plimsolls that Helen had given him.

A few minutes before the hour, the sound of the church bell rang out across the village. It occurred to Rusty that this must be the same bell that had been lost in the river so many years ago, the same bell that he had dived down to find, the same bell that had rung out across the fields the day he had watched the kestrel hovering in the sky.

Arriving at the church in his undersized formal attire, he felt constricted and uncomfortable and ill-prepared for his role as chief mourner. However, he managed the greetings and handshakes without mishap, and passively allowed himself to be ushered to the place of honour in the front pew. Although he suspected that it was not quite proper to do so, he then turned furtively around to scrutinise the small band of mourners. He recognised the old schoolmaster and felt warmed by his friendly presence. Granny Hopkins was at her usual place at the back of the church, looking particularly grim in her black veiled hat. Among the other mourners, Rusty spotted his old schoolfellows Colin Hopkins and his brother Sammy. They raised hands simultaneously in greeting. Doctor Gilbert, now looking quite unsteady, was squeezing his usual dour chords from the harmonium. Close by, watching him anxiously, sat a weary-looking young woman whom it took Rusty a moment to recognise as his former sweetheart Eileen. She noticed his stare, responded with a curt formal nod, then turned quickly away.

At that moment, Rusty's mental inventory-taking was interrupted by the arrival of the coffin, and he hastily turned to face the front in what he hoped was a respectful posture. A few moments later, the priest took up his position. He was just beginning his address when there was a sudden commotion at the church door. Decorum forgotten, everyone looked around to identify the late arrivals.

Taking their places at the back of the church was a group of about six ragged, dark-haired, sallow-skinned people. The men wore long moustaches and some of them had knives tucked into their belts. Rusty's heart pounded. He recognised them at once as wandering folk, and he knew that they must be his father's people.

After the service and the burial, the funeral party adjourned to the school hall, where the ladies from the church had prepared some refreshments. The stove in the corner was generating its usual sweltering heat, and Rusty was now feeling more uncomfortable than ever, but he knew that he would be expected to put on his bravest face as host and chief mourner.

He reminded himself to try and exchange at least a few words with each of the guests.

'She was such a hard worker,' said the priest. 'She really did a tremendous amount for the church. I don't know how we'll manage without her.'

'It's funny, though,' Rusty replied. 'I know she did a lot of church things, but it felt somehow as though she was only doing it all because she had to. Not because she wanted to.'

Wrongfooted by this unexpected candour, the priest took a moment to compose his reply.

'She came to the village as a stranger,' he said finally. 'She was born in another part of the land, one of the outer islands, I seem to remember. Perhaps she was trying especially hard to become accepted by our little community. People often do, you know. Belonging to a community is so important, don't you think?'

'From the islands. She never told me.' Rusty was thoughtful for a moment, then he managed to collect himself and continue. 'Actually, I've been living in a sort of community myself. It was good, being a part of something like that, but I did find after a while that I wanted to move on.'

'Well, you're very welcome back here,' replied the priest. 'Delicious sandwiches, by the way.'

The leader of the wandering folk introduced himself.

'My name is Luke Greening,' he said. He spoke stiffly, as if reciting a prepared speech. 'I am your father's brother. I have long known that my brother left a woman and child in this village, and although my clan has not passed this way for many a year, I have made it my business to keep myself informed of your doings. So when word reached me of your mother's passing, it fell to me to bring my people here to pay our respects. For, whether you knew it or not, Michael Brown, the blood of the Wanderer flows in your veins, and whether you like it or not, you are one of my people.'

'Thank you. I think I like it well enough.' Rusty had caught the older man's stilted form of speech. 'Is my father alive?'

'I cannot say for certain.' Luke Greening cast his gaze down
ward for a moment. 'Our ways have not crossed for many a
year, and I have heard no tell of his doings. But allow me to
introduce you to your other kinfolk. Here is my wife,
Alexandra – ' Rusty exchanged nods with the tall, courtly
woman ' – and my sons, Gareth and Martin.' Two strapping
young men offered Rusty their hands. 'And here is my cousin
Julia, and her sons, who unfortunately happen to be named
Martin and Gareth.' He smiled for the first time. 'I am sorry to
confuse you.' He was counting on his fingers. 'Is there anyone
else? Oh yes. My niece. Her name is Laurel.'

Facing Rusty stood a dark, upright, self-possessed young
woman. She seemed frighteningly serious and grown-up.

'Hello, Rusty,' said Laurel. She stepped forward and kissed
him formally. 'It's been a while.'

'Hello, Laurel,' replied Rusty. 'What have you been up to?'

'Well, this and that. Actually, I've got quite a lot of things to
tell you about.' Suddenly the formal mask split apart into a mischievous grin, and Rusty felt once again the tug of the old
enchantment. Realising what was happening, Laurel quickly
recomposed her features.

'But I really think you ought to attend to your other guests
just now. I promise I'll talk to you later. Go on.'

Rusty was still struggling to contain his excitement when he
found himself talking to the schoolmaster.

'So how are you feeling, young Brown?' asked the old man,
puffing as usual at his pipe.

'I don't know. Older in some ways.'

'Older?'

'Yes. But younger as well. Confused, I suppose.'

'What are your plans?'

'I hadn't thought. I suppose I shall sell the house and go away
again.'

'That would be a pity. You see, since I retired, there has been no schoolteacher in this village. The children have no schooling now, no learning at all. They are running wild. It is terrible to see, terrible.' For a moment, he seemed overcome. 'The school needs a new master.' He looked at Rusty meaningfully. 'Perhaps a young man with a little education? Or perhaps a young man who might have seen a little of the world?' The meaningful look continued. Rusty searched for a tactful reply.

'I'll certainly think about it,' he said eventually.

He was now feeling not only hot and uncomfortable, but flustered and confused. There were too many people, too many surprises, too much to think about.

'Please do think about it. The school could use a young man like you.'

At that moment, Rusty was startled out of the exchange by a harsh, abrupt chord of music. He looked around. The Wanderers had produced musical instruments from somewhere – concertina, pipe and fiddle – and had begun to play.

The schoolmaster whispered to him reverently, 'It must be their music of mourning. I've read so much about it, but I never dreamed I'd live to hear it.'

They listened, spellbound. As befitted the occasion, the music began solemnly with a series of long, wailing chords, but after a few minutes the tempo gradually began to increase, a rhythm established itself, and suddenly the four young men, Gareth and Martin and Martin and Gareth, gave a shout, leaped forward and started to dance. A ripple of shock passed around the hall, and one or two of the older people pointedly took their leave. The music grew faster and wilder, the young men now hurling themselves through the air in acrobatic leaps as the jagged rhythms and angular melodies interwove in ever more complex patterns.

Rusty was gaping in amazement when he felt a light hand at his shoulder, a soft whisper of breath at his cheek.

'It's the Funeral Dance,' explained Laurel in a silky whisper. 'Haven't you ever seen it? It's all about the journey to the next world, all the dangers on the way, you know the sort of thing. It's considered a great honour to have it performed. And if it's

to be done properly, all the guests have to join in as well.'
Suddenly she grinned again. 'But of course the chief mourner
is expected to take the lead.'

Rusty considered this.

'All right. Why not? But I'd want you – ' he swallowed ' – to
be my partner.'

In a sudden gesture of intimacy, she squeezed his arm.

'Silly boy. Of course I will. But don't let's rush. They'll probably play a waltz in a minute.'

From the Journal of Victor Lazarus

Tuesday 26th January (continued)

In a state of supreme agitation, I waited at the front gates of the
house with my book of accounts clutched in my hands. It was
only with great difficulty that I resisted the temptation to pace
up and down in the road. An hour passed, and another hour. I
could hear the music of the band as it rippled through the air,
and from time to time I could make out cries of delight and
bursts of laughter and outbreaks of applause. Resolute, I waited.
Finally, at the stroke of noon, a distant figure came into view
around the bend in the road. At first I could make out no
details, but as it approached closer I could see that it was the figure of a man in his middle years, a man who walked with a
rather uncertain, shambling gait. He was clad in a long, tattered
robe, heavy boots and a lopsided, broad-brimmed hat. At the
gates, he halted to draw breath and to brush the dust from his
garments. I knew at once (pray do not ask me how!) that this
was the owner of the house.

At last we stood face to face. Timidly I introduced myself,
tentatively I held out my account book for inspection. The
owner looked at me quizzically.

'Ah yes, the book,' he said finally. 'Excellent, Lazarus, excellent.

I suppose we'll need to have a look at that later on. But just now, if you don't mind, I should very much like to make a tour of the house, examine what you have done, assess the work, all that sort of thing.'

And with that, he passed abruptly through the gates and vanished into the throng. For the next hour I tried in vain to corner him, but every time I believed him to be within my grasp, he managed somehow to elude me. On one occasion I caught a glimpse of him emerging from the basement with Sam, doubtless deep in conversation about the details of the defective boiler. Later I saw him for a moment in the room of comics, chuckling with the little red-headed boy over a copy of *The Wizard*. Later still, I caught a glimpse of him ensconced in a quiet corner of the room of fossils, sipping a cup of tea with the old lady, who had seemingly awoken for the occasion. But each time that I approached him, he somehow managed to slip away. By the end of the afternoon, I was feeling close to despair.

However, at this point an unexpected diversion arose. I was making my way across the entrance hall, when suddenly a familiar husky voice rang out from somewhere above me, echoing through the house and instantly drawing the attention of all.

'My lords, ladies and gentlemen,' cried the voice. 'The Dance of the Shadow!'

Every head turned towards the source of the announcement, and simultaneously the breath caught in every throat. At the head of the staircase stood a tall, dazzling figure, a figure of startling grace and elegance, a figure lithe and sleek in form, a figure immaculately garbed in the chequered suit of the Harlequin. The feet were unshod, the lips were parted in an equivocal smile, and the eyes were concealed behind a sable mask. I became aware that my heart was pounding with apprehension.

Then, with delicate tread, Lee descended the staircase. The Dance of the Shadow had begun.

Rusty and Laurel

One by one the mourners took their leave. The leftover food was cleared away, the furniture was pushed back into position. Emerging from the kitchen, where he had been thanking the church ladies for their help, Rusty found himself face to face with Laurel. She seemed ill at ease.

'I really need to get away from my people for a couple of hours,' she said in a low voice. 'Any chance of dropping round to your place for a bit?'

And so, as night fell, Rusty and Laurel found themselves seated either side of the stove in Mrs Brown's parlour, sharing the last bottle of Mrs Brown's elderberry wine. Laurel drew a small clay pipe from her pouch and began packing it with the aromatic mixture of herbs that the Wanderers liked to smoke. She took a couple of fierce puffs.

'Here' she said. 'Try this. It should help you calm down a bit.'

Some time later, they were stretched out together on the rug in front of the fireplace, enjoying a companionable silence. Rusty was toying with a lock of Laurel's black hair, inhaling her rich, dark scent, filling his lungs with it. Finally, he broke the silence.

'Remember that little shelter at the top of the field at school? All those things you used to whisper to me?'

'How could I forget?' She turned the gleam of her dark eyes full on him. 'Nothing was the same for me after that. My whole life got turned upside down.'

'Nothing the same? Why? What happened?'

'Don't you know? Don't you remember what I told you?'

Slowly, Rusty shook his head.

'You whispered something . . . Yes . . . I could feel your breath . . . I'd never felt it before . . . And the smell in there . . . Wet raincoats . . .' Gradually he returned to the present, to the intense gaze of Laurel's dark eyes. 'So what was it that you said?'

'You never found out?' She giggled. 'I passed you the Gift.'

'The what?' In a neglected corner of Rusty's mind, a faint

bell chimed, but he could not at once attach a meaning to the phrase.

'The Gift,' repeated Laurel. She fidgeted uncomfortably. 'Look, it's complicated. I can't explain it all now. Maybe tomorrow. You see, I thought it was all right to tell you . . . but then my people said I shouldn't have. They said I'd broken one of our laws, and I had to be punished. That's how everything got upset.'

'All because of what you said to me. And I didn't even remember it. I still don't really know what it was. And what was the punishment? Were you beaten?'

'Only the once. No, it was worse than that. They sent me away to join the circus.'

'The circus? So it was you that I saw? But in any case, it hardly sounds –' he kissed the side of her neck '– like a punishment.'

'You really don't understand, do you? I didn't either, to begin with. But I learned soon enough. You see, among my people, it's the meanest kind of work there is, the lowest, the most humiliating thing that can happen to you. I had to do acrobatics, juggling, all that sort of stuff . . . Well, I suppose it does sound like fun, but after a bit I really came to hate it. And it got worse when I started, you know, to grow up, to become a woman. Those costumes.' She giggled again. 'They were really quite . . . quite immodest.' Now she was laughing aloud. 'And all those people staring, and the men shouting things . . . At first, I didn't understand them. But later . . .'

Her laughter infected Rusty, and for the next few minutes they were both helpless.

'So how long were you in the circus?' asked Rusty eventually.

She managed to calm down a little.

'Well, it was a severe punishment. My people take these things pretty seriously. So I had to stay at least until I came of age. And . . .' She hesitated. 'I hated myself for putting up with it. And I needed someone to blame. So I blamed you, Rusty. I blamed you. Because it seemed to me that it was all your fault. I wanted my revenge, Rusty. I wanted it so badly.'

Rusty's heart was pounding in his throat. Laurel was quick to sense his unease.

'No, silly boy, you're safe now.' She prodded the end of his nose with a finger. 'Things got much better when they let me do the knife-throwing.'

'Knife-throwing?'

'Yes. It was the only thing in the circus I ever really wanted to do. Madame Constanzas, she was my trainer, she said it wasn't a woman's act, but I kept on and on, and in the end she agreed. And the crowds loved it, especially the men.'

She ran a speculative finger down Rusty's breastbone, sketched a small circle just above his waistband.

'Of course, I was a bit older by then, a bit more of a woman, if you know what I mean. And after that I started to feel better about myself.' She stared into the fire for a moment, then looked at Rusty again. 'But I still hated the place. You don't know how I hated it, Rusty. I just wanted to get out. So as soon as I came of age, I ran away. And then I sort of went wild for a bit.' Suddenly she uttered a rueful laugh. 'Actually, I joined the bandits, so the knife-throwing came in quite handy in the end.'

Rusty's jaw dropped. Laurel spluttered with laughter again.

'And it certainly beat being in the circus. But you saw me, didn't you?'

'Yes, that's right. I did see you. In the mountains. And you spared my life.'

Rusty paused, thoughtful. Laurel took a long pull at the pipe, passed it to Rusty. He squinted at it doubtfully, took a tentative suck, inhaled a mouthful of ashes and was seized by a prolonged fit of coughing.

'Never mind,' laughed Laurel. 'I'll refill it in a minute. Where was I?'

'The mountains.'

'Yes. I could have had my revenge then, couldn't I? But somehow, when the moment came, I found I didn't want it any more. I looked down, and I saw that little dog looking up at me, and it was as if . . . as if something reached out and stopped me. Maybe something to do with the dog?'

Suddenly Laurel was no longer laughing. Her face was pale, her eyes large.

'You were the only one I ever spared, Rusty. I've got blood on my hands. So much blood.'

They stared wordlessly at each other, and for an instant it was as though each could see behind the other's eyes, deep into the darkness, deep into the hard fires that burned in the unknown realm beyond the darkness.

'I've got blood on my hands too,' Rusty replied finally. 'Let me tell you my story.'

And so they talked on into the night, sharing their secrets and their fears and their dreams. It grew late. The fire in the stove burned down. Rusty raked over the last embers, brushed the ashes from the grate, carefully closed the flaps. And while he was doing these things, dimly he was aware of Laurel standing, of Laurel turning, of the swirl of Laurel's skirts as she silently mounted the stair. Heart in mouth, Rusty bolted the doors, doused the lamps, and followed. On the landing, he unhooked the linen press beside the closed door, selected one of his mother's nightdresses. Then, hesitating for just a moment, he tapped softly at the door of his mother's room.

The door swung open. Laurel was standing beside the bed, already half-undressed. Seemingly unembarrassed by the intrusion, she made no move to cover herself. Suddenly, Rusty's clothes were feeling tighter than ever. He held out the nightdress.

'I'm sorry. I thought you might want . . .'

He tailed off in embarrassment. Laurel gave him a reproachful look.

'I don't think we're going to need that, are we? Here, let me help you with those buttons.'

Dumbly, Rusty accepted the assistance offered. After a moment, Laurel looked up at him with mock concern.

'Poor Rusty, you still can't keep your socks up. Let's just hope nothing else lets you down.'

She was drawing him onto the bed. Then, at the last moment, he froze. The coverlet still bore the imprint of his mother's corpse.

'Can we . . . ?' he stuttered.

'Can we what, Rusty?' Her eyes were imploring.

'Nothing. It doesn't matter.'

In silence I dance, and as I dance, each of you creates your own rhythm and your own harmony. Now I reach out to encompass the whole of the house, and all of the grounds around the house, and all of the woods and the mountains and the oceans beyond, and, leaping and curving and diving, I spin with my fingertips and the points of my toes an interlocking web of broad circles and shapely ellipses and sweeping hyperbolae that delineate my realm with enigmatic logic.

Arching and vaulting and spanning, gliding and dissolving from one attitude to the next, I sketch out in my wake the outline of an unseen moving sculpture, into which I breathe a graceful spectrum of hues that speaks to each one of you a language that your intellect cannot begin to interpret. Now you see me as the Harlequin in spangled suit, now the merciful angel swooping from the skies, now the wild beast poised to pounce.

And at last, after a spiralling cadence of twists and cartwheels and pirouettes that leaves you gasping for breath, my pattern resolves itself through imperceptible gradations to equilibrium, the delicate tracery of invisible architecture suspended in the air around me, slowly fragmenting into a multitude of pinpoints, gently drifting down among you in intricate mosaic, a fragment lodging at the heart of each of you, a fragment that you will carry with you long after you forget this day.

And even as my image dissolves, perhaps already you begin to forget.

★　　★　　★

In the Night

'Tell you a secret?' Laurel murmured drowsily. Rusty smiled.

'More secrets? Are you sure that's a good idea?' He was stroking her shoulder with a fingertip.

'Oh, you!' She kissed his cheek. 'No, it's just about the Gift. You see, there are rules.' Suddenly awake, she sat up. 'Rules. And one of the rules says that when you pass the Gift to another, you lose it. So when I passed it to you that day, I lost it. For ever. And I'm going to regret that for the rest of my life.' Suddenly a note of anguish scarred her voice. 'I think that's really why I wanted my revenge.'

She turned to look him full in the face. There were no fires behind her eyes now. They were the eyes of a frightened child.

'You bear the Gift now, Rusty. Learn to use it. You could do wonderful things.'

She had started to sob. Rusty drew her to him.

'It's all right,' he whispered. 'Talk tomorrow. Sleep now.'

And together they drifted away again into the blackness.

From the Journal of Victor Lazarus

Tuesday 26th January (continued)

Transfixed, I stood as one man among the crowd, mesmerised by the Shadow's dance, until, by and by, the dancer moved on to another part of the house. I shook my head in bewilderment. Slowly, I started to come to my senses. Then, with a jolt, I remembered that I still had a vital task to carry out. I turned around, scanning the room for some sign of the owner, but could see no evidence of him. I was about to move on to another room, when I was horrified to catch a glimpse of the ragged hem of his robe disappearing through the main doorway.

Abandoning all dignity, I took to my heels and set off in hot pursuit. From the porch, I could see the stooping figure moving at a steady pace down the path. Desperately I called after him, entreating him at least to make his inspection of the books. At the sound of my voice, he stopped in his tracks, turned around, and took a pace back towards me. I walked quickly down the steps. He seemed somewhat embarrassed at being waylaid in such a manner, and explained sheepishly that he could remain at the house no longer, as he was due to depart early on the morrow for a faraway destination. Even as he spoke, he was beginning to draw away from me again.

At that moment I lost control of myself and seized him by the arm, begging him at least to inform me whether everything had been to his satisfaction. He was clearly taken aback by my extreme state of agitation, but nevertheless managed a politely affirmative reply, following this with a gentle reminder to me of my obligation towards my other guests. While making these remarks, he contrived in some way to free himself from my grip, and, before I could gather my wits, he had begun to walk quickly away again. I attempted to pursue him but found myself rooted to the spot. It seemed that the last of my energy had deserted me.

Frantically, I shouted after the receding figure, desperate at least to discover upon what date he intended to return. But he had already passed through the gates into the road, and his voice was faint. Eventually I summoned the strength to drag myself down the path to the gates. I looked forlornly to left and to right, but he had already vanished from sight. Faintly, the breeze carried his last words back up the road.

'When my house is ready, I shall return.'

I walked slowly back up the path, astonished at the owner's behaviour, embarrassed at my own loss of control, in a state of utter confusion over whether the day had been a failure or a success. Our conversation must have continued for longer than I had realised, for the daylight was beginning to fade, and the festivities were coming to an end. At the front of the house, the bandsmen were packing away their instruments. At the rear, the canvas of the circus tent was spread out flat on the ground, and the swings and merry-go-rounds of the funfair were already in pieces. At the door, Harold was ushering away the last of the visitors, and from the cellar I could hear Sam turning the huge valves to shut down the boilers. I walked slowly through the empty rooms, silent now but for the echo of my footsteps. In the attic I chanced upon Lee, who was folding away the Harlequin suit.

Lee, it turned out, had had a conversation of some length with the owner, who, it appeared, had been quite delighted with the progress that had been made. A warm tide of relief flooded through me. To my surprise, I found myself grasping both of Lee's delicate hands and uttering fulsome thanks. Lee smiled a mysterious smile, then to my astonishment, leaned forward quickly and kissed me on the cheek.

'Thank you, Victor,' said Lee. 'It's been a hard day. Time for bed now.'

Face to face with Lee for a moment, it struck me that my shadow had grown in stature. Now the two of us stood as equals, each quite as tall as the other.

The Morning After

Rusty did not wake until the afternoon. When he reached out for Laurel, he discovered that the other side of the bed was empty and cold.

'Laurel?'

He looked in each room of the house, but there was no sign of her. And when he looked in the front parlour, he discovered that his mother's silver candlesticks had disappeared from their place on the mantelpiece. He looked in each room again, looked in the yard, even looked in the outhouses. But in his heart he knew that Laurel would not be returning.

★   ★   ★

At The Inn

'I found it.' The schoolmaster was lighting up his pipe when the magician joined him. 'Here.' He handed his companion an octavo-sized leather-bound volume bearing the title *Legends of the Forgotten Age.* 'It's a book of old stories,' he explained. 'I've made a bit of a study of them. There's a marker at the page you want.'

The magician had already located the passage.

'*The Legend of the Wanderers and the Islanders,*' he read aloud. 'What's this about? *At the beginning, the Great Being breathed life into the Land . . .*'

'You can skip the first bit,' his friend broke in. 'Start about halfway down the page.'

The magician grunted.

'All right, I've got it . . . *The secrets of the Wanderers and the Islanders were passed on from generation to generation. And the Great Being was glad, and so the Great Being saw fit to bestow upon the people a special talent.* This sounds more like it.' He read on slowly. '*And so it came about that each of the Wanderers learned how to look into the eye of another, and to see there all the pathways of her life, twisting and turning, both backward to the day of her birth and forward to the day of her departure. And those who learned this talent were said to bear the Gift.*' He grunted again. 'Could come in handy, I suppose. *And it likewise came about that each of the Islanders learned how to view the whole of the Land in one glimpse, as if through the eyes of a bird of prey hovering at great height, and so they learned to understand the ways in which the lives of all the men and women were woven together to form a never-ending seamless web. And those who learned this talent were said to see the Land through the Eye of the Kestrel.* Pretty turn of phrase, don't you think?' He read the passage again, silently this time. Finally he looked up, smiling faintly.

'I see what you're saying,' he said. 'In this story, a Wanderer can see the world through the eyes of another person. And an Islander can see the world from a great height. So, between them, the Wanderers and the Islanders have been blessed with just those qualities of mind that would be required to interpret the world through my Multiple Empathy engine.' He chuckled. 'Ideally, I suppose, one would require a subject who was half Wanderer and half Islander, assuming that such a person existed.'

'So it seems to me.' The schoolmaster was working up an impressive head of smoke on his pipe. 'There are more details, but they are mostly in other books. I could look them out, if you like.'

'No, don't bother,' replied the magician. 'It's an amusing fancy, but after all, it's only a story . . .' He noticed the school-master's raised eyebrow. 'Isn't it?'

'Good question,' replied the other. 'As I think I mentioned, I have made a bit of a study of the ancient legends. And, actually, I have become convinced that all of them have some basis in historical fact.'

The magician laughed.

'Come on now. You're talking about fairy tales, not about real magic! The only magic I've ever known is nothing more than engineering, pure and simple.' The schoolmaster attempted to interrupt, but the magician's flow was not to be broken. 'I know what you're going to say. Yes, of course we call it by the name of magic, but in the end it's not really magic, not in the fairy-tale sense, anyway. It's engineering. Nothing more than nuts and bolts.' He took a long draught of ale.

The schoolmaster puffed his pipe in silence for a few moments.

'Is it?' he asked finally. 'Personally, I am quite convinced that descendants of the two clans of legend are walking the land to this day.'

They stared at each other in temporary stalemate.

After a minute, the silence was broken by the arrival of another customer in the bar. It was a young man with an untidy shock of red hair. He was wearing a pair of grey trousers that were slightly too tight and slightly too short, along with a rather

dashing black leather jacket, which was decorated with an intricate pattern of brass studs. On his feet were a very battered pair
of plimsolls.

'Hello there, young Brown,' called the schoolmaster. 'Come
and meet my friend. This is Leonardo Pegasus.'

'Hello,' said the young man. 'My name is Michael Brown.'

'I do like your jacket,' said the magician. 'I once knew someone who had a jacket rather like that.'

From the Journal of Victor Lazarus

Monday 17th May

A period of three months has passed since the owner's visit, but
I have not until today felt impelled to make any entry in this
journal. From time to time I have pondered over the owner's
last, cryptic words, but still I have no notion of what he might
have meant when he said that he would return when I was
ready. For the record, however, I am pleased to note that the
house seems finally to have settled into a steady way of working. Thanks to the inspiration of Lee, and the dedicated work of
Sam and Harold, we have even started to acquire something of
a reputation as a haven for artists, musicians and other species of
creative persons. At any given time, there seem always to be several of them under our roof, resting or working for longer or
shorter periods of time. Harold is developing a canny instinct
for commercial opportunities, and has started to plan a long-
term programme of events to entertain our constant stream of
visitors. He now bears the title of Artistic Director, and continues to manage the collections as well as the performances.
Sam, meanwhile, bears the title of Estates Manager, and takes
care of both the day-to-day maintenance and the longer-term
development of the property.

So far as my own role is concerned, I have to admit that I

have lately been at somewhat of a loose end, although I would be reluctant to own up to this in public. I was therefore secretly relieved when Lee raised the subject, observing that I seemed listless, and suggesting that perhaps a short holiday might offer a welcome diversion.

I looked up from the marmalade jar that I had been scraping. (We were taking breakfast at the time.) On reflection, it seemed a good suggestion. As well as offering a welcome change of scene, it would afford me the opportunity to think things over, perhaps even to attempt to unravel the mystery of the owner's intentions. I enquired whether Lee had anything particular in mind. This enquiry was a mere formality, as I had by now begun to understand that Lee always had something particular in mind.

Lee's suggestion (it turned out) was that we should make a journey of exploration into the overgrown garden at the rear of the house. The garden had lain neglected over the winter and now stood in dire need of attention. My initial response was unenthusiastic, as it seemed to me that this was a task that fell more naturally within the remit of the Estates Manager, but Lee was persistent. In the end I relented, for in truth I have begun to place some faith in Lee's instincts in such matters. Lee has, after all, inhabited this place for longer than any of us.

And, of course, nobody is quite certain how far behind the house the garden extends.

And so we stride off together, packs on our backs, cheered on our way by all our friends. To begin with, the path leads us across the lawns and through the familiar tangle of overgrown shrubberies, but before long the terrain becomes wilder, and we find ourselves traversing treacherous forest and inhospitable moorland, before finally we arrive at the edge of the rugged mountain country. And there, hopping nimbly from crag to crag, I lead you each day along vertiginous ridges, up precipitous rock faces, through plunging ravines and across thundering rapids.

And each night, beside the campfire, I sing to you tenderly, and in your dreams I show myself to you, sometimes in my bright form, sometimes in my dark form, and sometimes as both together side by side, our two forms blending in unearthly harmony, our two voices lost in the darkness beyond the reach of the firelight.

And by and by we pass between unscaled peaks to the quiet land at the far side of the mountains, and at last to the very shore of the ocean that lies beyond.

From the Journal of Victor Lazarus

Sunday 13th June

For many weeks we have trekked across rugged and inhospitable country. From time to time our paths have crossed with those of other wandering folk – roadmenders, knife-grinders, even, on one occasion, a small circus – until finally we have found ourselves at a lonely and tranquil place, a place that lies in the shelter of the mountain peaks and that commands a panoramic view of the ocean. Scanning the horizon through my field glasses, I can discern many islands, scattered both far and near. I can even recognise some of their inhabitants.

On one island lies a sacred place, within which a group of people are conducting some sort of solemn ritual, chanting and striking extraordinary attitudes. On another island I see an old lady, fast asleep in her chair. Surely she has a familiar air about her? Can it be the same old lady who used to slumber in the room of fossils? On another island a graceful girl is dancing, while other, clumsier dancers cavort around her in a ragged circle. On another island I see a vigorous, moustached man leading an exercise class, people of various shapes and ages bending and stretching with stoical determination. On yet another, I see nothing but a kestrel hovering high in the air.

But on the largest island, the island nearest to the shore, I see only mist. Yet I somehow know that it is to this mist-shrouded island that we must go upon the morrow. Whatever lies at the heart of that mist, there we shall find the object of our quest.

Tomorrow we will attempt the crossing.

And tonight, in some way, has the air of being the last night of our holiday.

And tonight, Victor, you shall at last see my true face, for you have toiled hard and you have earned your reward. As you doze beside the fire, I shall enter your dreams for one last time, and there I shall show myself to you as I truly am, for as you have begun to learn, I have not one face but two.

One face is the dark face that once you feared, the face of the scarred and snarling Beast, the face with the burning eyes and the deadly fangs. But perhaps you have started at last to understand that this face is not the face of the predator, but the face of the protector.

For behind the dark face lies another face, the pale face, the face of that tall, remote incandescent Being, a fragment of whom abides within you and within each one of your kind, that Being that you so desire, but from which, in your fear, you seek the protection of the Beast.

Yet each of those faces is my true face, for I am both Dark and Bright, both Beast and Being, both Guardian and Gift. Yes, Victor. I, Lee, am the Guardian of your Gift. Tonight you shall know me. And tomorrow I must say farewell.

The Inside Pocket

'It's a useful jacket,' said Rusty. 'Plenty of pockets.'

'Jackets like that often have a hidden pocket, somewhere in the lining,' said Leonardo, trying hard to appear casual. 'How did you come by it?'

'Someone gave it to me,' said Rusty, vaguely. 'A woman.' He was feeling carefully inside. 'It's funny, I've never really looked in the lining. Oh yes, here we are. What's this?'

After a little fiddling, he slowly withdrew what appeared to be a tightly wadded bundle of documents. The magician was no longer able to control his excitement.

'Unfold them,' he panted. 'Carefully, for heaven's sake. Spread them out.'

The schoolmaster pushed some empty flasks to one side, knocking some of them onto the floor. Leonardo ignored them. The two older men watched as the yellowing parchment unfolded.

Rusty stared at the maze of lines as they spread themselves out before him. He was at the centre of a labyrinthine array of interlocking radial lines and concentric circles. And through this geometric array was woven a chaotic tapestry, a tapestry of snaking, tangling threads, a network of pathways diverging from a central point, connecting that point to every other point, spanning every divide, vaulting outwards into a boundless framework of invisible architecture that seemed to project itself from the very surface of the parchment, extending in every direction, backwards and forwards and sideways in time and space.

And somewhere, somewhere perhaps only just beyond the reach of his arm, there waited a tall, silent ring of stone forms, perhaps the tokens in some unfathomable game, each one with its head proud in the air, its foot firm on the ground. For here were the Stone of the Past and the Stone of the Future, here were the Stone of Impulse and the Stone of Reason, and here were the Earth Stone and the Sky Stone. And silently his being opened to the pull of the Stones, silently his being poised itself in fine equilibrium while the intricate mechanism of opposing forces ebbed and flowed through him and danced around him, until Instinct and Reason and Past and Future and Earth and Sky seemed to fuse into one and he floated, dancing weightless in the boundless ocean of calm.

And for a long, long time he remained there, until the awesome mass of the Earth Stone slowly reasserted itself, drawing him back into the ground, to the very source, to the hidden centre of the world where beat the deep and aching pulse of the Life Force itself, offering him once again a glimpse of the dark realm that it commanded, and of the hard fires that burned there. Finally, shaking his head slowly, he looked up.

'Oh,' he said faintly. 'That.'

'What is it?' asked the schoolmaster.

'Gentlemen,' said the magician, 'what you see before you is the original set of drawings for my Multiple Empathy Engine.'

Rusty had turned very pale, his eyes apparently focused on some distant object. After a while, he seemed to descend hesitantly to earth.

'Where do engines come into it?' he finally managed.

The magician gave him a long, puzzled look.

'Let's have another drink,' he said finally. 'I'll try to explain.'

Far into the night they talked. The magician talked of the city, and the Theatre of Magic, and the Empathy Engine, and the Multiple Empathy Engine The young man talked of the Wanderers, and the Wolf Boys, and the Eye of the Kestrel, and the Keeper of the Ground. And the schoolmaster talked little, but he listened spellbound to the other two, and he stared into the fire, and he dreamed dreams of the Forgotten Age.

Eventually, the landlord was forced to eject them from the premises. They were the last customers to leave. As the lights in the inn were extinguished one by one, the magician led his companions rather unsteadily towards the hayloft at the rear. At the foot of the ladder, he paused.

'Let me make you some coffee,' he suggested. 'I can knock up quite a decent brew these days. Assuming I can find the coffee engine, of course. And I've got something else that might interest you as well.'

'I think I've had enough excitement for one evening,' the schoolmaster laughed. 'We old folk like our early nights. I'll leave you to it.'

But Rusty was already halfway up the ladder. Hauling himself up into the gloom of the hayloft, he could sense the bulk of a massive structure looming above him but could at first make out no details.

'Hold on,' called the magician. 'I'll light a couple of lamps.'

And then he saw it. At the centre of the room stood a broad rostrum, about waist-high, that appeared to have been constructed from old packing cases and scraps of corrugated iron. Rusty could not make out what, if anything, stood on top of the rostrum, for it was surrounded on all sides by a tangle of strange machinery. Snaking cables, spider-like junction boxes, lamps mounted on rickety tripods built from old coat-hangers, cracked lenses, wavering ranks of gauges housed in battered sardine tins, clumsy-looking armatures wrapped around old biscuit-barrels. Everything seemed to be held together with pieces of knotted string and old bootlaces, and everything looked as if it might collapse at the touch of a fingertip. There was an overpowering smell of ozone and glue and paint and scorched dust.

'The Multiple Empathy Engine,' said the magician, with a slight hint of apology. He pulled a couple of wobbly levers, and the machinery shuddered into life with a disgruntled roar.

'What's that in the middle of it all?' Rusty was struggling to get a clear view.

'Be with you in a moment,' mumbled the magician, temporarily out of sight. 'I'm sure that coffee engine must be here somewhere. No, no, don't move that. Why don't you take a look through these?' Negotiating his way with practised ease between the stacks of machinery, he offered the boy a pair of battered brass eyepieces attached to some sort of extendable mounting, then carefully clamped a heavy pair of headphones over his ears.

For a moment, Rusty was marooned in darkness and silence. Then, slowly, he started to become aware of muffled sounds and blurred shapes and indeterminate colours. At first he could make no sense of what he heard and saw. Then, bit by bit, the scene came into focus. It was as though he were suspended in the sky, looking down . . .

He was looking down upon a large house. It stood at the top of a sloping patch of ground, enclosed by smartly painted iron railings, and surrounded by immaculately tended lawns and borders. It was a tall, imposing house, a many-windowed gothic phantasy of a house, a house of gables and chimney pots and weathervanes and gargoyles. From the windows spilled light and music and the sound of voices. And at the highest point of the house, seeming to act as a focus for all the light and music and energy, stood a tall, six-sided turret, with a window in each wall.

'That looks like Mum's old tea caddy,' Rusty murmured to himself.

'It may very well be just that.' Faintly, he could hear the magician's voice. 'But never mind the house. Try taking a look at the gardens. You see, the house was what I started with. But then I found I needed to add some grounds, and eventually I've had to design a whole landscape. Look over here.'

Rusty found his gaze directed towards the rear of the house. He thought he could see something moving, and fiddled with the eyepieces to give himself a closer view. Now he could make it out . . .

Two miniature people were emerging from the French doors, one sturdy, plodding figure wearing some kind of military uniform, and a companion, younger, more agile, who danced and skipped and somersaulted around the older one. As Rusty watched, they stepped out across the lawn and through the tangle of shrubbery. For a while they made their way between banks of overgrown shrubs, until before long the landscape started to become wilder, and they found themselves traversing forest and moorland and hill. And for days on end they continued, travelling through ever more perilous terrain, arriving at last at a rugged tract of mountain country. And there they continued along vertiginous ridges, up precipitous rock faces, through plunging ravines, across thundering rapids . . .

'Nice touch, those rapids, don't you think?' The magician's voice broke in upon Rusty again. 'I'm actually rather proud of them.'

Rusty nodded absently, his attention concentrated upon the

two characters and their adventure. They seemed larger now, almost life-size, and he could clearly see the expressions on their faces. In fact, it felt almost as though he himself were toiling along beside them. Without realising what was happening to him, he had become completely immersed in their story, inseparable from them as they strode silently along the hard mountain road, no longer aware of his real surroundings as they arrived at last in the quiet land at the far side of the mountains.

And there they descended the gentle slope to the shore of the ocean, in full view of the islands that lay beyond. That night, they made camp as usual, and at the campfire the young one sang to the old one, strange, unearthly songs of the forgotten age, and the music and the words and the fire wove slow rings of enchantment around them until at last they lay down together and slept. They slept soundly, and they dreamed deep, mysterious dreams.

At first light they awoke, and they walked down to the shoreline. Here, at a little jetty, they found a dinghy awaiting them. Without so much as a backward glance, they climbed on board and loosed the painter. The old one took the oars and began to row steadily out towards the nearest island, while the young one sat at the helm, effortlessly steering them through the shallows.

Gradually the island loomed closer, but before they could reach their goal they felt an alarming bump. The dinghy listed suddenly to starboard, and they realised that she had become grounded on rocks. They struggled to free her but, despite their best endeavours, she remained stuck fast.

'It's no good, youngster,' said the old one finally. 'I can't get you any further. From now on, you're on your own.'

At that moment, the dialogue faded away and the scene abruptly shrank to a pinpoint and vanished from sight. Disorientated, Rusty clumsily pulled the eyepieces and headphones from his head and slowly realigned his senses to accommodate the sights and scents of the hayloft.

'That's as far as I can get with it,' the magician was explaining. 'They start rowing across, then the boat gets stuck, grounded or whatever you call it. And then the story gets stuck as well, and I can't seem to get any further. It's the same every time I try it.'

But Rusty had begun to understand what was happening.

'I think I can probably help you,' he said after a long pause. 'You see, somehow I seem to know this part of the story. It used to come into my dreams. Actually, it still does, now and then.'

The magician was listening intently. For another long moment, Rusty remained sunk in thought.

'Here's an idea,' he said finally. 'I've got this feeling that we might be able to get the story moving again, but I think it'll need something from each of us to make it work. So I think we should both try it together. Do you have a spare set of eye-pieces?'

'I think so.' The magician started to rummage in a box of lumber, then gave vent to a sudden yelp of triumph. 'Here's my coffee engine! However did it get in here?'

And so, after a suitable pause for refreshments, they tried again.

They were back in the boat, the old one rowing, the young one steering. Gradually the island loomed closer, but before they could reach their goal they felt an alarming bump. The dinghy listed alarmingly to starboard, and they realised that she had become grounded on rocks. They struggled to free her, but, despite their best endeavours, she remained stuck fast.

'It's no good, youngster,' said the ferryman finally. 'I can't get you any further. From now on, you're on your own.'

So the ferryman steadied the craft as best he could, while the the young one rapidly stripped, dived cleanly into the water and swam in steady strokes towards the island.

The ferryman retrieved the young one's jerkin from the bilges, carefully folded it and laid it on the bench beside him.

He watched through his field glasses as the youthful figure receded rapidly into the distance. Then he trained his glasses on the misty shoreline across the water. After a short time, the young one emerged from the waves and stepped lightly up the shingle. And then, at last, the mist cleared and the ferryman could see what was on the island.

At the top of a flight of stone steps stood a tower. It was a tall, imposing, six-sided tower, a tower of grey stone, a tower with a window at the centre of each wall. And at the heart of the tower was a broad flagged chamber circumscribed by six tall windows beneath a beamed ceiling. And at the centre of this chamber was the owner of the house. He was seated at the controls of some kind of machine, busily making adjustments. So engrossed was the owner in his work that he had failed to notice the arrival of his visitor.

The ferryman watched through his glasses as, tiny in the distance, the young one half turned towards him, raised a hand in farewell, then, still dripping, mounted the steps, reached up and grasped the bell pull. After a moment the ferryman heard the note of the bell, chiming out transparently across the water. There followed a short delay, after which the door swung open and the young one stepped inside.

'Who's there?' said the owner, pausing in his work.

And then he saw the youthful visitor who stood bright and graceful at the threshold.

'Who is it?'

In a tide of warmth and energy and light, the visitor stepped softly towards him. The owner rose to his feet.

'Don't I know you?'

And now at last his visitor stood before him, still as a tree, head erect, fair hair framing pale, austerely sculpted features.

'Master Pegasus?'

It was a voice that he remembered from long ago, a voice that bore the soft accent of the outermost isles of the kingdom. The visitor stepped forward and took his hands.

'Hello, Alice,' said Leonardo. There were many things that he might have said then, but in his astonishment and confusion, only one thing came to mind.

'Can you still do that upside-down thing?'

'Whatever am I to do with you?' laughed Alice, despairingly. The magician regarded her gravely.

'You once promised that you would teach me to dance.'

'Well, I've just now been teaching those Wolf Boys to dance,' said Alice. 'Quick learners, they were. I'm sure I could teach you.'

'I'd like that. I think I'm ready for it now.'

She gave a small nod. Then, thoughtfully, she released his hands. She took a step backwards, pirouetted across the flagstones, turned an elegant cartwheel. Finally, she came to rest before him.

'So when do you want to begin?'

'Today?' suggested Leonardo.

'How about tomorrow? See, it's starting to rain just now. We ought to go indoors.'

The magician looked around him. Sure enough, it had begun to rain. He looked up, but could no longer see the ceiling of his chamber. Somehow he must have found his way outside. He looked down and discovered that the flagstones on which he was standing were engraved with a labyrinthine array of interlocking radial lines and concentric circles, like the cogs in a colossal piece of machinery. He scanned the horizon. He thought he could still make out the tall shapes of the windows, but now they appeared broken and irregular in form. And, somehow, they had become more solid, more substantial. They had begun to look, in fact, uncommonly like massive stone forms, positioned on the flagged ground like the counters in some unfathomable game.

The magician looked at the stones. The chiselled planes and intricate patterns of their surfaces were glistening with rain. He could feel powerful currents of energy beginning to weave around them. And was it his imagination, or did they lean inward towards him for a moment? Perhaps they had something to say to him? But no. Not yet. Not just yet.

He felt a gentle touch at his elbow, and realised that he had temporarily forgotten the presence of Alice. Now the magician allowed the girl to lead him with gentle touch to a place at the edge of the arena, a place where they could shelter. It was a special place, a place of safety, a place where they could sit in comfort and listen to the rain as it pounded the hard earth outside. It was a place where they could share all of their secrets and all of their fears and all of their dreams. It was a place where the air smelled, faintly, of wet gaberdine.

No longer a part of the magician's story, the boy drew back, allowed his viewpoint to soar away from the scene, up into the sky, up to a place where he could hover and look down upon the world again as if through the eye of a kestrel. Now he could see the house and the town, and he could see the mountains and the quiet land beyond the mountains, and he could see how they were all linked together by the network of tracks and paths and rivers. Now he could see the distant islands, now he could see how the islands were linked to the shore. And now at last, high above the ocean, he could glimpse for an instant the pattern that the islands made. And at the heart of the furthest island, in a silent, sacred place that bore the scent of clover and long grass and the sea, someone awaited him, someone he surely knew from long ago . . .

So that was it . . .

Slowly, letting out a long breath, Rusty pulled off the eyepieces and headphones. Suddenly, he found that he was utterly exhausted. He touched the magician lightly on the forearm.

'I'll have to go home now, I'm completely done in. See you tomorrow, maybe.'

'All right,' mumbled the magician, still immersed in his own story. 'I'll just carry on a while longer, if you don't mind. I quite like this bit. Oh, and thanks for your help, by the way.'

His fingers groped unconsciously for the eyepieces, straightened them on his face, adjusted them for a closer view.

Wearily, Rusty hauled himself down the ladder. Dawn was breaking as he emerged into the fresh air. At such an early hour he had not expected to see anyone about, but as he rounded the corner onto the village street, he was surprised to find himself face to face with Granny Hopkins. The old woman squinted at him suspiciously.

'Good morning, Michael. I'm just on my way to clean up at the inn. But what on earth are you up to at this hour of the morning? You should still be in bed. A young man needs his sleep, you know. Heaven alone knows what your mother would have thought.'

And, muttering to herself, she continued on her way.

From the Journal of Victor Lazarus

Monday 14th June

Eventually the tide rose sufficiently for me to free the dinghy and manhandle her back to shore. After making her safe, I sat for a long while alone on the jetty with my field glasses trained upon the tower, alert for the slightest sign of activity. For hour after hour I watched, until eventually the light began to fade, and I could watch no more.

I realised that it had become chilly. I drew Lee's jerkin around my shoulders. Then I laid down my glasses, settled back, and gazed up at the first stars, and, as I gazed, a warm feeling of repose and contentment began slowly to steal over me. And it dawned upon me at last that my task was done, my work at the house complete. My task, I now understood, had been to re-unite the owner of the house with the mysterious spirit who dwelled within. And that task I had at last accomplished.

It occurred to me then that there would be no further requirement for my presence at the house. Sam and Harold would be able to manage things well enough from day to day, and, if I chose to remain, I should only be in their way.

With my departure, the house will at last be ready for the owner's return. I shall sleep well tonight, and tomorrow I shall start to make my way back to the town. It is time for me to seek my next adventure.

Tidying Up

Granny Hopkins, who must by now have been well over ninety, hobbled around in the gloom of the taproom, polishing tables, straightening chairs, and retrieving, as usual, assorted items of lost property. There was an ugly-looking jacket, covered in studs, that she hung up on a hook by the door, shuddering at its sticky touch. And there was an old leather-covered book, which had probably been left behind by the schoolmaster. This she placed on the shelf behind the bar.

And then, on the floor behind an overturned table, she found a sheaf of yellowing parchment, covered with a maze of complicated, meaningless scribbles. When she stooped to pick it up, it began to disintegrate in her hands. Granny Hopkins shrugged. This could surely be of no use to anyone. She tossed it into the fireplace. The embers must still have been hot, for it flared up brightly at once.

The old woman watched the flames for a moment. Then, satisfied, she turned away and continued with her work. The bar always looked nice after a good clean.

★   ★   ★

From the Journal of Victor Lazarus

Tuesday 10th August

Upon returning to my lodgings, it came as a pleasant surprise to discover that my old room remained vacant. My landlady explained to me that she had rented it out briefly during my absence to a young student from one of the academies. This young gentleman, however, had apparently abandoned his studies quite suddenly, and had gone away without any warning. Eventually, his mother had called by to collect his things, and had removed everything apart from a number of curious charts or diagrams that I discovered pinned haphazardly across the walls of the room. I studied these for a time, but could make no sense of them. Eventually, with the good lady's help, I unpinned them, and she took them away for safe keeping until their owner should return.

Also awaiting me was a letter in a familiar hand. The landlady explained to me that it had been delivered to the house, not by the usual courier but by an old lady wearing a long costume of the old-fashioned kind. I broke the seal. The envelope proved to contain a cheque for a surprisingly generous sum. It also contained the following short note.

Dear Lazarus,

Many thanks indeed for all your hard work and for the time that you have devoted to the restoration of my house. I must apologise for my hasty departure on the occasion of our last meeting, but please rest assured that I am more than satisfied with the outcome of your toils. I hope that the enclosed remuneration will go some way towards compensating you for any trouble or inconvenience you might have suffered in the process. I thank you once more, and I wish you good luck in your future endeavours.

Sincerely yours,
L. Pegasus

At any rate the handwriting had improved! The name of the owner struck a faint chord in my memory, but I was unable at that time to recall in what circumstances I had encountered him.

After reading the note a number of times, it occurred to me that the owner had made no mention of Lee, and I fell to pondering, as I had done so many times before, on the nature of that extraordinary being. I wondered whether Lee continued to inhabit the little turret room at the top of the house, and I wondered how much, if anything, the owner actually knew about his mysterious tenant. And it occurred to me that on no occasion had I ever seen the two of them together in one place. Perhaps, after all, they had never met. But these are mysteries into which it is not my business to inquire.

I have been installed here for several weeks now, and have slipped back comfortably into my old routines. On my walks around the town, I sometimes pass by the gates of the old house. Perhaps on some suitable occasion I shall call in and discover what has taken place there since my departure. But at the moment the weather is pleasant, and I feel no sense of urgency.

It is hard to see the magician clearly from here. My view of him is obscured by the huge, crazy structure of lumber and litter that dominates the hayloft where he dozes, but, so far as I can tell, he dozes peacefully. He seems content in his work, he seems happy in his pastime, and he seems contented in his rest. And, one day soon, he will be ready to return to me.

Not so far away, the young man stands on a hilltop overlooking the country of his birth, and him I can see more clearly. Chart in hand, he gazes this way and that, surveying the diverging paths as they spread out across the landscape. Here is a path that leads him back to his village, to the inn and the church and the school, perhaps to the comfortable life of a schoolmaster. And here is a path that points him onward to the city, to a realm of wealth and temptation, to a realm of worldly power and strong magic. And here a third path beckons him, upward to the mountain country, and outward to the ocean, and beyond the ocean to the islands in the far, far distance, and to the silent one who awaits him there. I wonder for a moment which path he will take, but I know that whichever path he chooses, it will lead him, in time, back to me.

Before he can make his choice, I find that my attention has wandered. For it is pleasant here, back in my little six-sided room, hanging upside down from my beam, listening to the music from downstairs. There has been much work for me to do lately, and now at last I have earned my rest. I feel my spine elongate, my shoulders stretch, my eyes begin to close. In time, my strength will return to me, and I shall be ready for my next visitor. But until then, I am looking forward to spending a little time alone.

And you, Lazarus? You, who have glimpsed me at last in my true form? You have learned much, but still you have much to learn. And, in time, I know that you too will return to me. You will return, and I will be waiting.

For my name is Lee, and this is my house.